A GUY WALKS INTO MY BAR

LAUREN BLAKELY

LITTLE DOG PRESS

ALSO BY LAUREN BLAKELY

Big Rock Series

Big Rock

Mister O

Well Hung

Full Package

Joy Ride

Hard Wood

The Guys Who Got Away Series

Dear Sexy Ex-Boyfriend

The What If Guy

Thanks for Last Night

After Dark: The Gift Series

The Engagement Gift

The Virgin Gift

The Decadent Gift

After Dark: The Extravagant Series

One Exquisite Touch (Coming in October)

One Time Only (Coming in November)

One Alluring Chance (Coming in 2021)

One Shameless Secret (Coming in 2021)

The Heartbreakers Series

Once Upon a Real Good Time

The Sexy One

The Only One

The Hot One

The Knocked Up Plan

Come As You Are

Sports Romance

Most Valuable Playboy

Most Likely to Score

Standalones

Stud Finder

The V Card

The Real Deal

Unbreak My Heart

The Break-Up Album

21 Stolen Kisses

Out of Bounds

The Caught Up in Love Series:

The Pretending Plot (previously called *Pretending He's Mine*)

The Dating Proposal

The Second Chance Plan (previously called *Caught Up In Us*)

The Private Rehearsal (previously called *Playing With Her Heart*)

Stars In Their Eyes Duet

My Charming Rival

My Sexy Rival

The No Regrets Series

The Start of Us

The Thrill of It

Every Second With You

The Seductive Nights Series

First Night (Julia and Clay, prequel novella)

Night After Night (Julia and Clay, book one)

After This Night (Julia and Clay, book two)

One More Night (Julia and Clay, book three)

A Wildly Seductive Night (Julia and Clay novella, book 3.5)

The Joy Delivered Duet

Nights With Him (A standalone novel about Michelle and Jack)

Forbidden Nights (A standalone novel about Nate and Casey)

The Sinful Nights Series

Sweet Sinful Nights

Sinful Desire

Sinful Longing

Sinful Love

The Fighting Fire Series

Burn For Me (Smith and Jamie)

Melt for Him (Megan and Becker)

Consumed By You (Travis and Cara)

The Jewel Series

A two-book sexy contemporary romance series

The Sapphire Affair

The Sapphire Heist

ABOUT

A sexy, passionate, utterly addictive standalone MM romance from #1 NYT Bestseller Lauren Blakely!

Every bartender should follow one simple rule—don't go home with the customers.

That's been easy for me to stick to, until the night a cocky, confident, and sinfully charming hockey star walks into my bar. This sexy athlete is too hard to resist, especially when he makes it clear how much he wants the "sarcastic, witty, hot AF" guy behind the bar—also known as me.

Still, I'm not keen on breaking my own rules since I know where that can lead—no place good. But when that man makes his case with one bone-searing kiss on the streets of London, I throw resistance out the window.

What could go wrong with a hot, no-strings-attached fling before he leaves town in five days? Trouble is, soon our nights together lead to days, to long conversations, to getting to know each other, and to something I never expected—falling ridiculously hard for a man who's getting on a plane to America when I live a world away.

My life is here. His is there. And no amount of falling or feeling will change that one big problem.

Warning: contains hot hotel sex, loads of dirty talk, PDA all over London, and two sexy, witty, charming heroes...

A GUY WALKS INTO MY BAR

By Lauren Blakely

Want to be the first to learn of sales, new releases, preorders and special freebies? Sign up for my VIP mailing list here!

This book is dedicated to the women who insisted on this story. If it weren't for Kim you-did-tell-me-so B, as well as Kara, Kim L, Kelley, Jen, KP, Candi, Viviana, Helen, and so many others, this story wouldn't exist. You ladies get me and I love you all. And, of course, to Laurelin, for everything. I refuse to do it without you.

For the readers and listeners, you may notice as you experience this story that Dean and Fitz live in a world with zero homophobia. That is intentional and that's my wish for everyone. To have epic love stories and all the acceptance and joy everyone deserves. Love is love.

FRIDAY

Also known as the day I meet this guy who drives me absolutely crazy.

1

DEAN

I blame Maeve.

She's made me addicted to this game.

It's four o'clock on a Friday. I walked into work fifteen minutes ago, and I'm already in the mood to play.

We haven't even opened yet, but I'm in a winning kind of mood.

Victory is in my grasp.

Lately, my opponent has been weakening.

I've seen it in her eyes.

I've sensed it in her flirty attitude.

Tonight, it's time to go for broke—to pull out all the stops and get my damn prize.

What can I say? I'm a junkie, and I've got an excellent don't-sleep-with-the-customers streak going. We both do.

Time to goad her a bit.

"Have you seen the crowds out there? All those American tourists here for the British Summer Time music festival," I tell Maeve as we clean and stack glasses, preparing for another busy night at The Magpie. "I bet we'll have a full bar tonight."

"Hmm. I hadn't noticed," she says, in a way that tells me she certainly has.

"Teeming with lots of strapping, single men. Your favorite type. I'm thinking you're finally about to cave."

"You always say that," Maeve argues, shooting me a *you're so wrong* stare with her big brown eyes. "And you're never right."

"That's not true," I say in protest, grabbing a new glass. "Besides, I know you've come very close. The other night you seemed to fancy that table of businessmen in all those expensive suits. The night before, you were definitely flirting with that bad boy who kept ordering tequila shots."

An impish grin lights her face as she checks that all of the bottles are facing out. "He was highly shaggable. Plus, he was from New York. I do love an American accent." She takes a beat and arches a brow. "And yet I resisted."

"And so very many Americans will likely be streaming in tonight," I say, gesturing to the door that we'll open soon. "It's going to be soooo hard for you. If only you weren't this stubborn."

"Stubborn or smart? I choose the latter," she says, all saucy.

"It's a shame, your stubborn streak," I continue, sticking to my strategy of reminding her what she's losing out on. "Think of how many shaggables you've let just walk on out the door. Not to mention kissables. All because of a silly game we play." I shake my head like I'm mourning all the one-night stands she's let pass her by. Over the top, yes, but losing out on a chance with a fantastic guy is just cause for crying into your beer.

But a game is a game.

A bet is a bet.

And I won't cave.

Maeve sets down a pair of martini glasses on the shelf

behind her. "What about you, Mr. Checks Out All the Hotties and Pretends Not To? I've seen the guys who have caught your eye. It's only a matter of time before you spot one of them and—poof—you're in mad love, the game's up, and I collect my big winnings."

"And that is where you're wrong," I say, standing my ground. "Because I don't believe in all that rubbish."

"You don't believe in love? Get out."

I shrug, moving from organizing the glassware to wiping the bar down. "Oh, I believe in love. But I definitely don't have the time or interest in it."

Love is messy. It gets in the way of logic, facts, and hard work.

"Everyone has an inherent interest in love," Maeve says, heading to the tables to straighten up the coasters. "And someday it'll knock you on your arse. And I'm going to laugh so hard when it smacks you right in the face."

"Which one is it, Maeve? Am I going to be knocked on my arse or smacked in the face?"

Setting down the napkin holder, she parks a hand on her hip and shoots me a steely stare. "In your case, both. Especially since you've been so focused on business, business, business since we bought this place."

"As I should be. Because . . . loans. Also, because who has time for distractions when we have an empire to build? First stop, The Magpie. Next, world domination in the bar biz."

"But on the path to world domination, you might go home with a hottie, and then you'll be footing the bill for my big-ticket item," she says, a hopeful glint in her eye.

"When I win—and I *will* win—I'll give you a week to clear out a space for the pool table you're going to have to get me," I say as I spray down the bar. "Just to soften the blow."

She doesn't miss a beat. "When I win, I'll let you take out a loan for the vintage jukebox I've been eyeing. You know, I searched online, and it's going up in value. Sure you don't want to just buy it now and save yourself some cash?"

"That's sweet but completely unnecessary." I tap my chest. "Have you seen my willpower? It's pure iron."

"Something tells me that willpower of yours is just going to melt—and soon," Maeve says with a smirk as she snatches the rag from my hand and whips it at my leg. "And when it does, it won't just be money you'll lose. It'll be your heart."

"As if."

"Just you wait."

She sashays away, past the bottles of expensive booze that line the walls of our clean but elegant bar. She cues up the music for tonight, the usual jazzy standards, and then opens the doors.

Soon, the customers will come in. I imagine someone that's just Maeve's type—chiseled jaw, witty sense of humor, rugged good looks—walking in.

Walking in and securing me my pool table.

The thought gives me an idea.

Maybe I need to edge this bet in my favor.

It might be time I set a trap for my victory.

A tall, sexy trap that is the perfect fairy tale for Maeve.

2

DEAN

For the next few hours, I serve and chat, and I study the guys who walk into The Magpie. I look each of them up and down as I search for the type I need to finally sink Maeve.

A businessman with a tight suit and trim blond hair? No, she'll think he's too pretty.

Or maybe that guy with hipster glasses and ripped jeans? He's cute with an edge, but she'll think he's too grungy.

More guys weave in and out, ordering pints and whiskey sours, all of them too basic or too drab, too loud, or too impressed with their own jokes.

And then, I spot him.

A guy with so much potential it's practically radiating off him.

He strides in like he's walking into his bedroom at home, an effortless swagger to his movements. His large build is flanked by two women who giggle and laugh, already a little tipsy by the look of it. With inked arms and a trim beard, he has that rugged and dangerous quality she adores, right down to the dark jeans and tight white shirt.

He is the kind of man Maeve would call "sex on a stick."

In short? He's my new target.

I glance at Maeve, mixing a gin and tonic a few feet away. I catch her eye and mouth, *You're so going down*, then tip my forehead to the man in question, raising a brow. "Your type," I whisper.

She answers with an epic eye roll before returning to her customers.

She thinks no one here will tempt her tonight.

And I'm about to show her how wrong she is. If she kisses this guy, there's a list of chores waiting for her to pay up—painting that wall, sanding that table, reupholstering that stool. If she goes home with him, I'll be on my way to the pool table. The two-tiered system keeps us both in check. With a bar that's been a fixer-upper, the list of chores has been endless. The threat of a Saturday lost to scrubbing has kept me pretty chaste, at least in terms of customers.

And I intend to stay that way.

I check out my target. He's moving through the crowd, peeling himself away from the women as they head to the loo and he heads straight for me. I stare as he struts, jeans clinging to his body, hugging his muscular legs.

Oh yes, there is a definite strut in his walk.

And oh yes, Maeve will lose tonight.

Especially when she gets her eyes on his ink. I have a feeling that those tribal-band tattoos disappear somewhere beyond his broad shoulders.

And I wouldn't mind seeing where.

Shit, what am I thinking?

I need to focus. This is an acquisition for Maeve. Not eye candy for me.

I shake away thoughts of his full lips as the man sidles up and sits on the stool in front of me.

"Welcome to The Magpie. What's your poison?"

"Depends what's good around here," he says in a raspy American accent. His dark-blue eyes roam the taps.

I'm about to make a suggestion when he meets my gaze. There's a glint in his irises as he says, "How about a Bud?"

I flinch at this sacrilege. "No. Just no."

His lips twitch. "Maybe a Corona, then?"

"That won't happen either," I say, stern. "We have standards here."

"How about Pabst?" The question comes out thoroughly deadpan, and that's when I realize he's playing me.

And I can go toe-to-toe.

I point to the door. "If you keep this up, I'm going to have to ask you to leave."

He laughs, a warm rumble of a sound. "Beer snob. I like it."

"And let's be frank, beer snobbery is completely warranted."

"Couldn't agree more. What about music snobbery though? Is that warranted too?"

"Hell, no. Listen to whatever floats your boat. Jazz, show tunes, rap, or anything by Sam Smith, Daley, or Leon Bridges."

"Excellent choices. And how do you feel about book snobbery then? Is that acceptable?"

"Never. Reading is heaven, and everyone should do it often and indiscriminately." I realize that I haven't even gotten the man his drink because I'm having too much fun talking to him.

But I'm doing it for Maeve.

Still, I clear my throat and say, "Let's get you that drink."

"How's the stout selection? When in England and all."

I've officially struck gold. Maeve's not only a sucker for American accents and men quick with their wit, but she's especially keen on Americans who do their research and make classic choices.

Of course, I'm also into all of that, but that's not the point. I won't be Svengali'd by his easy charm again.

"We've got some great ones," I say. "What's your style?"

He runs his hand through his beard. *How would that beard feel against my face?*

Damn it, snap out of it.

"Surprise me," he says, his voice laced with daring.

He meets my eyes and winks.

And oh no.

Oh, no, no, no.

I made a critical error in my choice for Maeve.

He might be the perfect blend of sexy, rugged, and charming for her, but judging by the hungry way he's looking at me, she's not the right one for him.

So I should step away.

Get the guy his drink and leave him be.

"I'll get you something good," I say.

"I look forward to that."

Except I can't seem to stop flirting with him, and it seems he suffers the same affliction when it comes to me.

As I grab a glass for his stout, I tell myself what not to do.

Don't flirt anymore.

Don't trade quips and banter.

And do not exchange numbers, or anything else.

He might just be friendly. Bars tend to have that effect on people.

Besides, this is Maeve's night to lose, not mine.

I turn and hand him his drink. I should be scanning the

crowd for another target for Maeve, but he leans forward on the bar to grab the glass, making the muscles in his biceps tighten, and making it impossible for me to look elsewhere. I'm such a sucker for great arms.

"This is excellent," he says with a grin. "Seems you have good taste."

"Yes," I say, but I'm thoroughly distracted by those ridiculous bicep muscles that flex again as he puts the drink down. He catches me looking, and his grin goes crooked.

Crooked and wicked.

Look, I know the effect I have on men. With the game, it's never been a problem in terms of supply. Plenty of guys have asked, and plenty have tried. But ever since I decided I wasn't going to be getting distracted, I've been on a streak I don't intend to break.

The stakes are too high. Sure, we have our gotcha rules, but we implemented them because the business matters too much, and if we start sleeping around, The Magpie might get a reputation.

We don't want to be *that* bar.

And I know the price that distractions make you pay.

I won't let them into my life.

This man, and his mouth-watering arms, won't be any different.

"So, are you out here for business or pleasure?" I busy myself by cleaning a glass, keeping the conversation as standard as bartender chat can be.

The American leans back and takes another swig of stout. "Pleasure," he says with a twinkle in his blue eyes. "Fortunately, I don't have much work to do while I'm here."

It's bait. He wants to talk about himself. I should hate

how obvious that entrée is, but he makes it seem unbearably charming.

"What field are you in?" I ask, lifting my chin. "You look like you do a lot of lifting. Let me guess—professional mover?"

He smirks. "Not quite."

I arch a brow, studying him like I'm considering other professions. "Ah, I bet you carry water coolers. Do you work for the Water Cooler Association?"

"Do they have a Water Cooler Association, and if so, how do I get involved?"

"Oh, I'm sure we can find a sign-up form for you somewhere," I say, and bloody hell, why did I pick him? I need to stop right now.

But I don't. "Let me try again...carpenter. You're definitely a carpenter. Wait. No. You work in a timber yard."

"All excellent choices. All wrong too. I play hockey in the NHL. Defenseman in New York."

So that's where the hard body comes from. Professional hockey. And if his arms look like that, I can only imagine what the sport's done to his chest. His abs. His ass.

Best to put some distance between myself and this man who is far too much my type.

"Ah, that sport with sticks," I say, stepping back, a slight shift in body language toward other patrons.

He takes another swallow of his drink. "So, you're a sports snob."

"Yes. I like polo. Only polo," I tease. "And cricket."

"I bet you'd look good on a horse." And somehow that sounds filthy and enticing.

Must activate deflector shield.

"I prefer my feet firmly on the ground, thank you," I say, a telltale burn heating the back of my neck.

"Well, there's always hockey. That's definitely on the ground."

"Sure. Right. I should pick it up."

He laughs. "Have you even seen a game?"

I can't resist it—the challenge in his tone. I meet his gaze head-on. "Frankly, there's never been anything interesting about it to me."

He smirks. "I bet I could change your mind."

"And why's that?"

"Because it's the best sport there is, and because it's fucking awesome when I play it."

He is cocky, and it's too sexy for words.

But I won't let him best me in this battle of wits.

"I dunno," I say. "Isn't hockey sort of uncivilized?"

I expect him to recoil at my dig, but he just laughs. "All right, before you start ripping on my sport, I'm going to need your name."

Giving him my name feels personal. Giving him my name makes this go from flirty to dangerous.

But a name isn't breaking the rules or losing the game.

And I can pull back.

I always do.

"Dean," I tell him. "And I didn't intend to offend your sensibilities. I suppose I'm just surprised you aren't missing some teeth or something. I bet your dentist is pissed at you for not needing him."

He laughs so loud that it seems to fill up the bar. "Thank you for noticing my pearly whites. I make a habit of staying on *top* of things, both on and off the ice."

Ignore it . . . ignore the image of what he just said. No matter how hard it is.

"By the same token, shouldn't you be making martinis for James Bond and drinking tea? If we're playing stereotypes," he continues.

"Is that your way of saying you want a martini? Because I make a fantastic one that will go to your head."

A groan seems to rumble up from his chest, and he murmurs his appreciation. And I am skating on thin ice right now.

Must stop flirting.

"Sounds like my kind of martini."

I return to his sport before talk of martinis goes to *my* head. Besides, hockey is an innocuous enough topic, since I know nothing about it. "Speaking of sports with sticks, isn't the point of hockey just to get hit really hard all the time?"

"The point is to hit the puck really hard," he says. "Hitting the players is just a bonus."

"And you find this sort of heavy contact exhilarating, do you?"

The guy grins, leaning closer. "Oh, I find all sorts of heavy contact *exhilarating*. Given the right party, of course."

Shit. We just jumped firmly over the dangerous line.

And I need to reel this back in. Whatever it takes.

I'm not going home with the hottest man I've ever seen walk into my bar.

No matter what superhuman feats of resistance are required.

FITZ

I didn't come to England to get lucky.

I came here to support Emma, my brilliant little sister, who's earned the chance of a lifetime to study art in her favorite place in the world. I'm just here to be the best big brother I can.

But getting lucky along the way?

Well, I certainly wouldn't say no.

After all, I've worked damn hard to get here.

Hockey is the reason why I *should* be getting lucky in England. We're only one week away from training camp, and that's when our pact kicks in.

The pact that will expressly forbid getting lucky.

So yes, while I didn't come to England for a little action, I'm not opposed to it preseason.

Not at all.

I'm pretty much never opposed to physical activity, especially of the bedroom variety.

But I can tell I've got my work cut out for me with Dean, and that's exactly how I like it.

A little challenge.

A bit of a chase.

That's a huge fucking turn-on.

I settle in at the bar, ready to do whatever it takes to get this man back to my hotel room.

He's all Michael B. Jordan—hot as fuck and even better to listen to with that insanely sexy accent. I'm not immune to a hot-as-sin accent, or a man with a quicksilver tongue.

Because I've learned something about a man who isn't afraid to give and take in a conversation. A man like that?

He'll give and take the same way in bed.

In my pocket, my phone buzzes, and I check it to see a message.

Emma: Seems like you found someone fun.

I look down the bar and see my sister and her friend have settled there. A pretty brunette bartender is cracking jokes with them as she mixes a drink.

Emma catches my eye before pointing to where Dean's dealing with other customers. Then she's tapping into her phone.

Emma: I called it the second we walked in. You're so into him.

I roll my eyes. I'm used to the teasing about my love life. My three sisters have wanted to hook me up with every guy friend they've ever had.

But I'm happy playing the field.

Especially when there are hot British bartenders just waiting to be picked up.

Dean grabs two different bottles and whips them around to make a cocktail. He moves them easily, quickly, almost like he's performing a magic trick. The customers he's mixing the drink in front of ooh and aah, clapping as he does a long pour. He finishes and hands the glass to an older woman at the other end of the bar. Then he pivots and heads my way. As he walks over, my lips curve up in a grin. Sure, I'm his customer, but he could have sent someone else to see if I needed a refill.

I knew it. He's totally hooked on me.

He'll be the perfect guy to blow off steam with right before training camp. Before the pact.

He leans on the bar in front of me, eyeing my now empty glass.

"So, I'm guessing you thought that was better than a Bud?"

"Seems I did. You picked well for me," I say, crossing my arms over my chest, letting him see the muscles earned from countless hard-core workouts.

"I've done this for a few years. I'm good at reading customers."

"Yeah, I'd say you're pretty damn good at that."

"Some things are easy to read." His eyes are on me—where I want them.

"I like it when that happens," I say and the way this conversation is going right now, it's time to reel him in. I take a quick glance around, then I say, "Glad I walked in here tonight. I'm digging the whole *vibe.*"

Emphasis on vibe.

Dean's brown eyes spark in the light. "I'll be sure to let the owner know you like The Magpie."

"I do," I say. "Great bartenders too. Very . . . attentive."

Dean smirks, and the grin is so damn cheeky I want to kiss it off him with a punishing, devouring kind of kiss.

"He's very hands-on, the owner," Dean says. "Likes to know what's going on with the front of the house."

"Sounds like my kind of guy."

Dean grabs my glass for a refill without me asking. He's back in moments with the full glass. "Had a feeling you'd want more."

"That's *exactly* what I want." I take a drink of the fresh stout. "How late does this boss of yours have you working?"

Another smirk from Dean comes my way and leaves my head spinning as he says, "Late. My boss works us pretty hard."

I'd like to work him hard.

"I ought to talk to this guy. Tell him how impressed I am with his dedicated staff."

"I'm sure he'd appreciate that." Dean laughs. "Especially since you're already talking to him. I'm the owner."

"Oh, very clever. Well played."

"It was, admittedly, hard to resist."

I take a beat, then go for the close. "There are other things hard to resist," I say, my tone making my meaning clear.

For a second, it looks like it costs him something to say the next words, but when they come out, they're gravelly, smoky. "What sort of things?"

"Tell me what time you get off, and I'll show you."

He laughs, shaking his head, but it's not a no. It's more like *What the hell have I gotten myself into?* "But I don't even know your name."

I extend a hand to shake. He looks at it like he's considering it, then he clasps it.

If I said there was a spark, that'd be cliché. It's a goddamn handshake after all. I've given and received a million of them.

But I do like the way he feels against me.

I wouldn't mind feeling his hands all over me.

"Fitzgerald," I say.

He arches a brow. "Fitzgerald? Isn't that a last name?"

He says it like he's busting me, and I dig it, the way that he seems to want to question everything.

"Yeah. It is. But everyone calls me that."

"And what does your sister call you . . . Perhaps, is it James?"

I think I just blushed at the way he said that, all flirty. I glance down the bar and see my sister giggling with her bartender, both of them looking my way. Dean must have passed by them when he was working with the other customers and overheard Emma say my name.

"My sisters call me James, yes. But you can call me Fitz."

Dean glances at my drink, then down the bar. The bartender's smirking in his direction, looking pretty satisfied about something. Maybe even a little smug. Dean rolls his eyes at her, then turns back to me.

"Look, Fitz. I'm going to be blunt. You are pretty much the hottest man to ever walk into my bar. You're like one of those memes for a hot guy walking into a bar and all the ladies tossing their knickers at him."

"I don't want *their* panties."

"Yes, I'm clear on that," he says with a laugh. "But the thing is—I can't go home with you. I don't sleep with the customers."

I grin. "So, you're saying you *want* to sleep with me."

"You're relentless," he says like he's reining in a grin.

And he's right. Whether it's a man in a bar or a play on the ice, I am relentless.

And I *always* score.

Dean's grin disappears as he stares at me, heat in his eyes, giving me a look that I both love and hate at the same time.

Because that look?

It promises that challenge that turned me on in the first place.

And it also promises me that nothing is happening tonight.

"The thing is – it's a rule," he says. "And it's a rule I intend to follow."

For a second, I let him think he's won, that I'm going to walk away.

Then, in a low voice, I say, "Rules are made to be broken. Or bent," I say just for him. "You should bend your rules for me."

A twitch in his jaw.

He wants this as much as I do, even if he won't admit it.

He wants this because there's more here than insane physical attraction. There's a spark that'll make our physical connection out of this world. And I want what I want. *Badly.*

"What makes you think you should be the one I break the rule for?"

I give him nothing but the truth. "Because I'd make it worth your while."

His eyes stay on me like he's studying me, possibly even memorizing me. Maybe that's wishful thinking. Or maybe it's reality, because he leans forward, a mere foot away now, his chiseled face so damn close to mine. He lowers his voice to a sultry bedroom whisper. "Of that, Fitz, I have no doubt."

And I am officially an inferno. A speechless, hot, bothered, and turned-on-as-hell inferno.

Dean shrugs, grins, clears his throat. "But it's a rule I won't be breaking *tonight.*"

He walks away to tend to other customers, and I watch him. I cannot look away.

Because all I can think is—*Dean, your challenge is accepted.*

When I leave a little later, I hand him a tip, then say, "I'll see you . . . *tomorrow night.*"

He meets my gaze, his eyes locked with mine. "Is that so?"

"Yes. Yes, it is."

I walk out.

Tomorrow can't arrive fast enough.

SATURDAY

Also known as the day I don't expect to see him again.

Because, I swear, I'm not even thinking about him. Not at all. Not even a little bit.

Fine, maybe a little.

4

DEAN

I'm waiting for my award.

Top prize in Extraordinary Feats of Resistance.

Because what I did last night? There should be an entire fleet of people arriving at the door of my flat, ready to congratulate me for resisting the sexiest man to walk into my bar, let alone enter the damn country.

Thankfully, there's nothing in the rules forbidding getting off to a customer.

Nothing at all against thoughts of his hard body on mine. Or under mine—either image worked for me.

Trouble is, I can picture him sauntering through The Magpie's doors tonight, flashing those bedroom eyes my way.

Will I be strong enough to resist him a second time?

I better be.

I just need to forget his humor, his swagger. Erase his easy banter.

I have plenty more important things to dwell on anyway. Like the bar expo today, an event I've been eager to check out.

Business only.

I take the coldest shower I can stand, pull on some jeans and a casual polo shirt that I know looks damn good thanks to regular arm days at the gym, tuck my phone in my pocket, and head down three flights of stairs. London's warm as usual on this summer day, and by the time I've stepped outside of my flat, the sun's shining on the Thames a few streets away.

It's a short walk to Coffee O'clock, the perfect midway spot between my flat and Dad's. Inside, the intoxicating scents of coffee, tea, and flaky pastries greet me.

I haven't even made it through the front door yet when I catch the attention of Penny, Coffee O'clock's long-standing owner. She's behind the counter, making drinks. She gives me a smile as she chats up a regular, then waves me over after she finishes ringing him up.

When I reach her, I survey the board. "What are the chances I could get a decent cuppa in here?"

"Terrible, absolutely terrible," she says with a gleam in her eyes, crinkled at the corners.

"Also, can you please change the name to Tea O'clock?"

"Only if you can stop hating on coffee."

I pretend to consider that, tapping my chin. "Not a chance. So I'll take two of your special secret Stonehenge Breakfast Mix that you'll someday give me the name of the supplier?"

"Ha, as if I'd ever tell you where my tea leaves come from," she says, scooping some out.

"Someday you'll spill your tea secrets."

"And until then I'll happily brew them for you. Especially since I know you're taking one to your dad," she says with a smile as she brews the blend.

"Ah, I appreciate you giving me a pass on account of Martin."

"I trust he's still enjoying his retirement?"

"Considering I can't keep him off Tinder, he seems to be having a blast."

She drops her voice to a stage whisper. "Better tell him to swipe right on me."

"I'll be sure to pass on the tip," I say with a laugh, but something about the way Penny's eyes sparkle tells me she might not totally be joking.

She pours the tea, sets the cups down, then eyes the food case. "You know you want a scone today. Maybe two."

A quick scan of the options tells me the chia seed pudding and morning oats will be the best bet. Better on the heart for him, and, frankly, on the abs for me.

Penny bags up the healthy options and tells me to hurry back.

When I head outside, I'm already feeling the right amount of distance from Mr. Hockey Is Awesome and So Am I.

The walk to Dad's covers some of my other favorite spots.

There's the bookshop where, years ago, Dad bought me a copy of *Harry Potter and the Chamber of Secrets*, after I'd read the first book from the library. Where just last week, I picked up a new Silicon Valley exposé of a high-flying start-up. (Who can resist the fall of an upstart that gets too big for its boots?)

Up the street, I pass the park where I used to play rugby with my mates after school.

Next is the secondhand furniture store that my friend Taron runs, a place where I like to hunt around for old nightstands and tables to refurbish.

The walk settles me, and by the time I've climbed the flight of stairs to the place I used to live, my mind's completely clear of distractions.

"Tell me you didn't do it!" Dad says as he opens the door. His eyes go straight to the bag in my hand. "You did it," he says with a frown.

"Did what?" I ask ever so innocently.

He glowers at me. "Brought me Greek yogurt or a chia seed walnut salad with blueberries and quinoa that is going to make me twenty-five years younger."

"What did blueberries ever do to you?" I ask as I hand him the chia seed pudding and morning oats.

He eyes them skeptically. "What is this?"

I grin. "Breakfast. Sit. Eat. It's healthy."

"It's weird."

"Yes, but that's how we're doing it these days. Keep up with me, old man."

He rolls his eyes. "So much cheek."

"I wonder where I learned it from."

"It's a mystery to me too."

We sit at the table, where I dive into the chia seed pudding while Dad takes the morning oats.

He dips his spoon into the oats, looking at me like I've told him we have to remove his kidney. "Is it so hard to buy a scone?"

"It's not hard to buy a scone. It's quite easy. You take out the money, and you get the scone. But see, I can't eat scones for every meal. And you can't either. You need to look sharp for the ladies."

"And you need to look sharp for the lads. Speaking of—anyone catching your eye these days? Seems like it's been forever since that last guy. What was his name? Damian?"

I wave a hand. "Dylan, and that was ages ago."

Before Maeve and I bought The Magpie and made the pact, we were both just bartenders in our twenties. And, frankly, bartenders in their twenties—especially attractive bartenders—can get plenty of action.

Like when I worked at The Olde Shoe, and in walked Dylan, five years younger, clever and confident. He'd come by, flirt with me all night, and then we'd wind up going out to a club.

Then to my place, since he had twenty roommates or so.

Let's keep this simple, I'd said. *Just keep it fun.*

Of course, he'd said.

Soon it became more regular. He'd invite himself over to cook dinner. He'd stay the night, and he'd want to make breakfast, spend the day together.

Suddenly, Dylan wasn't just making dirty talk with me at the bar.

He was starting to hint at other things.

Other levels.

Levels like love.

That set off my get-the-hell-out-of-there radar.

I wasn't in love with him. Hadn't been with anyone, for that matter. All the guys seemed to want more than I was willing to give.

I cut things off with Dylan. And when Maeve and I bought The Magpie a few months later, she'd just come out of a bad relationship that had rattled her, so we'd decided on a pact to eliminate distractions.

The number one rule is don't mix business with pleasure. You can't run the risk of falling for a customer who might come back too often, show up at the wrong times, or leave a terrible review. Best to keep those worlds separate.

So we set our rules and our goals—focus on the bar and add in some friendly stakes to keep things interesting.

It's not like I'm celibate. A hookup here or there is just what the doctor ordered some nights. But I'm thirty-one now, and I steer clear of the younger guys who see a future in me that I'm not ready to share—they see someone steady, stable, with a business and a flat he owns and doesn't share with three, or twenty, of his mates.

It's a life I've worked hard for. One I've sought out. One I'm having at last, and I don't want to chance losing.

I take a bite of my breakfast as Dad continues on with his matchmaker routine. "Fine, not Dylan. But there are plenty of other men out there. A whole city full of fascinating people. That is, if you leave the bar."

I snort. If only Dad knew about last night.

Dad grins. "Oh? Perhaps you've already found someone?"

I shake my head. "Definitely not."

"Liar."

I huff. "How do you do that? See right through me?"

"I wonder. Maybe because I raised you? Also, did you forget I was a reporter for thirty-five years? I know how to read people."

"You know how to read financials and CEOs. You were a business reporter."

"And I know how to read my son. Who is the lucky fella?"

I laugh at his persistence. "No one. Just this absolutely frustrating American who walked into my bar last night and had the nerve to flirt with me."

Dad feigns shock. "Flirting with a handsome, quick-witted, sarcastic bartender. The goddamn nerve of the Yankees."

"Can you believe it? Some nights I have to beat them off with a stick."

He strokes his jaw. "It's the family curse, son. We have no choice but to live with it. I've had to spend my entire life fending off the ladies."

"Yeah, seems like Penny wants to work her magic on you. She was trying to get me to buy you a scone."

"I knew I liked her for a good reason. But you're not distracting me." Dad wags his oat-covered spoon in my direction. "Will you see this absolutely frustrating American again?"

I shrug. "I don't think so. It's all for the best. Too much going on at work. I don't have time for frustrating Americans. Especially ones who are too cocky for their own good."

"All I'm saying is, don't let all the opportunities pass you by. I've always admired your work ethic, but it's okay to get out there a little sometimes, meet that special someone."

I roll my eyes. I go out when I want to. I don't go out when I don't want to, and I'm perfectly content with that. "And it's okay to skip the scone. We're both full of sage advice today. Now, I should nip off, or I'll be late."

"Thanks for the breakfast. *I think*," he says as he puts down his bowl of oats. I've got a feeling it's going to end up either covered in brown sugar or tossed in the rubbish bin right after I leave.

"You're welcome. *I think*."

He waves me off with one last comment about "keeping my eyes open."

The man's stubborn, I'll give him that.

Maybe, possibly, I take after him in that regard.

But better him than the other person responsible for half my genes.

I leave and make the quick walk to the Tube. During the ride, I turn over his advice, weighing the pros and cons of it. I love the man, but it's a little ironic for him to be trying to encourage me to find a special someone, especially since he didn't date for years until I finally convinced him to get on the apps recently. Part of it is probably an old habit for him, thinking he still needs to be looking out for me and only me. Ever since Mum took off for Australia after a whirlwind affair with a man from Sydney when I was thirteen—one that went tits up a few years later—it's been Dad and me against the world. He did whatever it took to support us, whether it meant taking on extra free-lance assignments or avoiding romantic entanglements, something he claims he didn't do, but I know him—his focus was singular in those years, and I suppose it worked out as he'd hoped. He raised a good kid, and without him, I know the path off the rails would have been too easy.

More proof that sometimes you just need to stay the course and focus on what's important.

Business.

Friendships.

Family.

But love?

Seems to me that following your heart is foolish and leads to stupid decisions like abandoning your family to go halfway around the world.

Mum's on her fourth marriage now.

Every time, she says that guy is the one.

As if there's a *one*.

That's why I won't be the one to lose in my game with Maeve. And that's what I ought to be focusing on. Getting her in our game, since I suspect she was trying to trip me up last night.

It's like she hears my thoughts because the second I'm off the Tube and back outside, my phone buzzes with a message.

Maeve: Sure you don't need to pick up supplies for some chores later? You and that American seemed pretty chummy.

Dean: Further proof that you will be the one to lose this battle. If I can withstand that man, I can withstand anything.

Maeve: How can you be so sure that's the last you've seen of him?

Dean: Because I'm all business today. Now, about the bar expo. What am I looking for?

Maeve: You're all work and no play, Dean. What have I told you about that?

Dean: That it means I'll win our game?

Maeve: You nearly lost last night. But no worries. I understand why. He's quite foxy. Hard not to notice. Harder still to look away from. I'm curious though. Did you learn if his ink went all the way up to his shoulders? Down his back? To the V of his abs?

Dean: Has anyone ever told you that you're evil? Pure evil. Also, completely wicked too.

Maeve: Only you, ever since uni. Also, I'm soooo going to win. You think you're ice, but I know you.

Dean: Impervious is my middle name. Now, what's on your wish list, O Wicked One?

Maeve: See if you can find us some cool specialty food and drink options. I'll send you a checklist. Also, you should be on the lookout, too, for anything American. Foreign is an especially good sell. You know how HOT American goods are. Or should I say H-A-W-T?

Dean: I am a man on a mission tonight. Radar has been recalibrated to trip you up, witchy woman.

By the time I reach the expo at the edge of Bankside, the crowd's buzzing around the different stalls. I check them out, swinging by a booth with CBD-infused alcohol, another with vegan bar food, but nothing entices me.

The next stall features an old-fashioned jukebox, fifties tunes warbling from the speakers.

I snap a picture of it and send it off to her, along with a new text.

Dean: I'm sure you would have loved this baby. Too bad you'll have to buy me the pool table instead.

I'm still chuckling to myself when I look up from the phone and spot a familiar set of shoulders.

Maybe I'm seeing things at the end of the row.

Maybe he's just the one I *wish* I were seeing.

The same one who invaded my thoughts so damn inconveniently after I went home last night.

But when he turns around, I'm certain it's the frustrating American.

And he looks even better than he did last night.

This boozy festival wouldn't be my first choice to spend a Saturday afternoon in London. Checking out the Tower or kicking back on a riverboat cruise is more my speed for vacay.

But Emma insisted, saying getting the local feel would help her settle into the city, and this is local as hell, here in a neighborhood that feels very Old Blighty.

"So, after this, I think I'll head over to that used bookstore we passed earlier and see if they have the books I need for my art history class," she says as we pass a stall advertising bar art. "Plus, the vibe was *so Notting Hill.* Maybe I'll meet my own Hugh Grant."

"You don't want your own Hugh Grant. He's so old now."

Emma laughs, ponytail bouncing as she walks ahead of me. "I meant a young, cute Hugh Grant. Obviously. And don't act like those accents don't charm the hell out of you."

"Guilty as charged. Or charmed, I should say."

"Indeed."

"And listen, I'm all for you finding a younger Hugh Grant, but you don't have to buy your books used. You can just get the full-price ones."

"Yes, but I'd rather support a cool local business. Besides, just because you have the money now doesn't mean we need to spend it."

Of my three sisters, Emma's always been the most direct. Maybe it's because she's the baby of the family, but she has never had any problem telling me exactly how she feels about something, especially when it comes to money.

"I'm just saying that we don't have to be so frugal all the time," I say. "Old habits die hard, but you can afford to splurge a little. I want you to, Ems."

Emma's blue eyes soften a little. "I'd say me getting to go to the art program of my dreams is a splurge. And for that, James, aka NHL's top D-man, I'm extremely grateful."

I give her shoulder a little nudge as we walk. "Don't mention it. Nobody deserves to be there as much as you do. Plus, now you can live in the National Gallery like you always said you wanted to do."

"Mark my words. You'll find me camped out by the Vermeers someday," she says as she makes a beeline to check out a stall that's offering free mini sliders.

I love seeing Emma like this. She's here, and she no longer has to worry about nabbing a scholarship for grad school like she did growing up, when she knew she wanted to be an art historian and how much tuition would be.

For the last six years, I've been able to foot the bill, thanks to playing in the pros.

We're all still getting used to it, all three of my sisters, my mom, and me. But nothing could beat buying a house for my mom on the beach in La Jolla, a far cry from where we grew up in Lakeside.

And hell, I'm not going to lie—it felt damn good to tell

my little sister last year that she could go to England, no loan needed.

She takes a picture with her phone, then taps something into it before she grins as she catches up to me, with a "Soooo," dragged out and kind of coy, and I know where she's going.

Her favorite place.

She's going fishing for intel.

"So what, Ems?"

"So what's your plan for tonight?" she asks with a knowing look. "With the guy. That sexy AF bartender. His face is magazine perfection."

"Yessssss. Very *GQ*."

"Like if Idris Elba and Angelina Jolie had a love child."

A laugh bursts from me. "That's the image you're putting out there?"

"Idris is male perfection." She drags a finger down her cheek. "And Angelina has great cheekbones."

"You realize he looks nothing like Angelina Jolie and that, in fact, I'm not attracted to Angelina Jolie?"

"You're not? I had *nooooo* idea."

I haul her in for a noogie, since she deserves one. "Smart-ass."

When I let her go, she says, "My point is that he looks like two of the hottest celebs ever. Can you agree they're both quite pretty?"

"Yes, they are both quite pretty," I say, imitating her. "But maybe can we go with Idris and Chris Hemsworth?"

Her eyes light up. "Yes. In my dreams."

I sigh contentedly. "Yeah, mine too."

I linger on that image for a few more seconds, and I'm guessing she does too—because who could resist?—before she reconnects to the present. "Are you really going to go back there though?"

I nod decisively. "Absolutely. I'm going to go see him, and I'm going to lock that down."

Emma rolls her eyes. "Oh, you're going to seal the deal, James? And how exactly do you plan to do that, since he already kind of turned you down?"

I arch a brow. "Did he turn me down?"

Emma laughs, nudging me. "I believe what you told me last night was that he said it wasn't going to happen. That feels a lot like he turned you down."

I shrug it off. "Technically. But he also made a point of saying he wasn't breaking his rule *last night*. Leaving it open for *tonight*. All I have to do is work my magic this evening."

I glance over at her, waiting for the sisterly comeback I know and love, but Emma's not even listening. She's peering around like she's looking for something.

I stop in my tracks, waving my arms. "Earth to Emma."

She turns and gives me an adorable smile. "Right, please tell me all about the guy you're going after. I can't bear to miss a single detail, even though I've only been hearing about the hot guys you've wanted for the last twelve years."

"I don't think you've ever complained about it before," I say.

"Probably because I still find you far too amusing for my own good."

"See? I'm kind of irresistible to everyone, including my own sister. Therefore, I'm going to make sure this guy says yes to me."

I've got just the plan for tonight too. The right clothes. The right aftershave. I'll lay on my classic mix of cocky and charming, and then, before he even knows what's hit him, he'll be dying to take me up on my offer.

Hot hotel sex, here we come.

Pun intended.

"Well," Emma says, with a delighted tone in her voice, "it looks like now's your chance. There he is."

"What?"

My job is to anticipate. To be ready for whatever hits me.

But this surprises the fuck out of me.

I turn around and blink. I'm looking at the man I wanted to take home last night. And he's smirking at me.

"Better than Hemsworth. Better than Elba," I say to my sister.

Emma leans closer and whispers, "And I think now's the perfect time for me to go to that bookstore."

She makes a shooing gesture then adopts her best British accent. "Right. Cheerio. Carry on."

And before I can say anything more, she's gone.

And I don't miss her.

6

FITZ

Dean saunters over. He stops a foot away, appraising me, his dark eyes roaming up and down my body.

Yes, enjoy the view, sexy bartender. Feel free to enjoy the view.

"Seems like you can't quite stay away from me," he says, his expression a touch too close to unreadable.

And that could be a problem if he thinks I've followed him. That shit is not my style. "I didn't expect to see you here," I say, shaking my head, trying to course correct.

"It's okay, Fitz. Admit it. You were kind of stalking me."

I hold up my hands in a stop sign. "No, I swear. I had no idea you were going to be here."

Dean tips his head toward the next line of booths and gives me the slightest grin. "Oh, well, then. I'll just be on my way."

Like I'm letting him get away. Especially with that hint of a smile saying he doesn't want to leave me. Yup, I'm reading him loud and clear now.

"That's not necessary." I step forward, setting a hand on his arm. His strong, toned arm that looks fucking fantastic in that shirt. "I just didn't want you to think I was trying to engineer something."

His gaze swings to where I'm touching him. Damn, he feels good, but if I leave it there, I do look too eager.

I drop my hand.

His eyes return to my face. "Why would I think you were doing that? Are you that strategic? Or are you simply that determined?"

I square my shoulders, taking the bait. "I am determined. Make no bones about that. But I don't need to engineer anything. My guess is that my little sister is playing wingwoman. She was scanning the fair a few minutes ago, and I bet she knew you were going to be here."

"Ah, yes, of course. I did text your sister to give her a heads-up where I'd be."

I shoot him a look. "C'mon, man. Your bartender friend. Remember? I bet they were behind this. My sister was talking to her last night, and Emma has a little matchmaker in her."

Dean laughs, a sexy sound that turns me on then undoes me when he leans a little closer, lowering that deep voice. "Blaming your sister? Seems like a strange excuse when you could just admit you were dying for another opportunity to run into me."

"Pretty sure that's obvious, but I'm happy to spell it out if you'd like."

He pats the back of his jeans, his grin going crooked. "Need a pen?"

"Sure. Paper too? Or do you just want me to give you my hotel key card right now?"

Dean laughs. "So, that'd be a yes for both strategic and determined."

"Got that right. Incidentally, yes is my favorite word."

"I've no doubt it is."

Already the picture of Dean is filling in. He's the kind of guy where I have to read between the lines. And maybe he wants me to.

Because *how* he says something reveals more than what he says at times. The timbre of his voice, the way he moves closer to me—they give me plenty to read. "Has anyone ever told you that you are an insane flirt for a man who's already turned another man down?"

Dean strokes his chin, looking to the sky as if deep in thought. "No, I don't think anyone has told me that. Is that what you're trying to say?"

"What I'm saying is that you can't seem to resist flirting with me."

Dean's quiet for a moment, meeting my gaze. "If that's the case, it's only because you give me so many opportunities to do so."

"Well, trust me, I plan on giving you plenty more."

"Is that so?" We walk to the next stall, where he gives the cocktail mixes a once-over.

"Yes, that is so. That's what I told my sister a few minutes ago," I admit, because I'm easy to read. I lay my cards on the table.

Dean looks far too pleased with this new detail as he heads down the row, checking out other booths along the way. "And what exactly did you tell her?"

I exaggerate shock. "Dean, are you fishing for compliments? Trying to get me to tell you every little detail that I told sweet Emma?"

Of course, I could tell him that—or the things that I *didn't* tell my sister. The things that I kept to myself. Like how I am dying to get my hands on him. To *feel* him. I bet he'd like hearing that more than he lets on.

But now's not the time.

He glances at me out of the corner of his eye. "Hmm. Do I want a recap with every detail? That is a quandary."

I shake my head, amused at how he plays hard to get at times, then not at all at others. "Such a quandary indeed."

We come to a stop near a couple of booths featuring glasses. Dean's not looking at me, because he's checking out shot glasses.

But I'm not letting him off the hook.

I step closer, reaching past him to pick one up.

Letting my arm brush his.

I hear the slightest catch in his breath, then he looks at me, a little more serious for a second.

I wait for him to go next.

And he does. "I guess I do want to know some of the details. Tell me the good ones. Tell me the best ones."

My skin heats as I run my finger over the shot glass. "I told her I was going to return to your bar tonight. That I wanted to see you again. And that I was pretty damn sure you wanted to see me again too."

Dean's lips twitch. "You think so?"

"Yes."

"Your favorite word."

"Especially in this situation."

"And why do you think I want to see you again, Fitz?" His question doesn't come out as a challenge. It's an invitation. He wants me to tell him, to lay it out.

"Because I felt the chemistry, and so did you. And you know it'll be so good for both of us. Ergo, go out with me tonight once you've finished your shift."

There's that grin again. "Go out with you, or go to your hotel? Which one is it?"

"Both, Dean. *Both.*" I set the shot glass down and meet his gaze. "I don't know how to make this more clear. When I see something I want, I do absolutely everything to get it."

We're both quiet for a beat as he levels me with a stare that says he's studying me, trying to figure me out.

Or maybe trying to figure out what he wants from me.

What he'll let himself have.

Finally, Dean asks, "And am I that something?"

"You are that something, and you are that someone."

He gives a casual shrug. "You might not like me if you get to know me."

He walks toward another booth, and I match his strides.

"Maybe you could let me be the judge of that."

Dean seems to consider this as he segues to another topic. "What're you doing in England anyway? Are you and your sister on holiday for the summer?"

There's something more to the question. I'm not sure what exactly, but I have the sense that maybe he's making sure I'm leaving. Just a hunch. Funny, that he knows so little about hockey he'd think I might stay. Or even stay for the rest of the summer.

"Don't worry. I have a J-O-B calling my name in the States. My team isn't moving to London. I'm returning to New York in"—I stop, making a show of looking at my wrist even though I don't wear a watch—"five days. Thursday, I'm outta here."

Dean's eyes seem to spark when I mention the timing, or really, the expiration date. That is intel I file away because it tells me even more about him. "But I'm here now because Emma got into this incredible art program at the University of London. I thought I'd come over with her to get her set up and just have a good time."

"That's kind of you," he says, his tone genuine. "Looking out for her."

"Well, Emma's awesome. She's my baby sister. The others are a little older."

"How many sisters do you have?"

"Three."

"What's that like? Besides loud, I suspect."

"Are you an only child?"

"Yes. Is it that obvious?"

"Now it is. Only children are notorious for being extremely stubborn and often resort to playing hard to get . . . especially when they're pursued by the second youngest in a family of four."

A laugh bursts from his chest. "Was there a study on that?"

"Yes. By the American Journal of Why the Hell Won't You Have Dinner with Me. But the study found the more persistent the second youngest is, the greater the chance of a yes."

"Fascinating study. Do show it to me some time," Dean says, his grin widening.

"I'll be sure to look it up and send it to you."

We wander a little more, and he returns to the topic of family. "So, the second youngest of four. Sounds like you're close with all of them?"

"I am. I love all my knuckleheaded sisters madly, and I've managed to forgive them for the living hell known as trying to get to the shower in the mornings in a house full of double-X chromosomes. It's been my mom, my sisters, and me since my dad died when I was ten."

Dean's face softens. "I'm sorry to hear that."

I wave it off, since it's all I've ever known. "Couldn't have asked to be raised by better women. They all took a very personal interest in making sure I didn't turn into a total dick. I bet Emma's personally offended that you don't seem to be falling for my charms."

He looks away, then back at me, lowering his voice, and

it feels personal, like what he's saying is just for me. "I don't think that's completely true."

A smile spreads on my face, and my chest heats. "So you admit it—"

I'm interrupted by shouting and loud music from the booth up ahead. A small cheering crowd surrounds the booth. Dean and I edge closer, and it doesn't take long for me to figure out what's happening.

They've set up a small demonstration of softball, with a plastic bat and rubber ball. Different patrons are stepping up to try to hit a "home run"—hit the target in the back—for a free drink.

A brunette sporting a baseball cap that reads "The Foul Ball" bounces up to Dean, holding out the plastic bat.

She grins at him. "Looks like someone would be a natural! Fancy a hit?"

He shakes his head. "I'll pass, thanks."

"Not a fan of softball, either?"

"Not really. And definitely not in bar form."

"Have you played? Softball's a great fucking game."

Dean arches an eyebrow. "I thought hockey was the great sport."

"Believe it or not, lots of sports are great. Sure, hockey's the best. But softball's pretty awesome too."

I pause to examine his guns, making sure he sees where I'm looking. "And that lady might be right. With those fantastic arms, you might be a natural. And if you're a natural, you might like the sport."

A smile seems to tug at his lips from the compliment, and then his eyes slide down to my arms, covered in ink. "Maybe I'd be a natural, but I don't think it's my cup of tea."

Behind us, someone nails the rubber ball into the target, sending up a wave of cheers.

I take on the worst English accent I can muster. "Oh, do you just spend all day playing cricket?"

His eyes return to me. "So, you're going to mock my country for its sports choices?"

"I believe you started the sports mockery last night, or do I need to remind you of both your sports snobbery and your sports mockery?"

"You must. Because you just did."

"You kind of walked into it."

"And I stand by my case. There is no need for softball here in London. Why would we need it? We've never had it before; it's not an English thing. It's not *our* thing."

"But it *might* be your thing, because it's here," I say, grabbing a flyer from the table. "Look at that—a rooftop softball cage. Just imagine—if you went every day, you could become the British softball master."

Dean cracks up, a deep, hearty laugh that I dig. "Yes, that's just what I aspire to do. I'll just drop everything and focus on this instead."

"Everything?" I quirk a brow. "What exactly is *everything*?"

"Things that involve clothes." Dean shakes his head. "Things I do. The bar. Cooking classes with my mates. Furniture restoration with my dad."

I snap my fingers, his last comment triggering a memory. "That's an unusual hobby. My friends Summer and Logan have a cousin in New York who's into that. Guy named Leo."

"Yes. I know him. We're all mates, all of us who restore furniture around the globe. Maybe you have some friends there who like to cook too?"

"I believe I do. And we all agree softball is better than *cooking club*," I say.

He laughs indignantly. "It's not a fucking cooking club.

They're classes. I go with some friends who own an Indian restaurant. We learn different cuisines, new dishes. Don't you like food, Fitz?"

"Love it. And I love podcasts about unsolved mysteries, and I like hitting up the local indie and rock shows when I'm not on the ice. I also play paintball with my buddies back in New York. I bet you hate paintball."

"This may shock you, but I don't play paintball. And this may shock you too, since you seem to think I have no athletic prowess, but I could kick your ass at pool."

"Ohhhh," I say, dragging it out, loving the direction of this conversation. "I'd like to take you up on that."

"I bet you would."

My eyes drift back to his arms. Then down his chest, where I can tell, just tell, from the fit of his shirt that he's rocking a six-pack. "You look like you play sports. And that's a compliment."

He takes a beat, going quiet for a moment like he's weighing his thoughts. Maybe his wants. "You absolutely look like you do, and that is a compliment too," he says, his eyes drifting back to my ink, his voice hitting that low register it seems to linger in when he looks at me, and both the compliment and the eye-fucking do not go unnoticed. "In any case," he adds, "I'm a runner. I play rugby occasionally. Football, if I can."

"And by 'football,' you actually mean soccer."

"I mean the sport played entirely with one's feet. Meaning, *football*."

I see my opening and take it.

"Fine. I won't even try to convince you about football versus football or football versus rugby. But what I will convince you of right now is that softball is a hell of a fun way to blow off steam."

Dean laughs. "Sure it is."

"Wanna bet? I bet that right now, it would be the perfect way to take your stress away."

"How do you know I'm stressed?" he asks, and he's still laughing, and I love it. I can get this guy to laugh, and the sound lights me up, makes me want to keep going because, in his laughter, I can feel him bending. I can tell he likes talking to me as much as I like talking to him.

Do I want to get him under me? Abso-fucking-lutely. But do I also dig this? The talking? Hell yes. And it's one of the reasons I know it's going to be electric when I have my way with him.

Because we already have a rhythm. It's like being on the ice, in a way. He lines up the shot, and I shoot it right into the net.

I dig out my wallet and find a few bills. "How about this? Ten pounds says you love it. And if you don't, I'll throw in some drinks too."

"You do realize I own a bar, right? Drinks are literally on me every single night."

I run a hand over my beard. "Fair. How about dinner, then? That study said it was a good idea."

"I'm still waiting for you to show me that study."

"Oh, I'd like to show you a lot of things."

He tosses his head back, cracking up. "Fitz, do you ever take no for an answer?"

"You haven't said no. And if you do, I will walk away in a second, and you will never hear from me again. I respect boundaries. I respect the hell out of no. If you want to say no, say it." I wait. Arms crossed. Patient.

He looks at me, pinning me with an intense stare, one that has so much going on behind it.

If I only knew what.

He takes a small step closer, getting near me, and hell, I love being this close. This isn't the accidental brushing from earlier. He knows precisely what he's doing. Because even though he hasn't touched me, I can tell by the way he swallows, by the hitch of his breath, that he's affected by me being near him.

Good.

Same goes for me.

Dean takes a moment, like he's collecting himself before he answers.

When he speaks, his voice is low, just for me. "You might have noticed I'm not saying no to you. That, in fact, I'm having an incredibly hard time turning you down, Fitz."

I nearly groan at the way he says my name. Like he wants more of it, more of me.

"Good. I don't want your no. I want your yes. But right now, I would settle for showing you how awesome softball is." I take a beat. "Ball's in your court, sexy bartender."

He picks up the volley and serves it in my direction. "*Yes*, cocky athlete," he says. "Show me why you like softball."

"With pleasure."

And I'm patting myself on the back for having the self-restraint not to pump a fist.

But that's how I feel right now.

Like I just set up a beautiful play.

7

DEAN

They're going to take away my award.

All that resisting, all that attitude with Maeve, and what am I doing now?

Following this outgoing, determined, sexy-as-sin, and fit-as-fuck American to some cheesy, gimmicky bar.

I detest gimmicky bars as much as I loathe piña coladas. This kind of theme bar is an affront to everything I want for The Magpie.

Posters of ballplayers line the walls, all of them pitching or crouching behind a plate or running. Lots of thick mustaches. Loads of pinstripes.

Perhaps that'll kill the buzz I seem to have from Fitz. The intoxicating effect he has on me.

Maybe I should just home in on this bar's atmosphere, which should shore up my resistance—like the neon everywhere, and so much awful beer, endless taps of Bud and Corona. If anyone saw me here, I'd have to hang my head in shame. Lucky for me—or unlucky, considering I have a bet I've got to somehow hold on to—Fitz shows no interest in lingering at the bar.

We pay the attendant at the bottom of the stairs, then Fitz leads us right up them, following the signs for "Rooftop Batting Cages."

As he goes, he keeps looking back, watching me with those blue eyes that seem to get heavier with want with every step.

"Like the view?"

"It's not bad."

"Right back atcha."

I laugh at his way of speaking, his Americanisms that are kind of endearing.

All I'm doing is blowing off steam. Letting him teach me a little softball. That doesn't mean anything more will come of it.

He's just a man.

An insanely smooth-talking man with a fantastic laugh and a tempting beard.

A man that, unless I want to spend the weekend scrubbing walls, I have to resist.

On the roof, we grab the bat and balls ourselves, since this is a do-it-yourself setup, then head to the makeshift lane and its home plate. Maybe thirty or forty feet away, there are nets to catch the balls, so they don't pelt the Londoners on the street. Very considerate.

It's quiet up here, except for the whir of the bar down below.

I pick up the bat and swing it once for practice. "Easy."

"Easy and fun, right?"

"Sure. It's easy and fun," I repeat, and the weight of my words fully registers.

Something about being with Fitz is easy. Everything about being with Fitz is fun.

I bet getting him naked would be easy and fun too.

And in a filthy heartbeat, my threadbare resistance starts to unravel.

8

FITZ

Intense concentration etches on his brow. Dean swings the bat again with the same grace and power he used when he was mixing drinks.

Except…

"Your grip's all wrong," I say and because sports are second nature to me, I move in behind him, my arms over his, adjusting. Damn, he smells good. Like soap and pine and the man I want my hands on, my mouth on. The man I want to have my way with.

I take a breath. I have to make this count.

Something tells me it's now or never if I'm going to win Dean over.

And this is a match I don't intend to lose.

"There," I say, shifting his right hand one more inch. "You want to put your hands like that. Hold on to it. The power comes from the stance."

Dean doesn't say anything, but I can feel him breathing hard against me. I slide my hands along his arms, moving his hands slightly. Tightening his grip on the bat.

"From there, you just have to hit as hard as you can," I

say, and I'm hardly thinking about softball right now. I'm hardly thinking about what I'm saying. I'm just feeling—feeling the inescapable pull of contact. "That's it."

"That seems simple enough," he says, distracted, and clearly as uninterested in softball right now as I am.

And I know that I'm getting to him—little by little.

I can be very convincing.

"It's so simple," I say, then I run my nose along the back of his neck.

"I'm pretty sure that's not part of the game," Dean says in that tone that gives away his desire. A tone that says he wants more.

"No, it's not. But maybe it should be. Especially when the players feel like this."

I let my hands glide down from the bat, daring to graze his forearms.

"Ah, yes," Dean says, like he's trying for a laugh. "All ballplayers should have burly, pushy American men standing behind—"

His words are laid to waste the second I bring my lips to the side of his neck.

It starts as a soft kiss maybe.

For a second.

But then I bite him because he tastes so fucking good. I bring my teeth down and nip. His scent goes to my head, makes me lose my mind.

I crowd him with my body, my crotch against his ass, my arms around him, kissing and biting and sucking his neck, and the whole time he's tense in my arms.

But not quite.

Not quite at all.

He's slowly but deliberately giving in, his body veering the slightest bit closer. He pushes against me, and the sensation nearly drives me over the edge.

Then a loud clang of metal hits my ears. He drops the bat—or maybe I push it out of his hands—sending it clattering to the ground.

Dean spins around, and in a flash of a second, his hands are on my chest, and he backs me to the cage wall.

Oh yes, I like commanding Dean. I like commanding Dean very much.

"Has anyone told you that you had better finish what you start?" His lips are a straight line, his jaw set hard and his eyes fiery.

"That's what I want with you. Don't you know?"

"I mean, don't be a fucking tease with your kisses, Fitz." Dean levels me with a stare. "*Mean* them. Finish them. Kiss me all the fucking way, like I'm going to kiss you."

And then he grabs my face and drops his lips to mine and takes me. His lips are devouring, ravenous, and he kisses me like he's starving for me.

Sounds about right, since I feel the same damn way for him.

He grips me hard, kissing me passionately. He's greedy and pent-up, and I'm the object of all his wild lust. He pours it all into a punishing kiss.

It's deep, uninhibited, and so damn hot.

Normally, I like to lead, but hell, I will follow him anywhere right now. I take and take and take, and he gives it to me, his long, lean frame slamming against me. The outline of his cock, thick and hard and completely tantalizing against my pelvis, rubs against my hard-on, and it feels so incredibly good.

Like a dirty promise of what's to come.

And his lips—my God, his lips.

I am dead. Just fucking dead.

From the way he kisses me.

He fucks my mouth with his tongue, owning my lips, consuming me.

My hands race around him, grabbing that firm, tight ass, yanking him impossibly closer as he devours my lips . . . and we fit.

We fit together, and it's electric.

And I have no doubt when we finally make it to the bedroom—and we will make it to the bedroom—that it will be the hottest sex of my life.

Because my head goes hazy and my body heats to supernova levels just from the way he kisses me. From how he grabs my face and yanks me close. From the way he wants to resist me but can't whatsoever.

And the moans he makes with every stroke of his wicked tongue.

His lips are hungry, and his hands are strong, grappling at me the way I like, all rough and demanding. This kiss is frying my circuits, and I want nothing on earth more than to take him back to my hotel and do very bad things to him.

Seems he wants that too.

The need to get out of here wars with my need to kiss the breath out of him.

The door downstairs clangs, followed by voices, then footsteps on the stairs.

We break apart, panting, wildly aroused.

I smirk, glance down at my crotch. "Hope that goes down quickly, but that probably won't happen."

Dean laughs, shaking his head. "One of the many hazards of having a dick."

There's that dry sense of humor again. How is it possible to go from wanting to tear his clothes off to relishing his laugh?

But that seems par for the course around Dean.

The voices are drunken, unsteady, but working their way up the stairs.

Stepping away from him, I pick up the fallen bat as a group of twentysomething women bursts onto the scene, chatting with each other. A bartender follows them and glances our way. This wasn't going to stay private for long anyway.

"Here you go," I say, passing off the bat to a blonde.

She glances at me and blinks. "Hey, aren't you that guy from . . ."

She snaps her fingers, trying to place me. "From, ugh . . . it's on the tip of my tongue."

She's American and maybe a hockey fan, but it's hard to say.

My preferences are no secret, so I'm not trying to hide. Nor do I think Dean is. But I'd rather not chat with a fan while I'm sporting this kind of wood.

"Nah. I get that a lot though. Go knock in some homers, ladies." I wink at them as I head to the stairs, Dean behind me.

"Does that happen a lot? Being recognized or almost recognized?"

I shrug. "Sometimes. Not as much as basketball or base-ball players though." I gesture to my face. "Since we wear masks and all."

"Yes, I am aware of that aspect of hockey. *Masks and all*," Dean says, imitating my voice.

I shoot him an appreciative grin. "Ooh, aren't you so very cheeky."

"Charming, Fitz. I'm charming. Get it right," he says, then his tone turns serious, and he tips his forehead to the roof, indicating the girls. "But what I was getting at about being recognized is, did you deny it's you for a reason? Are you in the closet?"

I bust out laughing as we bound down the stairs, shaking my head. "Not in the motherfucking least."

Dean wipes a hand across his forehead. "Good, because I do not need to deal with that."

"Nor do I. Been there, done that, not interested. Closet's not my thing."

"Ditto. For a second, I thought maybe you came to England to avail yourself of opportunities to be . . . out of the spotlight."

"It's not a secret." I flash a grin. "I'm kind of known for it, as one of a handful of out players in the NHL."

"That's good."

The smile on his face tells me it's hella good, and I'm damn glad he's in the same sitch. But it's good to make sure. "I assumed you're out too. But if that makes an ass out of you and me, maybe tell me now."

He laughs. "You might be an ass on other counts, but not on that one. I don't care if anyone sees me turning you on. As I clearly do."

I roll my eyes, stop at the bottom of the stairs, and grab his waist. I wrap a hand around his hip. "You love to give me a hard time."

Dean's gaze drifts down to my jeans and back up. "Seems I'm quite good at it too."

"And that's why I said 'I get that a lot' to the blonde. Because I'm still insanely turned on from the way you attacked my face, and I didn't need anyone else seeing what you did to me."

His eyes take a stroll again. "Yes. You seem to be rather affected."

"Understatement of the century." I let go of him and head into the bar, where I gesture to the exit. "Let's get out of here."

"I'm still not going back to your hotel."

"Tease," I say as we edge our way onto the street.

"What? Didn't you like just kissing me, Fitz?" he asks, all mock-coy, since he knows I loved it.

But I'm a big believer in saying what you mean and meaning what you say. "I loved every single, solitary moment of it," I tell him, and Dean swallows roughly, then scrubs a hand across the back of his neck like he's processing that.

"The feeling is mutual," he says softly.

Pride suffuses me. "I'm going to convince you to check out the thread count of my hotel sheets tonight."

He laughs, runs his hand over his short hair, then mutters, "Why am I not surprised?"

"Oh, I have plenty of surprises left for you. And when you come over I'll show you."

We come to a stop on the street.

Dean chuckles, but when he looks at me again, that damn mask is back. He glances at his watch. "Listen. As much as I would love to accept, I do need to get to work tonight. It's getting on."

I study him and wonder if it's true or if it's an out. Wonder if he's playing hard to get or if he is hard to get.

Because as much as I like the chase, I do have my limits.

I want Dean.

But I also want him to want this thing between us as much as I do.

I have one more move, one way to tell. Make it crystal clear that this would have a beginning and an end. I have a feeling that's what he wants—an escape clause with zero loopholes.

"This was fun. And I know better than anyone how important work is. If you want to perform at the highest level, you have to eliminate distractions."

At that, he tilts his head, curious. "What do you mean exactly?"

I shrug like it's nothing, even though this is kind of a big deal—the pact I have with my teammates. "We came so damn close to making the playoffs last season and missed by this much." I hold up my thumb and forefinger. "All because we came out of training camp weak. We lost a bunch of games early on, and even though we had a killer second half of the season, it wasn't quite enough. So, we made a pact, some of the other guys and me. No distractions. No hooking up during training camp and into the start of the season. It'll let us focus on the game."

"Focus is important. A man needs to be able to do his job."

"Exactly. My job is everything to me because it means I can take care of my family. Make my mom's life easy. Give her all the things she never had when we were growing up."

"You do all that for her?"

"Hell yeah. I have since I started in the NHL after college. Six years later, she's living the life she deserves in the house of her dreams, and is married again to a good guy who respects her and adores her. As he should. So, yeah, making sure I can perform at the highest level on the ice is the most important thing in the world to me."

"That's great that you can do that. She must be proud of you."

There's no joking or teasing now, just earnestness, and I like it, so I continue laying it on the line for him. "For me, I'm over here with Emma being a supportive big brother. But I wouldn't mind one last red-hot, smoking night or two before I shut it all down before camp." I look at the sky, stroking my chin. "If only I could find the right guy. Maybe someone who doesn't want strings either."

My eyes sweep over Dean.

He draws a deep breath. "No strings?"

I slash a hand through empty air. "Nada."

"And you said you're only here for one week?"

"Not even. Only five more days and then I leave." I flap my arms like I'm flying away.

A flicker of a smile crosses Dean's handsome face as he asks, "Back to America?"

"Me and all of my charm. Gone, baby, gone."

"You're persistent. I'll give you that. Must be quite an asset for your job."

I stretch my arms above my head, my shirt riding up, revealing another one of my work assets. Or rather, a preview to six more of them. Let him watch and see what I've got going on in the abs department. I know what these cost me in crunches and gym time. All worth it for the fire in his eyes.

I lower my arms, because that's enough eye candy to whet his appetite.

"Speaking of jobs, you have to get back to work. And while you're mixing martinis, you should give some thought to my proposition."

"Is that what you think I'll be doing?"

"You're a thinker. Yes, that's what you'll be doing."

"And you're a full-speed-ahead kind of guy."

"Yes. Yes, I am."

Dean hums, and I can see him mulling over my offer, so I leave one last lure for him.

"Besides, I have a busy day tomorrow. I shouldn't be out too late anyway. Emma and I are going for afternoon tea at Fortnum & Mason. Aren't you proud? So English of us."

He laughs, sliding instantly back into that easy zone he lives in most of the time. His whole body moves with his laugh.

I just want him to do it again and again.

"I am quite impressed," Dean says, then his lips curve into the start of a grin, and I swear I can feel him bending. "But tea's not something we take lightly. You'll have to mind yourself."

There it is.

A spark.

"You're exactly right," I say, latching onto this potent possibility. "I'm going to be completely lost. Who knows what I'll mess up?"

"So true. I wouldn't want you to be overwhelmed by all the choices."

His smirk tells me this is the path to what I want—another chance with him, without him fully admitting that he's taking it. Maybe because of his rules, maybe for some other reason. I don't know why he's still reluctant, given our crazy chemistry, but I do know he's finding it harder to deny me.

"Do you know how hard it is for an American to have tea without an Englishman there to help? English breakfast, Earl Grey, blah, blah, blah. Who can tell it all apart without the help of a Brit?"

Dean's grin widens. "Right. It's just like being in France or Japan or Portugal and needing a translator."

"See? I knew you'd get it."

"I get it completely. You need an Englishman to help you decide whether it is the cream or the jam that goes first on your scone."

I had no clue there was a set order. "Yes, that. Exactly. As you can see, how else could a barbarian like myself enjoy a proper afternoon tea?"

"I can't even imagine how you would," Dean answers, then whispers, "The scone tastes the same either way."

"Whatever you say." I grin because it's looking like he's saying yes.

We stand on the street, as crowds walk by with their shopping bags and talk about the great weather.

This is it, my chance to seal this sort-of date with Dean. The man doesn't seem opposed to public displays of affection, so I go for it.

I grab the back of his head and bring him close, giving him a hot, hard, hungry kiss that I hope leaves him wanting more.

I whisper against his lips, "I will see you tomorrow."

Dean blinks, looking frazzled, maybe even as rattled as I feel. Then he nods. "Yes. You will."

And I want to punch the air. But I restrain myself, keeping it cool. "I'll need your number to text you the info."

Dean types it into my phone then takes a deep breath. "All right. Tomorrow, then." He licks his lips. "*Fitz.*"

Yes, there's my name again, and it sounds so damn good the way he says it—like sex and desire on his tongue.

He turns to walk away, but before he covers five feet, he spins around and returns. With a resolute expression and dark eyes fixed on me, he takes out his wallet and fishes around. He finds a bill and presses it into my hand, curling my fingers around it. "You won the bet. Softball is great." There's a pause, then he taps his finger to his bottom lip, humming in consideration. "Or really, I suppose there's something about how we played the game that worked for me."

As much as it goes against my nature, I don't touch him. I don't kiss him, and I don't say a word. I let my crooked grin do the talking as he enjoys having the last word—an admission that he wants me the same damn way I want him.

I watch as he walks away this time.

It's a great view.

I can't enjoy it too much, though, because a familiar voice pops up behind me.

"I'd say that was successful."

I whip around, and there's Emma with shopping bags full of used books.

"What luck that there was a used bookstore right down the road," she says. "And that I just happened to see my brother making out in the street."

I grin. "Why hide my talents when the public should see them?"

She laughs. "You're insufferable."

"And you're a little sneak."

"Not a sneak. Just an excellent wingwoman."

I want to disagree, but I can still taste Dean's kiss on my mouth. Then, of course, there's his number in my phone.

And tea tomorrow.

And the promise of something else too, if my kiss worked the way I hope it did.

9

DEAN

A man cannot survive a force of nature without rein-forcements.

When a hurricane barrels toward your city, you batten down the hatches.

The same strategy applies to Hurricane Fitz.

So I make sure that I squeeze in time for a run before I'm due at The Magpie. Running centers me. Clears my head. Gives me time to think.

After all, I'm a *thinker*, as he said.

I scoff at that label as I run alongside the Thames, logging another mile as I go.

But he's right. That's my style—I contemplate.

As I run, I imagine a sheet of paper, and I'm sketching out the pros and cons of a few red-hot, smoking nights with a visitor who's taking off soon.

On the one hand, I don't date younger guys.

On the other hand, we're not going to have a relation-ship. Also, he's only four years younger, as I learned today.

On the one hand, he's a customer, and that's against the rules.

On the other hand, he can't be a customer after the end of this week.

On the one hand, he's leaving in five days.

On the other hand, he's also *leaving in five days*.

"What's the worst that can happen in such a short time?" I ask out loud.

"That is an excellent question. Inquiring minds want to know."

I swivel around, slowing my pace as my mate Sam comes alongside. We started the run together, but I peeled ahead, and now he's caught up to me.

"Talking out loud? Still hearing voices in your head?" Sam's dark eyes glint as usual. He grins like he's got a secret that no one else knows.

"I was drawing an important conclusion," I say.

"Do tell. Was it about drinks or cooking or the state of the world? Or wait! Was it some piece of secondhand furniture you can't decide whether to buy or not? Or maybe a book you want, and you're going to go read twenty reviews before you pull the trigger on a nine-pound purchase?"

"Are you my friend? Or have you switched to my foe?"

He claps me on the back as we run. "In two short years of knowing you, I've learned that you deliberate on everything," he says.

I slow down as we near the edge of Jubilee Gardens. "If you must know, I was debating whether I ever wanted to play pool in your pub again."

"And you decided Sticks and Stones is the only way to go. Very nice, my man. Very nice." He narrows his eyes. "But I bet you're lying."

"Dickhead," I mutter.

"I see you're picking up our American lingo. Excellent."

"We use 'dickhead' here in the UK too," I point out to

my friend who opened a pub a couple of years ago with his then-wife, an English woman who just put him through the wringer in a hellish divorce. But hey, he got the bar. "On account of having so many dickheads here in London," I say as I wiggle my brows.

"Ouch. Who's the foe now?"

"Sorry, not sorry. You had it coming."

"That is true. Anyway, don't tell me what you're pondering. I'll just imagine it's whether you should buy new cookware or the latest political thriller."

"The ribbing. Dear God, the ribbing." I groan, scrubbing a hand across my face before I shoot him a look. "If you must know, I'm contemplating a hookup."

He scoffs. "What's to ponder? If you like the person, and the energy is there, go for it. But no clingers, K?"

"Never again."

He points to the edge of the park and the path leading to his flat. "Come by this week. Play a round. Try not to hustle all my patrons."

I bring my hand to my heart. "Me? Hustle your patrons? Never."

"You're the hustler. Catch you later, man."

After the run, I continue my contemplation over a shower.

Though the shower isn't the most conducive place for weighing pros and cons.

Showers, and the freedom to exercise one's imagination, usually lead to the pro column.

Once dressed, I head to work, where, fling or no fling, I have to pay the piper.

The piper glances at me all night while she mixes drinks, giving me *I know what you did this afternoon* eyes as she zips past me. But it's Saturday night, and there isn't a moment to chat or for her to harass me until after we close.

As I tally the receipts, I lose track a few times of the final take.

Thanks a lot, Hurricane Fitz.

"Hey, earth to Dean. Are you going to help me mop?"

I look up from the laptop and meet Maeve's gaze. She's put up all the chairs already. "You've been somewhere else all night, and I think I know why."

"Oh, do you now?"

Her smile's mischievous. "Someone's thinking about a certain customer."

I laugh.

If she only knew.

Except . . . wait. She does know. I shoot her my best death glare. "You tried to trip me up."

Maeve dares to look at me ever so innocently. "Me, who asked you to mop?"

"Yes. You. You engineered the whole thing at the expo today. You were talking to Emma last night."

"Ohh. You know his sister's name."

"Yes, he mentioned her today—"

Maeve bursts out laughing. "That is soooo sweet that you know her name."

"He was talking about her. It would be hard *not* to know her name."

"And now you're talking about her. Want to pick out monogrammed towels with him next?" She bats her lashes.

I shake my head adamantly. "Things that will never happen."

"Fine. Maybe not towels. How about sharing shirts?"

I arch one brow at her. "You were once my friend, right? Once upon a time, like in the dark ages?"

"You pegged him as *my* type and tried to trip *me* up.

That whole *you're so going down* and *your type* bit. Serves you right that now you can't get enough of him."

"That is not even remotely the case."

She points at me, glee written all over her features. "It is. So, pay up now. Did you shag him already?"

"No," I say, shutting the laptop.

"You didn't? I'm shocked. But you still owe me."

I tap my chin. "Is there anything in the rules about what happens when your business partner and *former* best friend tries to make you lose? I mean, why else would he have shown up at some random bar expo?"

She flashes puppy-dog eyes at me, trying so damn hard to school her expression. "I have no idea what you're talking about."

I don't blink. "Seriously? That's the best you've got?" I stare her down and imitate, *"I have no idea what you're talking about . . ."*

"Dean, maybe you've been working too much. You're starting to imagine things. Though if you're *admitting* that something happened between you and that guy . . ." She points at the mop.

I shake my head. "I'm not admitting anything. Not until you admit that you and Emma set me up. If I grabbed your phone right now, I bet I'd see a text thread about where I was at the expo today."

Maeve gives a satisfied Cheshire-cat grin. "If such a text thread did exist, it'd already have been deleted."

"You do know that's kind of playing dirty. Getting me like that."

She shrugs. "It's what you tried to do to me last night. I just happen to be better at the game." She hands me the mop. "You might as well get to scrubbing. And while you do, you can tell me all about your romantic make-out session on the streets of London. I want to live vicariously through you. Now, tell me. Was it swoon-worthy? Did he melt you? Make your knees go weak?"

"My knees don't go weak. And I don't melt. That's not a thing. Plus, it was just a kiss."

"Aha! So you admit it. Start mopping."

With a beleaguered sigh, I grab the mop, admitting she won this round. At least this is one of the easier chores on her list of consequences. And truthfully, I'd end up telling her everything anyway.

"Give me the details," she says as she cleans the counter. "When are you seeing him again?"

I dip the mop in the bucket. "It isn't like that. It was just a one-time thing," I say, though as I try that on for size, the prospect sounds awful. A few hot kisses were not enough. I want the whole hurricane, storm and all.

Maeve smirks. "Liar."

She's always been able to see right through me, ever since we met at uni more than ten years ago and hit it off straightaway.

"Why don't you just date him? I mean, yeah, you'd have to buy me my jukebox. And do a hell of a lot of chores. But it wouldn't be that bad. He's so delish. Plus, I looked him up. He has a great rep and contributes to a lot of charities —rescue animals, cancer research, LGBTQ teens."

I look from the spit-shined floor to her, impressed with this new intel. "Is that so?"

"Yes. He likes to give back. Which I happen to think is lovely. Along with his face," she says playfully.

"Yes, both qualities are quite lovely, Maeve," I say, and I mean it. His background is appealing, even though it doesn't matter much for a fling. Still, it's good to know he's not a selfish prick.

"But he's young," I say, moving the mop around the floor. "They always want more, and more isn't my style.

The bar, the loan . . . You know how it goes—more is distracting."

Maeve stops her cleaning, her tone softer. "You can't look at every guy you're interested in like he might be another Dylan."

Except I can, and I do. "I don't want to, but Dylan didn't start out saying he wanted more. He started casually. How can I trust this wouldn't be the same? That sooner or later Fitz wouldn't start talking about love?"

I shudder at the thought.

Love makes people do stupid things. It makes them lose sight of what matters.

Maeve closes the distance between us, curling a hand on my shoulder. "But this isn't about love, our least favorite four-letter word, my friend." She sets her head on my shoulder and sighs. I stroke her hair briefly, knowing that she's got her own issues with that word. When the last guy broke her heart, it took all my self-control not to knock him senseless when he walked in here and tried to make it up to her. Instead, I simply kicked him out and told him never to come round again.

"Definitely our least favorite," I echo.

She lifts her head, erasing the temporary spate of sadness, her eyes now glinting. "It's about other four-letter words, right? The good ones. The ones that mean fun."

"Right, of course," I say quickly. She's right on that count too.

"And along those lines, how long is he here for anyway? I thought Emma said he was only in town for a little bit."

"A week. Though I suppose five days is more accurate." I glance at the clock as if it's ticking down to his departure. Loudly. Insistently.

With wide eyes, she gestures to the door, shooing me. "Get on that. Now. Ride that man. Go, go, go."

I laugh. "You want that jukebox badly."

"Yes, but I also saw the way you two looked at each other." She brings her finger to her tongue and touches the air, making a sizzling sound. "You two are fire. And you have plenty of time for a fun fling. Plus, think of how great the bar will look once he leaves and you get on with all your chores. Sounds like a win-win all around."

"So I should bang him so we can have the bar done at last?"

"Yes." Then she shifts to a more serious tone. "Look, I've known you for more than ten years. We set up this bet to avoid distractions, and I know you want to avoid them, but you're also worried about being like your mum, and you're not."

"I didn't know you were going to psychoanalyze me."

She shrugs easily. "It's what friends do. And friends also remind friends to have some fun. After all, how many times is a hot, bighearted American hockey player going to show up here? One who, by all accounts, is insanely into you. The choice is easy as pie. No strings, no attachments."

She tosses a towel over her shoulder and leaves me to my thoughts. I push the mop around some more, running the possibility over in my mind. Sure, losing the bet nicks my pride, but more than anything, I need to stay focused because this bar—my business, the thing I've most wanted to do since uni—is my dream. Something of my own. Something I'm in charge of.

And dating can be distracting.

But if he's only here for a few days? He can't be distracting, because he can't be anything more than a fling.

I finish mopping, put the bucket away, and return to the counter, where Maeve is nearly done polishing the glasses. I pull out my phone and open my playlist. "Fancy a martini and some excellent music?"

"Always. But you make them—both the playlist and the drinks. Yours are legendary on both counts."

"That is true. I am the martini master and the greatest deejay this bar has ever known."

I put on some Miles Davis, since that's what I like in the bar, and mix some drinks. Then, I click open my texting app, deciding to add a little spice to tomorrow's tea.

10

FITZ

Later that night, I'm alone in my hotel room after I've worked out, showered, and had dinner with Emma. I slide into bed wearing nothing and grab my phone, tempted to text him.

But I don't. Instead, I turn to a podcast I've been hooked on, *Someone Knows Something*, catching up with some of my friends in New York as I listen.

First, I see a text from my friend Summer, who just opened a gym catering to the over-fifty-five crowd. I click on it, smiling at the picture she sent of some of her clients kickboxing, then read a message telling me she might just enlist me to teach them hockey next. I reply.

Fitz: I'll teach them to fight on the ice too.

I toggle over to a text from her twin brother, Logan, one of my good buds.

Logan: Some people are counting down till training camp. I am counting down till paintball league.

Fitz: That is because you know you have a secret weapon with me on your team.

Logan: Shh. Don't tell anyone. Also, Amelia says hi, and she wants a picture of you on London Bridge to make sure it's not falling down. Guess she likes you. Don't have any idea why.

Fitz: Because your seven-year-old has awesome taste. And I promise to get her a pic. Love that kid.

I close the thread, messaging next with Ransom, one of my close friends from the team.

Ransom: T-minus six days. NOT THAT I'M COUNTING THE DAYS till training camp starts.

Fitz: But is it counting that you're doing, man?

Ransom: Counting the babes.

Fitz: I'd expect nothing less from you.

Ransom: I'm heading to a club tonight in Soho. Wish me luck. Wait, I don't need luck.

Fitz: Good luck, you ugly bastard.

Ransom: The ladies love this mug.

Fitz: Some people have no taste. Anyway, be ready to kick unholy ass on the ice in T-minus six days.

Ransom: Nothing less, bro. Nothing motherfucking less.

I send him an emoji of a middle finger, and he sends five back to me, when lo and behold, a text arrives from Dean. I close the Ransom thread, since this one is way better than chatting with my friends.

Dean: English breakfast is a strong, robust flavor. Earl Grey is subtler.

There might be a hidden message in there. I reply, going fishing.

Fitz: Got a favorite between the two?

Dean: Generally, I prefer a strong tea.

Yeah, I had a feeling he might say that. Or maybe a hope, because I know I can come on strong. But that's who I am.

Fitz: Good to know. That's very good to know.

Dean: I thought you might find that intel useful. As a primer, if you know what I mean.

Fitz: I do know what you mean, and I do find that tip very, very useful.

Dean: Good. I'm glad to hear that it's handy.

Fitz: So handy. Also, in case you're wondering, I'm still thinking about the way you mauled my face this afternoon.

Dean: Of course you're thinking about that.

Fitz: No doubt you are too.

Dean: It's possible.

Fitz: You like to toy with me.

Dean: You like when I do it.

Fitz: Evidently I do. It was hot as hell how you went after what you wanted today.

Dean: I had a feeling you might have enjoyed it. But rest assured you weren't the only one.

Fitz: Ah, so you're saying the feeling was mutual?

Dean: The feeling was very much mutual. And I also very much liked what I felt.

Fitz: You are such an unstoppable flirt.

Dean: And this bothers you?

Fitz: No, it turns me on. That's the problem. I'm here in my big king-size bed, all alone, without a stitch of clothing on.

Dean: If you think I'm going to ask for a dick pic, that is not my style.

Fitz: If you think I'm going to send one, that is not my style.

Dean: Good. Now we've established that, thanks a lot for planting that fantastic image in my head. You in your bed with nothing on, and I can't fucking make a proper martini now.

I smile. Unbidden, it takes over my entire being. He's as affected as I am.

Fitz: And on that note, I've got business to take care of, and I will see you for tea.

I shut my texting app before I say anything else, because it's best to leave him wanting more. And I'm pretty sure that's exactly how he's feeling right now.

The same way I am.

SUNDAY

Also known as the day we make the rules we're sure we'll never break.

11

FITZ

My morning is packed.

First, a long workout at the hotel gym, where I push myself with weights, crunches, and push-ups.

Then, I hit the streets, AirPods in, blasting my usual hard rock jams as I pound out six miles across the city, soaking in the sights of Battersea Park and the Peace Pagoda.

As the playlist loops, I picture the season ahead of me, the performance I want to have, the stats I want to rack up.

The focus I need.

My contract is up at the end of next year, so it's a pivotal one. The better I do, the more secure I can make the future for Mom, Emma, Carrie, and Sarah, as well as their kids.

When I finish my workout, I return a call from my agent as I cool down, winding my way through the last few blocks back to the hotel.

"Just curious. How would you feel about an endorsement deal with an athletic wear company?" she asks.

"How would *you* feel about a lifetime supply of chocolate?" I toss back, since Haven and I made a deal once upon a time that if we hit a set goal, I'd set her up like that.

"Hmm. Let me think on that for a few seconds. Wait. Done. I'm in."

We review the details as I make my way into the lobby. "You're the woman. It all sounds good to me."

"This deal is going to keep you pretty busy when you're not playing. You good with that?"

"You know me—"

"The no-strings guy."

"Exactly." I say goodbye when I reach my room.

Checking the clock on my phone, I pump a fist that it's nearly teatime. Then I laugh at myself because I deserve to be laughed at.

Good job, man. You're stoked for tea—first time for everything.

I strip off my shorts and hit the shower.

But Dean's not the only reason I'm psyched to go to Fortnum & Mason. Being an Anglophile her whole life, Emma's had afternoon tea on her bucket list for a long time.

After the shower, I get dressed, checking out my reflection on the way out of the bathroom. I look sharp—pressed slacks, button-down. Not too shabby.

I head to Emma's room down the hall, rapping twice on the door.

When she opens it, she eyes me up and down approvingly. "I haven't seen you looking so spiffy in a long time."

I gesture to my clothes. "I have to wear a suit before every game. This hardly counts as dressed up."

She pats my shoulder. "Right. Sure. This is just like you following the club rules dress code."

I roll my eyes. "Are you or are you not the one who sent me the link to the smart-casual dress code for tea?"

"Hmm. That does sound like me. But I still know you have ulterior motives for looking so sharp."

"Yes. I do have ulterior motives. Which you played a part in engineering."

With a saucy lift of her chin, she says, "You're welcome."

She grabs her purse, slings it over her shoulder, then smooths out her pink sundress. "Let's go, Casanova. I'm excited that you've found a man to ask to tea."

I hold up my hands in surrender. "I didn't ask him, Ems. He offered. Told you. Your big brother is irresistible."

She ruffles my hair as we head down the hall. "A legend in your own mind. Though you are aware that we don't actually need an English person to navigate tea?"

"Of course we do," I insist as we step into the elevator.

She wags her finger at me. "I've only been prepping for this my whole life. I've studied every menu for tea in the city and read the reviews. But this will be extra special. I get to go with my brother"—she wiggles a brow—"and his new gentleman friend."

She gives me a wink as we head out into the lobby.

"Yes, he's a *friend*. I came to London to make new *friends*," I say, deadpan, as we hit the street.

"And I can't wait to meet your new *friend*. And learn all about your fabulous friendship."

I gaze at the sky. "Why must sisters be like this?"

She pokes my stomach. "I have to represent not just my interests in knocking you down a few pegs, but Carrie's and Sarah's too. It's not an easy job to handle all the ribbing on my own. I've got to channel theirs too."

"You seem to be doing just fine in that department."

"I'll let them know," she says as we walk through the crowds on a fine London summer day. She hooks her arm through my elbow. "I don't think I've met anyone you've liked since that guy in college. Marcus."

That name is another reminder why I don't do relationships.

He was the last time I was with someone for more than a few nights. Nearly a whole semester. He even met Emma when she and my other sisters visited campus for a game.

But it turned out he was more interested in experimenting. He returned to girls after me.

And asked for Carrie's number.

Yeah, that was fun.

As we reach Fortnum & Mason, my gut twists. I'm not worried Dean is after Emma, not for a second. Or that he's bi-curious. But is it a mistake to invite him along to a family thing? Shit. Maybe I got wrapped up in the challenge and the pursuit yesterday. I didn't think about the fact that I was mixing a fling with family—something I never do.

Should I cancel? Reschedule?

But when I'm inside and spot him at a table, I shove aside all thought of mistakes. Because I burn at the sight of him.

He stands, and he's absolutely smoldering in his tight black collared shirt and pants.

"Now that's smart-casual," Emma whispers.

"More like hot AF."

"Yes, that too."

As we walk over, his eyes run up and down me like I'm his next meal, and it's a huge turn-on.

Then he's smiling broadly at Emma and opening his arms to give her a hug and a kiss on the cheek.

When they part, she puts on her best sheepish grin. "I hope you can forgive me for my Machiavellian ways yesterday."

"You're a master puppeteer," he says, a twinkle in his

eyes. "And obviously, all is forgiven." His gaze swings to mine again. "Since I'm here."

"You're here," I echo, barely caring if my thoughts are transparent.

He looks down, swallows, then gestures to the table where we take our seats. "Let's get to your afternoon tea, Emma. Are you thinking Jubilee? Royal Blend? Earl Grey?"

Emma leans forward and rattles off five or six different combinations that she's been thinking about, and all I can do is lean back and watch.

Dean's witty with me, fast on his feet, quick with a comeback. With Emma, he's more charmingly inquisitive. Thoughtful. Truly caring. It's a welcome change of pace, seeing how he treats my sister, how he engages with this person I adore.

It's honestly hotter than if he'd shown up shirtless.

Though I do want that shirt off. *Stat.*

By the time they serve our tea and finger sandwiches, Dean has Emma eating out of the palm of his hand with his knowledge about the proper steeping times and his opinions on different flavor infusions.

"So, your art program," he says, lifting his cup of English breakfast. "Tell me what it is you're most anticipating."

Emma launches into the different classes she'll be taking, the symposiums, the art periods she wants to study. "I love modern, but in my heart, I think I'm drawn most to eighteenth- and nineteenth-century art. I feel it truly expressed society and all its unspoken wishes and wants."

"That's fair to say about a lot of English artists— unspoken wishes and all. I can see that in JMW Turner. Gainsborough too. Have you been to the National Gallery?"

Emma laughs. "It was the first place I went! The Nicolaes Maes work? Stunning. Normally, I'm not into seven-teenth-century work, but for some reason . . ."

"It speaks to you, right?" Dean leans forward. "You should have been here for the Vermeer exhibit recently. Loyalty to my countrymen aside, I'm partial to Dutch art. I love the realism they tried to capture—almost a hyper-realism."

Emma glances at me and bursts out laughing. "James, you didn't tell me he knows art!"

"I'm learning new things myself," I say.

Dean moves his teacup in front of his face to hide his laugh.

Emma smooths out her napkin. "How do you know so much about art? No one except art geeks like me know the Dutch artists well."

He waves a hand dismissively. "Mum worked in the field. Learned it from her. Before she left, that is."

My ears perk more. That's new intel.

"When was that?" Emma asks.

"Emma," I chide.

Dean's smile says he doesn't mind the question. "I was thirteen. She left for Australia. It's okay. My dad's great, and we did just fine without her. He lives down the street, and I see him a lot. Fortunately, he also likes art, and some-times we go to the National Gallery together. She didn't ruin our love of museums."

"Maybe I'll run into the two of you there some time," she says, and a momentary pang of jealousy tugs in my chest at how lucky she is to have the chance to run into Dean someday when I'm gone.

"Maybe you will. And you can teach me what you've learned. So, you've been to the National Gallery. What do you think about my hometown otherwise? Are you both enjoying London?"

"I think it's obvious that James is enjoying it." Emma nudges my elbow. "Thanks to you being his guide."

"Good thing I found one for us," I tease. "If you were in charge, we'd be lost, and we'd have ordered the wrong tea."

Emma lifts her teacup, laughing. "Okay, so I'm a little directionally challenged. Sue me."

"'A little'? Pretty sure a couple decades of family vacations would suggest otherwise." I drape an arm around her shoulder. "When we were little, she got lost at Disneyland."

"Hey, it's a big place!" She holds up her hands just as her phone buzzes. Grabbing it from her purse, she checks it and looks up, a little contrite.

"Oh, shoot. That's the guy from the company I'm renting the flat from. He wants me to give him a call. You two will have to handle the scones without me. James, can you meet me at the Tube station in forty minutes so we can go over together to get the key?"

"Don't go without me. I want to make sure it's all good."

"I know, I know," she says, then turns to Dean. "He won't let me get the key till he makes sure the guy renting it to me meets with his approval. He's protective."

Dean nods approvingly. "That's smart of him. Also, might as well put those ice-defender-or-what-have-you skills to good use."

She wiggles her fingers in a wave goodbye as she steps away from the table. I can't tell if she's serious about needing to take a phone call now or setting me up again, but in pure Emma form, she's hugging us goodbye and rushing out of the tea salon before I can ask.

And I honestly don't care, especially when I turn back to Dean.

"Ice defender? Really?"

He simply shrugs. "What can I say? Hockey's not my thing." He doesn't say it dismissively. It's more like he says it . . . *deliciously*. As if he's letting me read between the lines again, saying without saying that he's not into me for the number on my jersey, like plenty of guys in New York are.

And that's another point in his favor. Dean's not trying to bag a pro athlete. I kinda love it. But I'm not telling him that. No way am I revealing that yet. Instead, I say something else entirely true. "Thank you for chatting up Emma. Means a lot to me."

"She's lovely. Inquisitive mind—I can tell."

"Yes, that describes her perfectly. She's also always in motion. Never slows down."

He lifts a brow. "She seems to always be working the angles. She's quite a wingwoman for you."

I laugh. "I guess we'll see how good she is at it."

His eyes travel up and down my frame in that hungry way he has of looking at me. "I have a feeling she'll be quite good at it."

And I heat up again, the flames licking inside me as he cracks open the conversation I want to have. "Does that mean you're giving me another yes?"

"Your favorite word, Fitz. I wonder if that's the one I'll be saying to you today," he says, and holy fuck, this man is so damn sexy with the way he talks, the way he teases me.

I lean back in my chair, stretching out my arm across the edge of Dean's chair, toying with him like he's toying with me. "I wonder too. Or maybe you still plan to resist me."

He never looks away. Just keeps those dark eyes locked on mine. "As I told you, I have a rule about sleeping with customers."

"Ah, but I'm not one of your customers anymore."

"You were, though, and now I've lost the bet with Maeve."

I frown, confused. "What bet?"

"Maeve and I have an ongoing wager. Sort of like a deal about not going home with customers. If one of us does, we owe the other extra chores."

"Interesting. Did you have to pay up yesterday just for those kisses?"

"She made me mop. Such a taskmaster."

"Did that bother you? All the deep cleaning?"

He strokes his chin, like he's seriously considering the question. "No. Not in the least. I might owe her more though."

That piques my interest a whole helluva lot. "So, you really have to pay up if you sleep with me?" Just saying that aloud, getting closer to what I want, makes my skin sizzle and my dick throb.

Especially since he takes his time, licking his lips before he answers, punctuating each word. "So. Many. Chores."

The look in his eyes is driving me wild. The desire I see there matches mine.

I swallow roughly, my throat as dry as the Sahara, lust pounding through me. Lowering my arm, I slide it under the table, spreading my palm across his thigh. "Worth it."

A rumble seems to work its way up his chest as he widens his legs the slightest bit. "Possibly."

"Definitely."

He takes a deep breath, his tone suddenly serious. "But listen, this is just a fling. Nothing more. I want to make sure we're both on the same page."

"We are absolutely on the same page."

"I've had some exes get a little . . . clingy. I don't want that. I have the bar to think about. Maeve and I are just about to pay off our loan. I don't want anything to get in the way of business."

I grin. "I know the feeling. But trust me, Dean. I have training camp after this. Plus, I'm wrapping up a new sponsorship deal. I'll be so damn busy in New York, you won't even hear from me after I get on the plane on Thursday at two. I'll be in and out of your life like that."

"In that case, there's one more thing we ought to tackle."

12

DEAN

Rules are important. It's good to lay them out in advance. But so are expectations, so you're on the same page in the bedroom.

Returning the favor, I slide a hand up his leg, knowing it drives him wild because evidently *I* drive him wild. It's heady, this power. Addictive too.

Fitz's eyes darken as I touch him. Then I ask the necessary question. "So, how's it going to be if we do this?"

He knows what I'm asking, and he answers instantly. "I want to fuck you, Dean."

I had a feeling. It was clear from the second his eyes swept over my body at the bar. From some of the things he's said too. But it's best to be up-front. "I thought you might."

He lifts a brow in question. "That's not a problem, is it?"

"What if it is?" I toss back. I can't resist playing with him.

"Say it's not." It comes out as a command, his voice hot, desperate. He looks like he'll die of lust if he doesn't get his hands on me soon. It's a good look—a good feeling.

And I feel the same, but I can tell Fitz likes the chase, so I give it to him.

I smirk, then shrug, still revealing nothing.

He growls, bringing his face closer to my neck, his voice low and husky near my ear. "I want you so much. Want to get your clothes off. Get my hands on you. Feel you under me." Fitz's beard scratches my neck. He flicks his tongue against my ear, dropping his voice to a filthy whisper. "I want to be inside you."

His words scorch my blood, make me red-hot all over.

I release a breath, meet his gaze, then give him what he wants. Fortunately, it's what I want too. "Lucky for you, Fitz, I'm quite versatile."

His grin is wide, his groan deeply satisfied. "That is the sexiest thing you've ever said, and everything you say is sexy. Have I told you how much I like hearing you talk? Your accent turns me on."

"Seems everything I do does."

"It does. It absolutely does."

I look at my watch, the seconds ticking too fast. "You have to meet Emma soon. Where is your hotel?"

"Close. A couple of blocks away."

"Good." I take his hand off my leg and set it on the table. "Here's how this is going to work. You might want to fuck me right now, but that's not going to happen. Want to know why?"

He wastes no time answering. "Because we're going to take our time, make it last, screw all night long."

"Exactly. I want to enjoy every second of it. I want to feel you deep inside me. I don't want a quickie. I want to be driven mad with lust as you fuck me to the edge of pleasure. And that's going to take more than thirty minutes."

His eyes are drunk with desire, dark with lust. "A *lot* more than thirty minutes."

"But my calculations indicate we have just enough time for other things." I lower my voice. "Plenty of time for me to get on my knees and suck you off. Shall we go?"

Fitz scrubs a hand across the back of his neck, his voice hoarse. "You're killing me. You are the sexiest man I've ever met. You know that, right?"

People say things in the heat of the moment, but he looks like he means it.

"I suspect it'll be hard for you to walk right now. Why don't I go ahead and I'll meet you in the lobby, and you can think about tea cakes or the queen or something on the way over?"

He shakes his head. "Nope. Don't care. And I'm not letting you out of my sight."

He pays the bill and rises, an impressive impression in his trousers.

Well, I'm not complaining about that.

In the hotel, the elevator doors close, and we crash into each other. Fitz pushes me to the wall and kisses me hard. "You wind me up, make me feel wild," he murmurs when he breaks the kiss.

"You want me to drive you wild."

"I do, Dean. I really do."

This confirmation is necessary. Necessary for me. I need this verbal upper hand with him. It keeps me safe, protects me from the storm. Because it's a powerful one with Fitz, and part of me wants to be pulled into the eye of it.

A minute later, he slams the door of his room shut, and we collide. His hands are on my face, and mine are on his trousers, gripping his erection through the fabric.

Fitz groans his appreciation, then drops his hands to the hem of my shirt, tugging at it. We separate, and I unbutton it quickly, jerking it away as we toe off shoes and socks. Then I yank him toward me again, kissing him hard and rough, the way I know he likes it already. I walk him to the bed, stroking his insistent hard-on as I go, savoring the hot, hard length of him. He undoes his shirt, and I want to spend hours admiring his ink, tracing each tattoo with my tongue, but there will be time for that later. We reach the edge of the mattress, and I grab the zipper of his trousers, needing to get them off him right fucking now. "All right, Mr. Rules Are Made to Be Broken, let's see if your money is where your mouth is," I taunt.

Fitz laughs. "Oh, I think your mouth will like it all."

When I strip off his clothes, boxer briefs too, my eyes don't just like what I see. My entire fucking body craves it.

His cock salutes me, thick, hard, and eager to make my acquaintance. My palm reaches for him, curling around his shaft. The second I touch him, I'm rewarded with a throaty gasp, the sound of his lust sending a sharp jolt of pleasure down my spine.

"You drive me crazy," he rasps out.

"Yes, I can tell." I squeeze his dick, grinning as I run my hand along its length. I savor the feel of his arousal and the noises he makes too, as I indulge in the rush of touching him.

"So fucking crazy that you need to get down on your knees right the hell now."

I arch a brow. "Oh, I do, do I?"

"You want to," Fitz corrects as he pumps his hips, thrusting into my hand, so damn eager for me. His lust is like a drug, and I want another hit of it, of him. "You know you want to, Dean."

With my other hand, I give his balls a squeeze, then I

drop my hand to my length, steel under my clothes. "Hmm. What do you know? Seems I do."

He narrows his eyes and sinks onto the bed, jerking me to the floor, keeping my hand on his cock the entire time. Spreading his legs, he grabs my jaw, bringing me closer.

I'd like to take him in my mouth right now. Draw him to the back of my throat and show him what I can do to him. Almost as if I want to punish him with pleasure for making me break this one rule. As if I want to prove to him why I gave in.

Or maybe I want to prove it to myself.

Need to prove it to myself.

But I don't want to stop toying with him. This game Fitz and I play, this teasing—it's far more fun than any other game. And I don't want to relinquish playing. I bend my head closer, drawn by the heady smell of him, the feel of him. My mouth waters, but I resist wrapping my lips around his shaft, kissing his thigh instead.

"Mmm . . . and you say you like everything I do. So, do you like this?"

I lick a path up the inside of his leg, teasing the hell out of him, resisting, with my evidently iron will, his thick, hard cock I want to suck.

He shudders, grabbing my face with both hands, his voice a barren, demanding plea. "Just get your mouth on me and stop talking."

I narrow my eyes, then move closer, my jaw brushing against his pulsing length. "But I thought you liked my accent."

"I love it except when blow jobs are hanging in the balance."

My lips twitch in a grin. "Well, maybe you ought to give me one. That would be the best of both worlds."

"Come to think of it," he says, and before I even register

what he's doing, the man moves with the speed and grace of an athlete—of course—jerking me up from the floor, pushing me down on the bed, tearing off my clothes, and dropping his mouth down on my dick.

He deep-throats me in one swift move.

Electricity rushes down my body.

His expert mouth.

Holy hell, his delicious, expert mouth is working me over, sucking me deep, and it doesn't surprise me that Fitz goes all in, and oh yes, I want him to.

My hands rope into his hair, one palm curling over the back of his head. "That's right. Take it deep."

I swear I can feel him smiling against my dick as he sucks me ravenously, like he's starving for my cock.

But he's not simply brute-force strength or a magical unicorn throat that can handle being fucked.

His tongue is a sorcerer, and the way he spirals it along my shaft, the way he licks and flicks and strokes as he goes, makes my thighs shake and my breath come in fast, gasping pants.

"Fuck," I groan as Fitz slides his big hands along my thighs, up, down, and back up again. He cups my balls, playing with them as he devours me.

"Yes. Fucking yes," I say, and there's not much more talking I can give him while he does this, because I can't form words.

Curses, groans, grunts—that's all I'm capable of.

With the things he's doing, soon I won't be able to push out syllables. Lust barrels through my entire being, a punishing wave of agonizing pleasure as he blows my dick with so much enthusiasm it's like he's trying to blow my mind too.

Well, it's working. It's absolutely working.

My fingers tangle in his hair as my hips jerk, thrusting

up, fucking into his talented, relentless mouth—this man is ruthless as he sucks me to the back of his throat.

I'm losing all control and loving it—loving the heat in my body, the pleasure in my veins, his hands on my legs, my balls, my stomach.

Everywhere.

He explores me everywhere as he takes my dick on a trip around the world of pleasure, and my orgasm builds at the base of my spine, a pulsing, ravenous thing with a life of its own, with the power to pull me under.

"So fucking good," I say, as his tongue swirls up and down my length, as his fist grips the base, as lust rattles wildly through me. "Coming. Coming now."

And upon my words, I can feel him moan against my cock, can hear the rumble of desire in his throat. The sound and the hum and the vibration make my feet tingle, make my chest burn, make me shoot so goddamn hard in his mouth that I'm not sure I'm on earth anymore.

White-hot bliss knocks me into another world from the intensity of the climax he wrings out of me.

It's radiating through me, pulsing into every corner of my body as I groan endlessly—groan until I'm just panting, breathing, moaning.

That's literally all I can do as the aftershocks spread through every molecule, every atom. Fitz lets me fall from his mouth with a loud, wet pop and a most satisfied grin on his supremely handsome face.

Rising, he wipes a hand across his mouth. I try to see straight while my head is buzzing, my mind bathing in endorphins.

He lets his gaze travel down his body to his cock, thick and pulsing. Gripping himself, he runs a hand down his length, pushing hard along the crown, swiping his thumb across a bead of liquid on the head.

I lick my lips, wanting, my tongue begging for what he has to give. He heeds the call, stretching out his arm, running his thumb across my lips. I lick him off his thumb, and my eyes fall shut at that first intoxicating taste of him.

I open my eyes to see his hand is back on his shaft, stroking. "Well, then. I'm guessing it's my turn now," he says.

I push up a few inches, grab an extra pillow, and park it behind my head. "Then get up here and fuck my face."

13

FITZ

Take it easy.

Take it slow.

Enjoy it.

I repeat those guidelines. Not that I need a reminder to enjoy a fucking blow job—hell, blow jobs are life.

I say it because I don't want to shoot too early.

And I don't want to be too rough either.

I want to take time to enjoy the hell out of this.

I straddle him, settling in under Dean's shoulders, a knee on each side of the pillow. I'm so damn aroused after sucking him off, this delicious, tempting man, that I don't know how to take it slow.

I don't know if I want to.

I want release. I want to get off. I want to come in his throat as he watches me. But I also know this position is playing with fire.

I don't want to make him gag. But I also really want to fuck his mouth. *Hard.*

I wrap a hand around the base of my aching dick, and I offer him just the tip, rubbing the head across his lips.

His tongue darts out, and he groans as he licks. His moans and murmurs are already the sexiest sounds I have ever heard, and they send my pulse roaring.

With one hand braced against the wall behind him, I give small little thrusts, letting him lick and suck the head. That lasts a minute, maybe more, as I burn with desire.

Then he growls, a frustrated sound. His hands snake around my legs, big palms clasping my ass, gripping me. He opens his mouth wider, tugs me in a little deeper, his lips wrapping around the crown of my cock. I swear, it's a miracle I don't come right then. "Your lips are fucking fantastic," I rasp out.

He grins against my dick, pulling back. "But I've barely got you in my mouth, Fitz."

"So what? They're still sexy as hell. Look at you. Jesus. Just look at how sexy you are with my cock in your gorgeous fucking mouth."

And it's like those words do something to him. They affect him in a way I haven't seen, didn't expect. His eyes darken, etched with a brand-new intensity. He licks the tip, his eyes never straying from mine, and I don't look away either.

My God, how can I?

"Then don't hold back," Dean commands. "Give it all to me. If I can handle your enormous ego, I can handle your enormous cock."

I let go of my dick, grazing my hand over his face, and speak from the heart of my insatiable desire for him. Because I'm serious—no joking here. "No. It's me. I don't know if I can handle how hot this is."

His lips twitch. "Bet you can, Fitz. I absolutely bet you can handle it all. I bet you're dying to come in my throat."

I groan as lust tears through me. *This man. His words.*

He grips my ass hard, pulling me into his warm mouth.

Letting me know he's got this, he can take it, he can take all of me. His lips wrap around my shaft, and I'm right where I want to be.

And holy fuck.

Sparks sizzle across my entire body.

I swear, my skin is on fire. Pleasure floods me, touching everywhere as I slide to the back of his throat, watching as he takes me in. As he lavishes delicious attention on my dick.

I find a rhythm, set a pace, pumping into his mouth. "You're killing me, babe. Fucking killing me with that mouth. That tongue."

His eyes sparkle with desire, with satisfaction, saying that he's going to give me the best blow of my life. And no doubt he will, because he is.

Because I fucking love what he's doing to me.

Love his hands on my ass. Love his face. Love his sinful mouth that works me over, and most of all, I love that he wants it like this, that he wants me like this, fucking his sexy mouth.

I thrust a little harder, pump a little deeper, and he answers my every move with his fingers digging into my flesh.

And on an upstroke, my whole body lights up like a pinball machine, hitting a new high score as pleasure pounds through me, curling in my veins. I grunt, "Gonna come. Gonna come now."

I shudder as my eyes squeeze shut and my orgasm rips through me. Dean drinks down every last drop.

And as I'm coming down from the high, I pull out, slide down his body, and taste his lips with a hungry, possessive kiss. He tastes like us, and it drives me a little bit crazier.

But then, around him? Crazy seems to be my new state of mind.

14

DEAN

The clock is ticking as I zip up my trousers. I take a look in the mirror, checking out my reflection. "Well, looks like I'm going to have to confess to Maeve," I say, buttoning my shirt.

"Is that how your bet usually works? You go into the booth and serve it all up like she's your priest?"

I toss a glance at Fitz striding across the room in his briefs, but still shirtless. "I don't know how it *usually* works, since this is the first time I've broken the rule."

His grin is the size of the river, huge and filled with pride. He walks up behind me, sets his hands on my arms, and brushes a possessive kiss on my neck. "Good. I like knowing that. I like that a whole lot."

I do up the buttons, trying valiantly not to be affected by what he's doing to my neck. "But if you must know, she pretty much broke me down last night and forced me to admit it. And she told me that she'd set me up."

"I should send her a lifetime supply of top-shelf booze

for that." Another kiss on my neck. Another wave of lust through my body.

I stare at our reflection, at the way he's touching me even when he needs to get out of here. "Don't you need to get dressed and meet your sister?"

"Mmm. I do, but you taste so good." Fitz slides his lips farther down my neck. "I also happen to have a fantastic sense of timing. I know exactly how long it takes to get down the ice. By my count, I've got one-hundred-and-twenty seconds to leave you wanting more of me before I have to go."

Groaning, I lean into my American lover, taking his kisses, savoring his attention. At this rate, though, I'm never going to leave his room. Straightening my spine, I slide another button through the corresponding hole. "I suspect this time, however, that Maeve will read it on my face straightaway. She's smart like that."

He laughs as he draws his lips along my skin, rubbing his scruff against me. "Or are you that transparent, Dean?"

I arch a brow in the mirror as I finish the last button. "What do you think?"

Fitz raises his eyes, giving me a thorough appraisal. "I'd say that's the face of someone who's given it good and gotten it good."

"Great. Fucking great," I mutter, but I'm not annoyed in the least. Annoyance is impossible in moments like this.

He slides his hand to my ass, squeezing it hard. "I call it like I see it. And, Dean, you look like you've been sucked hard and well by a man who wants you."

His comment shouldn't do anything more than ignite another bout of lust. But the intensity of his desire is a life force. It's a light that draws me, and I want more of it.

"Hence my plan for preemptive confession," I say, and I can feel a smile tugging at my lips, the admission that I don't mind cleaning the floors or painting the walls or hauling rubbish or chopping wood or anything if it means another round with him.

It's not just his tongue or his mouth, though, or his fantastic cock. It's the other things he does with his mouth —it's the things he says and the way we are with each other.

He's the best time I've ever had.

I turn around so he can't distract me anymore with those kisses on my neck. "Listen, I have to go to the bar. Take care of some business." I look at my watch. "I'll be done before seven. Meet me at Sticks and Stones at eight thirty. It's nearby, and open Sunday nights, unlike The Magpie. I'll text you the address. Since I believe you had a study to show me, from the society of Why the Hell Won't You Have Dinner with Me. Tonight you should show me that, and then show me all the other things you want to do to me."

He grabs my face, drags me in close, and kisses me like he owns my lips. And if I stay any longer, he'll miss his appointment.

So I break the kiss, step to the door, and reach for the handle. I'm about to take off, when I stop, turn around, and close the distance between us again.

There are moments for games, and then there are moments for truth.

I'm not going to see him again after Thursday. He'll be out of my life for good. So, if I'm giving in now, I want to experience all of the pleasure, all of the chase.

And I want him to have a taste of the addiction he's giving me, to feel its power, to know its pull. I drag my hand up his chest, spreading my palm over his pecs, so firm under my touch. "I do want more of you, Fitz. I want all of you. I have since the night I met you."

His eyes are glossy with both lust and gratitude. "I'm so fucking glad you said yes to me."

"Ditto." I tip my forehead to the door. "And now I do have to go."

I leave, counting down the seconds till I see him again.

That's a good thing, this impatience, this intensity, but I have a feeling it could also become a bad thing.

A very bad thing indeed.

15

DEAN

After I do some work and go for a run, I head home, shower, and change for tonight. Jeans and a polo. Phone and wallet. That's all I need.

I catch the Tube, and when it lets me out near Sticks and Stones, I text my dad, checking in to see what he's up to. He replies immediately.

Dad: Poker. I plan to clean up with my mates from the old office. They're rubbish at cards.

Dean: And you're not.

Dad: I can bluff like nobody's business, and I can always tell who's trying to bluff me. What are you up to tonight?

Dean: Just heading out to see a friend. I'll see you Tuesday for dinner, right?

Dad: Friend??? It's hilarious that you think I don't know what that means. Have fun with that Yankee.

I crack up as I walk the short distance to Sam's pub, pinging Dad as I go.

Dean: How did you know?

Dad: Friend. You called him a friend. Not a mate. Good luck on your date.

Dean: It's official. I'm disowning you.

Dad: Too late. You're stuck with me.

Dean: See if I make it to dinner this week, old man.

Dad: You'll show, I have no doubt. You always do.

I look up from the phone to see the man of the hour walking toward me. He's freshly showered by the look of it, the ends of his brown hair a little wet. He wears jeans and a T-shirt that's just a notch above casual, revealing the tribal bands that wrap around his biceps and slide into sunbursts on his shoulders.

"Hey, you. Something funny?" Fitz nods at the phone.

"My dad. We were just texting."

"Ahh," Fitz says. "I nearly forgot to do this." He clasps

my cheeks and kisses me. It lasts all of two seconds, but it goes to my head.

When he breaks the kiss, he gestures toward my phone. "How's your dad?"

"He's good," I say, smiling, tucking my mobile away in my pocket. "He was just giving me a hard time about tonight."

"Why?"

"Because he's the world's most sarcastic person."

Fitz's eyes sparkle. "This explains so much about you."

"Why, yes, I do get my good looks from him," I say, deadpan.

He cracks up. "Exactly. So why was he giving you a hard time about tonight? Is he not supportive?"

It's my turn to laugh. "He's giving me a hard time because he called it a date before I did."

Fitz grins, then sets a hand on my back. "I like your dad. Also, yes, this is a date. I'm calling it that too. And your dad is a smart man."

"He's brilliant," I say, trying to rein in the grin that might reveal how much I want to be exactly where I am right now with the ice defender, the cocky athlete, the guy who walked into my bar.

He nods to the door. "Want some grub?"

"Since I suspect we'll be working up an appetite, the answer is yes."

We head into Sticks and Stones, a place I've been to a ton of times with Maeve, or with Naveen and Anya, my mates from cooking class who own an Indian restaurant over in Notting Hill. Or even with Taron, who runs one of the old furniture shops I haunt. They're my people—the ones I meet for a drink or a laugh at the end of the day.

Sam's behind the bar on the phone, and he gestures that he'll find me soon.

As luck would have it, Naveen and his wife are here, and they wave their hellos from the bar. I give Fitz the quick download on the couple. "Those are some of my good mates. He was born in Mumbai; she grew up in Auckland. They met several years ago at a café in Covent Garden when the staff mixed up their orders."

"That's quite a meet-cute," Fitz remarks.

"Just imagine if the server had given her the portobello mushroom sandwich and him the lentil soup like he was supposed to."

"I guess you've heard the lentil-portobello story from them before."

I give him a small grin. "Just a few times. But it's sweet. Come on over and say hi."

"Would love to."

I head over, kissing Anya's cheek and giving Naveen a clap on the back.

"Haven't seen you in ages," Naveen says.

"Yes, don't be such a stranger," Anya says with a flip of her blonde hair.

"I saw you just a week ago. But I get it— it feels like ages when you must miss me terribly." I park a hand on Fitz's shoulder. "This is Fitz. He's in town from New York for a few days. He's quite funny, he plays hockey, and if you see Taron around, you better tell him not to give Fitz so much as a second glance because he's already spoken for during his stay."

Naveen laughs. "I'll pass on the word that you got your claws into the American first." Then he extends a hand to my . . . date. Fitz shakes.

"Nice to meet you, Fitz," Naveen says. "Don't know how you put up with this cheeky fucker."

"I'm guessing a few days is about all you can take of Dean anyway," Anya weighs in.

"I can handle him for the short-term." Fitz smiles then kisses her cheek, European-style. "Good to meet you."

"Lovely to meet you too," Anya says. "And how are you liking London?"

Fitz glances my way, a hungry look in his blue eyes. "So far, I'm enjoying the sights quite a bit."

That sends Naveen and Anya into peals of laughter, and I roll my eyes as I move him along, heading down the bar to grab a couple of stools.

"I guess you come here a lot," Fitz remarks.

"I do. Since so many of my mates are here."

"And this Taron guy? Is he an ex?" There's a flare of jealousy in his voice, and it's endearing.

I laugh, shaking my head. "No. Not at all. One, he's not my type. Two, he's actually pretty serious about someone, so I was just taking the piss out of him, and he's not even around to defend himself. Poor fella."

"Why is he not your type? What's your type?"

I rake my eyes over Fitz. "Well, I happen to prefer a little rugged charm." I take a beat. "Or a lot, for that matter."

"Perfect answer." He grabs the menu, and as he looks at it, something occurs to me. Fitz is the first guy I've brought to this place where my friends congregate.

The whole time I was with Dylan, I never brought him here.

Never wanted to.

I kept him and other hookups separate from the people in my life I see nearly every day. Maybe because this place and these people feel like mine. I'd want to keep these friends in the inevitable breakup, so it was simpler not to let my worlds collide.

No need to intermingle.

Though I just did.

But Fitz and I have a natural split coming our way on Thursday. That must be why I'm comfortable with him being here.

Since he's leaving, this place will always be mine.

Fitz taps the menu. "What do you recommend? I have to admit, I haven't heard great things about English food. Outside of scones, of course."

"Which you missed in your overzealous haste earlier today."

"You missed the scones too," he points out.

I arch a brow, taking my time. "No, Fitz. I didn't miss the scones one bit."

"You have such a dirty mind, and I love it," Fitz says, dragging a hand over his scruff. I can still remember how it felt against my thighs.

Something I don't need to think about right now.

And yet . . .

"And when you do that," I say, gesturing to his jaw, "you cause the filthy thoughts to multiply."

His eyes seem to spark with dirty delight, and he lets out a low hum of appreciation. "You like my beard."

"You know I do," I say, then manage to veer the conversation back to the original topic. "And to answer your question—Sam doesn't offer typical English bar food. He was a chef before he broke into the bar business. He's a Yankee, like you."

"Ha! I knew it. So English food is terrible."

I roll my eyes. "That's not what I said."

Fitz wags his finger. "Then why did it take an American to fix it?"

He's deliberately trying to get under my skin, and I love it. All I can do is laugh.

"So, you admit the food here sucks?" he presses.

"Hello? Who is disparaging my fine cuisine?" The interruption comes from Sam, who's off the phone and has joined us at our end of the bar.

I hold up my hands in surrender, then gesture to my date. "Sorry, mate. We'll have to bar him for casting aspersions."

Sam hooks his thumb in the direction of the door. "Time to go."

Fitz clasps my shoulder. "His fault, man. He didn't defend you."

"Yes, I did," I say.

"No, you didn't. You only said he was a chef. You didn't say his food was great."

"His food is great." I practically shout it.

"Maybe I need to kick out Dean," Sam suggests.

"You would never."

"Seems like he might," Fitz says.

Sam grins, tipping his head toward the man next to me. "You from California?"

Fitz grins. "San Diego. Born and raised."

He and Sam exchange a thoroughly American fist-bump thing. "I grew up in New York but lived in LA for ten years. What brings you here?"

Fitz explains about Emma and her art program, and the two of them chat about tacos and burritos, beaches and surfing, hitting it off instantly.

Resting an elbow on the bar, I watch their volley, listening to their laid-back way of speaking, all those *dudes* and *mans* and *bros*.

"I miss the beaches something fierce, bro." Sam sighs a little wistfully.

"I don't get much beach time these days, being in New York. But when I go home, I soak up the rays."

"Your job is the opposite of the beach, isn't it?" I chime in.

"What do you do?" Sam asks.

"I play hockey."

Sam's mouth falls open, and a long "Ohhhhhh" falls from his lips. "Dude! I knew you looked familiar. That last game—you guys killed me."

"Trust me. It killed us too. We did not want the season to end like that."

"But this year, you're going to go all the way?"

"Only way to go."

"Get us the Cup, man. Get us the Cup," Sam says, pounding his fist on the bar.

They knock fists again, and Fitz turns to me. "You didn't tell me Sam was a hockey fan."

"Shockingly, we've never discussed hockey before."

"Well, discuss it now. I can talk about hockey all night," Fitz says, and I laugh because I'm sure he can, but he hasn't brought it up once to me. And I kind of love that he's not one to push his passions on someone else, and that he has plenty of other things to talk about too.

Sam shifts gears, gesturing to me. "Did he tell you he's a pool shark? I met him when he was laying down bets with some of my customers about two years ago."

"Is that so?" Fitz asks, enjoying these details.

"I can't resist a wager now and then." Then I look at Sam. "And who are you to talk? You bet me that I couldn't beat you, and I did. And the prize was—wait for it . . ."

Sam huffs, annoyed but not really, as he points at me. "This dickhead gets to eat free here forever."

Fitz gives me an approving nod. "So, Dean, you're a hot date, a smart date, and a cheap one. Excellent."

Sam laughs. "On that note, let me know if you're ready to order."

Fitz picks the chicken sandwich, hold the bread,

offering a faint apology of "I try to lay off carbs during the season."

"In that case, bring me all the extra bread you have," I tell Sam. "Just to taunt him."

"Do you want me to tell him you're a health freak too?" Sam asks in a stage whisper.

"No, please keep my secrets," I say, then mumble, "While you bring me the salmon and veggies. And a beer."

Fitz groans in frustration. "Now you're tempting me with my favorite carb. Fine, I cave. Beer for me too."

"Coming right up, gentlemen." Sam nods, then turns to Fitz. "Don't forget—get us the Cup."

"I'm on it."

As Sam leaves, I drum my fingers on the bar. "So, hockey. How did you get into it?"

"I thought hockey wasn't your thing, Dean?"

"It's not, but I still want to know how you got started, what about it makes you tick."

"My dad was Canadian. Loved the sport. When he moved to San Diego, he couldn't stay away from the rink. He took me there when I was four. Put me in skates and said, 'Let's see what you can do.'"

"And was it love at first . . . blade?"

Fitz smiles. "That's how my mom tells the story. She didn't want him to take me then, but he insisted, since apparently *I* insisted on learning at such a young age."

"Ah, that says so much about you too. Insistent from a young age."

"*Per*sistent," he corrects.

"And you loved it?"

He snaps his fingers. "Instalove. I had a ton of energy as a kid, and channeling it into skating was the perfect thing. It took focus but also intensity, and that's what I had."

"And still have, I presume?"

"Absolutely. And my dad was obsessed with hockey. He taught me some of my best moves. When to go for the goal and when to pull back. How to take a hit. And, of course, he taught me to always put the team first. That's when the best players do their best work."

The server returns with our beers, and I lift mine. "To your dad."

Fitz clinks back. "To my dad." He takes a drink, looking a little lost in thought.

"You miss him still?"

"From time to time. I think about him when I hit the ice though. I'm one of those guys who always does this," he says, then taps his chest and points heavenward, "before each game."

It warms my heart, that kind of remembrance. "It's good that you still honor him in that way." We talk a little more about his family, then as the waiter brings our food, we thank him and dive in. In between bites, I return to something Fitz said.

"So he was Canadian, and your mum is American?"

"Yup. He moved from Vancouver to San Diego after he met her. Fell head over heels in love."

"Sounds like my dad when he met my mum. The head over heels bit, at least, as he tells it."

"Is she from Australia? You said she took off for there."

I shake my head. "No, she's Swiss," I say, then gesture to myself. "I look more like my father. Mum's white, Dad's black."

Fitz shrugs. "And you're hot."

I laugh. "Thank you. And ditto."

As we eat, he glances around, taking in the decor—contemporary and sleek, a well-lit, modern pub in rich blues and greens.

"I like this place. But not as much as The Magpie."

"You're only saying that to get in my trousers," I say between bites.

A laugh bursts from him, and he shakes his head. "Don't mean to be cocky, but I think you're a sure thing. I said it because I meant it. I like what you're doing with The Magpie. It feels unique—a little vintage, a little modern. Like you've made it your own."

I can't help but grin. I've poured my blood, sweat, and tears into that place. "I love that bar."

"I can tell. What made you decide to go for it?"

"Maeve and I made a plan way back in uni. We always wanted to own our own business, someplace where we could have regulars and chat with them, get to know them, give them a place to come at the end of the day. And I'm chuffed we were able to do it."

"It takes a lot to pull something like that off," Fitz says. "How long's it been?"

"One year. Before then, I was merely a bartender. But this is something of my own."

"Hell yeah," Fitz says. "A man in charge of his own destiny."

When we're done, several shouts rise from the pool tables in the back. The group that's been playing there makes their way out, snaking through the bar.

Fitz brushes one palm against the other. "All right, I believe you said you'd kick my ass at pool. Show me how great you are with that stick."

I can't resist. "Isn't that what you're going to show me later?"

He shakes his head in admiration. "I am. I absolutely am. But first, this—I challenge you to a game. And I think you'll like the stakes."

"And why do you think that?"

With a lift of his brow, he licks the corner of his lips,

staring at me with a wicked intent in his gaze. "Winner picks the position."

A myriad of favorite ones flashes before me. "Well, then, when you put it that way, I better win."

I proceed to run the table, smacking ball after ball into the pocket, and destroy him. When I've annihilated the American athlete, I put the cue away, slide a hand around his neck, and preen. "Told you I'd win."

He bands his arm around my waist. "I'm pretty sure we both win here."

"Yes. I'd bet it all on that."

He brings his lips to mine, but he doesn't kiss me. He whispers, all hoarse and smoky, "Let's get out of here."

"Yes." I give him a salacious wink. "Because I know exactly how I plan to use my winnings."

16

FITZ

I let the door of my room fall shut, the sound of it closing so damn satisfying. It signifies the shift into the rest of the evening—the thing I've wanted since I first set eyes on this guy two nights ago.

Forty-eight hours.

But in libido time, it's eons. I've been wanting him every second of every day, wound up from the tension and rabid desire.

I want him even more now after having dinner with him, getting to know him better. Talking with Dean is one of the easiest things I've ever done. And that ease only fuels my lust.

I want to grab him, pin him down, have my way with him. But I also know we have all night, and I plan to make it last.

Inside the room, I kick off my shoes. He does the same.

We look at each other, poised, knowing what's coming. This is the calm before the storm, the moment of anticipation before the buzzer rings.

We aren't frenzied like we were earlier today. There

isn't that crazy collision like when we slammed into each other. But I can feel it in the air: a pulsing, a need.

It's palpable.

Like the low beat of a song. Some sexy, dirty number that gets you in the mood.

I'm already in the mood. Haven't left the mood in forty-eight hours. Still, I grab my phone and click on a playlist, something I figure Dean will like—the kind of smoky, sexy music from artists he told me were among his favorites the night we met. Sam Smith, Daley, Leon Bridges. Sex music —plain and simple.

"Good thing you have some music handy. Wasn't sure I'd be able to get turned on otherwise," he says, glancing at the bulge in his jeans, then to the matching one in mine.

"Yeah, same here."

"Good tunes though." His smoldering eyes lock onto mine.

"Yeah, I thought you might like." I'm not talking about the music.

"I do like. I like it all." Dean's not talking about the music either.

He's standing a few feet away from me, fiddling with the hem of his shirt, giving me a little hint, a preview of those abs. I lean against the bureau, cross my arms, and rake my eyes over the man I'm going to fuck.

I'm already an inferno just from looking at him. His jawline, his eyes, his lips. His body. "Take your shirt off," I tell him, my voice a raw husk already.

Grabbing the bottom, he tugs it up, revealing those cut abs, those firm pecs.

I breathe out hard.

Then harder still when the shirt goes up over his chest, his shoulders, then his head.

My God, he's so fucking gorgeous. All my resolve to

take it slow flies out the window, and I close the distance to Dean in a heartbeat. I can't *not* have my hands on him.

I grab his face and taste his lips. "*All night.* I want you all night," I say, my breath coming in a rush.

"So have me, Fitz."

I swear my body is on fire. There is no corner of me not burning up for him. I angle my face, kissing his neck in the way that drives him crazy. He stretches, offering me more access.

I take my time, giving him soft, tender kisses, coupled with scratches of my beard, till his murmurs turn to groans, the sounds so erotic that my cock strains against my fly. "You like that?"

"You know I do."

"Mmm. Me too. So much," I say, closing my eyes again, losing myself in the taste of him. My lips travel across his collarbone down to his pecs, where I flick my tongue then bite down on a nipple.

Dean grunts out a dirty *yes.* "Do it again," he urges.

I smile, biting him, then moving to the other nipple, giving it the same treatment. I roam lower, falling to my knees as I kiss the ladder of his abs, making my way to the waistband of his jeans. I flick my tongue along his stomach, licking and sucking and driving him crazy.

And myself too.

I swear I'm tripping. I'm awash in sensation, in lust, unlike anything I've ever felt. On my knees, I unbutton his jeans, slide down the zipper, and jerk his boxer briefs and jeans down his thighs.

His beautiful cock juts out, greeting me with a very eager hello. My mouth waters at the sight of him, the feel of him. I wrap a hand around the base and draw him between my lips, savoring the salty, sexy taste of him.

Moaning around him.

Getting drunk off him.

"Noooooo," he says. It has ten syllables, and he pushes my head away.

With my hand still on his shaft, I look up, smirking as his cock twitches against my lips. "Your dick seems to say yes."

Dean's hands curl around my head, locking me in place. "My dick is not allowed to make the decisions."

I smile at that intoxicating drop of liquid on the head of his cock. "Let me just make sure," I say, darting out my tongue and licking the taste of his arousal.

"Fuck . . . you," he grunts.

"Yes, that's the plan." I groan, my eyes rolling back in my head in pleasure as I kiss the crown, flicking my tongue over him. "Except I just don't know if I can stop sucking your cock, Dean."

"You better find the will to stop," he growls.

Another lick. "And why's that?" I know the answer, but my God, I am worked up. I am wound up. I am hot and horny and about to explode. And I want to know he's going wild for me too, that he's feeling the same kind of insanity.

Dean jerks me up, yanking me up from the floor. "Because if you keep doing that with your wicked tongue and your naughty lips, I'm going to come in mere seconds. Do you want that on your conscience?"

"Maybe not," I say, unable to contain a grin.

He grabs my chin, looking me hard in the eyes. "Now, do what I asked. Make it last with the way you fuck me. Make me go wild for you. And don't you dare touch my cock again until I tell you to, because I am not firing early."

I might, though, if Dean keeps talking to me like that. I'm on edge already from the heat in his words, the command in them.

"I'll try to be good, but I make no promises," I say with a crooked grin.

"I don't think you have it in you," he teases as he grabs my jeans, unbuttons them, and slides a hand inside my boxers, covering my hard-on with his palm.

I rock into his talented hand. "Fuck, babe. That's so fucking good."

Dean strokes my cock as I shove off my clothes, savoring the feel of him touching me the whole damn time. Then he lets go and pushes off his jeans and briefs.

When we're both in nothing, we lunge for each other, tumbling to the bed, two tigers ready to devour. We kiss like we're going to consume each other. Or maybe I'm already consumed as we slam our bodies together, and the sheer pleasure of contact with him is like an electrical charge surging across my skin.

We go at it like that for a few minutes of bone-searing, pelvis-grinding kisses, but then he pushes me flat on my back and rolls on top of me, his cock rubbing next to mine. I grab his ass, so firm and strong, the promised land where I want to be tonight.

He slides up on his knees so he's straddling me, his palms flat on my chest, his stare as hot as the surface of Mercury. "Now listen to me. We're going to fuck and fuck and fuck. I want it every way with you. Since I won the game, let me tell you what I'm going to do with my winnings."

"Tell me."

"I'm going to give you three choices, and you can feel free to pick your favorite," he tells me, as he rocks his perfect fucking ass against my erection. "I can ride you, Fitz. Ride your fantastic fucking cock till we both come so hard we can't think straight for days. Or I can get on my hands and knees for you, and you can fuck me to the edge of the bed. Or maybe, just maybe, you can throw me onto my back and drive into me till I beg for you to make me come."

I swallow roughly, trying to process those images, the filthy film of taking Dean in all those ways flicking before my eyes.

But I can barely move. Barely speak.

I can't breathe.

I don't know how he does this. I think I'm in control, but that's an illusion when he tops me with his words, his dirty mouth. He says the sexiest things in that English accent, and I can barely control myself. I can't contain this desire. Nor do I ever want to.

I breathe out hard, wanting, needing, craving.

"I want it all," I rasp.

"I know you do," he says, rocking that beautiful body against me, showing me what he'll do when he takes me all the way. Dean presses his chest against mine, and the contact, the exquisite contact, is some kind of erotic torture. So is choosing how to fuck him first. "But you better choose soon," he whispers. "Or I'll have to jack off in front of you, because I'm *that* aroused."

A breath shudders from me, comprised of a million tons of lust. This man is killing me.

But I know what I want. I know how I want to have him. I need to see his gorgeous face as I bury my cock in his body.

In one swift move, I push up, grab his hips, and flip him to his back. I pin his wrists above his head, bringing my face to his neck. And then I whisper in his ear, "Need to see your face when I drive into you, when I make you come so fucking hard you see stars."

Then I let go, grab the lube from the nightstand, and

move between his legs after nudging them apart with my knees.

He parks his hands behind his head. I take a moment to drink in the sight of his long, lean body, toned arms, and flat stomach.

His perfect dick—long, thick, and goddamn delicious.

But that's not all.

There's so much to admire.

His legs. Strong and muscled. His thighs. I drizzle lube onto my fingers, slide them along the length of his shaft, and watch him shudder as I move lower, then press a finger against his ass.

The look on his face is *nirvana*. It's blissful torture as I push inside, getting him ready—one finger. I pour on more lube then add two fingers, a third. My dick twitches, leaking at the tip.

Dean's eyes are closed, and he lets one hand glide down his chest, the other drifting to his shaft.

"Uh-uh. Don't touch. Can't have you coming too soon. You want me to fuck you to the edge of pleasure, remember?"

His eyes snap open, and he pushes up on his elbow, his gaze full of fiery intent. "Then get inside me now. I really can't wait any longer before I take matters into my own hands." He grabs the condom from the nightstand, opens it, and thrusts it at me.

"Put it on me," I tell him.

With a satisfied grin, my sexy Brit sits up, slides the protection on the head, then rolls it down my length. I groan from his touch, even like this, even in this necessary action.

When I'm covered, he lies back down. I set my hands on his thighs, spread him wider, then rub the head of my cock against him. He pushes his hips up, letting out the most carnal groan I've ever heard. From that. From that tease of a touch. Just the press of me against him.

My skin is tight. My chest is a furnace, and I'm so goddamn aroused as I push in farther, breaching him.

We both groan at the same moment. That electric moment when I move past that ring of muscles, when his ass grips me so nice and tight, and I never want to leave.

I'm braced on my palms, placed on either side of his chest. Like that, his hands travel up my pecs and spread over them. His eyes glimmer with desire. "Give it all to me," Dean commands.

"With pleasure." I shove inside, all the way, and we both sound like animals.

Groaning, grunting, growling.

"You feel so fucking good," I say, my bones vibrating from the intensity.

"So do you," he gasps, his hands wrapping around me, grabbing hard onto my ass, tugging me farther into him. "That's how I want you, Fitz. Nice and deep and so fucking hard."

This man. I can barely wrest any control from him. Even when I try, he takes it all from me with that filthy, beautiful mouth. If I thought it was sexy when he said my name before, that's nothing to how he says it now, in the heat of the moment while I'm inside him.

I try though, thrusting into him, stroking out. We find the perfect rhythm in seconds and keep it going. But the need to get closer consumes me. I lower myself, bracing on my elbows, my chest inches from his. Sparks tear across my body, and I fuck him like that, thrusting, pumping.

Filling him.

As his hands clasp my ass.

As his face, his gorgeous face, twists with pleasure.

As his lips, full and decadent, part while he breathes out hard with every thrust.

Dean lets himself savor every second of it, of us.

And the sounds he makes burn me up.

Yes.

So good.

Fucking yes.

I can barely take it.

I can barely last with the way he is, how he responds, how much he wants me.

He seems to want me as much as I want him, and I can't count that high.

There isn't a number big enough to define how much I want this man.

Pleasure roars through me, intense wave after wave, and I want to just fuck into blissful oblivion, till we are drowning in orgasms.

But Dean set the bar high earlier, and I am not going to fail.

I am not going to come too soon.

I rise up so I'm kneeling, grab his hips, and slam him hard on my cock.

Which doesn't help matters.

But that's okay. I know what I'm doing. I know how to slow down. And that's what I do, stealing control back from him. I downshift like the music, like the low pulse of the playlist.

I slow-fuck him like this, with long, leisurely thrusts, taking my sweet time, driving into him, then pulling out, almost, almost all the way, but not quite.

The whole time I watch him, savoring the pleasure in Dean's eyes, the way his lips part, how his chest moves, and how insanely hot and hard his perfect dick is.

I grab his cock, wrapping my fist tight around it,

stroking as I fuck him. He feels so damn good in my hand, and the anguished twist in his features tells me everything.

"You like that? When I do this while I fuck you?" I give his hard shaft a tight squeeze, sliding my hand up to the head, then back down again.

Dean groans. "Yeah, just a little."

"Or maybe if I do this," I say, sliding out halfway, still stroking him.

His hips jerk up, trying to bring me back to him. "You fucking tease," he moans.

I wiggle my brows. "You like just the tip?" Letting go of his dick, I pull nearly all the way out, then pause, holding us in place just like this. "You like it like that, when I drive you crazy?"

Dean rises onto his elbows, his eyes furious. "I liked it better when you were all the way in me," he says, sliding a hand down his perfect chest, headed straight for his cock. He grips himself, toying with his dick—teasing me now. "Do you enjoy being teased, Fitz?"

My eyes lock on the man under me, his hand curled loosely around his thick shaft, his fist leisurely, languidly gliding up and down his length. A shudder wracks my body. I am shaking as desire rips through me. Watching this man pump his beautiful cock is unraveling me.

Whatever tenuous hold I had on fucking him spirals away as Dean taunts me.

I'm pretty much a lost cause.

My balls tighten, and pleasure barrels down my spine. "You want it hard? You want me deep?"

"I do."

"Then come with me. Come with me really fucking soon," I rasp as I drive back into him, burying my cock so deep that the sound he makes is obscene. It's the most delicious, fevered sound I've ever heard, a groan ripped straight from his chest.

"Fuck," Dean pants out. "Yes, that's so fucking good."

And it's more than good.

It's electric and wild and mind-bending as I take over for him and grip his hard shaft in my palm, pumping him as my orgasm marches through my body.

Taking no prisoners.

Leaving nothing behind.

"Coming," he groans.

"Me too, babe. Coming so fucking hard." I grunt as my release takes over, my vision blurring, my brain firing a thousand million pleasure receptors as my whole body succumbs to the release.

And Dean's right there with me, shooting into my hand, on his chest. And, when I collapse onto him, on my chest too.

I can't think.

I can't speak.

I can only feel.

And I feel amazing.

Like I knew I would. Because I knew from the second I met him that sex with Dean would be the hottest sex of my life.

We're both panting, sweating, and I bury my face in his neck, inhaling his scent that drives me wild. I don't even know what it is. It's just his soap mixed with him, but my God, does it do it for me. I kiss him, working my way to his ear. "I cannot wait to do that again."

"Me too, Fitz. Me too."

He slides his arms around my lower back, and we're quiet like that for a few seconds, maybe more.

I could get used to this. I could get used to *him*.

But before we get too cozy, I need to take care of things.

"Be right back." After I ease out, I head to the bathroom, where I clean up, dispose of the condom, and grab a wash-cloth. I wet it with warm water and return to the sex-drunk man stretched out on the mattress.

I wipe his chest, his stomach. I dip my face to him, planting a soft kiss on his clean pecs before I return to the bathroom and toss the washcloth on the floor.

Seconds later, I'm back in bed, and I need to feel him against me. I need the contact. So I wrap my arms around him, pulling him close, his back to my chest, and I sigh.

Happily.

So damn happy.

"Stay the night," I say.

"Was kicking me out previously on your list of options?"

I laugh. "No. I just didn't know if you would stay. Will you? Spend the night with me?"

He shifts around to look me in the eyes. "What part of *all night long* made you think I was leaving?"

I shake my head, still a little too blissed-out to think straight. "I dunno. I just want you here, whether we're screwing or not."

He doesn't say anything to that—just gives me that studious once-over. "'Or not' . . . what will we do with the 'or not' part?"

I wrap my arms tighter around him, nuzzling him. "This. Just this."

"The things we do," he says, filling in the dots.

"Yeah, the things we do," I say, then brush a kiss to his cheek. Even after what we just did, my chest still does some kind of flip just from kissing him.

Dean slides out of my arms, shifting to his other side, facing me. "I never planned to leave."

And my chest flips again. "God, you make me want to kiss you again."

I grab the covers, pull them up over us, and get close to him again, kissing him in the way you kiss someone after that kind of sex, that kind of intensity.

Tender, gentle, a little wrung out from the Os.

And hungry for more of him.

Although ravenous is more like it.

In the morning, all I want is to spend the day with him, so I ask in the best way possible if he'll do just that.

MONDAY

Also known as the day it starts.

17

DEAN

On the list of surprises in my life, I would not count this—
a middle-of-the-night session with the tireless Fitz.

I absolutely expected it.

Wanted it.

Craved it.

The man can truly go all night, which is a
complete *unshock*.

And though he has the stamina of a pro athlete in the
bedroom, I have an equally large appetite between the
sheets.

For him.

And for our visit to the three-a.m. club, I pick the position, choosing one I quite enjoy, getting on my hands and
knees. It works spectacularly well for both of us, especially
when he presses his hand between my shoulder blades,
pushing me down to the perfect angle.

And I conk out shortly after.

Hours later, when the sun rises and I stretch awake, he's
there with a "Morning, sunshine" that's facetious and

sweet all at once. He leans in for a smooch, and when I smell his minty breath, I shake my head.

"I don't think we'll do that when you smell like springtime and I'm a swamp." A quick trip to the bathroom, where I brush my teeth with an extra hotel toothbrush and take a piss, and I'm back in bed. Then he gets his morning smooch. "There." I grab the covers, turn on my side, and yawn. "Go back to sleep, Fitz. I'm sure you're Mr. Crack of Dawn, but I enjoy a morning lie-in."

"Fine. If you insist."

And he insists on wrapping his arms around me, which I don't mind at all.

But I only drift off for a little while before I'm woken again—this time by something worth waking up to.

Fitz between my legs, sucking me off.

Well, good morning to me.

It's the perfect wake-up call, an unhurried blow job that I luxuriate in, enjoying every single delicious second of it.

After, he slides next to me, his eyes flirty. "What are you doing today?"

I shrug happily as I stretch, enjoying the aftereffects. "I'm off work."

"Spend the day with me."

I shoot him a suspicious look. "Did you give me a morning BJ just to get me to say yes to spending the day with you?"

He wiggles his eyebrows. "I did. Did it work?"

I give a sigh—the deep, contented kind. "Seems it did." I prop myself on my elbow. "What about Emma?"

"She has orientation stuff on campus. I'll catch her in the early evening."

"All right. What do you have in mind? Eager to see Kensington Palace? The Tower of London and the Crown Jewels? Or more of my crown jewels?"

"The latter, obvs. I have a riverboat cruise booked tomorrow with Ems, but today I was hoping to go to London Bridge. I've been instructed by my buddy Logan's seven-year-old to take a photo on it, and I can't turn Amelia down."

"Ah, she wants to make sure it's not falling down."

Fitz taps his nose. "Bingo."

I stroke my chin as if deep in thought. "And you find yourself in need of a tour guide again."

He grins a little evilly. Deliciously evilly. "Yes. Yes, I do."

I nod like I'm absorbing this info. "Let me get this straight. You came to London to find a hot English bloke to bang. You found one straightaway. And now you're looking for a twofer. You want me to be your fuck buddy *and* your tour guide?" I arch a brow.

He props himself on his elbow. "Sounds like a win-win for me. So, yeah. Let's do it."

I roll my eyes. "And meanwhile, I have to do a shitload of chores."

"But not today, since you have the day off. What better way to spend it than showing me around before we go for another round?"

"Another? Just another? I might want more than one more. Especially since I'll be working off my debt to Maeve forever, it seems, given your appetite."

He slides a hand down my chest, tracing my abs. "Your appetite matches mine."

"Hmm. There is some truth to that."

Fitz dips his head and kisses my pecs. "It's all true. And you will get everything you want. Say you'll show the poor Yankee the sights of your town."

I heave a sigh as if this is the toughest choice in the world when, in fact, it is the easiest. Spending the day with this man, showing him some of the city I love, then fucking again, sounds like the recipe for a perfect summer's day. "Fine, I'll be your tour guide, but the first thing you need to know is *this*." He pops his head up and nods, like an eager student. I tap his chest. "It's not London Bridge you want to see. It's Tower Bridge. That's the pretty one."

Reaching for my phone, I quickly google "Tower Bridge" and show him the iconic symbol of the city, two bridge towers tied together with two walkways. "That's the more picturesque of the two."

"Then let's go there." He grins, so easy to please. "Wait. Can we see the Harry Potter bridge too?"

I crack up. "You mean the Millennium Bridge? The one the Death Eaters destroyed in *The Half-Blood Prince*?"

Fitz's face contorts with the strangest look—possibly excitement, maybe thrill, then he lets out a long warrior cry. He grabs his head, tugging on his hair. "Shut the front door. You're a fucking Harry Potter fan?"

I chuckle. "Yes. I mean, obviously."

"Why is it obvious? Because you're English?"

"No, because the books are bloody awesome." Then I pause, arching a skeptical brow. "Wait. Please don't tell me you're just a movie fan. Shit. You're a movie fan, aren't you? You've never read the books? You had a crush on Radcliffe when you were a curious teen?"

He clasps his hand to his bare chest. "You wound me. I mean, yeah, I had a crush on Radcliffe when I was twelve, like every other gay tween. But as for that insult . . ." He pokes my chest. "Are you saying I don't know that Hermione blackmailing Rita Skeeter and Neville leading the DA during *Deathly Hallows* were two of the best parts of the books that the movies left out?"

I slow-clap. "Bravo. The reduction of Neville's role in the films was a travesty."

"An utter disgrace."

I sink back into the pillow and let out a long, relieved breath. "All right. I've decided. I'll keep fucking you."

"Uh, yeah. But you seriously thought I was a poser? I read those books to Emma. All of them. In my best English accent, thank you very much."

I sweep out my arm in an invitation. "By all means, let's hear it."

He clears his throat and affects a British sound— vaguely. *"Mr. and Mrs. Dursley of number four, Privet Drive, were proud to say that they were perfectly normal, thank you very much,"* he says, reciting the first line of the first book.

It's not half bad. "So that's your Harry Potter accent?"

"Yes. I sound just like you, don't I?"

I slide into my riff on an American accent. "Yeah, man, like, that beach was totally rad."

Fitz cringes. "Never do an American accent again."

"Let's just agree that the accent thing goes both ways."

"That sounds fair."

I park my hands behind my head, savoring this morning-after time. "So, is it a tour of London you want? Or just a tour of all the Harry Potter locations?"

"All of that." His eyes sparkle. "Seriously, just Tower Bridge is fine. But I'm game to see anything. This is my first time here."

"Yeah? And do you like London?"

"I do. I like it a lot. Have you always lived here?"

"Born here. Raised here. Went to university in Leeds. That was the only time I've lived anyplace else. But I've traveled around Europe."

"Favorite place?"

"I went to Paris with my parents when I was eleven. And Amsterdam when I was twelve, when Mum was doing some work for the Rijksmuseum. Don't remember a ton, except I loved Amsterdam."

"Me too. Great city," he says with a happy sigh.

"When were you there?"

"Last year. The NHL has an event called the Global Series, and my team played in Amsterdam, Prague, and Copenhagen."

"Copenhagen is great. Maeve and I went there right after uni."

He sticks out his tongue, panting. "The men in Copenhagen are superhot."

I roll my eyes. "Wow. Tell me more about your European trysts. I would love all the details."

He laughs and nuzzles me, kissing my jaw. "I didn't bang anyone, you dick. I'm just saying it would be fun to go with you. We could ogle the eye candy together and then go back to our hotel and screw."

I laugh. "You fucking pervert."

"C'mon. That'd be fun, right? Go to a bar. Get some beers. Sit outside, drink, and check out all the tall, strapping Danish men walking by. We could tell dirty stories about what we'd do to them, then go back and fuck each other like horny penguins."

"Are penguins horny?"

"Have you ever seen them walk? You tell me that penguins aren't taking it up the ass."

And I have no choice but to crack up, with deep belly laughs that expand to fill my body. Fitz smiles, looking pleased with my reaction.

When I finally collect myself, I say, "So, fine, we'll perv on hot Danes together in this fantasy world of yours. Where else have you been enjoying the scenery?"

"Ha. Mostly I've gone with my family on some fun vacays."

I gesture to myself. "As I said, you go with your family and enjoy the scenery."

"I don't usually"—he stops to sketch air quotes—"'enjoy the scenery' when I'm with them."

I give him my best smolder. "I see. I'm irresistible. You broke your look-don't-touch rule for me."

His expression shifts to serious. "I don't hook up when I'm with my family, so yeah, you must be irresistible." He runs a hand over my hip and along my thigh in a lazy, decadent way that makes my skin come alive. "And to answer your question, we've gone to a bunch of places. We never traveled when I was growing up. Didn't have the money at all. So, in the last few years, I've tried to make up for it. I took my mom and sisters to Colorado to go skiing, then to Costa Rica a couple of years ago. My sister Sarah loves to surf, so we surfed and zip-lined and hiked, and it was awesome. My other sister, Carrie, is a huge fan of Japanese culture, so I took her and everyone else to Tokyo last year. Had a blast checking out the temples, tea gardens, and shrines."

There's such genuine affection in Fitz's tone as he talks about his family that a grin takes over my face. "You're good to them," I say, keeping it simple.

"They're good to me. And hey, it's no hardship to travel to some amazing places. I loved all that stuff in Tokyo too, since I was a history major."

"Then I definitely will show you some of our sites here in London, and I'll pretend I'm not jealous that you've been everywhere."

"I'm lucky I've been able to travel. Have you ever been to the States?"

I shake my head. "No. Haven't made it that way yet. But it's all good," I say, then trace my fingers down his arm. "I keep meaning to ask you about your ink, but every time we get naked, I'm distracted by other things."

"My dick is super distracting."

"It actually is. But I won't be sidetracked now. So, what's this?" I draw my finger across the tribal band on one arm, barbed lines woven intricately across his biceps.

"Strength, family, wisdom," Fitz says, letting out a soft rumble as I touch him. It's heady to know even a curious trace can make him tremble.

"Your pillars?"

"Yup. Exactly. They're what matters."

"Couldn't agree more. And this?" My fingers follow a geometric design like spokes spiraling out from his biceps, winding around his shoulder and upper back.

"Passion. Intensity," he says, shutting his eyes, breathing out hard as I map his ink.

"And is that for the way you play hockey?"

He opens his eyes, those blue irises glinting. "Yes. That's how I try to play. Give it my all every time I hit the ice. Nothing less."

"Your teammates are lucky to have you."

"Goes both ways. I couldn't do what I do without them. They're my guys." He lets out a low growl as my hand spreads to cover the sunburst. "And this one?" I lower my face, pressing a kiss to the ink.

"Light, truth. It was Emma's idea."

"Yeah? Why'd she suggest it?"

"She said I was like that. That I was always outgoing, always up-front, always open."

I smile. "Sounds like you."

"It came from a quote she found when she was studying religions in college as part of her core curriculum. 'Three things cannot be long hidden: the sun, the moon, and the truth.' Buddha said it, and she shared it with me. I like it."

"And then this last one?"

My fingers travel to his chest, where his skin bears an

inscription under the left pec. It's small and simple, just two words—*No Regrets*.

"That's how I try to live. It's a good mantra," he says.

"I can't disagree with you on that. I like it. I like them all. I like the way they look on you. So much that I don't mind mopping the floors or scrubbing the toilets."

Fitz snakes a hand around my body, squeezing my ass. "You're going to have to do so many chores after the things I plan on doing to you."

"At this rate, I think I might be building a new bar from scratch."

He wiggles his eyebrows. "I should feel guilty, but I don't." He pauses for a beat. "Do you want me to help you though?"

I scoff. "You're not going to pitch in and clean the floors. I make my own choices."

"I'd do it for you. If you wanted me to." The earnestness of his offer is almost too much. It tugs on my heart, the sweetness in his voice. I believe he'd really grab a paint-brush or a hammer and happily work off my debt with me.

"I'm sure you'd look fantastic with a tool belt, but let's focus on these tools instead," I say, sliding a hand under the covers and squeezing his cock.

"You can use that for anything you want."

"And I plan to. Since evidently you need to get all these horny penguins out of your system before you go whack some moles or whatever it is you do on the ice."

He cracks up as I let go of him. "I will get you to like hockey, I swear."

"If it's the last thing you do," I tease, shaking a fist.

"I'm going to make sure you love it. Mark my words, Dean."

"And I suppose I'd better make sure you like London. So, on that note, I should shower and change." I glance at the clock on the bedside table. "I'll meet you at Tower Bridge at twelve thirty."

"That's two hours away. How will I make it until then? I'm like a penguin, and in penguin time, that's years."

Laughing, I toss the covers aside. "So rub one out in the shower. That'll tide you over for a couple of hours."

He pouts, grabbing my thigh. "You rub one out with me right now," he says, grabbing my hand and wrapping it around his cock.

Which is ready to go.

And feels *amazing*.

That's the problem. He feels too good, turns me on too much. I'm getting hooked on the drug that is Fitz.

Even though I know better. Addictive feelings lead to choices that have far-reaching consequences, like leaving your family, leaving your world.

Things I would never do.

But I won't be tempted.

Because that's not what flings offer you.

They don't dangle before you the chance to skip out of town.

They don't encourage you to say *see you later* to all that matters.

Flings have a beginning, a middle, and, most importantly, *an end*. You can enjoy the hell out of them because of that immutable fail-safe known as an expiration date.

A fling is a perfect container for these unruly feelings Fitz evokes. Flings are supposed to be wildly intoxicating. They're meant to consume you for a few days, like a star that burns twice as bright, but half as long. You can bathe in the intensity for a few days, drape it over you, roll around in it.

You can drink it up and swallow it down, savoring every drop, knowing it'll be gone soon enough.

Fitz is dessert, all the decadent chocolate cakes in the city, and I will devour him for days.

Then, I'll return to my normal diet.

No more cake, no more him.

So I should eat my cake while I can.

I get back in bed, grab some lube to make this easier, and slide my palm along his erection, loving the hot, hard feel of him, the velvet-smooth skin, the steel length, and, most of all, the sounds he makes.

Yes.

Fucking yes.

Love it like that.

Love it hard and tight, and yes . . . Just. Like. That.

I dip my other hand lower, cupping his balls, playing with them, then I bring my mouth to his and suck on his bottom lip, drawing it in, knowing that kissing will send him over the edge.

And it works.

He's coming in my hand, rocking and thrusting and moaning my name.

After I wash my hands, I get dressed, say goodbye, and tell him I'll see him soon.

As I leave the hotel and hit the streets of my hometown, I vow to use these hours away from him to remind myself how much I *like* being away from him.

Since that's where I'll be in three more days.

I can't get accustomed to having him around.

No matter how much I like it.

Or him, for that matter.

There's only one thing to do—forget about him for the next two hours.

* * *

I pop into Coffee O'clock and order my usual.

"And one for your dad too?" Penny asks.

I tap my chin. "Hmm. Does he deserve a tea? He was quite cheeky to me last night."

"Sounds par for the course."

"True, true. I suppose I won't cut him off just yet."

"That's good of you. No wonder you're his favorite son."

I wink at her. "Exactly."

With the cups in hand, I thank Penny then head to Dad's flat, where I find him locking the front door on his way out.

"Personal tea delivery service is one of my favorite features of adult children," he says with a crooked grin, taking the tea.

"Where are you off to, old man?"

"Heading to the furniture shop. Taron got a new chair he thinks I'll like. Or an old one, I should say. Want to work on it with me this weekend?"

I take a drink of my tea. "Sounds like the perfect way to spend a Saturday or Sunday afternoon."

After all, I have no plans besides work—there won't be a soul demanding anything of me after Thursday.

My schedule will be clear.

I'll have no one to shepherd around town during the day or to hunker down with at night.

Just loads of time for my favorite things.

When we reach the shop, Taron greets us with a huge grin and a clap of his hands. His colorful red shirt billows in the summer breeze. "You are going to die when you see this piece. It reminds me of all the chairs we had growing up in Johannesburg."

"You had so many Victorian-era chairs in South Africa," my father teases.

"We were teeming with them. Working here is like being back home," Taron says, and when my dad heads straight for the rear of the store, my mate pulls me aside. "So, I hear you're into someone."

I furrow my brow. "What are you talking about?"

He tuts. "Naveen and Anya told me about your American. Sounds like the two of you were quite cozy."

I straighten my spine. "It was a date—that's all."

"You keep telling yourself that, but someday you're going to fall hard, and it's going to be so spectacular. Trust me, I know."

"Trust me. It won't happen with him. He lives across the ocean."

Taron waves a hand dismissively. "Details."

I shoot him a hard stare. "It's a three- or four-thousand-mile detail. A *transatlantic* detail. But besides that, he's not interested in more than a fling, nor am I. But I'm very interested in this chair."

I divert his attention away from talk of Fitz.

Any talk of him would go nowhere, which is precisely where Fitz and I are going after Thursday.

And that's fine by me.

18

FITZ

Sex burns calories, but those are just extra ones as far as I'm concerned.

Bonus calories.

That's why I hit the hotel gym, lifting weights for an hour and trash-talking Ransom via text in between reps. I send him a picture of the bar.

Fitz: You wish you could lift this much.

Ransom: I lifted that much when I was five, asshole.

Fitz: You wish you had my stats.

Ransom: I had your stats when I was in peewee league, dickhead.

Fitz: I was never in peewee league. Skipped it. I'm that good.

Natch, I finish off the thread with a GIF of Wile E. Coyote dropping an anvil on the Road Runner, because we're mature like that.

He replies seconds later.

Ransom: How's Emma? Is she still hot for me like she was the first time I met her?

Fitz: You ass.

Ransom: Burned.

On that note, I leave the gym, shower, and get ready to meet my tour guide. I drop my shades on, and along the way to Tower Bridge, I text Emma.

Fitz: Are you orientating?

Emma: Yes, I am pointing north now. Oh wait, that's orienteering.

Fitz: We'll sign you up for a map-reading class next.

Emma: I've mastered the Tube though. I'll be an expert at zipping underground in no time.

Fitz: And how's the flat coming along? It looked good yesterday.

Emma: Furnished flats overlooking quiet lanes and old bookshops are a dream come true. And speaking of dreams come true . . .

Fitz: Emma, the Stanley Cup is in June.

Emma: As if I'm talking about sports. How's your man?

Fitz: He's not my man. He's just a guy I'm spending time with.

Emma: Oh, cool. So you can meet me in thirty minutes for a quick jaunt through Kensington Palace after I finish my next session? My day is over early.

Fitz: Umm . . . no. I have plans.

Emma: Because you're seeing him. :)

Fitz: Fine. Yes. I am. We're going to Tower Bridge.

Emma: Knew it. Called it. You two were so cute yesterday.

Fitz: We are NOT cute.

Emma: Whatever. You seem enamored with Dean, and he seems quite taken with you.

Fitz: Yeah?

Emma: Yeah, but what do you care? He's just a guy you're spending time with. *insert winking emoji*

Fitz: Exactly. That's what I meant. I don't do relationships.

I don't do boyfriends. We're simply two adults enjoying each other's company.

Emma: Yes, enjoy his company at Tower Bridge. That's sooooo something you'd do with a hookup.

Fitz: Emma . . . I can see you have hearts and arrows in your eyes, but rest assured, this is just a good time. That is all.

Emma: Right . . . and on that note, I have a full afternoon of orientating. I'm not really done in thirty. I said that to bait you, and you revealed that you're going to spend time with Dean. Ha!

Fitz: You remain Machiavellian. Goodbye, Emma. See you for dinner. BTW, you're not into Ransom, are you?

Emma: The hella hot forward on your team with the smoldering eyes, great body, and face carved by angels?

Fitz: *facepalm*

Emma: Don't ask a question if you don't want to know the answer. And have fun with your new man.

Fitz: He's not my man.

I close the text app on the little stinker and enjoy the walk through the streets, savoring the busy vibe of this city.

My man.

Please.

No one has been my man in years, not since college. Not since Marcus, and that barely counts. I mean, yeah, it hurt like hell at the time—he was my first real boyfriend.

But whatever. He wasn't into me the same way I was into him, and that experience taught me I'm better off focusing solely on the things that matter—my job and my family.

I've been laser-focused on those twin cornerstones of my life ever since.

My mom worked too many jobs while I was growing up. Now, I need to take care of my family, and I won't throw away that duty for a guy.

Any guy.

That's why I like playing the field. I like flings. I like zero commitments.

Dean's a fling.

Nothing more.

A no-strings-attached arrangement that I intend to enjoy the hell out of until I leave.

Then, come Thursday, this tryst in London will be behind me, and the season and my team will be in front of me.

That is all.

As I walk along the river, I check the time of my flight on Thursday.

Two in the afternoon.

Then the time on the phone.

Almost twelve thirty.

That's seventy-four hours from now.

Fine, it's seventy-three-and-a-half hours till I'm gone.

My muscles tense the slightest bit. But I don't know why I'd feel any sort of frustration. I roll my shoulders to let loose some of the strange tightness in me.

There's no need to be tense when I'm doing everything

I'd intended when I walked into Dean's bar on Friday night.

Having him.

When I look up, I see the man himself resting his forearms on the railing of the bridge, sunglasses on, watching the Thames.

Waiting for me.

My skin sizzles as I near him.

He looks so damn good—all cool and relaxed in jeans and a T-shirt that fits just right as he gazes out over the water.

He's got AirPods in, and when he spots me, he turns, takes them out, and clicks on his phone. He gives me a grin that says he knows what I look like naked and he likes the look very much.

"Hey, you," I say. My hand twitches and reflexively reaches out to take his.

What the fuck?

I'm not going to hold his hand.

I mentally slap my hand away, tucking my thumbs in my jean pockets.

We don't hold hands. That's not what this is between us.

We screw, we have fun, nothing more.

Just to prove we aren't some touchy-feely couple, I don't even plant a kiss on his delicious lips.

He doesn't seem to miss it, since he smirks as he says, "Good afternoon, James."

I shoot him a curious grin. "You're using my first name now?"

"Thought I'd try it on for size."

"And how's the fit on your tongue?"

He screws up the corner of his lips like he's deep in thought. "I think I'll call you James when I'm mad at you."

I laugh. "You could never be mad at me."

"And why is that?"

"I make you laugh, and I'm good in bed."

He tosses his head back and cracks up. "That's all it takes to prevent someone from being cross with you?"

"What else is there?" I ask with a wicked grin. Banter is good, more like the level that Dean and I are—fuck buddies who have a great time together.

Nothing more.

"I can't think of a damn thing," he says. I take that as proof that he agrees, and that we're on the same page we were yesterday when we made our deal at the world's sexiest tea party. We set the rules, and we outlined all the expectations for this fling that ends in seventy-three-and-a-half hours.

Or, really, seventy-three hours and fifteen minutes.

I shove off the reminder of the ticking clock, since who cares? Clocks are supposed to tick, and I'll be so damn happy when I get on that plane to training camp. All the hot hotel sex will have satiated me, and the only thing I'll be hungry for is ice time.

I keep my foot on the gas pedal of this no-strings arrangement. "Seeing as you're *not* mad at me, and *won't* be mad at me, since I plan to keep making you laugh and keep making you feel good, you should just call me Fitz. I like that better for you."

"Why?"

"Because my teammates call me Fitzgerald. Well, they say, 'Yo, Fitzgerald.'"

"Something you will never hear me say."

"Also, I like the way you say Fitz."

"Why's that?"

I drop my voice to a whisper. "It's sexy, the way you say it in the heat of the moment. It's like my name tastes good on your tongue."

Dean lets out a low rumble, leaning closer to me as crowds stream by, tourists and Londoners alike weaving past us. "*You* taste good on my tongue, Fitz."

A bolt of lust slams into my chest, heating me up. This is what I'm talking about—lust, desire, pleasure.

"Right back atcha, Dean." Then I drape an arm over his shoulders. That's not holding hands. It's not as intimate. It's just a normal thing for us to do as we walk along the river then turn onto the bridge.

I survey the Thames from this vantage point, savoring the view of the ribbon of water as it snakes through the city. We stop in the middle of the bridge. I check out the setting, enjoying everything about it. The gray stone towers, like something out of Cinderella, complete with turrets, are flanked by a light-blue walkway and suspension railings. "Fine, you were right. This is hella pretty."

"Hella," he says, shaking his head in amusement. "Your Americanisms kill me."

"Knackered bloody wanker. Same to you, bro."

Dean rolls his eyes. "*Bro.* I die a slow death."

"Has anyone ever told you that it's easy to rile you up?"

"No. No one has. Maybe because no one likes to do it as much as you do."

"True. I kinda love it. Pushing your buttons is my new favorite hobby." I stop, park my elbows against the railing, and drink in the sights. "Yep, I can see why you like this one."

"It's lovely, isn't it? Like a fairy tale."

"Yeah, it's got a very storybook vibe." I punch his arm—that's friendly, pals-y. "Good call."

He shoots me an amused smile. "So, is this how we're doing it? With *bros* and arm punches?"

My cheeks flame as he calls me out for trying too hard to be ultracasual. To treat Dean like one of the guys on the team, like Ransom, trash-talking each other to show we care.

"Sure? Why not?" I ask with a shrug, keeping it up because it feels necessary.

"Okay, wanker," he says, staring at the water, his lips curving up in a grin. "Piss off," he adds, punctuating the words, having fun with them.

"Aww. Are you gonna call me James next? Are you mad at me?"

He laughs, shaking his head. "You said it was impossible to be mad at you."

"And is it?"

He turns his face to me. "No. I bet you could piss me off." Dean's voice is low, a little smoky, a hint of challenge in it.

"Why's that?"

"I just think you have it in you." It comes out even and offhand, but I'm not sure what to make of it.

I narrow my eyes. "Are you saying I'm a dick?"

He shakes his head, his tone more serious than I expected. "No. I'm just realistic. I think we as human beings have it in us to irritate each other. Even if you're funny and make me come ridiculously hard, you can still piss me off."

"That's why I think it's smart that we set rules for this," I say as a reminder to us both. I need the part of my head that's counting the hours to shut the hell up. Laying down the law will quiet that nagging part of my brain. "Boundaries are healthy. So everyone knows what to expect," I add for good measure.

Dean flinches almost imperceptibly, but still, it's there. "Of course, especially when we're"—he stops, seems to almost let the words roll around on his tongue—"*enjoying the scenery.*"

I nod, making sure we're both clear on the sitch. "I like scenery. I like to enjoy the scenery. But I also like to make sure everyone knows what to expect from the scenery. Know what I mean?"

He jerks his gaze to me, his eyes saying *Oh no, you didn't.* "Pardon me?"

Uh-oh. I might have overstepped. "I'm just saying I'm busy, as you know," I say, going for diplomacy before I quickly add, "So are you."

"Very busy. So this is very temporary." It comes out clipped.

And it feels like this conversation is veering straight out of riling each other up and right into pissing-each-other-off territory. But I don't stop it from heading in that direction.

Instead, I pat my chest. "Don't worry. I don't do serious."

"I don't either," Dean says, straightening his spine.

"Then we're all good," I say, my jaw tight, because he agrees so quickly, and that's good, but it irks me too, for some stupid reason.

"So good," he adds quickly.

I square my shoulders, unable to let this go. "For the record, I'm not interested in relationships. I'm not interested in anything more than what this is," I say, pointing from Dean to me and back.

His jaw ticks. "This *is* what it is, Fitz. It's not anything more." His dark eyes narrow, like I've gone too far and he needs to correct me. "You don't have to act like I'm one of your boys on the road who doesn't know any better. Who thinks he can shag an athlete and keep him around."

"I'm not acting that way," I say indignantly, wrapping my hands around the railing.

Dean gives a nonchalant shrug, but his words aren't casual. "You kind of are. You're acting, for some utterly absurd reason, like I'm some sort of lost soul, looking to attach myself to you." He doesn't raise his voice, doesn't shout. He simply speaks in a cool, calm tone here on Tower Bridge. "I have a life here, one I love," Dean says, taking off his shades, and his eyes aren't hot like I'm used to. They're ice-cold, and they're chilling my blood. "I have my bar— that's my home. I have my father and the things we do together. I'm having dinner with him tomorrow night, and this weekend we're restoring a chair. And I have Sam, and Naveen and Anya, and Taron. And Maeve, most of all. You don't need to keep reminding me that this is a fling. I was there yesterday when we made the rules. I'm not going to break them." He draws a deep breath, then goes quieter when he finishes with "James."

The way Dean says my name stabs me.

Like an ice pick in the chest.

It's cold, and I deserve it.

Because I did piss him off. I started this. I pushed us into an argument by drawing a line in the sand over and over, by saying, *Don't step over this, no, really, don't step over this.* I should have stuck to sex and laughter, to what I'm good at. I'm shit at anything more because I don't do anything more, not with anyone.

But I also know this—I don't want to be the guy who puts that look in Dean's eyes. Because he's staring at me like I am a dick.

And I'm pretty sure I just acted like one.

My chest pinches, and regret swirls inside me.

Even though we won't ever be anything more, I want the *now* of us to be as good as it was last night, and this morning, and in between.

I speak to him in the one language I'm most fluent in—the physical.

I grab his face, hold his cheeks, and meet his gaze. "I'm sorry," I mutter, then I kiss his luscious lips, trying to say I'm sorry that way too. When the kiss ends, he still looks annoyed, but not as much. "I just want to have fun with you. I didn't mean to go overboard about the rules. I know you get it. Sometimes I worry because—"

"Because others have wanted more from you?" he asks gently.

I nod, thinking of the times a hookup has asked to go home with me, to stay for breakfast, to go to the movies or brunch. "Yeah. But I bet that happens to you too. You're a catch, Dean. I'm sure all the guys want you."

"I'm sure they all want you," he says, and the chill has begun to thaw.

I drag a hand through my hair, hunting for the best way to make it clear that I'm a happy camper with the status quo, and that I bet he is too. "I don't want to make it seem like you're like them. I get it. I get you. You and me," I say, patting his chest, then mine. "We're the same. We're happy with our lives as they are. No need to change things, right?"

A tiny sliver of a smile seems to tug at his lips. "We are the same. No strings, no expectations. We'll just enjoy the next few days. I won't call you James again."

I offer a fist for knocking. "Knock me, bro."

He folds his arms across his chest, but he smiles. "No. There will be no 'bro.' No knocking."

"Hey! I just realized I don't even know your last name."

His brown eyes twinkle. "Ah, maybe it's better that way. So you can't track me down after the affair is over."

I roll my eyes, sighing heavily. "All right. Serve it up. You know I'm not tracking you down."

"Collins. Dean Collins," he says. Then he extends a hand. "Let's make a deal. I won't use James when I'm mad, because you won't make me mad, and you won't have any need to use Collins. Because neither one of us will do anything to piss off the other in the next seventy-two hours."

I rein in a grin that threatens to overtake my face. He's just as aware of how many hours we have left as I am.

I take his hand, clasping mine around it. "I won't use it in anger. But I do think it's hot as fuck. Much like you are." A rumble works its way through my throat as I savor the feel of his full name on my lips. "Dean Collins." I don't let go of his hand. Instead, I yank him to me, his chest inches from mine, his pelvis so close. "Dean Collins," I say again, his name heating me up. "I'm going to fuck you so good tonight."

In a flash, he's back. The heat in his eyes. The parting of his lips. The signs that he wants me.

"Show me," he says in that challenging tone he uses. "Kiss me right now the way you want to tonight."

"Gladly." I grab the back of his head and plant a hot, fierce kiss on his lips, on Tower Bridge in front of everyone walking by, not caring in the least.

When we separate, I wiggle my brows. "Okay, you ready to take my picture?"

He laughs. "Yes, I want to be completely turned on when I snap your pic."

I clap his back. "Just think of tea cakes or the queen, *mate*," I toss back at him.

More laughter. Then Dean schools his expression,

clears his throat, and mutters, "God save the queen." He gestures to his crotch. "Voilà. Done."

"So impressive, your deflation technique."

"Thank you very much."

I snap a quick selfie in the middle of the bridge to show London Bridge – not falling down – up the river. Then we walk to the other side of the bridge as it wraps around the water. "More pics. Amelia will like this one better anyway since it looks more like a bridge in a book and she loves to read. I practically read her a whole Calvin and Hobbes book at a softball game earlier this summer when we were sitting in the bleachers while everyone else was playing."

"Because softball wasn't her thing either?" Dean teases.

"Ha. No. Because I'm a good guy and I was watching my friend's kid."

He flashes me a smile. "She likes you. That's sweet."

"She likes Calvin and Hobbes now too. And hockey. I've been training her to like hockey from a young age."

"And you've succeeded?"

I give him my best cocky grin. "I have. Don't worry." I curl a hand around his shoulder. "I'll convert you next."

He grins. "Stranger things have happened. All right. Let's get on this."

Lining up the shot, I stand on the walkway, the bridge behind us, the water too. It's a good shot, but the thing is, it'd be better with both of us. It just would.

"Join me in the pic."

He shakes his head. "I don't think your friend's daughter wants to see me."

"Get in here," I say, motioning him closer. "She'll be impressed I'm on the bridge with a real Londoner."

He arches a brow. "You truly want me to join you?"

"It's a photo. It's not a promise ring."

"You ass," he mutters under his breath, but he's smiling

again, and we're us, having a good time, riling each other up.

Dean slides in by my side. I angle my phone out so that I can see both of us perfectly positioned in front of the famous landmark.

And we look good together.

Damn good.

For a flash of a second, before I take the pic, a series of images flicker before my eyes.

Unbidden.

Out of nowhere.

I don't ask for them, but they arrive fully formed, and I can see us like this. Checking out the world. Going to Amsterdam. To Copenhagen. To Paris. Taking pictures in front of tourist icons.

Pictures for my sisters, for Amelia, for my mom.

And for me. Most of all, for me.

That's why I want this shot.

Amelia doesn't care. That was a half-truth. I wanted to see how I looked here with him, with this man I can't get enough of.

Something about the way the two of us are together makes me feel like we could have that life. Those times. Those days and nights.

That he could be my man.

Then I blink the insane thought away.

Because what the hell?

That's not me. That's not what I want.

That won't happen.

And as soon as I'm fully aware of that thought, I squash it, keeping it far, far away.

I snap a couple of pictures.

"There. Done," I say, then tuck my phone away before

even looking at them. "I'm starving. Want to grab some lunch?"

He says yes, and I focus on food, not on the runaway thoughts that briefly, only briefly, invaded my brain.

They return later that day, and I do my best to quell them, to keep everything light and breezy.

But it's not as easy as it was even a few hours ago.

19

DEAN

After we eat, we roam around the city. I ask him about hockey. Even though I don't see myself becoming a fan, I'm genuinely curious how the game works, what the best strategies are. I like learning new things, and Fitz is an excellent teacher when it comes to his sport.

As we walk, he shares the ins and outs with me, and I can start to appreciate his passion for the game.

He asks about my dad and the things we do together. I tell him I see my dad often and that we have dinner once a week, sometimes more. I mention Penny at the coffee shop, and how I think she has her eye on him.

"Is your dad into her?"

"I dunno. I'd love to see him date again."

"He hasn't dated since your mom left?"

"He has. But nothing too serious. A few girlfriends now and then. It would be nice to see him fall in love."

"I hear ya. I was pretty stoked when my mom met her new husband a few years ago. He's a genuinely good guy, and he treats her like a queen."

"The Fitz seal of approval."

"It's good to see her happy. I hope your dad finds that."

"Me too."

I ask about his friends in New York, and he goes on about some guys on the team, then tells me about Summer and Logan. "He's a cool cat. Very intense and driven, but with a great deadpan sense of humor. He met this woman a few months ago and he's head over heels in love with Bryn. And then his sister Summer is hilarious. She's involved with Oliver, another good bud of mine. He's English too," Fitz adds.

"Oh, you know another Englishman?" We walk along a side street, passing a newsstand.

"Yes, we have Brits in New York. He's lived there since he was thirteen or fourteen though."

"A transplant."

"Does that still count in your book?"

"Sure. As long as he's loyal to . . . *proper football,*" I tease, then tip my forehead to another side street.

Fitz scoffs. "Too late. I've trained him to love hockey, as it should be."

"Of course you have."

We turn down the street and reach Leadenhall Market, a covered market with an ornate roof. "Here you go. This is the Leaky Cauldron."

His blue eyes widen, sparkling with delight. "Diagon Alley." He wags a finger at me. "I knew you could never stay mad at me."

I hadn't been terribly mad at him.

Just irked that he thought he'd cornered the market on cool and casual. I'm as cool and casual as he is. That was why I stood my ground during that conversation. Because I am every bit as invested in this ending as he is, and he needs to know that. I'm not clingy, I'm not a hanger-on, and I'm not a star-fucker.

It's all for the best that we reset the rules.

If you don't have rules, that's when you run into trouble.

"I'm not mad in the least," I say.

I show him around the market, and he insists on snapping more pictures, and I join him in a few.

"You're like a teenage girl, with your addiction to selfies."

"Pictures are more fun when people are in them," Fitz says. "Now smile for my cell phone, sexy bartender."

"Here you go, cocky athlete," I say, giving a grin for the camera.

He snaps the shot, then tucks his phone away.

Along the way to the nearby Millennium Bridge, he demands more photos by the river.

Photos of us.

I wrap my arm around him. "Are you starting a collection now? Working on a photo album of your trip?"

"Yes. I'm going to post stickers of unicorns next to you." He smacks his lips to my cheek and captures the shot. Then he looks at the picture. "Aww, you look so peeved you had to pose for a selfie."

"Please tell me that's not for your friend's kid."

He gives me a salacious look. "That's for the spank bank."

I roll my eyes again. "I seriously doubt you're going to whack off to a shot of me rolling my eyes."

"But it captures your essence so perfectly."

I laugh as we reach the Millennium Bridge. "Here you go."

He regards it with eager eyes, a tourist's delight, and it's good fun to see him take in for the first time the sites that are so familiar to me.

"What do you think?" I ask. I hope that he likes it, that he likes all of London.

"Love it." He turns to me. "London is great. I can see why you love it here."

"I do love it here," I say with a smile, feeling understood. "It feels like home. It *is* home."

"That's a good feeling."

We cross the bridge, and soon enough, the long rays of the afternoon sun bounce off the windows of the red phone booth next to the Tube station in front of us.

"I need to go see Emma," he says, a tiny hint of reluctance in his voice, then quickly adds, like he needs to clarify, "I *want* to see Emma."

"Of course you do," I say, though the distinction is not lost on me. I wouldn't mind wandering some more with him, walking on into the evening as it spills into night.

But time apart is good.

It's wise.

And it's inevitable.

After all, we have less than seventy-two hours of this tryst remaining. Wait. No. More like sixty-eight or sixty-seven, since we just whiled away several hours.

In the blink of an eye.

My chest squeezes as I hear the clock ticking toward tomorrow, and the next day, and the next.

Fitz scrubs a hand over his beard. Takes a beat. "Dean."

"Yes?"

"Come over tonight?"

It doesn't come out as a command. It's a question. Like Fitz thinks there's a chance I might say no.

There isn't a chance in hell I'd say anything but yes.

"I will."

"When?" He sounds relieved but also eager.

"When are you free?"

"Nine. I can peel away by nine."

I smile playfully, keeping it light, since that's the order of the day. Since those are the rules. "So far away."

He breathes out hard, rubs a hand over the back of his neck, and shifts his gaze back and forth like he's thinking. For a few seconds, he seems lost in thought, or maybe indecision. But then his eyes sharpen, and he grabs my hand and jerks me against him on the street. "I really want to see you again tonight."

"You will. I'll be there," I say, reassuring him.

"I know," he whispers, but his voice isn't cocky this time. There's a note of urgency to it. He presses his forehead to mine, his voice going smoky, whispery. "Fucking you was incredible . . . it was better than it's ever been."

The words come out like a heated confession.

Like they can't be anything but the truth, so help him, God.

I feel the same, and the memory of our time in bed flickers before me in a burst of heat and desire.

"Same," I murmur. "Same for me."

His hand curls tighter around mine, squeezing my fingers. "You and me. In bed. It's intense, man. Isn't it?"

"It is, Fitz." I feel lightheaded, drugged from this conversation.

He pulls back slightly, meeting my gaze. "You feel it too?" His eyes are vulnerable, as if he desperately needs this confirmation.

And I want to give it to him, because I can, because it's safe. Admitting the truth of our chemistry can't hurt me. "I do. I do feel it."

Fitz's breath shudders. "It's kind of mind-boggling."

"It's a little bit crazy."

"Or maybe a lot," he says, then he lets go of my hand. "I

should go, or I'll never see Emma. I'll just get in a black cab with you and get seriously randy."

He says it like it's a joke, and it likely is, but there's something in his voice that makes it sound like he needs to get away from me.

Maybe to recalibrate.

That's not such a bad idea.

When you want someone so badly, spending all your time together borders on dangerous.

And with him, I'm feeling more than a little bit dangerous.

He turns to head into the station, then he doubles back, grabs my forearm, and spins me around to face him. "Spend the night again?"

"I will." Some little part of me is cheering, glad he asked now, glad I won't have to assume anything.

"Are you working tomorrow?"

"Later in the evening. After an early dinner with my dad."

Fitz runs his hand down my arm. "Spend the morning with me too."

"I will."

And I want to. And that feels like a new kind of danger. But it's a risk I'm diving into headfirst, no parachute.

At nine o'clock, I knock on the hotel room door. I have my gym bag with me, a change of clothes in it for tomorrow. My temporary fling opens the door, and I'm gobsmacked.

Fitz wears only jeans. He's barefoot and shirtless, all those carved muscles and ink on display. He's got a glass of amber liquid in his hand.

He lifts a brow, holding up the tumbler. "Fancy a nightcap?"

"Why, yes, I would."

I step inside, drop the bag, and head to the bar, where he's cracked open a bottle of scotch.

"You trying to get me pissed? Don't you know I'm a sure thing?" I ask as I pour the scotch.

He comes up behind me, aligning his body to mine, his erection already evident as he presses against my ass. "I want to taste the scotch on your lips."

My skin burns. I lift the glass, knock some back, then set it down. With my back against his stomach, Fitz raises an arm, grips my jaw, and turns my face to claim my lips in a heady, electric kiss.

It makes my head swim and my skin feel too tight for my body.

It torches my blood.

My God, how can kissing do this to me? I want so much more. I want all of him inside me, and yet I don't want to stop kissing him.

I swivel around, and I'm in his arms, my hands looping around his neck, his around my hips. Arms and hands move everywhere, grasping, gripping, feeling.

I groan as I jerk him closer, needing the contact, needing to feel his body firm against mine.

We kiss like it's all we've thought about since we separated a few hours ago.

His lips are hungry, and he sucks and nibbles and torments. Then he spears his tongue into my mouth, and I groan from the wicked pleasure of his touch, since he's grinding against me too, the outline of his cock finding mine.

And my head drifts into a passion-fueled haze.

Lust travels down my spine, echoing across my whole

body.

And I *want*.

I want Fitz so much I can feel it in my lungs. I want him ferociously, with a desperation I haven't known in ages.

Or maybe I've never known it could be quite like this.

This intense.

This . . . *devouring*.

And my God, I want to devour him.

I want to toss him on the bed, strip him naked, and just have him, *fuck him*. Do what I want to him.

But I know he needs us a certain way, and I can do that for him. I can give, and I can take.

What I can't do, though, is wait.

I break the kiss, panting, eyes wild, I'm sure. I clasp his face and say the words. "You need to fuck me right now."

He growls. That's all. Just a carnal growl that heats me up even more.

Fitz jerks at my shirt, then rips it over my head. "Need you naked. Need it now."

"Same. Same to you," I say, my breath already ragged with desire as I grab at the waistband of his jeans, unbuttoning, unzipping, pushing them down.

I lick my lips the second I see his hard cock, ready for me, a glistening drop of liquid at the crown. I run my thumb over it, bring it to my lips, lick it, and savor the taste of him.

"You taste so fucking good," I tell Fitz as his blue eyes go glassy, like he can barely handle the sight of me reveling in his flavor.

"Touch me again," he groans, long and powerful.

"Like I'd do anything else," I say, lowering my hand to his shaft.

He thrusts against my fist. "God, you're driving me crazy, Dean. I'm so fucking turned on by you," he says, wrapping his palm around my hand, so we're both stroking him. "You do this to me. You just fucking do this to me."

Anticipation zaps through my body like a current as I indulge in several long, tantalizing strokes. Touching Fitz, sending him to this frenzied state is such a high. I don't want to stop at all.

But soon he swats my hand away with a feral grunt, so he can shove at my clothes, stripping me to nothing too.

Then he takes two steps backward and sits on the edge of the bed. His hand goes straight to his cock, and he grips it roughly, savagely. "Get on me. Ride me so fucking hard. *Please.*"

My dick twitches at his filthy command that's almost a beg. Fitz grabs the lube he's left on the bed, next to a condom. As I straddle him, he flips open the bottle, slides two quick, eager fingers into me. I stroke myself as he gets me ready, and it's all so damn intense I don't know how I'll last.

But I'm willing to find out.

Oh hell, am I ever willing.

For a few seconds, I let myself get lost in the sensations of what his fingers are doing, but I know something so much better is coming, so I focus on what's next, grab the protection, and slide it on his thick shaft.

Then I rise up, my knees on either side of his thighs as Fitz takes his cock in his hand, holding the base, rubbing the tip against my ass.

My head falls back as the unholy pleasure begins. "Yes, fucking yes," I groan while my body seeks him out, takes him in the slightest bit, lets him breach me.

The second he does, wild want overwhelms me.

And, in one swift move, I drop down on his dick.

The world turns into a scorching blur.

"Oh fuck," Fitz grunts as his hands grab my ass hard, holding me in place, just holding on, so he can push even deeper into me.

"God, that's good. That's so fucking good," I say, adjusting to the delicious burn that comes first, then the way he fills me.

My hands press against his chiseled chest. Everything about him is hard, rough, and muscled, and I fucking love it.

My cock juts between us, and when he slips a hand down, grabbing me, I shake my head. "Don't. I'll come too soon," I warn.

"Can't have that."

Fitz grips my ass again, as I lift up, swiveling my hips, then pushing back down. Every inch of my body is sizzling, sparking. Lust jolts through my cells as I show Fitz how I like it, how I intend to ride him to our next release.

His eyes lock with mine for a hot second. In that flash, I see so much need, so much urgency in his irises. That look makes me want to give it to him harder, hotter, deeper.

I let him know with my body, with how I move, with the grinding and the pressing as I ride his cock.

He licks his lips, breathes out hard, and stares down at us, at where we connect. "Fuck, Dean. I'm dying here. You are so fucking hot like this."

His words fuel me, drive me to roll my hips expertly, to take him in deeper, then slide up, so he's barely in me.

He squeezes his eyes shut, and a groan seems to rip from his throat. When he opens them, he grips me harder. "I want to watch us. Want to watch my dick slide in and out of your ass."

I glance at the mirror on the wall. "I believe that can be arranged."

20

FITZ

I am combusting.

I am a brush fire that shows no signs of letting up.

The flames lick my skin, and I fan them.

"Shift around. So I can watch in the mirror," I tell my sexy Brit.

We move from the foot of the bed to the side, his gorgeous body on me, my cock nestled in its favorite place.

Inside this man.

When we find the perfect position, his arms rope around my neck, and he whispers in my ear, "Now watch, Fitz. Watch as I fuck your cock."

I shudder, grabbing his back, watching over his shoulder, imprinting onto my brain the most erotic sight I've ever witnessed.

Dean Collins, riding me, giving me the view I want, taking his time.

"Oh, hell yes," I grunt as I catch sight of him rising, my cock almost sliding out of his fantastic ass. Then, in slow motion, he lowers himself, and I can barely breathe as I watch his ass draw me in. "Nothing," I pant out, trying to form the words. "Nothing is sexier than that."

"Then, you better not look away."

"I can't look away."

Forget the brush fire. The entire forest is burning down from the Dean show and tell, from the way he grinds and dips, from how he rises and lowers, from the tantalizing way he takes my dick inside him.

And how he shows me, making sure I can watch us in the mirror.

What I see floors me.

My hands are all over Dean, sliding up and down his muscled back, gripping his perfect, delicious ass.

"You're killing me when you do that. Just fucking killing me," I rasp out.

"Don't die before you come, Fitz," he taunts, and how he can tease me when I am hovering on the edge of the cliff is a mystery to me, but I don't need to solve it, don't want to solve it.

I just want to gaze at the two of us fucking, at his body taking me over and over. "Dean, babe. We're so fucking hot together. I can barely handle it."

I smash my lips to his, needing to kiss him, needing to feel his mouth on mine. He kisses me back hard, fierce, all teeth and lips and fire.

When we break apart, I'm even drunker on him than I was before. I'm high, so damn high as I jerk my gaze back to the mirror. "I want to watch this filthy fucking view all night, of you riding my dick."

"Then do it," he says, slowing down, turning the pace into a sensual striptease, a visual feast.

My skin is tingling everywhere. Beads of sweat slide down my chest. And my hands feel so good wrapped around his ass, squeezing those strong, firm cheeks as I stare at the two of us.

This man owns my pleasure.

And he's determined to wring every last drop from me.

That's all I want. To be consumed by what he's doing to me. Because he's doing everything. He's giving and taking and fucking my cock so damn good that the switch flips in me.

"Dean," I warn. "I need to come really fucking soon. Are you almost there?"

"Seconds away," he says.

"Good. Let me fuck you hard now," I say, then smack his ass. "Get on your hands and knees."

"Only because you asked nicely," he says.

Keeping the condom in place, I pull out, my dick whimpering at the momentary loss of contact.

Then, after Dean's in the perfect position to finish, I get behind him, slide right back home, and I know—I just know—this is how sex should be.

It should always be this intense.

This electric.

This *out of this world*.

Because I am out of my mind with desire, eaten alive by it as I kneel behind him, thrusting into him, taking his hard cock in my hand, where it belongs.

And I stare at the two of us in the mirror, my body curled over his.

But then, I get the bright idea to yank him up so we're both kneeling, his back pressed tight to my stomach, one arm of mine looped under his. My other hand is on his dick, my cock buried deep, so damn deep in his body as I fuck this sexy, filthy, fantastic man to release.

As I come so damn hard inside him.

As he climaxes all over my hand, groaning my name.

The pleasure just crashes over me in wave after wave of never-ending bliss.

We collapse, a hot sticky mess on the bed, and I don't care, I don't care, I don't care.

I slide out, keeping the condom on, but not wanting to let go of him as we pant and breathe and moan.

And I tell myself it's just the sex I'll miss.

It's just the hottest sex of my life that I'll long for.

And I almost believe it.

Almost.

But not quite.

21

DEAN

A little later, I down a glass of scotch, savoring the last satisfying drop. "A shag, a scotch. What could be better?"

Fitz sets down his empty glass, reaches for the remote, and flicks on the TV. "SportsCenter?"

I sink onto the bed, flinging a hand over my eyes. "Dear God. No. Just no."

Fitz cracks up. "I'm not that much of a dick. I won't subject you to SportsCenter." He tosses the remote on the floor. "Do you really hate sports?"

I remove my hand from my eyes. "Sports are great. I just don't want to watch sports news in bed with you."

He wiggles a brow. "I get it. There are better things to do."

"Yes, that. And I'm sure we'll be recharged shortly."

"So, what do you want to do in bed with me, then?"

I glance at the tumbler. "Drinking scotch is fun. But if you really want to watch television, I'd rather watch a comedy on Netflix or something."

His blue eyes twinkle. "Dark comedy?"

"Love it."

"British comedy?"

"Of course."

"Sitcoms?"

"With no laugh track."

Grinning, he offers me a hand to high-five, and I smack it back. "Laugh tracks suck," he says. Stretching across me, Fitz reaches for his phone, clicks on Netflix, and scrolls through the newest comedies. We find one that interests us both, a show about a group of friends too tangled up in each other's lives.

Fitz clicks play and then settles in next to me, his head on the pillow beside mine. His body fits snugly against me, his arm draped across my shoulders.

Everything about this moment screams *opposite of hookup*, yet that calendar mercilessly flipping forward reminds me that it's safe to enjoy this moment, since it'll end soon.

Still, I can't resist teasing him.

"You realize we're both over six feet, and we're in this little sliver of the bed," I point out, staring at the other unused side of the king-size bed.

He grins, inching closer to me. "Are you saying you don't want to snuggle with me after I fucked your brains out? Or are you trying to tell me diplomatically that I suck at snuggling?"

I crack up. "Because that would be an insult to you? Being rubbish at snuggling?"

"I am not rubbish at snuggling, and you know it. I am an awesome snuggler," he says, squeezing me harder.

"You're not too bad."

"You hate snuggling. Admit it," he says, dipping his head into the crook of my neck and planting a loud, over-the-top kiss there as a soft *thunk* registers in my mind.

"Yes, I despise it. Please stop," I say as I do the opposite, somehow scooting closer to him.

"I can't stop. I can't help myself," Fitz teases, then grabs me hard, yanking me into his arms.

"Okay, now you're being ridiculous," I say, but I'm laughing, even as I gently push him away, the sound of the show playing in the background a little more distant now.

He raises his head, furrowing his brow. "What happened to my phone?"

"I think it fell on the floor." I peer over the side of the bed and reach down to grab the phone from the carpet. I hand it to him, the show still playing.

"So, good show, huh?" he asks dryly.

"It's fantastic. I could write an essay on it."

"We could do a trivia night about the show."

"Yes, I know so much about it. Let's find a pub and do a quiz, and we'll ace it."

Fitz laughs, clicking the end button on the show. A notification pops up on his phone—a new text message.

I look away, not wanting to pry.

"You can answer your messages. It doesn't bother me."

"It's from Logan. He thanked me for the pic," he says, then shows me the text.

Logan: Amelia loved the pic. Thanks, man. Anyone who makes my kid that happy is good in my book.

Fitz smiles, then scrolls to the next message. "And this is from his sister, Summer. She's also one of my friends in New York."

"They're the ones with the cousin I'd surely be mates with because of our furniture hobby?"

"Yes, that's them," he says with a laugh, then clicks on Summer's message.

I don't look at his phone, but I can't help but notice the way his eyes light up, how a smile seems to tug at the corner of his lips as he reads her note.

But I say nothing. It's not my place, even though I'm curious about what makes him look like that, what a friend says to him that puts that happiness on his face. Of course, it doesn't seem hard to make Fitz happy. He's wired for it, like a golden retriever. Happiness seems to be the natural state he gravitates to, yet another thing to like about him.

That list is getting far too long for my own good.

"Summer says you're a smoke show," he says, nudging me, breaking my momentary daze.

"She does? Why would she say that?"

"I showed her your picture. A different one than I sent to Amelia. I sent Summer one where you look hot AF."

I sit up straighter in bed, intrigued, maybe even a little delighted. "You did?"

The look on his face is sheepish as he confesses, "She wanted to know what I was up to, so I sent her some pictures."

"Ah, and did you say, 'This is what I'm up to—banging this hot English bloke'?"

"Something like that," he says, still clutching his phone. The look in his eyes, the sound of his voice almost makes me think he wants me to dig further, to ask what he said about me.

I don't entirely know if I want to go down this road, but I don't want to turn away from it either. So, with a little bit of nerves, I ask, "What did you say?"

He shows me his phone so that I can see his response.

Fitz: This is what I did today. Had the best time.

Three pictures are attached to the message—a shot of us by the Millennium Bridge, another by the Tower Bridge, and one more by the Leaky Cauldron. We look happy together, like a couple. I'm having a hard time looking away from the images.

I read his text to her a few times, and each time my chest warms a little more, and words stick in my throat. Words I want to say. Words I'm terrified of saying.

I meet his gaze. He looks like he's waiting for something. A confirmation. A departure. *Something.* And none of this feels like it fits our earlier conversation on the bridge, but all of it feels necessary.

Like we're stepping over those lines we drew again so firmly this afternoon.

Especially when I say the words that scare me and electrify me all at once. "Same. Same for me. I had a great time too."

His shoulders relax, and his grin ignites. "Then Summer said you were a smoke show. And I said, 'Trust me, I know. He's the hottest guy I've ever met.'"

I laugh, shaking my head, even though inside I'm preening from the compliment. "I bet you say that to all the guys."

Fitz props himself on his side, his head resting in his hand. His lips go ruler-straight. "No. I don't. It'd be a lie."

I roll my eyes because that's easier than to accept he means it. Besides, what does it matter if he's attracted to me more than anyone else? It doesn't—not in the scheme of things.

"I meant what I said earlier."

"On the bridge?"

"By the Tube station," he says, an intensity to his voice. "I meant it all. And yes, I meant what I said on the bridge earlier too." He stops, sitting up, dragging a hand through his hair. "Fuck," he mutters.

I sit up too, some self-preservation telling me maybe it's time to go. My fight-or-flight is kicking in.

"Don't go." He reads my mind, grabbing my arm.

"I'm not going to leave," I lie.

"I meant what I said on the bridge, Dean. I don't do relationships." He exhales heavily. "But I meant what I said outside the Tube station too, about wanting to see you. And I meant what I said to Summer. I meant all of it." He lets go of my arm, grabs my hand again, and threads his fingers through mine. "But the thing is . . ." He sighs. "I really like you."

Fitz shrugs, a little helpless. A little aimless.

And a whole lot endearing.

And so damn likable.

That's the problem. When he says these things, my heart thumps the slightest bit harder. I wish I could say it was from the exertion, from the sex, but that was a while ago. This is just from talking.

That's why my heart is hammering—because I feel the same way.

And there's no room in my life for this.

But I don't have to rearrange my life for him. All I have to do is rearrange the next three nights and two days.

I squeeze his hand back harder. I can't believe I'm about to say this, but I can't quite believe I feel it this soon. Or at all. "I like you too," I say, then give him a matching *what can you do* shrug.

My reward comes in the form of a tackle. He pushes me down on the bed and smothers me in kisses and laughter, and then he rolls to his back, breathes out hard, and says, "I feel like I just ran a marathon."

"Why's that?"

"I don't say that. I don't, Dean. I haven't. But I guess it doesn't matter. This is ending when I leave, so I don't need to pretend you're like everyone else. You're not," he says, shifting to his side again to look at me, his hand sliding down my waist, over my hip. "You're not like any other guy. And I can say that because it's going to be over in two and a half more days. And I want to enjoy the hell out of this time with you. But I'm not just a player. I mean, I am, I have been, though there's a reason I've avoided anything serious."

"What's the reason?" I ask.

"Look, I'm out. I have been since I was fifteen. It's not a secret. But because of that, because I've been open, that's how people saw me for a long time. The gay hockey player. The openly gay division-one star. The openly gay first-round draft pick. The openly gay rookie."

"Are there other openly gay pro hockey players?"

"Yes. I'm not even the first. But I am the best."

I shake my head, amused. "There's that cocky side I adore."

He laughs lightly, then continues. "And that also meant I was seen that way for the longest time. Not by my stats or my performance on the ice, but by my identity."

It's not tough to be out in my profession. But for Fitz, it must have been difficult. "That must be hard. I can't imagine, because my life is so different. There are plenty of gay bartenders. It's not something anyone makes a thing over. I'm no one's hero."

"Look, it's not like I think I am anyone's hero. But I didn't want to be identified by who I liked, but how I played. That's why I just have hookups. Why I avoid entanglements. I don't want the media talking about that. I don't want to be seen on the reg with so-and-so. *Oh, that's New York defenseman James Fitzgerald and his boyfriend.* I want it to be, *Oh, that's one of the league's best players, out playing paintball with his friends, or at a concert with his buddies.* That's why I don't do serious."

"Self-protection," I say, understanding him more.

"Exactly. I just want to be the NHL's top D-man."

"Well," I say, with a wry grin, "I don't know if it helps that I still barely know what that is."

"You'll understand all the nuances soon enough."

"And you'll know how to mix a perfect martini."

"One that goes to my head? Like you told me the night I walked into your bar?" he asks, reminding me of the conversation we had just three nights ago.

"Exactly. I'll teach you my secrets."

He smiles, but then it fades away, and he stares at me, that hungry look in his eyes. But it's a needy look too. Almost desperate, but in a wildly sexy way—not a clingy way. Not a way that scares me.

Fitz slides his thumb along my jaw. "You go to my head."

I lower my eyes as my chest fucking flips. As this wild warmth spreads through me dangerously, like a wave. And this feels nearly as good as fucking him.

Or maybe as good.

And I think—no, I'm sure—he's going to my head too.

So I look up, take a breath, and say, "The feeling is mutual."

His grin is huge, and he sighs, relieved. "Thanks for understanding why I'm a dick."

"You're not," I say, laughing.

He tips his chin at me. "What's your story? Why do you avoid relationships? You just like playing the field?"

"Ah, the million-dollar question."

"I take it there's not an easy answer?"

"Is there ever?" I toss back, dancing around the truth.

"Hardly ever."

I draw a fueling breath. Answering this question isn't my favorite thing to do, but he opened up to me. I can do the same.

"I suppose I could tell you it's because of the last guy I was involved with. He wanted too much too soon, and I didn't have it in me. I wanted to focus on my future, on the bar, on what I wanted to build with Maeve," I explain. "I found my attention wavering, and I didn't feel that deeply for him. Once I ended it, I was able to focus on this—what I want. My life, my dreams, provincial as they are. I mean, I'm sure they seem small next to yours. Global Series and worldwide recognition."

"Stop it. That's not the point. The point is they're your dreams. They matter to you."

"They do, and that got in the way. I don't want things to get in the way. That's what my mum did. She let love get in the way. Took off for Australia with a guy, and she's not even with him anymore."

"It didn't work out?"

I shake my head. "She's married to someone else now. Her fourth marriage. Her choices, right? I just don't want to make the same ones."

"I hear ya," Fitz says, leaning back on the pillow. "But that's why it's good we feel the same way. We dig each other, but we also know it's ending soon. We can have fun. We can have a great time together."

I poke his side. "'Great'? Just 'great'? I thought you said it was 'the best time'?"

He smiles, then yanks me toward him. "You know what would really make it the best time?"

I grin wickedly, knowing what comes next will be dirty. "Wait. Let me guess. Does it have two numbers in it?"

His eyes twinkle with naughty mischief. "It's like you know me."

And maybe I do. And I like knowing him.

And touching him.

And I really like sucking him off while he does the same to me, since the numbers are sixty and nine. That's how we finish a night that's pretty much perfect—more so because it caps off a perfect day with him.

With this guy who is not at all like Dylan. Not at all like anyone I've ever been with.

But if he lived here, I don't think I'd stop at Thursday. I don't think I'd stop in a week or a month. I'd want more of him.

I could see us being a thing.

A real thing.

And that's why it has to be good that he's leaving. It just has to. There's no other way to see him and me.

TUESDAY

Also known as the day I know.

22

DEAN

For the second day in a row, I wake up next to Fitz.

For the second day in a row, it feels entirely natural.

And for the first time, I'm aware of the need to seize every moment.

But he's still asleep, so I do something risky.

I text Maeve.

And I call in the biggest favor I've ever called in.

Dean: Gorgeous, wonderful, kind, all-knowing best friend of mine . . .

Maeve: You obviously want something.

Dean: I do. I need your help.

Maeve: Oh. You're not joking. You're serious. Hit me up.

Dean: What are the chances that you'd cover for me over the next few days? Call in one of our backups?

Maeve: IS THIS WHAT I THINK IT IS?

Dean: What do you think it is?

Maeve: You. Falling. Hard.

I scoff lightly at her note. Then I look at the man next to me. The ink climbing over his arms, his back. The scruff on his face. The way his hair sticks up as he sleeps.

Some kind of storm brews in my chest as I watch him, and I silently curse my best friend for being right.

Dean: All I'm saying is I would love a few days off. I will do any chore in the universe. I will get you your jukebox.

Maeve: Oh my God! You have no idea how much I want to say I told you so, but even my cold black heart won't let me. I am just happy that you like him so much. (That IS why you want the time off? You want to spend it with the hockey hottie?)

Dean: Yes. I do.

Maeve: I'll do it under one condition.

Dean: Name it.

Maeve: I want to meet your man.

Dean: He's not my man.

Maeve: Don't even try that poppycock with me. He so is. Bring him by. And yes, go have fun. I'm happy for you.

Dean: It's just fun. It's just a fling. But I'm enjoying it. And I want to enjoy every second of it.

Maeve: Sometimes a fling is all we need.

Maeve: To get a jukebox!!! Ha, I told you so!

Dean: You did. And I'm so glad.

When I set down the phone, Fitz is stretching, eyes floating open. "Morning, sunshine," he says, all sleepy sexy.

A pang twinges in my chest because I want that *Morning, sunshine* again and again and again.

"Morning."

He reaches for my waist, slinks an arm around me, then murmurs, "Don't go."

"I wasn't leaving," I say, laughing. "You always think I'm leaving."

"Maybe because I always want you to stay."

And that pang becomes an ache.

But I have a temporary balm.

"Speaking of not going . . ." I take a deep breath, because this is huge for me. This is not something I ever saw myself doing. This feels like the riskiest step of all, and I don't want him to slap back like he did yesterday.

But I understand Fitz more now.

And today already feels like an entirely new ball game.

He yawns, then waits for me.

Nerves crawl up my throat, but this hardly seems like the thing to be nervous over. He wants this. I want this.

And I'm the one who can make it happen—two full days together.

"I hope this isn't presumptuous, but I arranged to take the next two days off."

And the smile that takes over his face is the biggest reward ever. "Spend them with me."

"Obviously, Fitz."

* * *

A little later, I step into the shower, turning the tap as hot as it can go.

I grab a bar of soap and lather it across my chest. Steam fills the space, and I breathe it in.

Seconds later, the man I want opens the shower door. "Mind if I join you?" Fitz asks.

"I would mind if you didn't."

He steps in, giving me that incredible view that I'm already addicted to. I do more than admire.

I touch.

I rub the soap over him—first his pecs, then those perfect abs. I trace the grooves, my fingers traveling over every hard plane.

He groans his appreciation, and I move my hands to his broad shoulders, down his firm biceps, then along his roped forearms. I map his body, his muscles, his strength.

Taking the soap from me, Fitz does the same for me, and I savor the treatment, the attention from his talented hands. He sets down the soap in the soap dish as the steam enrobes us. His hands travel down my chest again, lazily tracing my stomach, and he moves closer, wraps his hand around my length, his fingers curling nice and tight.

I return the favor and give the man what he wants. Contact. With me. Touch. From me.

He shivers the second I grip his hard-on, then lets out a long, contented rumble. As the water streams over us, we stay like that for a minute or two, taking our time, playing and stroking. *Enjoying* each other.

As I linger in the sensation, my mind wanders ahead to where this might lead. To blow jobs? To sex? To more of whatever this is? Then, I catch sight of something fun out of the corner of my eye.

On the shower shelf, amid the shampoo and conditioner samples, is another bottle of lube. I tip my head toward the bottle as I slow my pace on his shaft. "You're always prepared."

"I was hoping to get you into the shower at some point. Have my way with you."

"Don't you always?"

Fitz laughs—a big, rumbly sound. Then he leans in and bites my earlobe. "I do, and I think you like it. Am I right?"

He pulls back, waiting for a response, an unfamiliar vulnerability flickering across his blue eyes.

Do I like it when he has his way with me? Is there really any doubt?

Not about that, but I have a question of my own.

Something I want to know about him.

Letting go of his cock, I answer him first. "Yes. I like what you do to me so fucking much. But I think the more important question is this . . ."

I cover his hand and take it off my dick so I can spin him around. Pushing his back against the tiled wall so he's facing me, I cage him in as water pounds down on us.

I grab the lube, pop the cap, and pour some on my finger. "Would you like it if I had my way with you?"

His blue eyes widen, and desire flashes across them. I

turn the tables, wanting to be the one in control, the one pushing. I'm not going to push too far. But there are things I can do to him.

I whisper in his ear, telling him exactly what they are.

Hoping to hell that he can handle it. That he'll let himself *take*. Because I want to give.

Fitz shudders all over. "Try me," he commands.

Those two words spur me on. My hand slips between his legs, traveling down to his balls, giving them a squeeze first, then to his prostate. My fingers tease, press, massage.

Instantly, he lets out a strangled moan, adjusting his stance, giving me more access to where I want to be.

Where he clearly wants me.

Then, my fingers travel farther, and I push in. A little at first, as he hisses, then farther, deeper, and he unleashes a wild groan.

"Yes. That. Oh, fuck yes."

Pleasure twists inside me from his unfettered reaction. After a few minutes, I add more lube, then another finger, crooking it inside him while rubbing my thumb against him too. Right there. Where it's magic for a man.

"Love that," Fitz groans. "Fucking love it."

He rocks against my fingers, and it's so sexy, so wanton the way he moves, the way he seeks. My whole body hums. It's utterly crazy, the addictive, heady pleasure I get from him.

With some one-handed finesse, I pour lube into my free hand, drop the bottle to the tile floor, then wrap that slicked-up hand around his shaft. Tight, rough, just the way he likes it. The way I like touching him too. But then, I like everything with him.

"So good," he grunts, moving with me. "So damn good." He brings his lips to my ear, breathing out hard. "You make me insatiable."

"Insatiable seems like your natural state."

His eyes drift down between us, and mine do too, admiring the view, the erotic sight of two hard, thick cocks throbbing right next to each other.

Yes, insatiability rules the day.

"My natural state is hungry and horny for you. Only you," he says, and somehow, the fire in me rises another thousand degrees.

"Finish us off, Fitz," I tell him hoarsely, as pleasure ricochets through my body.

"Fuck, yes." He jerks our cocks together as I fuck him with my fingers. And as he strokes up, harder, tighter, his head falls forward, resting against my shoulder, his words in my ear. "You feel so good. Don't stop, don't stop at all."

As if I could.

I can't stop touching him any more than he can stop talking.

I don't think I've ever been with someone so expressive, who just lays it all out and so freely voices all his wants and desires. Not only his physical needs, but also his overall craving to see me, to have me, to be with me. It's so damn intoxicating. More than I ever knew it could be.

"I won't stop. I can't stop," I say, and I'm talking about this—hands, fingers, fists—but I'm talking, too, about *this*. Whatever this is between the two of us.

This temporary fling with my American lover. A fling that is going to consume me. I can sense it building already. I can tell where it's going and what it'll do to me.

My orgasm edges closer, and I'm overwhelmed by desire, by the crush of agonizing bliss as he takes us both to the edge, where we're moaning and groaning and coming once again.

Whatever this is—I don't want it to stop.

23

DEAN

Later, at Coffee O'clock, Fitz grins as I list all the chores I'll have to do for Maeve. She doesn't need to know the *specifics* of how I came to owe so many, but Fitz is privy to the X-rated exchange rate of dirty deed to necessary chore.

And each one is worth it.

I show him on my phone the jukebox I'm buying for her. "As soon as I slept with you, I owed her that."

"Love that jukebox," he says with a naughty grin.

As he eats a very late breakfast of yogurt and blueberries, he points to the task list marching down the paper. "Ooh! I know something else you need on there. Add 'sanitize the ice bins,'" he says with wicked glee.

I arch a brow. "And why am I adding that?"

He leans across the table, his grin all crooked. "That's so you can pay up for what I'm going to do to you tonight."

I roll my eyes, then wiggle my fingers. "Serve it up."

"It's pretty dirty."

"You think I can't handle it?"

"I don't know if you want me to say it out loud."

"Bet I do. Be a big boy. Just use your words."

"You sure?"

"If you can't say it, you can't do it," I challenge.

Fitz lets out a faint growl, jerks his chair closer to me, then brings his bearded jaw close to my ear. His whiskers brush my cheek, sending sparks across my skin as he whispers low and smoky words detailing his plans, then flicks his tongue across my earlobe, a promise of how he'll make good.

I close my eyes, letting the image flash in my mind before I open them again, a little woozy already. "Why, yes, I think that will be worth sanitizing the ice bins."

"I. Can't. Wait."

We leave, saying goodbye to Penny, and head to meet Maeve at her favorite park. She's lounging on a green bench, wearing a huge pair of sunglasses, a bouncy brunette ponytail, and a cat-that-ate-the-canary grin.

She holds open a paperback, but she's not reading. She's gloating as she watches us striding toward her. I decide to let her enjoy her moment. It's the least I can do for her.

I take Fitz's hand and link my fingers through his. He shoots me a surprised but thoroughly delighted look, then squeezes back.

Maeve's brown eyes pop, and her smile is worthy of a GIF. Setting down the book, she leaps up from the bench and swings her gaze from Fitz to me to our hands. "I'm just going to say it. Emma and me and the expo—you're both welcome."

Yup. She's a tabby feasting on canaries today.

"Anything you need," Fitz says, "ever. You let me know." Then he kisses her cheek. "I owe you big-time."

She pumps a fist. "Knew it. Called it. Also . . ." She points from Fitz to me and back. "You two are seriously cute."

"We're not cute, but thank you."

Fitz stage-whispers, "We're cute. Just admit it."

"Not cute. In any case, Maeve, this is James Fitzgerald. But you can call him Fitz." I give him a deadpan look. "Or should she call you 'Yo, Fitzgerald'?"

"Fitz will do just fine, smart-ass," he says, grinning.

Maeve whistles her appreciation. "Oh my God, shut up, you two. Just shut up with your smiling and your flirting."

All I can do is laugh. "Thanks again for covering for me." I drop Fitz's hand, dip my fingers into my pocket, and give her a piece of paper.

She arches one brow. "What is this?"

Fitz claps me on the back, looking too proud for words. "I offered to help with his chores, but he refused."

"It's my to-do list. They're the chores I'll owe you."

Her eyes twinkle with delight as she unfolds it and reads aloud. "Scrub the bar tops, clean out the glass washing system, sanitize the ice bins, wipe down the bottles in the speed wells, brush on a fresh coat of chalk-board paint for our specials, hang up Maeve's art that I keep swearing I'll put up one day, and install the new sound system." She clutches the paper to her chest and looks up with cartoon-character-size eyes. "The one that's compatible with a certain jukebox?"

I wave a hand dismissively. "Yes. At this rate, I'll owe you ten."

Fitz scoffs, muttering under his breath, "More like fifty."

Maeve slow-claps. "Well done, gentlemen. Well done. Or should I call you, as the Americans say, horndogs?"

"Penguins," Fitz says. "Call us penguins."

Maeve arches a questioning brow.

I shake my head adamantly. "Private joke. Moving on. Want to walk around the park and grill Fitz like I know you're dying to?"

"I do," she says with a smile.

But she doesn't interrogate him as we wander past lush green trees and budding orange lilies. She asks him questions about New York, about Soho and the East Village, where he likes to go to see live music. She asks where he lives in the city, and he answers that it's a spot called Gramercy Park. His favorite things about New York are all of his friends and he tries to see them as much as he can.

He asks her about me, how long we've known each other, and if she can handle my sarcasm.

"I manage him fairly well," she replies. "And you?"

Fitz looks at me and winks. "Yeah, I can handle him too."

I roll my eyes, and when Maeve happens to look away, I mouth, *Manhandle.*

He replies under his breath, *And soon.*

"And when do you leave again?" she asks.

"Thursday at two," he says, his voice ten tons heavier than it was three seconds ago.

Maeve frowns. "That's soon."

Fitz shrugs, unhappily. "Yeah, about forty-eight hours from now."

My chest tightens, the reminder making an uncomfortable knot inside me. I don't want him to go.

"I wish I could slow down time for you," she says, a little wistful.

"Same here," Fitz adds, then looks my way and slides a hand up my back, rubbing. "Same here," he repeats, and my heart squeezes with the same wish—the one that won't come true.

When we near the edge of the park, Fitz's phone rings. "It's my agent. Excuse me for a second."

He walks away several feet as he takes the call while Maeve looks at me with *what now* eyes.

"What?" I ask.

"Dean . . ." There's a note of worry in her voice.

"What's wrong?"

She cuts to the chase. "This is more than a fling."

I glance over at the man I'm spending the next forty-eight hours with, and the pang returns, stinging a little more this time. "Yeah, it is. Wish I could tell you otherwise. But that'd be a lie."

She reaches for my arm, clasping it. "You don't owe me anything."

"Oh, stop it, woman. I did the crime. I'll do the time."

She shakes her head. "I mean it. I don't want you to pay up. But what are you going to do when he leaves?"

I swallow roughly, lifting my chin. "Same thing I always do. Get up, go to work, live my life. I'll be fine."

"You don't have to pretend it's going to be easy. This is serious. And that's okay."

But it can't be serious.

He's returning to America.

Yes, it feels like it could be something. But it won't.

His life is there. Mine is here. There is no in-between.

That's not even on the table.

I sigh and scrub a hand over my jaw, catching a glimpse of Fitz before I turn my attention back to Maeve. "What can you do? You meet someone. He lives across the ocean. You live here. And nothing will change that."

She just smiles softly, knowing I'm right, knowing that this fling will end. "I know," she whispers, and there's a hitch in her voice, like she's already sad for me.

I'll have none of that. I reject it by slicing my hand through the air. "Don't be sad. I'm having the time of my life."

She nods, swipes a hand across her cheek, then fixes on a grin.

Fitz returns, clasping his hands, squaring his shoulders. "My new sponsorship deal is a go. My agent said the company has big plans for when I return."

"That's brilliant," I say, and as the three of us stroll on through the park, I do my best to savor every second of it.

24

FITZ

Dean and I wait by the river for my sister, the London Eye circling behind us. Emma's usually early, but it's almost two, time for the riverboat cruise, and she's not here.

"Where is Emma?" I scan for her blonde head, her blue eyes.

"Are you sure you want me to go with you?" Dean asks as I survey the crowds again. "If you want it to be just you and Emma, I understand."

I whip my gaze to him. "*Yes.* Just yes. I already bought you a ticket. Don't ask again."

"So sensitive," he teases.

I turn to face him. "Don't you get it, man? I want as much of you as I can have."

"I know, but I don't want to encroach on your time with your family."

I grab his cheeks, locking my eyes with his. "Encroach, Dean. Encroach all you want."

"That sounds dirty and erudite at the same time."

"Hey," I say, smirking. "That sounds just like a hot guy I know."

Dean huffs, but he's not mad. I let go of his face and spin around right as someone taps on my shoulder.

It's Emma. Smiling and a little out of breath.

"Where were you?" I ask, relieved.

She points to the ticket counter for the riverboat cruise. "I was just returning my ticket."

I blink. "What? I thought you wanted to do this?"

She shakes her head. "No. I want *you two* to do this. You don't need me."

"*Emma.*"

She looks to Dean then waves. "Hi. Good to see you again." She points at me. "He likes you a lot."

I groan because she is such a devil. "He knows I do."

Dean shoots Emma a smile. "Good to see you again too, Emma. And the feeling is quite mutual."

Emma squeals, nearly jumping for joy. I want to drop her in a headlock. Instead, I give her a noogie. "You are a troublemaker."

"No. I'm a matchmaker, like I've been from the start." She squirms away. "And listen, thanks for inviting me. Thanks for getting me the ticket. Under other circumstances, I'd hang out with you two, but you really should enjoy the day together."

I sigh, but I'm not unhappy. I'm incredibly, ridiculously happy. I love my sister, but I'll see her for the rest of my life. Time with Dean is finite, and once I get on that plane, I won't see him again.

"I love you, Ems," I say, wrapping her in a bear hug.

"I love you, James."

I haul her in tighter, then let her go. She immediately gives Dean a huge hug too, and it's insanely endearing to see them embrace as if they've done this many times before.

When she lets go, she waves goodbye. "Enjoy your

riverboat cruise," she says, then, like the smart-ass she is, she adds, "lovebirds."

"We are so not lovebirds," I say when she's gone.

"So not at all," he says. To prove it, I don't hold his hand as we walk onto the boat. Instead, I drape my arm around his shoulders.

Well, that *does* give me more real estate of Dean to get close to.

* * *

Dean leans against the railing, gazing out at the water as the boat glides along the Thames. "So, on a scale of one to ten, how touristy, cheesy, or eye-rolling is a riverboat cruise to a Londoner such as yourself?" I ask.

He strokes his chin as if deep in thought. "Let's see. Let me think back on all the riverboat cruises I've done." He casts me a side-eye stare. "One."

"You've done one cruise?"

He laughs lightly, holding up his thumb and forefinger in a circle. "I've done zero. I was rating it a one on the touristy cheesy scale you mentioned. Not cheesy at all."

"Whoa." I stumble back dramatically like I'm shocked, then I move closer again. "For real? You've never done a riverboat cruise here?"

"Never have I ever."

"Is that because it's touristy and cheesy?"

"Have you been to the top of the Empire State Building?"

I shake my head.

"Statue of Liberty?"

I shake my head again, then raise a finger. "But I have been to the Museum of Natural History countless times. Because . . . dinosaurs."

"Well, sure. Dinosaurs are cool. And I would probably go there too. But see, if I visited New York, I'd see those other places as well. Empire State Building and all. It's just what you do when you visit."

"I'd take you there." I bump his shoulder, savoring the notion of showing Dean around New York, taking him to wherever he wanted to go and to my favorite places too.

"Yes, I'd expect you to return the tour-guide favor," he says, and I'm tempted to float the trial balloon, to see if he'd ever come see me, maybe spend a weekend together in my city.

But that would be true insanity.

No way am I going to try to have a long-distance relationship with this guy. Hell, a relationship isn't in the cards for me at all, for all the reasons I laid out last night.

Plus, there's the pact, the damn pact that kicks in soon. I won't be the one to break it. I made it with my guys, and I'll keep it.

I swipe away the dangerous thoughts. "So, are you enjoying the cruise?" I ask as the tour operator warbles into the mic about the landmarks we pass, historical structures alongside modern skyscrapers.

Dean meets my gaze. "Yes. I feel like I'm seeing London in a new light. It's a great view."

And my stomach fucking flips. Because he's not looking at the city. He's looking at me.

The way he stares feels different than before.

Deeper.

More important.

There's more connection, more closeness, and it's doing a number on my head.

Thank fuck for the pact. Thank fuck for training camp. If I didn't have those natural stops, I'd be falling so damn hard on my ass.

But I do have those, and they'll cushion the blow. Make it easier to get on that plane on Thursday.

But until then, there's this.

This raw, sexual energy vibrating between the sexy-assin Brit and me.

"Yeah, it's a fantastic view," I say, my eyes on him.

For a few seconds, we stare at each other like we're going to pounce, like he wants to tear off my clothes and get his mouth all over me. It's a great look.

But we're surrounded by people and water and landmarks, and everything is getting in the way of what I want —alone time with this man.

Dean breaks our gaze and slides his arm around my waist. "Now, before we maul each other on this boat, tell me something innocuous. Why did you want to take this cruise?"

I laugh. "I've always liked boats. My dad worked in shipping. Maybe it's in my blood."

"I bet it is. A connection to him."

"Yeah. I think so." I take a beat. "My turn. Why do you like London so much?"

He gives a shrug and a smile. "It's home. It feels right. Like where I belong. Is New York that way for you?"

"I think I'll always be a California guy, but New York suits me now. I love the energy, the pace, the people. It's loud and dirty and awesome, and you can find anything and do anything." I survey the city unfolding before me, the view of Big Ben, the iconic city skyline. "It's a lot like London, I suppose. And I like it here. A helluva lot."

"It's the good-sex effect."

I shake my head. "Get it right, man. It's the great-sex effect."

"Excuse me. It's the hashtag Best-Sex-Ever effect."

"Yes. Thank you for the clarification." I pat the railing

of the boat. "Looks like we both popped our Thames river-boat cruise cherries," I say, letting my tongue loll out like a dog's.

"We're no longer riverboat virgins."

Which raises an interesting topic. "Speaking of, when did you . . .?"

Dean shoots me a wry grin. "I was eighteen. Just finishing school. You?"

"Same. Summer before college."

"Was it good for you?"

"Eh." I shrug. "It was necessary."

"That's a fair way of putting it."

"I know where I'd like to put it right now," I whisper.

He shoots me an *oh no, you didn't* stare. "You picked an hour-long cruise. You're not shagging me on a boat."

I slide a hand up his back. "I know. I just want to. Remember?" With my other hand, I tap my chest. "Insatiable."

"Yes. I know. And yes, I like it. Now, enjoy the cruise, because before you know it, we'll be getting off." Dean's lips curve up in a grin as he takes a deliberate beat, then adds, "And then getting off."

An hour later, we dock, grab a cab, and head back to my hotel, where we get naked so quickly, we set a record.

Then he's bent over the bed, I'm inside him, and I'm so fucking happy and so damn horny that I decide it's official —I'm living my best life ever.

When we're done and recovering from the #BestSex-Ever effect, Dean's phone rings.

Lazily, he reaches for it, then when he sees who's calling, he sits up quickly.

"Shit, I almost forgot." He answers with "Hi, Dad."

I listen as he laughs with his father, drops his face into his hand, and then covers his phone and looks at me.

"We're having takeaway at my flat. He wants you to join us for dinner."

"Hell, yeah," I say, and after a shower, I leave the hotel with my lover to meet his father.

It's completely surreal and completely real at the same damn time.

Not gonna lie.

I feel like I just gained entry to a secret land.

A special place.

And it is awesome. When Dean unlocks the green door to his flat, I want to pump a fist because I get to see inside.

Instead, I turn around, drink in the view of the quiet side street where he lives, then follow him into the foyer.

"It's just like *Notting Hill*," I remark.

"Except it's in Bankside. And I don't live with a crazy man who wears goggles and eats expired apricots."

I poke his side. "Dean. Are you a closet rom-com fan?"

He swivels around, stopping on the steps, arching a brow. "Closeted? Oh no, not at all. I'm totally out on that front and all fronts."

I laugh. "Yeah, *Notting Hill* is just a good flick."

"That it is."

I follow him up the stairs to the third floor, and he unlocks the door to his place. It opens with a faint groan, and I catalog that sound.

It's like the opening theme song to a movie, and as the credits roll, I step into the world of the man I want to spend all my time with.

"It's small, but it's home," he says, almost like he's apologizing for it.

And it is tiny.

A kitchen with a sliver of space that opens right into a living room with exposed brick walls.

My eyes are wide, and I take it all in, like I can learn even more about him from the place he lives. It's neat, tidy. His couch is dark gray, and there are books on the coffee table—nonfiction, from the looks of it, current titles on scandals and business. His walls are minimalist but decorated with prints of artwork—one looks like a Rothko, and another a Vermeer—and I smile privately, knowing where this comes from. His mom. Even if he's not close to her, she left a mark on him, on something he loves.

As I turn around, Dean's looking at me a little expectantly. Like he's waiting for me to render a verdict on his home.

"I love it," I say, then my gaze catches on some bookshelves. Framed photos line the top shelf. I walk over and pick one up. "That's you and Naveen and Anya," I say, studying the picture of them all at some sort of street fair. A candid picture of Dean with his friends, laughing and carefree.

"Yes."

"When's it from?"

"Two years ago, I think."

I set it down, this piece of Dean's history.

Then I find a picture of Dean and Sam crossing a finish line in a race. Looks like a 10K, and the date is a year ago. Their arms are raised. From the race banner, I see it's a fundraiser for a local children's hospital, and that tugs on my heart even more, another piece of his past. I'm looking through a window into his life, and I want to know it all, see it all.

The next shot is Dean lining up a pool cue and aiming it across the table. The guy he's playing with has dark skin, much darker than Dean's. I kind of love that he has friends from so many places and so many walks of life. "Who's that?"

Dean moves next to me. "Taron."

"Ah, the one who's *not* your type."

"Exactly. He's a good mate though. Outgoing, vibrant. I wish you'd met him the other night."

"I wish I had too."

My eyes drift down the row of photos, ravenous to see more of his life, to gobble up all this insight into who he is, what makes him tick, and his world. Pictures of him and Maeve at the bar, then a posed shot of them outside The Magpie, arms wrapped around each other, smiling, and an OPEN FOR BUSINESS sign behind them.

"Last year?"

"Yup."

I pick up more pictures of him and Maeve, including one of her lifting a pillow to swat him. He's holding up his hands as if to defend himself. They're in a tiny room, and he looks younger.

My heart thunders. "That's you in college, isn't it?"

"Yes."

"You didn't room with Maeve, did you?"

He laughs, shaking his head. "No. But we spent a ton of time together."

"You guys are really close," I say, stating the obvious as I stare at the picture of Dean and his best friend like I can't get enough of it.

"We are," he says, then moves in behind me, wraps his arms around my waist, and brushes a soft kiss to my neck.

I set down the picture, close my eyes, and let myself enjoy the sensation of being in his embrace, feeling his lips, his touch, his strength.

I grab his hands clasped around my stomach, and clutch them so he won't let go of me.

But it's not just him I'm holding on to.

It's the last shred of my resistance.

It's so threadbare right now.

I don't know if I can hold out much longer.

We stay like that for a minute or two, quiet as his lips travel across the back of my neck, and I try—I try so damn hard—not to say everything I'm feeling for him.

Stay in the moment, I tell myself.

So I do, just savoring Dean's tender kisses on my neck, his arms wrapped around me, and the way he seems to know what I need right now.

Him.

Just him.

This moment is as close to perfect as any moment has ever been. I don't want it to end. I don't want anything to end.

But all of it has to.

Every moment, every second will be over in less than two days.

Soon enough, he lets go. "My dad will be here any minute with the food. And as cool as he is, I don't want him to see me like this—looking like I'm about to take you to my bed."

I manage a laugh, turn around, and drag my fingers through my hair, a makeshift comb. With a deep breath, I center myself. "Agreed." Then I furrow my brow, focusing on the practical. "Want me to grab some wine or something? I can run to the store. Pick up a bottle."

Dean waves a hand, dismissing the offer. "The one thing I have plenty of is liquor. You can help me find a bottle if you'd like. He enjoys red wine."

I join him in the kitchen, rubbing my palms together. "Let's find some red wine for Dean's dad."

The hunt briefly takes my mind off this train rattling down the tracks.

A train that's gathering speed, and I don't think I can stop it.

But I also don't think I want to stop it. There's a part of me that wants to be walloped by it. To feel it. To feel everything for him that's coming my way.

* * *

Dean's father deals the final cards. Empty takeaway boxes and the remnants of dinner—he brought a curry from Naveen's restaurant, and it was amazing—are strewn on the kitchen counter, but my attention is on this game of poker.

I pick up my cards, considering my hand.

My sucky, shitty hand.

Maybe I can bluff though. Yeah, I do that on the ice. I can do it here. I want to impress Dean's dad.

I slide another chip across the table, staying in.

His father arches a brow, then pushes in two more chips to join mine. "You're bluffing."

I blink, and try to keep my tone neutral. "Not bluffing."

Dean reins in a laugh, covering his mouth.

"You think I'm bluffing?" I toss out to my guy.

Dean just shrugs and smiles.

"I guess we'll find out," I say, with more bravado than my cards call for.

His father shoots me a skeptical stare. "All right. What have you got, Yankee?"

Smiling, I lay down my cards, loving that his dad calls me Yankee. Nicknames are a good thing in my book.

His father cracks up, leaning back on the couch, clapping a hand on Dean's shoulder. "Your friend can't bluff for shit."

"No, Dad. It's that *you* can always tell when someone is bluffing."

His father nods solemnly. "That is true. Very true."

"Fine, fine. Maybe I suck at poker," I admit.

"No, you just need a better poker face," his dad tells me, as he squeezes Dean's shoulder. "This one? He has a great poker face. I taught him well."

"Those are important life lessons, sir," I say.

They both laugh.

"What's so funny?"

"You don't have to call him 'sir,'" Dean says.

"Just use my name," his dad says. "Martin."

"Okay, Martin," I say, but it's still weird. Maybe it's only because this is the first parent of a lover I've met.

Ever.

"Or just call me 'old man,' like Dean does."

"I call it like I see it, old man," Dean says.

"Yes, I suppose you do. And I've been meaning to ask, would you like me to tell your friend embarrassing stories about you from your younger days?"

My eyes widen. "Tell me everything."

Dean shakes his head, staring daggers at his dad. "Reveal nothing, or I will march into Coffee O'clock tomorrow and tell Penny you've been pining away for her."

Martin laughs loudly. "Dean, she already knows. We went out last night."

"You scoundrel."

He wiggles his brow and looks at his watch. "And on that note, I should get out of here. We're going out again."

"Double scoundrel."

"Takes one to know one," his father says, then rises and heads for the door.

"I want a full report tomorrow," Dean says.

"Maybe I'll tell you. Maybe I won't."

"Tease," Dean says.

I follow them, clearing my throat. "It was great to meet you, Mr. Collins."

Another laugh bursts from him. "You're good with the formalities. I wasn't expecting that."

"Well, my mom and three sisters made it clear that manners matter."

"They taught you well." His father claps me on the shoulder. "Pleasure to meet you, James. Maybe we'll see more of you."

I wish, I want to say.

But instead, I say thank you.

When he leaves, Dean turns around and gives me a smile full of gratitude. "Thank you."

"For what?"

"For being great with my dad."

"It was easy." That's true of nearly everything with Dean.

Except for being with him the way I want to. Which is starting to feel like . . . *every day*. That's how I want to be with him, and that makes things the opposite of easy.

The thought scares the shit out of me.

And kind of doesn't at the same damn time.

As the door creaks shut, Dean's gaze drifts to a book his dad left behind. He grabs it and tells me he'll be right back.

"I'll be here." As his footsteps sound on the steps, I say those words again to Dean's flat around me. *I'll be here.*

Wishing there were a way, but knowing there's not.

I'm going to just enjoy every last minute with him. That is all I can do.

DEAN

I find my dad on the street and hand him the book. "I'm sure you'll be too busy with Penny to read, but one never knows."

"Same goes for you," my dad says. He tips his head toward the door, glancing upstairs. "I like him."

Three words, that's all, but they make my heart glow. I didn't realize until just now that I wanted them from my father. Needed them—his seal of approval.

"Me too," I answer.

"I can tell."

"Yeah?"

"Yeah, and it's a good thing."

"Feels like a good thing."

Or really, a great thing.

He heads down the street, and I return to my flat to see that Fitz has cleared the table and is already washing the dishes.

I grin, ridiculously happy that he thought to do that. I grab a towel and start drying the dishes he's already washed and rinsed, and we fall into an easy rhythm.

"I like your dad," Fitz says, glancing at me.

"Thanks. So do I."

"I can tell. You guys have a great relationship."

"I'm lucky. We're a lot alike, and honestly, we're good friends too." I take a beat, setting down a plate in the rack. "My dad said he liked you." Once I speak the words, they feel *significant*. Bigger than I expected them to, like I'm opening up to Fitz in a whole new way.

I swallow roughly, waiting.

He looks at me out of the corner of his eye as he rinses off the last dish, puts it down, and wipes off his hands. He's quiet, which is unlike him, so I fill the silence with another question. "Are you close with your mum like that?"

"Not in the same way exactly. But we're open, and we talk. I call her every week. She texts me before each game and wishes me luck. She texts me *after* every game to say either 'Congrats' or 'You'll crush them next time.'"

"She sounds amazing," I say, then I cast about for something more, something to fill this conversational void. "And have you talked—?"

He runs a hand along my arm, then at last answers my unspoken question. "She'd like you too, Dean. My mom would like you."

Sparks spread across my skin. Only this time, it's not from the contact—it's from the admission that parallels mine.

"Is that so?" I put down the towel.

"Yes, *it is so*," he says, imitating me.

"And why do you mock me for that?"

"Because it's easy. And because you walk into it sometimes, so I can't help it. Like the way you say, 'Is that so?' as if you doubt everything anyone says."

"Perhaps I do. Perhaps I like facts. So, tell me. Why

would your mum like me?" I ask, and we're treading dangerously close to the deep end again. Lately, that seems like what we do with each other. Like we're dipping our toes in the water all the time. Maybe soon, one of us will jump.

Or maybe we won't. Maybe it's safest to keep this on the safe, dry, *limited* ground where it belongs.

He shrugs easily. "Because I do."

"It's that simple?"

Fitz smirks before leaning over and kissing my cheek. "And because you're adorable."

I lift my chin. "I'm not adorable."

"A little. You're a little adorable," he teases in his Harry Potter accent.

"Now you're mocking me again."

"I am, but you walked into it, man," he says, shaking his head, amused.

"You really like taking the piss out of me, don't you?"

"I really, really do," he admits. "Anyway . . . after meeting your dad, I can tell, too, why you resisted me at first."

I laugh as I grab the now-dry dishes to put away. "What does that have to do with my dad?"

"He's skeptical . . . like you."

Fitz makes a fair point. "It's the reporter in him," I say. "He looks at everything from every direction."

"You're the same. You looked at me that way."

And he's hit the nail on the head. "Yes. I don't trust easily. I don't give in easily." I set the last dish in the cupboard and shut the door.

"Because of your mom?"

I lean against the counter. "Because of my mum. Because of my dad. Because of everything. It's better to be skeptical, to be sure of what you're getting into."

"I get that. I respect that. You like to check out all the angles."

"Exactly. Know what they are. What I'm walking into."

He runs his hand down my arm again, then over my abs, toying with the waistband of my jeans, tugging me closer. "So, tell me. Why did you give in to me? Is it only because I'm leaving?" His tone is more earnest than I've ever heard it. It's hard to concentrate, though, with his hands on me.

"What do you think?" I ask, my fingers curling around his ass as I inch closer to telling him why I gave in.

Fitz shakes his head. "I think that's the reason why you started, but it's not why we're here now."

I know where he's headed. I ought to steer this conversation in a safer direction, but I can't seem to resist this path. I want our motives to be out in the open.

"What's the reason *you're* here, then?" I ask as I kiss his neck, nibbling and biting.

Fitz breathes out hard, rocking his hips against me. His moans grow louder as I kiss his jawline, his cheek, and then nibble on his earlobe, trying to tell him with my body, with my lips, with the way I kiss him that there are other reasons.

"What's the reason?" I ask softly again. Then I bite his skin. "A pact?"

Fitz shakes his head.

"Last chance to get your rocks off?"

"You ass," he growls.

I laugh. "You love my ass."

"I do. I really fucking do. But that's not why I'm here." We're tangoing closer and closer to the dangerous edge we've been resisting. I could make another joke about this crazy chemistry, and part of me wants to, because I'm having so much fun with him. But I don't joke. This is no longer a fling. We both know it.

The man I've spent the last few nights with looks at me intensely, like this moment could tip into something much more than an interlude or an affair. Maybe it already has.

And because he's taken so many steps to me, I make this one toward him. "Why are you in my home? Why are you having dinner with my dad? Why do you want to meet my friends?" They aren't questions though. They're statements about where we've found ourselves. His eyes never stray from mine as I run my thumb along his jaw, ready to be completely honest. "Maybe it's because there's much more here than chemistry. More than the hashtag Best-Sex-Ever effect."

Fitz lets out a breath like I've freed him, like I've given him everything he needs. "So much more," he echoes, his shoulders relaxing, his arms looping around my neck, and his lips zeroing in on mine as he repeats "You are so much more" against my mouth, kissing me.

I close my eyes as those words reverberate in my head. *You are so much more.*

They're the chorus of a song, and they don't stop playing, and we don't stop kissing for a long time.

When he breaks the kiss, he says, "You know, sometimes talking to you is like leading a horse to water."

"Are you going to make me drink?"

"I'd like to make you take my cock."

"What do you know? I'd like to have it." I put a hand over the front of his jeans, where he's hard and ready for me. "Because I like you and your cock so very much."

"The feeling is mutual," he says, tossing my pet phrase back at me.

As we slide back into the games we play, the teasing, the never-ending flirting, the dirty words all feel bigger too.

More necessary.

They cover up what's simmering, all the next steps and possibilities we can't have.

The only thing we can have is the *now*.

And in the *now*, I want contact. I want it desperately, and I need the sex to drown out the refrain in my head.

You are so much more.

Except the volume knob is broken, and those words can't be turned down, even as I take his hand, lead him to my bedroom, and strip him naked.

But I try hard.

I try so damn hard to just zoom in on the sex.

I pin him to the bed, my hands on his shoulders, our bodies aligned. "Do you realize I haven't had you in my mouth nearly enough times?"

"Are you worried you'll forget what I taste like?"

"So damn worried."

His eyes glint with dirty deeds. "That'd be such a shame."

I grind against him. I'm still in my clothes, and for some reason, I like this inequity. It gives me a chance to be fully in charge of his pleasure.

His eyes squeeze shut, and his lips part on a heavy breath. "You should fix that now."

"I should. And I will. But I'm giving you fair warning about something."

"What's that?"

I lean in even closer, bringing my mouth to his ear. "I'm going to tease the fuck out of you."

Fitz groans. "I'd expect nothing less."

I slide down his body slowly, taking my time and kissing him as I go. A brush of my lips on his shoulder. A kiss on his throat that makes him groan. A flick of my tongue across his pecs. A bite of his right nipple, then the left, then a lick across the words *No Regrets*.

"I think I'll trace this letter by letter," I say.

"Please do."

My tongue coasts across the ink, then down to his abs, where I savor the landscape of his body, the grooves between all those hard muscles, licking and kissing and wanting never to stop.

"You're killing me, babe. What are you doing to me?" he rasps.

It's a valid question. And I answer it in my head. *Imprinting you on my mind so I don't forget.*

As my lips glide across his flesh, I say, "Just making sure you don't forget me."

"As if I could."

I reach the V of his abs, and he's already rocking his hips, seeking me out, begging for my attention.

My head goes hazy with his longing, and my own too, as I move closer and closer to where I want to be.

When my mouth reaches his shaft, he's pulsing, and there's a bead of liquid at the tip, just waiting for me.

I lick it off.

"Fuck," he groans, his hands shooting to my head, curling around me like a vise.

I can tell he wants me to take care of him straightaway, to get him there fast, but I know, too, how much better it'll be if I drive him crazy, so I reach up to loosen his hands.

"Just let me," I say quietly. "Let me do this slow. Let me enjoy every second of having you in my mouth."

He huffs, but then relinquishes his grip, hands going slack but still holding my head. "Okay. Do your thing to me, babe."

I look up at him. His eyes are hooded, desperate. "I will."

And I return to kissing his shaft. No. I'm *adoring* it. I lick him like he's the most delicious thing I've ever tasted, because he is.

With a hand wrapped around the base, I travel down to his balls, sucking until he's writhing against me.

When I have Fitz panting and wild, I move back to his cock, flick my tongue over the head, and take him all the way to the back of my throat.

"Yesssss," he groans, and it lasts forever, the sound of his relief becoming the sound of his wicked pleasure as I draw him in deep. "God, your mouth. Your perfect fucking mouth."

His words are going to be the death of me. A sultry, mind-bending death. I spread my hands across his thighs, pressing and squeezing his legs as I suck.

"You are so fucking good," he rasps out as he thrusts into my mouth. Lust rockets across my skin from tasting him.

This time when his fingers curl around my head, I let him grip me in place. He holds my head tight as I lavish attention up and down his cock, flicking my tongue as I go and sucking him hard, the way he likes it, the way I like it when he does it to me. I want him to feel extraordinary pleasure, to go back to New York and never fucking forget how I made him feel.

I revel in every moment of his taste, his scent, his bliss. With each move he makes, I'm more aroused. That seems like it should be impossible, but my body says it's not.

His palms clasp harder, and he's fucking up into my mouth. "Dean, babe. What are you doing to me? Jesus. What the fuck are you doing to me?"

His words come out strangled. I know he's close, and hell, I feel close too. I'm actually rocking my hips against the bed, desperately seeking my own pleasure. But his first. I want his first.

And I crave his words.

The things he says to me in bed.

The things he's saying right now.

"You," he rasps on a wild thrust. "You're so fucking good to me." Then he just grunts and calls out, "Coming."

Seconds later, I'm tasting him, drinking him down, and losing my mind with lust, with desire, and with something else entirely.

Something I never wanted to feel when we started.

But something that I can't stop now.

The feeling that he belongs to me. Just me. Only me.

When I climb up his body, I kiss him deeply and passionately. I know he likes that after a blow job, and hell, so do I. We go at it like we can't get enough of each other's lips. We go at it like time is running out. We go at it like we're trying to consume all the kissing in the world, so we don't forget how each other tastes.

Or maybe that's just me.

Maybe it's all in my head, this rush of emotion that pummels me, these impossible thoughts running rampant.

When we stop, with bruised lips and chins rubbed raw, he strokes my face, his eyes locked with mine.

For a second, maybe more, I see everything reflected back at me, and it's terrifying.

But it's thrilling too.

"I'm fucking obsessed with how you touch me," he says, his voice low and rough. "I swear you suck me off like you love it. Like you can't get enough of it. Of me."

Nailed it. "Sounds about right."

"Yeah?" The weight he puts in the question says it's about more than mouths on body parts. It's about this obsession we've given each other. This shared addiction.

So I answer without teasing, only with truth. "Yes."

I don't know what to do with this torrent of feelings. I fight the urge to say something that would reveal all. To say why I love it now, how it's changed from the pure desire of a few days ago to something richer and deeper.

But it's hard to keep it inside when Fitz repeats what he said when he was fucking my mouth. "Dean, what are you doing to me?"

He strokes my jaw and gazes at me, and this isn't the heat of the moment.

He's saying it *after*.

I swallow and try to look away, but I can't unlock my eyes from his. "What *am* I doing to you, Fitz?"

His fingers trace my face. "That's the question, isn't it?"

"That's definitely the question."

For a few seconds, a heaviness descends on us, but I don't want the pressure—not when time is running short.

Maybe he doesn't either, because the next thing he says is light and easy. "I could do that every night with you. Every damn night."

"A blow job?" I ask, a little relieved we're returning to familiar territory.

He relaxes into the pillow for the post-orgasm sex talk. "Yes. But it goes both ways, babe," he says. "You. Me. Every night. A blow job, a handjob, fingers, tongues, cocks. Everything. I want everything every night with you."

Or maybe this is how we make the talk manageable. He's talking about sex, but he's also not talking about sex. He's talking about every night. How he wants this, us, me.

Fitz wraps an arm around me and drops a possessive

kiss onto my shoulder. He does everything possessively. His entire body seems wired for possession.

I arch a brow and fire back at him. "Every night? You sure about that?"

He nods vigorously against me, his beard scratching my neck. "Every night. Every morning. Couldn't you?"

"That's a tall order. You would want to go every night and every single morning?" Goading him is easier than dealing with this strengthening storm in my chest. And because of course I could fucking go every night and every morning. Of course I'd want to with him.

"Yes," he says with certainty, then he shifts, looking into my eyes. "With you, absolutely. I would fuck you every night and then I would fuck you every morning."

Well, I can't back away from one question that comes up. I drag a hand down the hard planes of his chest, trailing it toward the V of his abs. "But what if I wanted to fuck you, Fitz? What would you do about that?"

His eyes darken, and the sound that emanates from him is an animalistic rumble. He drops his face to my neck and licks a line up to my ear, making me shudder. "I would let you, now and then," he murmurs.

I want to laugh, arch a brow, and say, *Let me? You'd let me?*

But he pushes up on his elbow, expression serious.

This matters to him.

This is a big deal.

I can see it in the set of his jaw, the vulnerability in his eyes.

So instead, since I want to understand what this means to him, I say evenly, "Is that so?"

"Yeah, I would. I wouldn't let anyone else do that. I haven't in years. But I would with you."

I sit up and take notice of this. "Why with me?"

Fitz lets out a deep sigh. "I've always liked the control, needed it, even. But with you, Dean, I already feel reckless."

"You seem pretty in charge."

He shakes his head. "I'm hardly in control with you."

"So when you pin me down and have your way with me, that's not control?"

"No. Not at all. Because everything's different with you. And I don't just mean how great the sex is." He snakes an arm around me, dragging me close. Fitz is the most tactile person I've ever known, seeming to crave constant contact.

"How? How is it different?" I press. This tells me volumes about Fitz. "Why would you switch for me?"

"Dean, I don't think you're getting it." His tone brooks no argument. "I would do that with you. Because you're you." He hauls me in for another possessive kiss. "You"—he kisses me hard—"make"—sucks on my bottom lip—"me"—jerks my body against his—"feel"—levels me with his intense gaze—"so damn much."

My heart thumps a little harder, a little faster.

And that pisses me off.

My reaction to him is highly inconvenient.

I know he's just saying this because he can. He's saying it because it's easy. He's leaving, and I'm his final fling. That's all this is and all it's going to be.

What do stupid hearts know?

I tell mine to settle the hell down, that it doesn't matter that I feel the same way about him, that I can't get him out of my head.

That doesn't matter, since this—*us*—is just a game.

Just pillow talk and pretend.

This is fantasy. Nothing more.

And none of this conversation matters because he's leaving, so I decide to give him a little bit of what he wants.

He wants the fantasy of him and me, and so do I. Time

to spell it out for him as I slide a hand down his chest, my fingers traveling through the hair on his pecs, then to his stomach.

"We could do that, then. Every night, every morning. And I'd go to your games. I'd cheer you on when you scored or blocked or what have you."

His smile lights up. "I stop goals. I crush the other team."

"Yes, that. I'd cheer for you when you did the stopping goals thing you do."

His mischievous blue eyes seem to delight in this scenario. "And before the games, I'd get on my knees for you, take you deep, and suck you off," he says.

I smile. "Excellent. I get blow jobs before *your* games. Lucky me. Sign me up."

Fitz arches a playful brow. "Dude. It'd go both ways. Hello. I blow you; you blow me."

"Ah, the old tradesies game. Fine, I can live with that. Since you do give spectacular head."

His grin is magnetic. "You do too. We'll call it a good luck charm."

I lift a finger. "I only have one issue with this scenario."

"What's that?"

I move my mouth to his ear, nipping his earlobe. "Don't call me 'dude.' That is a horrid word."

He cracks up, big and warm and so very him, and my heart does that annoying stutter again when he pins me, hands on my wrists, stares down at me, and says, "I like you so much that I won't say 'dude.'"

When he lowers his mouth to mine for another scorching kiss, it reminds me how utterly screwed I am.

Especially when he breaks the kiss and adds, "In fact, it's more than like, Dean. You know that, right?" He levels me with a stare I can't escape. "Tell me you know that."

And I don't know if we're playing games still, if we're giving each other the fantasy of us, or if we're jumping into the deep end of the hard truth.

But I can't lie. Not when he looks at me like that, like he's laying it on the line.

I swallow and then nod. "I know that, Fitz. I absolutely know that."

When we kiss again, it's tinged once more with desperation. So much that I don't care if he calls me *dude*. I just like him calling for me. Wanting me. Surrounding me.

I want as much as I can get.

"Now, about that matter we discussed earlier," he says in a naughty tone.

Fitz seems intent on making good on his list of dirty deeds.

Especially when he has his wicked way with me a few minutes later, getting me to arch my hips, and bow my back, and say his name in strangled, hoarse breaths, because what he's doing to me is wild and carnal and worth cleaning all the ice bins in the city.

The trouble is, it's worth so much more.

Because I think I'm falling in love with him.

* * *

When the sun streams through the window the next morning, warming me, waking me up, I stretch, yawn, and smile.

We have one more day.

I reach for him, ready for the last twenty-four hours to start.

But he's gone.

WEDNESDAY

Also known as the day it hurts, and the day it hurts so good.

27

FITZ

It's five in the morning, and I can't breathe.

I scrub a hand across my face, and I try to draw in air.

But my lungs can't fill because my heart is slamming against my chest, and I have no fucking clue what is happening to me.

I sit up in bed as the dark of night streams through the open blinds.

Dean's sound asleep on his stomach next to me, his back on display.

And I still can't breathe.

Being near him is too much right now.

It's too hard.

I can't think straight with him this close.

I have plans. So many plans for my family. For my team.

For myself.

And I can't sleep.

I never have trouble sleeping.

I sleep like the dead. Like the guilty. Like a cat.

But I've been waking up every twenty minutes. I can't think straight, and all I can do is *feel*.

I clench my teeth and drag a hand through my hair, willing this to stop.

This incessant beating in my chest.

This too-fast, too-hard pounding.

And the ringing in my ears. Loud and unavoidable, with no way to turn the volume down.

But the noise and the thumping aren't going away.

I look at the window, jaw clenched, trying to figure out what to do. Then I glance at Dean.

Sleeping so damn peacefully.

I lift a hand, wanting to slide it down his back, along his arm.

That's the problem. All I want is to touch him, be with him.

And I can't deal with this intensity. It's strangling me. It's cruelly stealing my blood and my breath.

This isn't what I wanted.

This isn't why I came to England.

I didn't come here to *feel*.

I came here for Emma.

And maybe, just maybe, to fuck.

And now I *am* fucked.

Because I *fell*.

And I can't handle it.

I swing my legs over the side of the bed, find my boxer briefs, and tug them on. If he wakes, I'll tell him I'm going for a run.

But he's quiet, still sound asleep as I pull on my jeans, my shirt, my socks. I stuff my phone in my pocket.

I push my fingers against the corners of my eyes, pinching the bridge of my nose, trying to decide.

Should I stay, or should I go?

But my feet choose. They take me to the door, where I grab my shoes.

I'll text him later.

Tell him I'm working out.

That's plausible. That feels reasonable.

Even though, as I open the door quietly and let it fall shut behind me before I put on my shoes, I know what I'm doing is something else entirely.

I'm running.

28

DEAN

At first, it seems like a miscommunication.

I wake up. The other side of the bed is empty. So is the living room, the kitchen, the bathroom.

Fitz is gone, and so are his clothes.

His shoes aren't by the door.

His phone isn't on the nightstand.

Fine, fine. He could have gone for a run or maybe had somewhere to be. He didn't want to wake me, but he'll have texted with an explanation. If I grab my phone, I'll find a message saying he had a meeting, a workout, a breakfast with his sister.

So that's what I do. I pick up my phone and ignore the sense of impending doom hanging over me.

I slide open the screen, wanting a note, *needing* one. When I click on my text app, the sinking feeling returns like a leaden weight in my gut.

There are no new messages.

He left.

He fucking ran.

I drag my hand across my jaw, heaving a sigh.

I want to believe this is a misunderstanding. That there's an easy explanation. That his absence makes perfect sense.

So I click on the app again, opening the last text he sent me—before I arrived at his hotel on Monday night. I told him I was on my way, and he'd replied with *Can't wait.*

No texts after that because we spent the next thirty-six hours together.

Thirty-six hours, during which I fell in love with the fucking jackass.

Now what?

I could start a conversation.

I could say, *Hey, where are you?*

Or *Everything okay?*

Or *Where did you go?*

But the thing is, if he wanted me to know, he'd have told me.

Gritting my teeth, I stare at the screen again.

Give it time. Maybe he just left. Maybe he ran to the store to surprise me with tea.

That sounds grand.

I set the phone down, head to the bathroom, brush my teeth, shave, and take a shower.

Surely he'll have returned when I get out.

He'll definitely have texted.

But my phone is still empty.

"You fucking prick," I mutter.

A small part of me thinks I should reach out, make sure he's okay, but I know he's okay. Nothing happened to him in the middle of the night in my flat. Nothing happened to him this morning.

The only thing that happened is he left.

And I'm not going to fucking chase him.

No way.

I get dressed, pulling on a T-shirt and jeans, then I stare at the bed.

It's a mess, tangled sheets, scrunched-up pillows.

All the evidence of us.

How we were.

I sneer at it.

I hate it.

I grab the sheets, toss them in the laundry bin, get out fresh ones, and make the bed.

I strip the pillowcases, throw them in the bin too, then put on new ones.

I toss on the cover, straighten the corners.

It's like he was never here.

I smooth a hand over the bed. "There." I draw a deep breath. It's shakier than I would like.

Then I head through the kitchen and leave.

The door groans shut behind me.

I don't want to be here.

I don't want to be in my own damn home because it's the last place I saw Fitz, and now it reminds me of him.

I bound down the stairs like I'm going to run a race, and when I reach the landing, I clench my teeth, let out a muttered "*Fuck*," and yank open the front door.

The worst part?

My stupid fucking heart is hoping he'll be on the other side.

Waiting for me. Walking down the street. Carrying breakfast. Smiling. He'll give me a kiss, head inside, and tell me he just stepped out for a bit.

But I scan the street for signs of him, and there are none.

"God damn you," I grumble. "God damn you, James."

I turn and walk, unsure where I'm even headed.

All I know is I want to get away.

Maybe that's how he felt too.

Except it feels a whole lot worse to be the one left, rather than the one leaving.

29

FITZ

Answer.

C'mon, just answer.

I ring the buzzer on Emma's door one more time.

A tinny sound rattles through the box. "Hello?"

"I called you three times. Can I please come in?"

"Oh, lovely to see you too."

I huff. "Well, you didn't answer, so I came over."

"James, it's eight in the morning."

"You're an early bird." I glance down Emma's street as a black cab rushes by. "You gonna let me up?"

"Yes. Of course." She presses the buzzer and lets me in. I hoof it up the steps two at a time till I reach the fourth floor. I rap on her door, and she opens it, still clad in her pj's.

"Can you get ready quickly? I'm hungry."

She blinks. "Are we having breakfast today? I thought you were with Dean."

His name is like a punch in the gut. But I absorb it like it's a hit on the ice, and I keep skating, focusing on my motherfucking job—*not feeling*. "Nah."

She shoots me a quizzical look. "You're *not* having breakfast with Dean? You're not spending the day with Dean? The guy you really like who you went on a riverboat cruise with? The guy who took two days off to spend with you?"

Stab me in the heart, why don't you?

"I wanted to see you before I leave tomorrow. I'm starving. Can we go?" I point to the clock on the wall behind her.

She rubs her eyes, then shakes her head. "I'm getting dressed. Only because I can tell you royally messed something up if you're trying to convince me we had a breakfast planned, when I know you really want to be with the guy you're falling for."

I bristle at her words, then try to shrug them off. "Time's a-ticking for scones, Ems."

* * *

A little later, we grab a table at a café near her flat, and I open the menu. I scan the items, reading each one carefully, letting eggs and toast and sausages and tea and Emma totally take my mind off the man I can't let myself think about. His eyes, his sarcasm, his laugh . . .

Shake it off.

I study the menu harder, like I can memorize it.

There. Eggs.

Perfect. I look up.

Emma parts her lips, about to say something, when the server swings by. We place our orders, then I fire off questions at Emma.

"So, you ready for your program to start? How's the flat? Do you need anything? Want to swing by the store?" I snap my fingers. "Hey, should we go to the Tower of London today?"

She holds up her hand as a stop sign. "James."

"Fine. We can go to the National Gallery." I flash my best supportive-brother smile. "How about the Tate too?"

Adamant, she shakes her head. "How about we start this impromptu bonding session with you telling me why you are hiding from the fact that you're falling in love?"

My heart lurches.

It kicks and screams.

It flings itself to the ground in an epic temper tantrum.

Then, it stops, goes quiet, as emotion clogs my throat. I swallow it down, drag a hand through my hair, then cover my face. "I'm so fucked, Ems. I'm so fucked."

She moves next to me, sets her hand on my back, and rests her cheek on my shoulder. "Why are you running? That's what you're doing, James. You know that, right? You don't need me. You need to figure out what's going on in here." She taps my heart.

I look up, feeling nothing but misery and not trying to hide it from her. "Because he lives here, and I live there, and that's not going to change. I have a job in the NHL. I can't and I won't give it up. And he has a life here, a family here, a business, friends, a loan. Everything. This is his home." I gesture wildly to whatever direction Dean lives in. "We don't work. We can't work. It's not possible."

She nods, smiling sadly. "Can't you try long-distance?"

I shake my head. "No. I can't. I barely get time off during the season. We play three games a week. We travel constantly. He works weekends. Hell, he works six days a week. This was a huge exception for him to take off two days to be with me."

She scoffs. "Why are you with me, then?"

I grab her arm, desperation wracking my body.

"Because I don't know what to do. I don't know how to be with him and not tell him I'm absolutely fucking crazy about him."

She hauls me in for another hug and ruffles my hair. "You're such an idiot. He's so obviously crazy about you too."

My heart slams against my chest. "Yeah?"

"Yes, and you're stupid if you can't see it."

For a few seconds, a sliver of happiness sneaks under my skin. I didn't think I was alone on this slippery slope. I had a strong feeling he'd been sliding along with me.

But even if he feels the same way I feel, that doesn't change the almost four thousand miles between us.

"I don't want a long-distance thing. I want to see him and touch him and be with him. That's how messed up this is."

She takes a beat. "I don't know how you solve it either. But I know how you *don't*."

"What's that?"

"By being here with me. You should be with him. Talk to him. Tell him what you told me."

"I don't want to scare him away."

"You already ran, James. Go see your man."

My stomach rumbles. "I'm kind of hungry though."

She rolls her eyes. "You don't deserve breakfast. Go fix this. Now. You have one more day with Dean."

I stand, open my wallet, hand her some bills, then drop a big kiss on her forehead. "I love you."

"I know. And I love you slightly more than I did before because now I have breakfast for my lunch."

The second I leave the café, I call Dean.

But he doesn't answer.

30

DEAN

"It's mad if you think about all the people that company hoodwinked." I pause my rant to take a bite of my breakfast.

"Yes, just mad," Anya says, with a curious lift of her brows.

"I mean, who thinks that's okay? It's not. It's not okay," I add, then finish my eggs and take a drink of tea.

"It's absolutely not," Naveen puts in, but then he clears his throat and looks at his wife. "So, Dean. Did you want to have breakfast with us to rant about some Silicon Valley company that tricked all its investors?"

I frown, confused. "You liked the book too. Right? I mean, it was captivating. It was a brilliant exposé."

Anya laughs lightly. "We talked about it two weeks ago."

"Right." I scrub a hand across the back of my neck, then shake my head. "I guess that proves my point. It stuck with me."

"Are you all right, mate?" Naveen asks.

"You're all amped up. Wired," Anya adds.

I lift the cup. "All this bloody tea."

Naveen's face is lined with skepticism, his voice dead-pan. "Yeah, you've been drinking it your whole life. I don't really think the tea has you in this mood."

I glance at my watch. "I should go. It's Wednesday. There's a . . ." I say, then drift off, trying to remember what I normally do on Wednesdays. Run errands for the bar. Pick up supplies we need. "There's an order I need to fetch." I check my watch. "I should be getting on."

"Dean." The no-nonsense tone comes from Naveen.

I look at him. "Yeah?"

"If you need to talk . . ."

"We're here," Anya finishes.

A wave of self-loathing crashes over me. I don't want to talk. I already feel stupid enough. Telling them won't help. Listening to my gut five days ago would have helped.

But still, they're my friends. They'll be here. Hell, they *are* here. And he's gone.

I tap the table. "Thanks. Listen, I appreciate it. I just need to sort some things out in my head. I'll be fine."

"And if you're not, we're still here," Anya says again.

"And if you are, we're here too," Naveen echoes. It's become a refrain.

I give a half-smile, which is all I can muster. "I know. Goes both ways."

I open my wallet to pay, when Naveen waves me off. "Your money's no good here."

I stand, thank them, and take off.

I cross the street and head down the stairs into the Tube. I wish I could say I feel better than I did when I called them a little while ago then crashed their breakfast together.

I don't.

But at least I feel like I'll get through this, reassured that I have everything I need right here.

* * *

When I exit a few stops down the line, I pop into a supplier's, say hello, grab a box of vodka samplers, return to the station, then head back home. I'll leave this at my place and take it to The Magpie tonight.

Because I'll be back at the bar.

I'll do what I usually do on Wednesdays. Exercise in the morning. Grab a bite with Taron. Work on the books then mix the drinks and talk to the customers.

Everything I'm supposed to be doing.

As I get off the Tube once more in my neighborhood, my phone buzzes once, like it's just caught cell service after trying to connect underground.

And for a few fantastic seconds, my brain tricks me into thinking it's Fitz.

That he's been calling all morning.

That the phone went to voicemail while I was on the Tube, where there's no cell reception.

That maybe he knows how I fucking felt when he took off.

But I don't grab it in time, and the ringing ends in my pocket. Checking it is too difficult as I juggle the box and head up the steps. The missed call will be there when I get home, and besides, it's not going to fucking be *him*.

I've been ghosted, and I can't wait till tomorrow at two, when I know he'll be gone from my country and out of my life for good, and I can truly erase him from my head and heart.

I walk down the street, passing the shops I know, saying hi to a few neighbors, then I turn down my road.

And I stop in my tracks.

He's sitting on the steps of my building, leaning forward, elbows on his knees, staring at his phone. One hand scrubs his chin, that thing he does when he's thinking, trying to figure out what to say, what to do.

Even from this many feet away, I can tell what he's feeling.

It's in the set of his jaw, the angle of his shoulders, the language of his body.

He's miserable.

Like I've been all morning.

Then, he raises his face and sees me, and something like hope flickers across his eyes.

But I steel myself to feel absolutely nothing.

The second I see Dean—the damn nanosecond—I'm up, walking down the street toward him. I need to apologize.

I don't think it's going to be easy.

His face is the definition of implacable as he carries a box under his right arm.

I rush over to him—not quite running but definitely moving faster than a walk. When I reach him and he keeps going, I turn around and head with him toward his flat.

"Hi," I say, my stomach roiling with nerves, with fear, with something else too—this crazy hope that he might feel the same way I do.

"Hello." He's cooler than he was on the bridge.

I deserve it. I clear my throat, trying to figure out what to say. I've been sitting on his stoop for twenty minutes, practicing, but nothing has stuck yet, so I blurt out the obvious. "I left this morning. At five or something."

"I noticed." His tone is expressionless.

"I'm so sorry." But that barely covers it. The trouble is, saying more could make things worse. I could risk whatever this is now. But I have to say something beyond a simple apology for what I did.

His mask gives zero away as we walk. "Nothing to be sorry about," he says. "I figured it out."

"*Dean.*"

We reach the door, and he hardly looks my way. "It's okay. You're not obligated to stay. You're not obligated to do anything at all. It's all fine." His tone is flat. He could be talking to me about a contract to clean the carpets.

But nothing is fine. *Fine* is how I feel about a turkey sandwich, or a piece of furniture, or a haircut, or the new blanket Carrie bought me.

But *fine* is not how I feel about Dean.

It's never been how I felt, and now, it's the furthest thing from what I feel.

And I've got to let him know. "I just freaked out. I couldn't sleep, and I freaked out," I say, starting to get to the heart of things.

He reaches into his jeans pocket. "I don't know why you would." His voice is so distant, and I'm such an ass for leaving.

"Because everything is happening so quickly," I say, trying that on for size as he finds the keys in his pocket and palms them, meeting my gaze briefly.

"And everything is ending quickly, Fitz," he says, matter-of-fact to the bone, as we stand in front of his building.

My heart hammers ruthlessly, its breakneck speed a reminder that I have to do this. I have to find the guts to let him know.

But how?

How do I express this emotion when I barely understand it?

This is all so damn new to me. The last person I had

any feelings for was my college boyfriend, and that was more than six years ago. This is entirely different. We're adults. We're busy in our careers. We have lives and jobs and families and responsibilities. This is flying blind.

"That's why I left. Because it is ending. And that sucks," I say, taking another small step.

Dean's expression remains stony. He's more inscrutable than he's ever been. "Fine. It was always ending. You ended it sooner. Doesn't really matter, does it?"

I drag a hand through my hair, wishing I could get out all the words, but I'm terrified they'll scare him away.

I purse my lips, hunting for the right sentences, when Dean does something unexpected. He fills the silence. He never does that. He always waits.

"Look, Fitz. Relationships end. It happens. It's normal. They don't last. I never expected anything. Stop acting like I did." His tone is crisp, but his eyes look hurt.

I know that look. I feel it deep in my bones. I understand exactly what he's not saying, what he maybe won't let himself say.

But I have to say *something*. I'm the one who freaked out, the one who left. I'm the one who wants him back, if only for a day. And I have to let him know what he's done to me.

Here in the doorway, in front of his home, I peel off a layer of truth, and it's scary as hell, but it feels wholly necessary. "What if I do? What if I want more?"

Dean meets my gaze fully this time. His brown eyes flare with possibility, but pain too. He looks away, then back at me, shaking his head. "You can't have that."

"I still want it." I sound desperate. I *feel* desperate. I tap my chest. "Do you think I came here to feel this way? Do you think I came to London to feel anything?"

"No. You came here to get laid, and you did it. Plain and simple."

"That's not why you're mad."

"Why am I mad, then?"

I reach for the box in his arms so I can set it on the stoop, but he doesn't let go of it. Fine, I'll do this with a physical barrier between us. I clear my throat. "Because in the last forty-eight hours, it's become more than that, and you know it. Hell, it was more than that the first time we slept together, and you know that too."

He breathes out hard, licks his lips, then in a quiet voice that gives me hope, he asks, "What did it become?"

I grab his shoulder to bring him close. "You know what it became."

I inch closer like I'm about to kiss him. To tell him with my lips what *this* is.

He holds up a hand and presses it to my chest, a powerful stop sign. "You're not kissing your way out of this, James. You're not fucking your way out of this. I'm thirty-one. I'm not swayed by that. If you're trying to say something to me, just say it. Don't kiss it. Say it and mean it."

His words are fire, and they ignite me. They're the last straw between my actions this morning and what I hope my actions will be for the next twenty-four hours.

My jaw is tight; my chest is heavy.

I hold my hands out wide and rip off the remaining layers of truth. "You want to know what I came here to say?"

"Yes," he bites out.

I shake my head, pissed and sad and frustrated all at once. "I'm crazy about you, Dean Collins. Just completely crazy about you. I didn't plan this. I didn't expect it. But it happened. *We happened*," I tell him, and it's both easier and harder now that I've said *that*. Easier because I feel like I can breathe again. I feel like I can fit inside my body without trying to crawl out of my skin.

Harder because he's expressionless. I grab at my shirt, my chest, to make my point. "I feel so much for you that it scares me. I don't know what to do about it, and I wish this thing between us could last well beyond tomorrow. I wish I didn't have to leave. Because I just want to see you and kiss you and touch you and be with you, and it's driving me crazy. Because you're not a fling at all—not one bit. You're the opposite, and I don't know what to do about it."

For several anguished seconds, he's impervious.

His lips barely twitch.

His face remains impassive.

Then he breathes out hard, sets down the box and his keys, pushes me to the other side of the doorway, and kisses me.

My God, does he ever kiss me.

He kisses me like he feels the exact same way.

His hands clasp my face, and his body slams against mine, and he crushes my lips in a searing, bone-melting kiss that knocks all my senses out of whack.

His lips devour mine—rough and demanding, like he's telling me all the same things with the fiercest, most passionate kiss ever recorded in history. One hand slides down my body, along my waist, traveling to my hip. The other ropes through my hair. And he's yanking me closer, even closer, and holy hell, I guess I haven't fucked up too badly.

If I get to have him for even one more day, I will be the happiest man alive.

Because Dean is kissing me like he's crazy for me too, and I can breathe, and I am lit up, electric and alive again.

When he breaks the kiss, he still has me caged in. His

hand clasps my face; his lips are a ruler. "Don't do that again, James."

"I won't," I say, shaking my head, relief flowing through me.

"I mean it. Don't do that. I don't like being ghosted. I don't like you taking off without telling me. We both know what happens tomorrow. We've both known from the start. I know what I signed up for, and I can handle it. But if you want to be with me until then, you've got to be all in. No running."

I swallow roughly. "I'm all in. I'm so all in with you."

A sliver of a smile tugs at his lips, and he tips his forehead to the door. "Good. Get inside."

"And can I show you how I intend to make it up to you?"

That earns me a devilish smile. "You damn well better." He bends, picks up the box, then finds his keys and unlocks the door.

He opens it, and I follow him in, relieved in a whole new way. Thrilled that I didn't fuck up the best thing to ever happen to me.

I trail him up the stairs, happiness washing over me because I have this time with him. A little more than twenty-four hours, and I plan to make the best of them.

As soon as we're inside his flat, he lowers the box, pulls at the hem of my shirt, and jerks me against him. "Now listen, Fitz," he says, and I can't stop grinning because I'm Fitz again. I'm out of the penalty box.

"I'm listening," I say.

His eyes blaze, and he's dirty, bossy Dean once more. "We've got a day. I would rather fuck and have fun. And right now, here's what that means." He licks his lips while he slides his hand under my T-shirt, up my abs, making me shiver.

"Tell me what it means," I rasp.

His hand spreads over my pecs. "It means I want you to show me what it's like when the man I'm crazy for makes up to me properly."

Oh. My. Fucking. God.

Forget *all in*.

I am so in love with him, it's insane. It's going to eat me alive. And I am going to let it. I am going to let this feeling take over my body and mind.

I grab his face. "I'm so damn happy you feel the same way."

"I do. I do feel the same," he says, and my heart soars. He keeps me close, his hands on my face too, as he toes off his shoes. Then he lets go of me and walks to the couch, stripping off his shirt and tossing it to the floor. He parks himself on the sofa, stretches his arms across the back of it, then spreads his legs for me.

He's wearing his jeans and nothing else.

And he's waiting for me to take care of him.

Oh hell, do I want to. Do I ever want to show Dean how sorry I am.

I kick off my shoes. My mouth waters as I walk over to my man and tug off my shirt.

I climb onto his lap, my hands settling on his shoulders then traveling down his firm and muscled arms.

"Let me grovel. Let me show you how sorry I am," I whisper, as I bend my head to his neck, kissing him there in the way that drives him wild.

"Mmm. That helps. That helps a lot," Dean says, sinking deeper into the cushions as I trail my tongue and my lips across his neck, the way I did the first time I ever touched him.

His fingers thread into my hair, and he tugs, pulling me down.

Making his intentions so damn clear.

I smile against his body as I follow his lead, my lips sliding along his chest as I kiss a hot trail along his pecs then down to his abs.

"How about this? This help too?" I lick a line along the grooves of his abs, across, down, traveling closer to his erection.

"That's pretty good," he pants. "But it might help a little more like this . . ."

His hands move to his jeans, unbuttoning the top button. I slide to the floor, kneeling between his legs as I work down the zipper. "I can definitely be of assistance."

He lifts his ass and pushes the denim down to his thighs, his fantastic cock springing free and greeting me with a very happy hello.

Dean runs a hand down his stomach, takes his cock in his fist, then rubs the crown against my lips. My eyes roll back in my head as I lick him.

"Show me how you grovel, Fitz," he says, all rough and commanding as his other hand curls around my head, yanking me close to his dick.

"With pleasure. With so much fucking pleasure." I wrap my lips around the head, and I groan against his length because he tastes so damn good.

I want all of him in my mouth, want him to fill me up. I want to show him that he deserves all the pleasure in the world from me, only me. So I draw him in, inch by inch, spiraling my tongue along his shaft as I go, taking him farther.

"Fuck, that's good," he mutters as he slides to the back of my throat.

And that's where Dean wants to be, judging from the sounds he makes. "Show me how much you love sucking my cock," he says, and my dick throbs in my jeans at his dirty words.

I do love sucking his cock.

So damn much.

And I show him. Sucking him hard and deep and ravenously. Letting him grab my head, pull me down on his dick, and rock his hips up against me. Letting him fuck my mouth, my face, my throat.

I suck him hard and deep because it feels so good, because it drives him wild, and because I want to let him know what I'll do for him. That if I have to, I'll get on my knees for him.

No. Not just because I *have* to. Because I *want* to.

Because this guy—my God, this guy is mine, and I want Dean to feel every second of pleasure in the world from me.

As I devour his length, he bucks against me, dirty words falling from his lips. "Yes, fucking yes. I fucking love that." Then just a long, choked out, "Coming."

He shoots into my throat, salty and intoxicating, and I savor every drop of him.

When I let go of his dick, I look up to see a very satisfied man.

He's supremely content, his lips parted, his breath coming fast. He reaches a hand to my face, runs a thumb along my jaw, then says, "Take your cock out. I want to watch you get yourself off."

Fire roars across my skin. I rise and strip off my jeans in seconds flat as he lies back on the couch, parking his hands behind his head, and I straddle him.

My dick is aching for relief, heavy in my hand as I grip myself. I'm close to the edge already from having him in my mouth, from him coming on my tongue.

The second I slide my hand down my length, I shudder.

I've never enjoyed jacking myself off more than right now, never more than when I'm looking at Dean, my hand shuttling at a fevered pace up and down my length.

His eyes are locked on my dick. He stares as I stroke myself, as pleasure crackles in my veins, as it spreads relentlessly across my whole body.

"You better come on my chest," he instructs. "Shoot all over me."

"Yes, God yes. I want my come all over you."

My orgasm rattles down my spine as my balls tighten, and I jerk faster, harder, until I'm coming so damn hard on his chest.

Then, as I'm panting and groaning, he reaches up to me, both arms tugging me close, pulling me against him. My release smears between our bodies, and neither one of us cares.

All I want is to get close to him. And that's what I do as he wraps his arms around me, pulls me to his chest, and kisses me.

Soft. Tender. Gentle.

I'm forgiven.

When he breaks the kiss, he whispers, "Thank you for coming back to me."

"I'm so glad I did," I say. Then I rise and grab his hand. "Let's clean up."

He pulls up his jeans, and we head to the bathroom, where he grabs a washcloth and wipes off my chest, and I do the same to him.

I walk into his bedroom, flop onto his bed, and beckon him to me.

"You're ready to go again?" he asks as he climbs over me.

"Soon," I say as I pull him on top of me and wrap my legs around the back of his thighs. "I told you so."

"Insatiable," he says, shaking his head.

"And you love it," I add.

"I do love it," he says.

I curl my hands around his neck as I hook my legs tighter around him, loving the contact after being intimate with him.

"But mostly, I just want to make out with you for a little bit."

"Like this?" he asks, bending closer and brushing his lips to mine, sending a wave of tingles through me.

Tingles. Jesus. I get tingles from the way he kisses me. I am so far gone it's unreal.

"Yes," I say on a moan, as I draw him closer.

As I bring my lips to his, I try to tell him everything that I'm dying to say.

Everything I learned today.

I tell him in the soft but urgent way I kiss him that I want him again and again.

As I tighten my legs around his body, I try to tell him without words that I'm in love with him.

And I hope he's kissing me back the same way.

32

DEAN

It's a little after twelve, and I make lunch. It's weirdly domestic, but I like it. I cook a chicken and veggie stir-fry, since I know Fitz tries to eat as healthily as possible, same as me.

Fitz stands in the kitchen, leaning against the counter, drinking an iced tea and watching me.

"I could get used to this," he says.

I eye his jeans, his bare, muscled chest. "Yes, me too. Please walk around shirtless literally all the time," I say as I turn the heat down on the pan.

"I will if you will. Speaking of, why are you wearing a shirt?"

"Oh, you know, that thing called cooking. Figured it'd be better with clothes on."

He scoffs. "I beg to differ."

I shake my head as I plate the food. "Sit down. Time for lunch."

Fitz pats his belly. "Good. I'm starving."

I arch a brow. "You're not starving. You're several days and many meals from starving. You're just hungry."

He finds cloth napkins in the cupboard and utensils in the drawer, and sets them down at the table. "No. I'm definitely starving. I didn't eat breakfast. I skipped out on Emma when I realized what an ass I was, and then I came straight here."

I move to the table and set down the food. "So next time you'll have learned your lesson. Don't do a runner before the cook wakes up," I say, sitting and picking up a fork. "I'm an excellent cook."

Fitz digs in, moaning around the food. "Damn. You are. This is amazing."

"Glad you like it."

"I guess your cooking club comes in handy," he says, deadpan.

"Cooking classes," I correct.

"Whatever it is, it's working. You can definitely make me breakfast tomorrow," he says, then takes another bite.

"Gee, thanks. I was hoping you'd let me."

He sets down the fork and leans across the table to give me a kiss.

Then he returns to his meal, and as we eat, he asks, "So, what do you want to do today? Besides fuck?"

"Well, that. Obviously."

"Obviously," he repeats.

"I think the more important question is—what do *you* want to do?" I toss back at him. "Is there something you want to see? Tower of London, St. Paul's Cathedral, Borough Market?"

He screws up the corner of his lips, thinking, then he shrugs. "What would you do?"

"If I were you?" I ask.

"Yeah. If you were me, and you had one day left to spend here."

"I'd just walk around the city," I answer.

"Then let's do that."

We straighten up and leave, and when we hit the street, I take his hand.

Fitz looks at our hands, then at me, and he smiles.

My heart trips over itself with happiness.

And sadness too, since this is all over tomorrow.

* * *

Time takes on a surreal quality as we walk along the river.

The clock ticks louder with every step, but I also can't escape the sense that I'm living in a cocoon of time. That I'm wandering through a dream state of what it's like to live one perfect day.

The blue sky above blankets us, the river rolls beside us, and the sun warms my skin. It feels as if this could last, as if this could be my life.

Here with him.

I want so badly to believe in this illusion as we walk past the Tate and the Globe and I tell him about growing up here, as he tells me about California and New York. When we stop at the railing, elbows resting on the stone, watching the boats glide by, the illusion feels wholly real.

He loops his arm around my lower back, yanking me a little closer to him as we stare at the water.

"Do you ever get tired of this view?" he asks, gesturing to the Thames.

It's a murky brown, but that's beside the point. It's not the color of the water that matters. It's the way it weaves and bends through the city, how it's the city's highway, bringing fame, fortune, respite, and certainty.

I shake my head. "No. But I do think sometimes I take it for granted. I walk by, head down, lost in my own world, and don't even bother to glance up, because it's too familiar."

Fitz nods as he stares at the water. "You've got to remember to look up. To see what's around you. I try to do that in New York."

"Yeah? How so?"

"Just try not to spend all my time on my phone as I walk around. To look at the restaurants and stores, the people, the buildings, the parks. To pay attention, you know?"

"I do know what you mean." I glance around. No one notices the hockey star, or us. We are anonymous. "Do you get recognized there?"

"Sometimes I do. Sometimes people come up to me on the street."

"Does it bother you?"

He shakes his head. "No. It's cool, actually—kind of a dream. My whole life, I wanted to be a pro athlete, and now I am. Having fans is a gift. So, when someone stops and says hi or asks if it's me, I try to chat for a minute. Unless there's some reason I can't, like I have a raging boner, as I did at that softball place with you."

"Fair point. And I can see that. You interacting, sans erection. So, if some fan came up to you here, you'd chat for a bit?"

Fitz glances around at the throng of people passing by, at the families, the fathers carrying young children on their shoulders, at the men and women in suits marching past us, at the couples—men and women, women and women, men and men—walking along the river.

"Absolutely," he says. "But I'd make sure he wasn't giving you sex eyes. If he was, I'd be all possessive and *mine, mine, mine.*"

I crack up. "Yes, exactly. No doubt loads of gay men are

giving you sex eyes." I hold up a hand. "Wait. Don't answer that. I don't want to think about all the guys who'll be hitting on you in literally a day when you return to the States."

He squeezes my waist. "Jelly, much?"

I roll my eyes. "Jealous a lot," I mutter, but I don't say what's tangoing on the tip of my tongue. *What happens when you meet someone else? What happens when you want to go home with someone else?*

Those thoughts curdle my stomach.

I wince.

"Hey," he says, regarding me closely. "What's wrong? You look like you just swallowed a jalapeño."

"I like jalapeños."

"Yeah, me too. Wrong analogy, then. You look like you swallowed a cockroach."

I pretend to retch.

"Exactly," he says. "So, what is it?"

"Nothing."

Fitz pinches my waist. "It wasn't nothing. What was it? Talk to me, babe."

I sigh, running my hand over the back of my neck. "It's stupid."

"It's not stupid. What is it?"

I shrug, then tell myself, *Why the fuck not?* "I was just thinking about when someone does want to take you home in a week or a month or whatever."

His smile downshifts then disappears. "Won't happen."

"Please. It will happen," I scoff.

"First, I've got the pact with my guys, and I'm sticking to it, so it won't happen."

"But the pact ends eventually. In a month or something, right?"

"About a week or so into the start of the regular season."

"So, that's the only reason?"

"You ass. The reason is you. I fucking want you. I don't want anyone else." Fitz turns to face me, looping both hands around my waist, tugging me against him. I wrap mine around his neck.

"Yeah, I get that, Fitz. It's just, down the road . . ."

He leans in close, nuzzling my neck. "I can't think about anyone else. Not now, not tomorrow." He brushes the lightest kiss on my neck, then moves back to look at me. "Dean, do you want to talk . . ."

"Yes," I say, and my heart slams against my chest because I think I know what's coming.

The talk.

The *Can we do this?* talk.

And I want to have it, but it's crowded and busy here.

"Let's go sit on a park bench."

"That's so rom-com," he remarks with a roll of his eyes.

"Yeah, and if this were a movie, we'd both watch it."

"We so would."

I take his hand, guiding him away from the water and toward a nearby park. We find a quiet bench, away from foot traffic, among the grass and the trees.

Fitz speaks first. "What are we going to do after tomorrow?"

"I don't know," I answer honestly.

"Do you think about it?"

A laugh bursts from me. "Are you kidding me? I think about it all the time. If you were here, I'd make sure no one gave you sex eyes." I furrow my brow and reconsider. "Well, I can't make sure no one would do that, because you're the hottest guy who's ever walked into my bar, so

I'm sure tons of guys would. But I'd damn well make sure everyone knew you were taken."

His smile is the stuff of legend. It's like I've given him his greatest wish. "You'd go all caveman on me?"

"Fuck, yes."

"What would you do?" Fitz asks, a little low and dirty. "Like, if we were in public, what would you do?"

"Same thing I do now. I'd have my hands all over you. I'd drape an arm around your shoulder," I say, demonstrating. "I'd make sure all the guys knew you were going home with me, and that no one else would get to touch you."

Fitz closes his eyes and lets out a needy rumble, swaying closer to me. When he opens his eyes, those blue irises are full of desire. Like they usually are. "You being possessive is my new favorite thing." Then he blinks and shakes his head. "But stop distracting me." He clears his throat and gives me an earnest look. "What can we do?"

"I honestly don't know. I imagine your schedule is ridiculously busy. You know mine is too."

He runs a hand over his beard. "We play three games a week. We're on the road a ton. You work every day but Sunday and Monday."

I nod. "I do."

He's quiet for a minute, eyes turned toward the people stretched out across the lawn, but not seeing them. He looks lost in thought. After a beat, he says, "But honestly, New York's not that far from London."

I shoot him a skeptical stare. "Not *that* far?"

"Well, it's not San Diego-to-London far."

"Fine. True. But it's still far, Fitz."

"Yeah, I'm just trying to work through scenarios," he says, leaning back against the bench, rubbing his hand on my shoulder. "Like, if I had a couple days off and they lined up with your days off, would you come over and see me?"

Would I? I know the answer, but I also can't resist the chance to toy with him. "Depends." My voice is coy.

"Depends on what?" he asks, indignant.

"Are you getting me a first-class ticket?"

Fitz laughs, sliding a hand up my thigh. "Well, you have a first-class cock. I'm definitely going to miss this first-class cock."

I grin. "I get it. You'd be willing to fly me and my first-class cock over when you are horny."

He smirks, licking the corner of his lips. "Fuck, yeah."

I nod a few times. "I can live with that. My first-class cock and I can definitely live with that."

He pumps both fists. "Problem solved by the power of dick."

All I can do is laugh. We both do. We crack up, and it feels great to laugh with him.

But soon, the laughter fades, and we're back to the same place.

The *Will we?* The *Can we?*

"Seriously though, Dean?" he asks.

I sigh, wishing there were an easy answer. "I think we just have to see how it goes. I mean, I don't know. It doesn't sound ideal, to be honest. Do you *want* a long-distance thing? It sounds kind of awful."

"It does. But I also don't want *zero* of you."

"I feel the same. But I don't want two percent of you either." I turn and meet his gaze. "And look, I can't just up and leave my world." Before Fitz can say a word—because I am *not* taking a chance on him freaking out again—I hold up both hands. "I know you're not asking me to. I'm not saying you are. I just want to be clear. I'm putting my cards on the table. There's no bluffing here. My mum did that, and I won't do the same."

He reaches for my hand, squeezing it. "I get it. I do, I swear."

We sit and stare at the park, looking for answers and finding none.

"Do you want to go?" I ask after a few minutes.

He shakes his head. "No. I want to stay."

I know what he's saying, and I want it too.

But that's not in the cards. Still, I sit on the bench with him for a little longer before we leave with nothing decided, because this is one of those problems that doesn't have a solution.

33

FITZ

Emma calls this the golden hour.

It's not sunset. It's a little before, when the light is perfect, and every photo has that perfect hazy glow.

Natch, I take plenty.

Dean's stopped giving me a hard time, and I've stopped pretending they're for Amelia.

They're all for me.

As we drink our five o'clock beers, I hold up my phone. "Smile for the camera."

"You mean for your wank bank, Fitz."

"I call it the spank bank. You call it a wank bank. Whatever. Just get over here."

My sexy Brit takes off his shades and gives me the best *fuck me* smolder ever. I snap that pic so fast.

"Damn," I say, looking at his dark-brown eyes on the screen. "That's my new favorite shot of you and me. I am going to be looking at this a lot."

"Just not in the locker room, please."

My brow knits. "Dude, this is my bedtime viewing. I'm not looking at this in the locker room, because then I'd have a boner in front of my teammates. That is not going to happen."

Dean laughs. "Good. Let's keep it that way."

As I take another swallow of my beer, a tall guy runs by, earbuds in, exercise shorts on, Nikes pounding the pavement.

"Shit," I mutter.

"What's wrong?"

"I didn't work out today. Or yesterday," I say, slumping in the chair. "Fuck."

"And your training camp starts in a few days."

"I can't skip a workout."

"It makes a difference? Every day?"

"This close to the season, yeah, it does. Cardio, at least."

Dean reaches into his wallet, grabs some bills, tosses them on the table for the beers, then says, "Let's go for a run."

"Seriously?"

"Yes. I try to work out every day too."

"And it shows. But seriously, you want to run with me?"

"Are you worried I can't keep up? Because I don't think that's going to be a problem. Also, I weigh about twenty-five pounds less than you, so I might have the advantage there," he says, taunting me with a quick survey of my bulkier frame.

"Oh no, you didn't just unleash your secret competitive side on me."

He lifts a single brow. "Was it a secret?"

I laugh, clapping my guy on the back. "No, but the thing is, I don't have my running shorts or sneakers, and I don't want to go back to my hotel and get them."

"Well, you won't fit into my shorts," Dean says.

I snap my fingers, aw-shucks-style. "Damn, I was hoping we could start borrowing clothes."

"I have an idea though. What size shoes do you wear?"

I smirk. "Big ones."

He laughs. "Yes. I can tell. Because you have big feet. Seriously though. What's your shoe size?"

"Twelve. US size."

"Same. I have a couple of pairs of running shoes. You can borrow some." He nods toward the end of the block. "Athletic store. Let's get you some shorts, and we'll run."

"You really want to spend our last afternoon together going for a run?"

"It's what you'd do at home, right? That's kind of what we've been doing today."

"That is true." Maybe that's why I've loved it so much, because it feels like a normal day in our normal life where we do all the things we want to do—eat, fuck, walk, run, play, talk.

Everything I want.

* * *

The man did not lie. Dean keeps pace with me at a fast clip as we run through the park. Only difference is he wears a T-shirt. I do not.

"Do you always run shirtless?" he asks. "Or just when you leave your clothes behind at the hotel?"

"Does it bother you?" I ask. "Or just distract you?"

"Yes, it bothers me terribly to see you half-naked." He roams his eyes up and down my frame as we cruise along the path. "Correction: *mostly naked.*"

"And still *all the way* distracting," I toss out.

"Yes, exactly. I can't focus at all, which is why I'm keeping up with your NHL arse."

"Cocky," I say. "And I like it."

"Thought you would. Anyway, tell me more about how

that ice-defender thing works," he says as we round the
next bend.

"You want to know?"

"I want to understand hockey better. I truly do."

And I swoon.

Then I tell him all about my favorite thing.

Except he might be my favorite thing now.

* * *

The golden hour is over. Twilight falls, and we're in his flat
again. I've got a towel wrapped around my waist, and my
hair is wet, slicked back from the post-run shower. Dean's
the same, towel across his hips, and I stare at his reflection
next to mine in the bathroom mirror. He slicks on deodor-
ant, and then I wiggle my fingers in an unsubtle request.

He rolls his eyes and tosses it to me, even though I'm a
foot away in this tiny space. He doesn't have to say a word.
I know we're thinking the same thing, laughing at the same
thing. We're sharing all our shit.

Still, I just shrug as I slide it on. "What? TaskRabbit isn't
here yet with my stuff."

His buzzer rings. "Guess it's here now. I'll take care
of it."

Dean unhooks the towel, lets it fall to the tiled floor,
tosses me a *feel free to stare* look, then gives me a perfect
view of his naked ass as he leaves the bathroom. I stare at
him shamelessly as he grabs fresh boxer briefs and pulls
them on, along with jeans and a polo.

This view. My God, I need this view in my life.

Need it badly.

I pick up his towel, hang it on a hook, then put mine
there alongside his.

A minute later, he's back with the delivery of my suit-case from the hotel. He sets it on the floor.

"Your valet," he teases, and I open the suitcase and tug on briefs and jeans.

I look at the clock on his nightstand. It's a little after seven thirty. Time is unwinding, but I'm going to make the most of tonight. And after today, and after last night, and after the other morning, I already have some ideas.

An agenda, if you will.

As I button a short-sleeve shirt, I imagine those things, how they might be. Things I need, things I want. Things that, even a few days ago, I didn't think I wanted.

But now I'm pretty sure I do.

I'm pretty sure I can see them happening tonight. When I'm dressed, I catch his eye. "Want to hit the town, sexy bartender?"

"Let's do it, cocky athlete," he says, and we leave his place together.

When I look back at his flat before I shut the door, I have a crystal-clear image of what I'll want when I walk back in here later tonight.

But first, food.

34

DEAN

After dinner, we find our way into a night club I've wanted to check out.

"The drinks here are supposed to be fantastic," I say as I order at the bar. "Classic cocktails. Good and strong."

"Then pick something that'll get me in the mood," Fitz says with a wink, gesturing that he's going to hit the men's room while I order.

"So that's . . . pretty much anything?"

He salutes me as he heads off. "You know me so well."

I order the bar's Snake Bite shot for myself, which is Canadian whiskey and lime juice, and the Godfather for him—bourbon and amaretto. I pick it because I know he'll like the name.

I carry them toward the back and claim a circular booth as pop music emanates through the dark club. Seconds later, Fitz saunters over and slides in next to me, his hand on my thigh.

"Godfather for you," I tell him, and he knocks some back.

"Excellent. Don't forget, I still want your martini."

"You'll get it. Someday," I say.

He takes another drink then drops his lips to my neck. "I want that someday, Dean."

"I know you do," I murmur as I take a swallow of my drink. It burns, as it should—a good burn.

He finishes his drink, then tells me he needs another. "Wait. I want something else. Another classic. Pick for me. Perks of dating a bartender."

That goes to my head quicker than any alcohol. Because whatever happens tomorrow, it does feel like we're dating.

Hell, it feels like way more than dating.

When the server swings by, I call her over. "We'd love some more drinks."

She flashes a bright smile. "What can I get for you gentlemen?"

"He's no gentleman," Fitz mutters under his breath.

I roll my eyes. "Ignore him," I tell the redhead.

She's all pink lip gloss and straight teeth. "He's hard to ignore. So are you."

"Thank you. Rusty Nail for my . . ." I pause, then meet Fitz's gaze, knowing what I say next will make the man ridiculously happy, and it's a privilege to be able to do that. "My insanely hot date."

She wiggles her brows. "He is."

"And I'll have an Irish Threesome."

She sets a hand on my shoulder. "Excellent choice. And you're just as hot."

"Thanks, love," I say, then return to Fitz as she leaves.

He stares at me with wide eyes. "'Thanks, love'?"

I crack up. "Are you jealous again?"

He shakes his head. "No, but I've literally never heard you do that whole British thing—*hi, love; thanks, love*—and now you're breaking it out with abandon?"

"I said it once. I wouldn't say I'm 'breaking it out with abandon.'"

He nods exaggeratedly. "That's abandon, my friend . . ." He moves closer to me, even though there's hardly room to get closer. "Also, did you get the feeling she wanted to have a sandwich with us?"

I laugh again. "I did get that distinct impression."

"Who do you think she'd want on top? You or me?"

"Does it matter? I don't think she's getting either one of us." Then I pause for a split second, a tiny bit of panic wedging itself into my chest. "Wait. You're not saying you'd want that?"

Fitz rolls his eyes, then slides his hand around the back of my head. "Dude. Shut up. I'm not even going to dignify that with a response. Now get your lips on me, you sexy fucking man."

I dignify that command with a hot, wet kiss that lasts until the redhead returns with our drinks.

"Here you go, gentlemen," she coos as she sets them down. Then she lowers her voice. "And I'm Vicky. I'm off at one if you two want to make it a fun night."

Fitz clears his throat and wraps an arm around me. "Thanks, love," he says in his Harry Potter accent. "But we're going to pass."

She wiggles her fingers. "Maybe another time."

And when she leaves, he mouths, *Maybe another time, my ass.*

I lift my glass. "I will drink to that, for sure."

He gestures to my cocktail. "Also, you think maybe your drink gave her the idea we'd take her home? What's in that thing?"

I look at the glass. "Irish cream, Irish whiskey, Irish stout. The only threesome I want."

My date clinks his to mine, then he dips into his accent

again, muttering, *"Thanks, love."*

And I imitate him when I say, *"But we're going to pass."*

We finish our drinks as the music slides into another round of pop, until "The Time of My Life" plays, and his blue eyes twinkle with mischief.

Fitz nods to the corner of the club. Men and women flock to the dance floor, some of them coupled up with arms around each other and some shimmying in groups, all of them eager to get their groove on to one of the most cliché dance songs of all time.

Fitz wiggles his brows in an invitation. He expects *me* to be one of those people.

"Not a chance," I say.

"You don't dance?"

"Not to this song. And not well."

"Who cares? Not me. Not about either of those things."

"I do," I say, but Fitz has started making circles on my thigh, making it very difficult to argue my point.

"Come on," he says. "Let's dance."

"Let me guess—you're a spectacular dancer."

He shrugs with a cocky grin. "I'm not bad."

"Liar," I say. "You're good at everything, with your perfect body."

He leans in and whispers close to my ear, still making those circles that move dangerously high on my thigh. "You're one to talk, with your smoking-hot bod," he says, and the song shifts again. The DJ used a crowd-pleaser to lure more clubgoers to the floor, but now the music shifts to a slow but steady beat.

Leon Bridges.

"Now you have no excuse," Fitz insists, standing up. "Even you can dance to this."

"Do you always get your way?"

"I got you, didn't I?" he says wolfishly.

"Maybe I'm easy," I tease.

"Maybe you're hard," he fires back.

"Around you, that's an accurate assessment."

He glances down to where he was tracing those maddening circles on me. In an imitation of my accent, he says, "Why don't you let me assess it right now?"

I groan, trying to suppress a laugh at his humor, his insistence. "And you think that's going to get me to dance with you?"

He leans in and nips my earlobe. "I want to dance with you, babe," he whispers, then flicks his tongue against me, letting out a low, husky "Please."

And that's enough. I'm evidently powerless to resist him.

I take his hand and let him lead me to the dance floor. His arms circle my hips. Mine land on his shoulders as we sway together.

Around us, some of the groups of friends have peeled off, but most of them have paired up. They lean into each other, some more closely than others.

Fitz nods at the couples around us. "Do you care if someone looks at us?"

My brow knits. "Because you're famous?"

He laughs, then turns serious again. "Do you care because we're two guys?"

"We are? News to me," I say, being cheeky.

He yanks me closer. "Smart-ass. But do you?"

I laugh, shaking my head, but I'm truly shocked that he's asking something he must know the answer to. "Is that a real question? You kissed me in the booth ten minutes ago. The server propositioned us. You have your hands on me constantly. You've been kissing me in public since I met you. You kissed me on the street outside that wretched softball bar, and on Tower Bridge. You had your arm around me on the boat. We made out in the doorway of my building. All we do is touch all the time. You think I'm suddenly shy?"

He smiles, almost like he's embarrassed. "I know, babe. It just makes me happy to do it. It makes me happy to know you like it."

My heart stutters. "Just being ourselves?"

"Yeah. It's like a reminder of why it's good to be out. To be open, you know?"

I nod, more serious now. "I do know. I get it."

For a moment, we just dance, then Fitz asks, "When did you come out?"

"I was sixteen. And you were fifteen, you said?"

"Yup, and when I was seventeen, I went to prom with Brian Levine. A real catch at the time."

I smile, loving that he knew then. That he was confident. That his family supported him.

"Lucky Brian," I say. "How did that come about?"

"I asked him with one of these cheesy signs, and he said yes."

"And your school was cool with that?"

"Benefits of growing up in San Diego, I guess. When I told my mom I was gay, she hugged me and said, 'I'm so happy for you,' then she asked me to mow the lawn."

This thrills me—the lack of drama, his certainty—and not just for fifteen-year-old Fitz. I've been the first for some guys. The experiment. That's dangerous and sexy. It's intoxicating for the ego but hell on the heart.

"That's perfect. And sounds just like my father. He said something like 'Great, and did you finish your essay?' then asked if there was anyone I had my eye on, and it's been that way ever since."

"We're lucky," Fitz says, a massive understatement I don't take for granted.

"We are." I tip my head toward the redhead. "Have you ever been with a girl?"

He shakes his head. "No. Never even kissed a girl. You?"

"Same. Unless you count Louise Abernathy during Seven Minutes in Heaven when I was fourteen."

He growls.

I toss my head back, laughing. "You're jealous of a girl I didn't even enjoy kissing, an experience that helped me realize I was and am very, very gay?"

"Fine, when you put it like that," he grumbles.

"Don't worry. It was pretty clear she was not my type."

Fitz smirks. "And your type is?"

"Just this inked, bearded, cocky, charming, and addictive hockey player."

He smiles, a crooked, delicious grin that makes my heart flip. "Good. Because it turns out I've got a thing for this sexy, sarcastic, strong, and stubborn British bartender." He takes a beat, then adds, "But I'm actually glad you knew nothing about hockey."

His tone is vulnerable, and I latch onto that sound, asking, "Why's that?"

"Because my job never factored into this thing between us," Fitz says.

There's a look in his eyes telling me he needs something from me. He needs me to answer the question he didn't ask. Because *this* fact, this underpinning of the night I met him, is part of what's happening between us. This is part of the *why* of what's happening.

My fingers play with the ends of his hair. "This thing between us was never about *that*. It was never about a name or a number on your jersey. I don't even know what your number is, and I've never watched a hockey game. You could run a sandwich shop, and I'd still want to see you. You could collect rubbish. You could be the head of a company, or you could work in the post room. I don't care." It's an unexpected rush of words tumbling from my lips, but it feels important to say them, to tell him this truth. "None of this is about what you do. All of it is about *you*."

For the first time since I met him, the man is speechless. Maybe I've stunned him. Maybe I've said too much. But he's never quiet for long, even if he's speaking with his body.

Fitz slides his hands tighter around me, and there's a rumble in his throat, an appreciative sound that seems to say *thank you* in some wordless language.

He's so close to me right now, so unbearably close, and yet I still want him closer. I don't want this moment to end. I don't want any of this to end.

He slams his mouth onto mine, and it's heady and wild, and we need to leave really fucking soon.

Fitz breaks the kiss, clearing his throat. "I've been thinking about something all night," he begins in a rough voice full of intent.

"You have?" I ask.

"Been thinking about this since the shower yesterday morning. What you did to me."

The moment slows. The music warps. Everything comes to a pause with this man and his hands on me and the words he's saying. What they might mean.

"Yeah?" My mind is buzzing.

"And since last night too. What we talked about," he adds, a little breathless, a lot hot and bothered.

His blue eyes are intensely focused on me. His hand wraps more tightly around my hip. My skin sizzles.

"Tell me," I say, desperate to know.

He takes a breath, like it fuels him. "Remember what I said about how I'd let you fuck me?"

All my nerve endings come alive, flickering with possibility, with promise, and the promise of pleasure rushes through me. "I remember it perfectly," I say in a voice like smoke.

His hand slides up my back to my neck, gripping me. "I want that."

My mouth is dry. My head is hazy. My entire body is an electric grid lit up.

The prospect of fucking Fitz is going to make me lose my mind.

"I want it now. Tonight," he says.

In seconds, we are gone.

35

DEAN

The door to my flat barely has time to shut before we're tearing off clothes. We stumble our way to the bed.

Fitz strips off his boxer briefs, the last of his clothing. I watch him greedily as he sinks down on my bed, looking like he belongs there.

He lazily strokes his cock as I shed my boxer briefs and grab the lube and a condom, setting them next to him.

I straddle him, then bend closer to ask something important. "When was the last time for you? Like this?"

"College."

I blink, drawing a deep breath. This is almost too much. What he's giving me is a gift, and I want it to feel extraordinary for him. My hand skates over his erection. "Then I'll need to spend a long, long time getting you ready."

He thrusts up against my fist. "I don't object to that."

Savoring the feel of him in my hand, I kneel between his legs, his naked body on full display for me. My eyes drink him in, from the planes of his abs to the muscles in his thighs, then up to his powerful arms. His tattoos snake along his biceps, all those armbands and sunbursts, the edges of them visible as he parks his hands behind his head. He lets his legs fall open more, and I am undone with desire. It consumes me, even as it fills every cell in my body.

This man feels like mine.

Hell, he doesn't *feel* like mine.

Right now, Fitz is mine.

I tighten my fist around him, the feel of his hot, hard length sending a wicked thrill down my spine. His moans and *yeses* set alight a dozen fires inside me. After a few more mind-bending moments of stroking him, I let go so I can lube up my fingers and slide them against his ass, teasing him. He groans in anticipation as I push one in while my other hand focuses on his cock.

"Yesssssss," he growls as I rub my thumb against him at the same time, right where I know it feels amazing.

After only a few seconds, his hips roll up, and he's seeking me out, his body asking for more, more, more.

I push farther.

He's tight and hot, and I relish every shiver and groan as I watch the pleasure ripple across his perfect body. My dick aches, hard and heavy between my legs, but my dick can wait.

I want to make sure he's ready.

"More," Fitz whispers, a plaintive plea.

I add more lube, then slide in another finger. His jaw tightens, and his eyes squeeze shut. His cock twitches against my palm, the evidence of his desire on the head of his dick.

His lips open, and he's panting. "Fuck, babe, that's so fucking good. I want you so much."

I bend down and kiss the tip of his cock, savoring the taste of him. "The feeling is mutual."

Fitz rocks his ass against my fingers. "Give me more."

"More mouth, more fingers? Be specific," I tease, licking his shaft.

"You cocktease," he growls.

"Just the way you like it." I draw the head between my lips for a delicious suck before I add even more lube then give him the three-finger treatment.

He writhes, letting loose a long "Oh fuckkkk."

The groans he makes as I thrust into him—obscene, carnal, the hottest sounds I've heard in my life—make my head hazy, my skin red-hot. I am burning everywhere for this man.

He thrusts up against me with abandon, with wild need. "Dean," he groans, his whole body begging me. "I need your cock. Please fuck me. Get in me, babe. Get in me now."

I combust into a roaring, five-alarm blaze.

I pull my fingers out as he shoves the condom at me, desperate, aroused beyond words, and such a sight.

I sheath myself, adding more lube to the condom, and settle in between his legs again, nudging them farther apart.

For a second, I wonder if those are nerves flickering across his eyes.

But no, it's desire I see. Want. Lust. And so much need. As much as I have. As much as I feel.

"Just tell me if it hurts," I say gently. "Promise me, okay?"

Fitz slides his hands over my chest. "I promise. But it's not going to hurt. It's going to feel fucking amazing."

I run a hand along his shaft as I press the head of my cock against his ass and push in a little bit. There's a moment, I swear, when everything stands still. When I'm barely in him, and his eyes are wide, almost shocked.

"Breathe," I whisper as I move my body forward, my free hand braced on the bed by the side of his chest.

He nods, takes a deep breath, then exhales. His eyes stay locked with mine as his hands settle on my abs, his fingers spreading over my hips as I go a little deeper.

"Ohhh God," Fitz grunts, and I stroke him again then sink in farther, his ass gripping me so tightly, so intensely, that I tremble all the fuck over. I let go of his length, setting both palms on the bed.

His fingers curl around my hips, and he's holding on tight, caught between pleasure and pain.

"Say the word, and I'll stop," I say, calm and soft, letting him know I'll listen to his needs, what he can take, what he can't.

"Don't want you to stop," he mutters. "Just give me a sec."

I bend my head, brushing a kiss across his jaw. He lets out a deep breath.

Then another as I kiss his earlobe. "I'm not going anywhere," I whisper.

I can feel him relaxing under me a little more with each breath.

My body heats, and I'm dying to move in him, but I'll wait till he gives me the word.

I raise my head, and I do wait for him.

Until he's ready.

Fitz lets out a low moan, easing me closer with his hands. "I need you so fucking much," he says, answering me with words then with actions. In a split second, his hands take full control of my hips, and he jerks me close, driving me deeper into him. More than halfway now.

"Oh fuck, babe. That's so fucking good," he rasps.

I can't even speak. It's more than good. It's out of this

world. It's in another solar system, as his ass grips my cock in the most intense sensation ever.

Pleasure sizzles across my skin, and I'm a live wire, burning and sparking.

Fitz breathes out hard, then meets my gaze, his lips parting. "All of you. Gimme all of you."

As I sink inside him, his legs wrap around me. I lower myself so I'm inches from his chest as I bottom out in him.

Nothing exists but him and me and us.

And *this*.

This intoxication of a long, slow slide into him and the look in his eyes as he takes me all the way at last.

The sound on his lips . . . *Yes*.

His body lifts, rolls, and arches against me. He's so fucking sexy, so beautiful, his cock thick and long, jutting between us.

Reaching down with one arm, I hook his right leg tighter around my body.

As I start to thrust into him, reality slams into me—I won't last long. It feels too good, too perfect.

He is too much of what I want. He is all I want.

He is *it*.

The shattering truth of that clobbers me. There is no more falling. The falling is done, and I'm here.

I'm in love with James Fitzgerald, this man I didn't even know a week ago. And now he's the *only* one I want.

Desperately. Everywhere. In my body, in my mind, and, inconveniently, in my heart.

Focus on the physical, I tell myself as I stroke in, out. I try to form words of sex, so I don't stupidly blurt *I'm in love with you* in the middle of fucking him. My voice comes out rough, gravelly. "Everything good for you?"

"You're good for me," he murmurs, so open right now,

so vulnerable, and it's cracking open something inside of me, a piece of my heart that I can't afford to lose to him.

But I lost the battle.

Days ago.

I didn't want to feel this, but *this* couldn't be stopped. I feel it all. I feel everything, even as I try my damnedest to focus on the physical.

On the heat. On the burn. On the tightness of his vise-like thigh muscles wrapped around me. I focus on the hard planes of his abs, his chest, the thickness of his cock between our bodies.

The way his body seeks me out. Asks for more.

And his hands too, gripping my ass as I rock into him, squeezing like he needs me deeper in him, so much deeper.

I rise a bit, sliding a hand between us to take his shaft in my palm. The second I touch him, he's moaning and groaning, but shaking his head too. "You can't do that yet. I'm going to come so fucking hard if you touch me. Want this to last, babe." Fitz shoves my hand off him, then pushes up on his elbows, getting closer to me. "I need to kiss you. Kiss me while you fuck me."

Wildfire spreads through me from the intensity of his words, his gaze. How can I resist him? I've never been able to. Even when I tried, I couldn't. I can't resist anything with him, with this man who strutted into my life and insisted on me. Who chased me, challenged me, found me.

And found my heart too.

As my hips swivel, my cock throbs inside him, aching for release, but I fight it off as he grabs my head and pulls me to him. He attacks my mouth ferociously, fucking me with his tongue as I fuck him with my cock.

His pulsing shaft is hot and hard, pre-come slicking between us. The feel of him like this, near the edge, sends bolts of lust down my spine.

Fitz slows the kissing for a second, murmuring against my lips, "I love kissing you so much. Gonna miss it so much, babe."

"Me too," I whisper, feeling too much, wanting too much.

I'm on the edge of the world right now. My body is nothing but pleasure, nothing but bliss.

My mind enters a wonderful, ecstatic haze as I move in him, rock my hips, stroke deeper.

"I love fucking you," Fitz says with another hard kiss. "But I love this too. You fucking me. Want it again and again." His hands grab me harder, while his legs grip me so damn tight. "Just love it all," he whispers between bites and deep, hard kisses.

He's not saying certain words exactly.

But it hardly matters. I feel them deep in my chest. And I know in my heart, I absolutely know what's happening. I hate it, and I love it too. I love it so much.

This connection.

This incredible, intense intimacy that's physical and so much more—more than two bodies smashing into each other. It skates far past chemistry and molecules and organs.

We are in this.

And I don't know how we turn back.

His face shifts with pleasure, like he's breaking.

"Babe," he grunts. "I need to come."

He drops his hand from my head, grabbing his cock. The moment shifts back to the physical plane as I swat his hand away.

"I'll get you there," I say, feeling possessive, needing to take him over the edge. Wanting to be the only one to ever do this to him, for him, with him.

And I do. I stroke him as agony twists his features—

mine too, while I try to stave off my release. But it's point-less because he's growling and grunting, and his sounds unleash my own pleasure.

"Yes. Coming," he says, and I watch as he explodes with desire, come spurting in jets over his stomach, up his chest. The sight of it pushes me over the edge. My own pleasure detonates, searing my blood, torching my veins, and taking over my whole being.

I groan, as my climax blinds me in an electric neon haze until both of us are gasping for air.

I sink onto him as he kisses me.

"I love kissing you," he whispers again and again, like he can't not say it, like he can't stop doing it. "Love it so much."

It's all he's saying, but I know what he's not saying. I know what he's feeling because I'm feeling it too.

"I love it so much too," I tell him, and he loops his arms around my back.

And we know.

We both know what happened in such a short time in London after the night he walked into my bar.

Trouble is, I have no clue what happens tomorrow when he gets on that plane.

* * *

But I have to figure it out.

In the middle of the night, while Fitz is sound asleep and I'm unable even to nod off, I look up flights. I look up details. I run through scenarios.

I chase every possible permutation, and I make a list in my head of pros and cons.

I feel both hopeful and ridiculously foolish.

And then hopeful again as I look at Fitz, his chest rising

and falling, his breath coming in that steady, peaceful rhythm.

Softly, without waking him, I run a hand over his hair, flashing back on the last few days, remembering Sunday at Fortnum & Mason when we laid down the law.

This is just a fling. Nothing more, I'd told him.

I'd believed it fervently that afternoon. It had felt like a fact, like nothing would change it.

We could police our emotions.

We could make the rules and never break them.

I shake my head, silently laughing at the two of us. How little it took for us to bend.

I set my phone down, trying once more to sleep.

But then I remember what he said that day. It slams back into me with the force of a hurricane.

My job is everything to me because it means I can take care of my family. Make my mom's life easy. Give her all the things she never had when we were growing up.

That's the heart of the problem. I care about him too much to get in the way of his everything.

THURSDAY

Also known as the day we say goodbye.

36

FITZ

Dean keeps his word.

He makes breakfast the next morning—a mushroom omelet with fresh-cut strawberries on the side—and my stomach is in heaven.

"I will never mock you for cooking club again," I say as I sit, setting down my coffee.

Then I wince.

Dean arches a brow above his cup of tea. "A little sore?"

I laugh lightly. "Yeah. Someone I know is kind of well-endowed."

He sits across from me, smirking. "Sorry. Not sorry."

I tap my left pec. "No regrets, babe. No regrets. It's a good sore."

His fork dives into his breakfast, and he takes a bite, chews, then swallows before he adds, "You know, there's one surefire way to deal with that predicament."

My nose crinkles. I don't want to hear about weird remedies. Call me suspicious. "And what is that?"

Dean leans a little closer. "Do it again." He takes another bite. "And again." One more bite. "And again."

Admittedly, I could go for that. "There's only one little problem with that cure."

"Your incessant need to top?" he asks with an arch of his brow.

"No," I say emphatically. "Also, hello? It's not incessant at all. Do I or do I not recall your dick in *my* ass last night?"

Dean pretends to consider this deeply. "What do you recall about it?"

I move closer to Dean. "I recall loving every single second of it," I say, and his eyes darken, locking with mine.

"Every second?"

"Every single second," I repeat, a little surprised at the strength of my own reaction to him topping me, at my own desire to try that again, to explore that possibility with him in bed, something I honestly never wanted with anyone else. "I did." I slide my hand over his, running my finger over the veins, a spate of nerves reappearing briefly in my chest. But fuck them. Fuck those nerves. I shed them like I do in games—there's no place for nerves in my world. "I want to again."

"You do?" His voice sounds raspy.

I swallow, then nod. "I do. With you. Only with you. It felt fucking incredible." I run my thumb along his knuckles. "But I don't think it was just the physical."

"It wasn't . . ." he says.

I have to finish the thought. I'm the one who set that rule— of how we would be in the bedroom.

I required control.

I've needed control in the bedroom because it gave me control of my identity, control over how I was seen, some kind of control over my career.

But I don't need to control everything with Dean, and there's one reason for that. "No. It wasn't just physical. It's .

. ." I stop, breathe in, dig deep into my fears, but face them anyway, speaking from the heart. "It's because I trust you."

He turns his hand over and holds mine. "You should trust me."

I do. More than I expected to. And it feels damn good. "So what are we going to do about it?"

Dean's lips quirk up. "Of your newfound interest in switching?" He grins wickedly. "Explore the fuck out of it."

I laugh, shaking my head. "Dickhead."

"You're so sweet, Fitz. Don't let anyone tell you you're not sweet. Because you're the sweetest."

"Switching is easy. I'm talking about the *big* issue." I gesture broadly, like that can encompass the endless miles between London and New York. "The nearly four-thousand-mile thing. Because that's the real problem with your proposed cure for my new affinity for switching," I say, then take another bite of this decadent meal. "Also, dude, you can cook."

"Thank you." Dean takes a bite too, then finishes before he adds, "And it's three thousand, four hundred, and fifty-nine miles. To be precise."

I murmur my appreciation for his due diligence, then do my favorite imitation of him. "Is that so?"

"And about six hours and fifty minutes by plane," he adds.

I set down my fork, raise my coffee cup, and take a long drink, then give an appreciative hum. "Someone has been doing research."

"You said it yourself. I'm the thinker."

"Did you make a pros and cons list too?" I return to my breakfast, but as I lift a forkful of strawberries, I have the strangest sensation—sort of like déjà vu, but not quite. It feels like I'm remembering something that is *going* to happen. Or rather, that I can start to see it lying ahead, like when I envision the trajectory of objects on the ice.

"Sometimes I make pros and cons lists," Dean answers. His voice is distant as my mind latches onto this image. It's hard to make out—the picture is hazy around the edges—but it feels like something I want.

I shake my head, trying to make sense of my brain. "Do you ever have forward vu?"

"Come again?"

I make a rolling *stay with me here* gesture. "Like déjà vu, but for something that's going to happen."

His brow furrows. "That's a premonition. Are you having premonitions?" He sounds concerned.

I shake my head adamantly. I probably sound crazy. "No. It was more like a feeling, a sensation of something that *could* happen."

His voice goes serious. "And you felt it just now?"

"Yeah, I did."

He simply nods and takes another bite. "Interesting."

"Why is that interesting?" The question sounds more defensive than I intended.

He laughs lightly, then sets down his fork. "Fitz, you brought it up. I'm simply remarking that it's interesting."

I scratch my jaw, trying to sort out these nascent ideas, these stick figure sketches in my head. "Yeah, sorry, babe. I think I'm just distracted. The flight and all. My mind is kind of like a train station right now."

"Understandable."

I return to the important issue, since I want some clarity before I go. I *need* it. "Did you make a pros and cons list for us?" I ask, my stomach flipping a little with nerves. Because I want him to have found all the pros. I want him to tell me he'll do a long-distance thing, even though I *don't* want that at all with him.

That's the irony of this unworkable sitch with Dean.

I want all of him, and I don't know how to be content with whatever scraps I can scavenge.

I'm an *all-in* kind of guy. A *go for it* person.

Don't do anything halfway when you can give 110 percent. That's how I've been my whole life. It's what I had to do for my mom when my dad died. Maybe not right away, maybe not even for a few years. But once I was a teenager, once I heard from enough coaches that I had a shot at the NHL, I knew I had to give every ounce of blood, sweat, tears, luck, and talent to hockey.

So I did.

That drive brought me where I am today—a place where I can finally make a difference for my mom.

Where I can be the man of the family.

I *know* how to do that. I've trained my entire life to give my all.

But to give only some? Sparing a bit of myself when we manage to make our schedules line up? I don't know how to do that.

Except I've got to figure it out. Dean's worth it.

Maybe pros and cons are the way to start. As I stand and clear the plates, I say, "Tell me about your list, babe."

"Here's a hint." His English accent sounds a little melancholy as he joins me in the kitchen. "It's all cons, except for one thing."

My stomach dips in fear as I brace myself for the cons. "Give me the bad news first." I set the dishes in the sink then turn to face him.

Dean moves next to me, jerking me close. "It's a lot easier if I tell you the pro."

The pro.

Only one damn thing.

I have a sinking feeling I know where this talk is going.

We are going nowhere, a plane sputtering out of the sky.

I steel myself for rejection. "What's the pro?"

He slides his arms around my waist, probably to lessen the blow, as he says, "You're the only pro."

That should make me happy, but it doesn't. "Dean," I say, and I hate that I sound enamored of him. I sound like a guy with an unrequited crush.

"Fitz . . ."

"Are you . . .?" I don't even know how to say it. *Ending things?* Because *things* were always ending, and I've got to remember that.

But yesterday, last night—it felt like a new start, like another chance to figure out how to do this.

He presses a tender kiss to my lips. "No. I'm not ending things," he says, following my thoughts. Then he pulls back. "I've been thinking though."

My stomach roils again, and I need to get myself under control because feeling this way is foolish. I knew a split was coming. Knew my time with him was ending. But the end, it fucking hurts.

I clench my teeth.

I will keep my shit together.

"I think you need to focus on training camp," he says, calm but not clinical. He sounds like he's been thinking on this for a while, turning this over in his head.

"I know. I will. But what are you getting at?"

Dean clears his throat. "On Sunday, you told me your job was the most important thing to you. The last thing I want is for you to go home and lose sight of that. You said you had this pact with your teammates because you came close last year but didn't make it. You said your teammates are depending on you."

"They are. That's all true."

Dean runs his hand along my face, and I move with his hand, like a cat seeking him out. A desperate fucking cat. That's my fate. God help me.

"So let them depend on you." His voice is kind, loving, even. "I think you need to focus on that when you return home, and not on me. You and me—we don't know how to do halfway. If we start calling or texting or talking every day, that'll knock you out of whack."

I furrow my brow. "You're saying this for my benefit?" Then I put my finger on what this sounds like. It sounds like a breakup line.

But he doesn't look at me like he's handing me a line.

"I care for you too much to be the reason you're distracted. And I think that would happen right now."

"You want to cool it?"

"I don't *want* to," he says, holding my face. "But I don't want to stand in the way of your career. Your success." He offers me a small smile. "Besides, I know you. You'll call me in a few days. We'll talk, we'll dirty talk, we'll video chat, and we'll be getting each other off in no time."

I groan. "You realize that sounds red-hot?"

"I know. That's the issue. We'll combust. But you made your pact for a reason. You need to honor it. I want you to honor it." His hand slides down to my shoulder, along my arm. "I'm not going to be with anyone else. I can't."

"I can't either."

Dean squeezes my arm. "Do you get it? Why I'm saying this?"

I swallow roughly, getting it. "I do. You'll be all I think about, and I need to focus on the ice, on the game plan." I draw a deep breath. "But what then? After the season starts?"

"Maybe when you've done your thing, whatever this pact thing is and however it works, then call me. Text me. FaceTime me. We'll do . . . *something.*"

I manage a sliver of a smile. "Something?"

My guy roams a hand over the fabric of my shirt. "Something good."

I can smile again. The prospect of his *something, someday* is enough to keep me going. "Yeah? You mean it?"

Dean pushes his pelvis against mine. "Of course I mean it, dickhead."

I laugh and slide a hand around the back of his head. "You sure?"

"Yes. And I don't know what happens then, so don't ask me now. I don't have a crystal ball. All I know is I care about your career and your job and your family, and I don't want to be the reason you can't focus, or that your teammates toilet paper your locker or whatever it is that you guys do."

I smirk. "You think they'd TP my locker if I got distracted by the sexy British bartender I left behind? That's what you think they'd do?"

He shrugs. "I honestly have no clue."

I laugh. "Maybe they'd throw eggs at my car?"

"You have a car?"

"No. I don't have a car." I clear my throat. "They won't TP my locker, or throw eggs at my car, or pour glue in my shampoo. They'd do something else if I was all fucked in the head."

"What would they do?"

"My captain would give me words. He'd sit me down, tell me to focus. To get my head out of my ass. He'd tell me to do more passing drills. More shooting drills. More one-on-one drills."

"That last one sounds fun," Dean says, wiggling his brows.

"One-on-one drills with you and me sounds hella fun." I cup his cheeks. "I thought you were ending this."

Dean shakes his head. "No. I don't think I can." He lets out a long exhale. "But, Fitz, I still don't have any idea how to make us work. I have no more answers today than I did yesterday. All I know is you need to focus on your job for the next thirty days or however long, and I think you can do a better job at that if you're not doing naked stripteases for me over FaceTime."

I let out a low rumble, then tug on the waistband of his jeans. "Let me show you my striptease right now."

And that's what I do.

* * *

Still, the morning marches to a cruel end.

I pack my bag, zip it up, and unplug my phone from the wall where it charged this morning.

A message from Ransom sits on the screen.

Ransom: You ready? You better be. We're gonna bring it.

I send a quick reply.

Fitz: Let's fucking do this.

Ransom: World domination, bro. World domination.

Fitz: Nothing less.

I close the thread, one more reminder that Dean is right. Best to shut this thing with him down for now. For a while.

Fifteen minutes before I need to go, Emma rings the buzzer. She comes upstairs, where I give her a hug and tell her I expect regular updates.

"You'll get more than you can handle," she says.

"I can always handle your updates," I tell her.

She stands on tiptoes to give Dean a kiss on the cheek. "I'll see you around."

"Be sure to come by some time," he says.

"And let me know if you ever want to go to the National Gallery."

I roll my eyes, cutting in. "Are you guys trying to kill me here? You're making me ridiculously jealous."

"Don't worry. We'll livestream the Van Goghs for you," she teases.

"It's not the Van Goghs I want to see," I tell her.

She shoots me a *duh* look. "I know, James. I know."

We walk out together, the three of us, and as I wait for the Lyft to Heathrow, I walk with Emma a few feet away. "Thanks again," I tell her.

She smiles. "I had a feeling about the two of you."

"You were right," I say.

"Call me when you figure out what you're going to do."

"There's nothing to do."

"Like I said. I'll be here."

She waves goodbye and leaves, and I return to Dean and the Lyft that's pulled up.

I nod toward the car. "Come with me to the airport."

"Ah, the old airport goodbye."

"Give me the airport goodbye, babe."

"As if I'd do anything else."

He locks the door to his flat, and we get in the car to head to Heathrow.

37

DEAN

We stand in front of security at the airport. The man I just spent the most fantastic six days of my life with is boarding a plane in less than an hour. He is leaving, and this is ending, and my stupid heart aches.

It aches more than I ever imagined it would.

If this is heartbreak, I don't ever want to feel it again.

Goodbyes are awful.

He's inches away from me, looking somehow even more handsome than the night he walked into my bar. Because now I know him. I can see beyond that cocky grin. Beyond that swagger. Beyond all that charm. I've seen inside his heart, and I know how incredibly big it is. He gives me this look, a look that seems to say everything. *This sucks, why am I leaving, why aren't you coming with me, why can't I see you every single day?*

A look that says *What's really happening in a month? What will things be like after this . . . pause?*

Part of me thinks maybe I'm reading too much into his expression. But part of me knows that's exactly what's on his mind.

"I guess this is it," I say.

Fitz grabs my face with both hands, pulls me close, and rests his forehead against mine. "You have no idea how much I'm going to miss you," he whispers, all rough and packed with emotion.

As I loop my arms around his neck, I answer him. "No, you're wrong. I have every idea because I feel the same."

He presses his lips to mine, a soft, poignant kiss that sends sparks through me. I try to make light of it. "Trying to get me aroused at Heathrow?"

He growls in my ear. "This is so much more than arousal, and you know it."

There's no point fighting it. No point denying it. "I know, Fitz. I know."

He inches back so he can meet my gaze. "You know what this is." It's a statement, not a question. His lips curve up in a helpless grin, his expression sad. "I fell in love with you."

My eyes float closed for a second, as I absorb the intensity of his words, the weight of them, the strength of them. I let them weave their way through me, filling every corner, making me feel alive in a way I have never felt before.

Nothing has come close.

No one.

Ever.

And now I feel it everywhere, and he's leaving.

I open my eyes, part my lips, and grab a fistful of his shirt in frustration. "I can't believe you did this."

His lips crook up in a curious grin. "Did what? Fell in love with you?"

I tighten my grip on his shirt. "Walked into my bar, walked into my life, walked into my fucking heart. I can't believe you did this to me. And now you're leaving."

Fitz smiles at me again. "Why does it bother you so much, Dean?"

He knows what he's doing. He's goading me.

Fitz has always been the one to go first. Fitz has always been the one to open his big heart to me. Damn him for doing that. Damn him for making it so hard to say goodbye.

Letting go of his shirt, I grab the back of his head, my jaw tight, my body tense from the horrible reality of him leaving. *"Because,"* I answer. "Because you know what happened. You know because you feel it too."

There's the intensity in his gaze that must drive him on the ice. He brings that to this moment as he demands, "Tell me."

I'm stoic for a moment. Maybe if I keep this truth inside, if I keep my feelings to myself until he gets on the plane, I won't stumble and screw up my whole damn life.

I now get why I've avoided love.

I understand why I chose men like Dylan, guys I knew on some level I'd never be serious with. If I never got serious, I'd never face *this*.

And now, I am.

Now I'm taking an absolute walloping because I fell in love against all my better judgment.

Against my brain.

Against my rules.

Against my pros and cons.

Once I say it, I don't know how I'll be able to stop myself from getting on that plane with him, stowing away in his luggage, and doing whatever it takes.

That's the problem. I want him so much. Too damn much. I've never been able to resist him, even though I should have, even though I know what giving in can lead to.

And now, I don't think I can resist telling him the truth.

More than that, I don't want to. In spite of my fears, I want him to know what he's done to me.

I slide my hand along the back of his neck, tugging him close. "I fell in love with you too," I whisper.

The second the words leave my mouth, he crushes my lips in the most wonderful and terrible kiss of my life. Wonderful because it's with the man I love, and terrible because he's leaving.

"I have to go," he says, when he breaks off.

"I know."

"I'll be thinking of you the whole time."

I shake my head. "Don't think of me. Just do your job."

"Can't help it." He taps his temple. "You're here." Then his chest. "And here."

I give him my most wry grin. "The feeling is mutual."

He holds his hands out wide. "I fucking love you. That is all." He heads through security, looking back at me nearly every second.

I don't move. I stand, hands in my jeans pockets, eyes on that man as he sets his carry-on on the conveyor belt, as he walks through the scanner, then as he grabs his bag on the other side.

Then, one last raise of his hand. I do the same.

I watch him walk around the corner and out of sight, where he'll board a plane for America, where he'll return to his busy life, to three games a week, to constant travel, to life on the road, to teammates who need him, to family who depend on him.

And I go back to my little corner of this city I love.

The only place I've ever lived.

The only home I've ever known.

And it's a little bit grayer without him.

NEXT WEEK

Also known as misery.

38

FITZ

I am spent. Officially drained. Thoroughly exhausted.

But it's a good kind of tired, one I feel deep in my bones and in every damn muscle in my body. It's the tired that comes from sprints and more sprints and then still more.

From drills, to work with rookies, to time in the conditioning room doing cardio, weights, and more weights.

I only break for meals and to see my teammates and catch up with Logan, Summer, and Oliver.

All the following week, I do everything to stay in the zone.

Our latest session is open to fans, and when we finish up, a handful of peeps cheer as we head off the ice.

Ransom nods to the folks at the edge of the rink. "Ready to sign some shirts and pucks?"

"Always," I say, knocking fists with my teammate.

A bunch of us skate over to the stands, chatting up the superfans, which anyone who comes to training camp absolutely is. A brunette is particularly chatty with Ransom, while an older dude who used to coach talks up the goalie. A guy my age asks me to sign his jersey.

Finally, there's only a mom and her kid left, waiting for Ransom and me.

"You two are my two favorite players." The kid is maybe twelve, with a mouthful of braces.

"You have excellent taste, then," Ransom says, signing a hockey stick for him.

"You like to play?" I ask, as I take my turn to sign.

The kid nods. "I do. I can't decide if I like defense, though, or being a forward."

"Being a forward," Ransom says in a stage whisper. "It's the best. You get to score points."

I shake my head. "Defense, man. It's the way to go. You get to stop the other team. And hello, you get to score now and then too."

The kid shrugs and smiles. "But I also like basketball. Maybe I can play both sports. Thanks, Ransom. Thanks, James."

He turns to leave, his mom tucking an arm around him as she guides him out of the rink.

"'Play both sports.' It all seems so possible," I say, drifting off for a moment, thinking of other possibilities, never far off in my mind.

"Dude, are you going all philosophical on me right now?"

"What?" I ask, distracted.

Ransom shoots me an exaggerated, wary look. "You sound . . . weirdly contemplative."

I laugh once, then stop. It's harder to laugh these days. What the hell? Is that a by-product of falling hard? There ought to be a warning pamphlet for love—side effects include pangs in your heart, a runaway mind, and finding very little funny anymore.

"I feel weirdly contemplative now and then," I admit.

"There's only one cure for that."

* * *

The cure is barbecue.

It's messy and delicious and completely distracting.

Until Ransom finishes his story about what he did this summer—going zip-lining in Costa Rica, followed by cliff diving, then parachuting.

I snap my gaze up from the plate, setting down the rib, then wiping the napkin across my mouth. "You went zip-lining *and* cliff diving *and* parachuting? Isn't that—oh, I don't know—against your contract?"

"No. My contract allows it," he says, mocking me.

I flip him the bird. "Asshole."

"Dude, what is your story? I made all that up to see if you were paying attention. Are you ever going to tell me about your summer vacay and why you're so fucking distracted all the time?"

I furrow my brow. "I'm not distracted. I'm killing it on the ice. I guess you're just jealous." But even that one little word—*jealous*—reminds me of Dean. The way we teased each other over jealousies. Him saying he'd be jealous over guys hitting on me, and then me busting his chops over the waitress who hit on us.

"You're fine on the ice, man," Ransom says. "That's not even what I'm talking about."

"Then what are you talking about? Try English. Because you're making zero sense."

He arches a brow, pointing his thumb back in the direction of the rink. "That guy who wanted you to sign his jersey? Before the kid?"

"Yeah?"

"He was hitting on you. So was the waiter at the burger joint last night. You didn't even notice."

What? This is news to me. "The waiter too? And the guy today?"

He rolls his eyes. "Yes, like this is a surprise. You get hit on almost as much as I do."

"More," I mutter.

"Whatever. But now you're off in la-la land, and hanging out with you is killing my mojo with the ladies, since you aren't pairing up anymore."

"Aww. I'm so sorry you can't score a date. Have you considered looking in the mirror and maybe getting a face-lift?"

He nods appreciatively, clucking his tongue. "That's what I'm talking about. That's the first joke you've cracked in a week. What's the deal? You're kind of . . . joyless. And that's on top of how you don't notice the dudes anymore."

"Well, hello. The pact?" I say, pointing to the obvious explanation, even though it's not the reason.

"Yes. Same pact, bro, but I still notice the babes. I might not *do* anything about it, but I sure as shit notice them." He shoots me a *what's up* stare. "What's your deal? Did you go to England and fucking fall in love?"

I freeze. Is it that obvious?

Do I say something to my bud? Ransom and I get grub, play ping pong with the guys, and shoot the shit on the team plane, occasionally mentioning a hookup, but we don't do deep-dive relationship talks. Never have. He hasn't been in one for as long as I've known him. A woman broke his heart once upon a time, and he's been devoutly single since then.

But now, we're charting new friendship territory, and I'm not entirely sure how to tread. I've only ever talked about Dean to Emma, but she's a continent away.

I'm not entirely sure what to say to Ransom, so I try to deflect. "Why are you asking?"

"Because you might be a focused Zen master in the rink, but off the ice, you're kind of lost." He parks his elbows on the table. "You okay, man?"

I heave a sigh. He's right. I know he's right. I might be in the zone physically, but mentally I am elsewhere. I have been since I left London six days ago. Even if Ransom and I haven't been *let's make a quilt and talk* buds, maybe that's only because we've never needed to.

Pretty sure I need to now. "Yeah, I did fall in love," I say heavily.

His jaw hangs open. He lets out the most shocked *whoa* in the universe.

"No fucking way!"

"Yes, way."

"No kidding?"

I hold up a hand like I'm taking an oath. "It's all true."

He offers a fist for knocking. "Knock me, bro."

"Not sure this is a knock-me thing," I remark, but I knock anyway, since you don't leave a teammate hanging.

"Fuck yes, it is. The player falls hard." He leans back in his chair, beckoning me to serve it up. "So, what's the story? You keeping it wrapped up till our pact ends and then . . .?"

"And then what?" I ask. "He lives in London. I live here. There's not really much to do."

The waitress swings by and asks if we need anything, smiling at Ransom. He says no, but when she leaves, he nods in her direction. "And if you're not going to see this guy again, does that mean you're gonna get back on the market after the season starts?"

I cringe, shaking my head. "God no."

"Dude, you have it bad," he says, and the look he gives me tells me I'm a sorry-ass lovesick bastard right now.

"No shit."

* * *

I know how to follow orders. I take them seriously. I abide by them. So I'm a very good boy at resisting talking to Dean.

At avoiding his photos? Not so much.

That night when I'm alone, I crank up the tunes in my place, take a long, hot shower—during which I entertain *all* the thoughts of him, because that's what I do in showers—then dry off and flop down on my bed.

My big, empty bed.

I turn my gaze to the unoccupied side of this vast California king, wishing I could see him sliding up against me.

Or the more likely scenario is me tackle-hugging him and making him snuggle with me after a good, long fuck.

A shudder wracks my body at the thought.

I grab my phone and click on a folder.

If Google could report me for looking at pics, I'd have been handcuffed six million times already.

And I have no regrets.

I click on my favorite—the one at Tower Bridge—first. I smile as the memory shimmies in front of me. That was the day I knew we could sort shit out, because we did that during our first fight.

Then the picture at the Millennium Bridge. That was when I knew I could always have fun with him, because we had a blast.

I slide my thumb over another. It's the picture I took the last night there, at the sidewalk bar, drinking brews. He gave me the most smoldering look, a look that said *I want you so much.*

"I feel the same, babe," I say to the image. "I feel the same."

Great. This is what I do now. Talk to pics of the guy I wish were my boyfriend.

But it's not that red-hot desire that makes me flip through the shots again.

It's the other part. The part that Ransom saw.

The *I have it bad* part.

Because I absolutely do.

39

DEAN

My dad pats the back of the finished chair. "Admit it. I missed my calling in furniture restoration."

"It's never too late to start a new career, even in retirement," I say, but my voice sounds a little hollow.

He gestures to the chair's new home across from the couch. "Maybe I could be an interior designer. The chair looks good here, doesn't it?"

I glance around his flat, pointing to the corner by the window. "Better over there. Let's move it."

We move the chair by the window, and sunlight streams in over its whitewashed wooden arms, the perfect place to sit.

It's Wednesday afternoon. We finished the chair last weekend.

That . . . passed the time.

It was . . . somewhat enjoyable.

I just wish someone had given me the memo that missing the man you love sucks.

But I guess some things you have to learn on your own.

I stare out the window, watching the traffic trudge by, checking out the passersby on the pavement below.

Plenty of tourists, from the looks of them—white trainers and khaki shorts, some wearing shirts from their favorite sports teams. What's that one? I peer at a cluster of college students walking by, laughing, taking selfies. A blonde in the group wears a jersey. A hockey jersey. I want to shout at her, *Hey, I know someone on that team.*

I don't.

Instead, I pinch the bridge of my nose, riding a wave of self-loathing at the idiocy of feeling connected to a random fan on the street who's sporting a jersey for some other player on Fitz's team.

I've officially hit a new level of pathetic.

Or maybe I'm pissed at myself for recognizing his team colors, for having checked them out online. What is wrong with me? Turning around, I drag my hand over my face.

My dad stares at me, sympathy in his dark eyes. "Let's get out of here. Grab a beer."

The specifics of the beverage suggestion do not go unnoticed. "What? No offer to get a cup of tea, old man?"

"You don't look like you need a cuppa. You look like you need a drink."

"A stiff drink."

"Okay, so maybe not a beer. How about a shot?"

I manage a mirthless laugh. "Getting shots with my dad. So this is how it goes."

"Could be worse."

I'm sure it could, but at the moment it's hard to see how.

We hit a nearby pub, an old-time place that's so London, I feel like I walked into a movie set. Everything is wood and dark, which seems fitting.

We order a round, and Dad lifts his glass to toast. "Let's

drink to . . ." He pauses, glancing around the pub, and I can tell he's hunting for something hopeful. Something to cheer up my sorry arse. Perhaps he finds it. "Let's drink to this pub."

And it works. I do laugh at the ordinariness of the toast. "And why are we drinking to a pub?"

He scans the joint like he's studying every angle. "This is very England."

"Well, we are in England." Those words taste a little bitter, a little less sweet than they would have a week ago.

"And this place, it feels like home," he says, lifting his shot glass then knocking it back. I do the same, letting the tequila burn, as tequila does.

I make note of the pub's pool table in the back, the trivia games too, and all the endless taps. It's so standard London it's beyond standard. "Yeah, it feels like home," I say, echoing his sentiment, wishing that home could comfort me.

* * *

When we leave, I'm a little drunker than when I went in. So is my dad.

Okay, we're buzzed. Let's just call a spade a spade.

"So, are you going to see your lady friend now?" I ask as night falls over the city.

"Maybe I am. Maybe I'm not," he says, but the grin gives him away.

"You are indeed a scoundrel." I squeeze his shoulder. "What am I going to do with you? Driving all the ladies crazy at such an old age."

"Just one lady," he says.

I shoot him an *I gotcha* grin. "So you and Penny are a thing?"

He laughs. "Seems we are."

I wag a finger at him. "It's about time, old man. It's about time."

"Yes. Yes, it is."

While we wander down the street, his phone buzzes. He snags it from his pocket, slides open a text, smiles, and taps out a reply.

Jealousy seizes me like a monster, thrashing inside me. I'm envious of my own damn father for texting his lady friend. I draw a deep breath, trying to settle the dragon, trying to be happy for my dad.

Because I am happy for him, just sad for me.

He nods to a side street. "I'm going to take off."

"To see Penny," I say, forcing a smile that's mostly legitimate.

His eyes twinkle. "I am. She makes me happy." He draws me in for a quick embrace. "Good to see you. Text me tomorrow."

"I will." I watch him as he heads down the street.

Is he . . . whistling?

He's bloody whistling.

My dad is whistling a happy tune, and I am a sorry sack, getting pissed on a Wednesday night and heading home alone.

* * *

Once I'm inside my flat, the door groans closed, and the emptiness enrobes me.

I turn to a playlist, but as I flick through a few songs, I decide I hate them all now.

I think, as I flop down on my couch, that I actually hate everything.

Opening my text app, I scroll through the names on my

recent threads.

Maeve, telling me about the jukebox she's been eyeing.

Maeve: I'll add all your favorite tunes to it!

Then Taron, inviting me to check out a street fair this weekend with him and his boyfriend. I actually groan out loud. Not that I don't like hanging with him and his guy. But I don't want to go to a fucking street fair, because nothing could top the last one.

I find a note from Naveen next.

Naveen: This is not a drill. We are going to this new Greek place Sunday. The whole crew. Making rezzies. I know you have the night off. You're going to be there. No excuses.

Sam's text is next.

Sam: Round of pool tomorrow?

That's all for new messages.

None from Fitz—not that I was expecting any.

Still.

With my chest feeling hollow and my apartment

sounding far too empty, I stick my finger in the fire. I click on the last note from him, the one he sent me when he got on the plane last week.

A picture of him in his seat.

Fitz: Thought you might enjoy this for your "wank bank." It's me in first class. You'd look good in first class, babe. Also, I fucking love you.

As my chest aches, I run my thumb over his words, then the image. I've read it ten thousand times. I'll read it ten thousand more.

Then, my own reply.

Dean: Keeping it. Definitely keeping it. Also, I fucking love you too.

I want to reply, to add a new message, to start this up again. But this is where the thread ends.

I let the phone fall to the floor with a dull *thunk*.

A WEEK LATER

Also known as the time I figure it out.

40

FITZ

Fourteen days.

I must be made of iron. I've lasted fourteen whole days without talking to Dean.

Or texting Dean.

I killed it in training camp. I'm crushing it in the preseason games, and I am feeling good. I tell Ransom as much when we leave through the player's entrance after our second win.

"Guess it's working. Our pact," he says.

"Seems to be," I add, then tell him I'll catch him tomorrow, since my agent is waiting for me.

I jog over to Haven, give her a kiss on the cheek, and grab a Lyft across town with her.

"You were on fire tonight," she remarks.

"That's my job," I tell her.

She pats my thigh. "I like it when you do your job."

I laugh. "Because when I do my job, I make you money."

She smiles wickedly. "Exactly. But also because it makes you happy. You look happy."

"Hockey makes me happy," I say, but it's not the only

thing. Something else does. Rather, *someone* else, and I wish I were seeing him tonight.

I try to shake off thoughts of Dean so I can stay present. Haven deserves that much.

The Lyft lets us off in Chelsea at a restaurant she picked. "I've been dying to try this place. I hear great things about it," she says as we head into the swank eatery. "The curry is supposed to be amazing."

That's all it takes. One stinking mention of a meal I had with Dean, and my mind trots back to London. I picture him there, wondering if he's out having dinner with friends on a Thursday night, if he's laughing, smiling, happy.

I hope he is.

But a part of me hopes he's not.

Which is terrible to say, but honest.

That I would understand because that feels like my life right now.

Not quite happy. A little bit empty.

I should be having fun with Haven. She's a goddess and a brilliant agent. But all I can see is the calendar. All I can *feel* is anticipation and the wish that time would accelerate. In one more week, the regular season starts. If we kick ass, I can call Dean. See Dean somehow. Have that *something.*

"And I thought it'd be perfect for you. Since you always like to try new food," Haven says as we reach the table.

She might have said something on the way. I have no idea what she's been talking about.

After we order, I do my best to focus on Haven and the details of the sponsorship deal she inked for me.

But when Sam Smith comes on the sound system, I don't know that I can pay attention to anything with "Dancing with a Stranger" burning a hole in my mind. It's on my goddamn playlist for Dean, the one I made when he came over to my hotel that first night.

And I can remember—my God, I can see it so damn clearly—the way I crushed his lips, the way he said *Make it last*, the way we did.

We made everything last.

And hell, there has to be a way to make *us* last.

I drag a hand through my hair, trying to slam the door closed on all these images of him. But I can't. I just can't, and I don't want to.

"You like this song?" I ask Haven, my voice a little hoarse.

She tilts her head. "Yeah. I do. What about you?"

"It's great. I love it." I let out a deep sigh, and then hold my hands out wide, admitting defeat before I even start. "Haven, I have no idea what you've been talking about."

"You don't?"

I shake my head. "No clue. This song, this place, everything here. It's all making me think of . . ."

She nods sagely and reaches out her hand, squeezing mine. "I've noticed you've been a little distant. And 'distant' is not a word I'd ever use to describe James Fitzgerald. What's going on? Do you need to talk?"

The song floats through the restaurant, the chorus about not wanting to be alone tonight, and I swear it's mocking me. It's taunting me. And it's tempting me too.

Then, in a flash of brilliance, I have an idea that snaps all my attention back to her.

"Would you be able to help me with something?"

"Anything."

I tell her what I need, and she nods approvingly. "All in a day's work as an agent."

She grabs her phone, we hatch a plan, then place a rush order. It'll be in London Saturday afternoon.

41

DEAN

The Greek place is great and wholly necessary.

Spending time with my friends roots me in London when parts of me—namely my heart—are elsewhere.

I don't tell them as much, but I'm pretty sure they sense it.

After that dinner, Naveen declares he's making a reservation for a sushi restaurant the next weekend. I spend the week counting down because it gives me something to do. It gives me a goal.

Time with them distracts me from thinking of Fitz. It's the only thing that keeps my mind off him.

When Saturday rolls around, sixteen days after Fitz departed, we all go to lunch. We laugh and talk, and the entire time I keep thinking what a lucky fucker I am to have such great friends.

I have to keep on living. Keep on enjoying my life as best I can.

After we finish, Taron taps my shoulder, his eyes wide and curious. "So, whatever happened with that guy?"

Before I can answer, he shouts, "*Ouch*," his face twisting in pain, like someone just stepped on his shoe.

Laughing, I glance at Maeve across the table. "Did you just ram your heel on Taron's foot?"

"You evil, evil woman," Taron hisses at her. "That smarts."

Maeve slices an imaginary knife across her throat, staring sharply at Taron. "We're not bringing him up."

I lean back in the chair, cross my arms, and regard her with a smirk. "So, this," I say, gesturing in a circle to the whole table, "is part of some plan you cooked up to induce amnesia in me?"

"No. We're just trying to keep you happy," she says, squaring her shoulders.

"A plan. Like I suspected," I say, having caught her in the act.

"He's onto us, guys," Sam chimes in, then stares at me with inquisitive eyes. "But the more important thing is—is it working?"

"Fabulously," I say, deadpan. "Also, thanks for making me your charity case. Appreciate it."

"Oh, stop," Maeve says. "We love you, and we want you to be happy here."

"I am happy here. I promise. And I'll stay happy as long as people aren't constantly asking about him."

"Speaking of never bringing up the NHL all-star," Sam says, "he's killing it in preseason."

"Is that so?" I pick up my drink like it's the most fascinating concoction in the world.

"His stats are great. His gameplay is top-notch," my American friend adds, then rattles off stats I already know by heart. Points, goals, assists.

"Why are you smiling like you have a secret?" Maeve asks me with narrowed eyes.

"No reason," I say, trying to rein in a grin.

"You are a certified fanboy," Sam says, wagging a finger at me. Then he leans toward Maeve, a little closer than I've seen him get to her before. "I think your best friend just developed an interest in hockey."

And she inches closer to him too. "I think he did."

Taron's jaw drops as he gawks. "You, of all people, know hockey now?"

"A little."

Sam points at me. "Do you know how many assists Fitzgerald had last night?"

I hold up a finger. A little sheepishly, but a little proudly too. I am proud of my man.

"Fitzgerald is very good," Sam adds, then looks at Maeve. "And it seems Collins is still quite taken with his American man."

Maeve sets her chin in her hands and bats her lashes at me. "Yes, it seems you are, Dean."

I shrug, *what can you do*–style. "Well, it's not like the common cold. It wasn't going to go away after a week." *Or at all*, I add silently.

Sam shakes his head. "No. It's not going to go away when you research him, Dean. But maybe it *shouldn't*."

"I for one think you should get on a plane tonight," Taron offers.

I shake my head. "That won't happen." But the idea is insanely tempting.

"He might be your portobello mushroom sandwich," Anya says.

Maeve stabs the table. "Dean, why don't you call him?"

"You know why," I tell her. She's privy to the details of what Fitz and I decided the morning he left.

Anya rolls her eyes. "Enough of this nonsense. Just send the gorgeous man a text. The night we met him, he looked at you like he was already falling in love with you," she says, and I have to hide a grin.

Maeve nods savagely. "Text him. I bet it'll make him incandescently happy."

When she puts it like that, there's no question. I do know a simple note from me would make him happy. I'm as sure of that as I am that the sun will rise tomorrow. I know Fitz. I know that man so well. It's heady to possess the power to make another person happy.

It's a gift, truly.

One that should be used with care.

But I'm not only doing this for him.

I'm doing it for me.

Making him happy makes me happy.

"Fine." I hold up my hands in surrender, and maybe I really am. But maybe that's what I need to be doing—surrendering to the grip the past has had on me, to the fear that I'll make the same mistakes.

Then letting go of everything past.

I take out my phone, open the last text thread, reading his words yet another time, then tap out a message.

Dean: Nice assist in the game yesterday.

In seconds, my phone buzzes.

Fitz: You watched my game? You have no idea how happy that makes me. Also, where are you? There's a delivery guy at your bar.

DEAN

Maeve's grin may never disappear.

"This is the best jukebox ever," she says, resting her cheek against the brand-new jukebox in The Magpie a half-hour later, stroking it, petting it. "And this makes our bar the best bar ever."

I stand back, surveying the scene, still amazed at what Fitz pulled off. He actually found the jukebox she wanted—the one I showed him at Coffee O'clock—ordered it, and sent it here via rush delivery. I was going to buy it for Maeve, but he beat me to it, doing something incredible for my friend.

"Why are you not on a plane right now to go see him?" Sam asks, flapping a hand in the direction of Heathrow.

"He's on the road tomorrow," I explain, still dazed from the enormity of this gesture. "You should know his schedule, since you're the hockey fanatic."

"Yeah, whatever. You're the hockey fanatic now. And more importantly, what are you going to do after that, Dean?"

"Yes, Dean. How about after that?" Maeve seconds.

"Guys, I need to sort things out," I add, but I'm grinning, and I can't stop, not at all and not when Maeve hits the first tune on the jukebox. Music fills the bar, and everything feels okay in the world again.

At least for now.

But most of all, I can't stop grinning because I know what I need to do now, and it's not hang out with my mates.

I step outside and call Fitz. He answers in less than a second.

"Hey you," he says.

The sound of his voice is like melting chocolate. "Hi. The jukebox is amazing. That's an incredible gift."

"I miss you," he says, cutting to the chase.

My stomach flips, and briefly, I lean against the brick wall of the bar so I don't stumble off the earth, pushed by this rush of emotions. "I miss you too."

"I miss you so damn much. And then when you sent that text just now, do you know how it made me feel?"

I step away from the bar, heading down the street, smiling. "How did it make you feel?"

"Like I knew how to be happy again." He sounds relieved, but his tone holds a tinge of sadness.

I wince, walking along the street. "I know the feeling," I say, an answering sadness in my voice. I don't want that to color our time talking, so I strip it away and laser in on something good. "So, you're playing great."

"I am."

"The pact is working."

"Maybe, or maybe we're just a good team. And hello, when did you become a hockey fan?"

"I've taken an interest in it lately."

"You researching hockey is hella hot, babe."

I turn the corner. "You know what else is *hella hot?*"

Fitz moans, all raspy and sexy. "Tell me."

"You, me, video chat. Are you home?"

"Yes."

"I'll be back to my flat in fifteen."

"Good, but let's keep talking now," Fitz says.

"Obviously. I'm not letting you go," I say.

"When you say that . . ."

"When I say *what*?" I tease. It's so easy to flirt with him, it's like we never hit pause.

His voice is rough and needy. "Do you know what it does to me when you say that?"

"Why don't you tell me?"

His answer comes in a long, appreciative rumble. "*Everything*. It does everything to me. Turns me on, makes me happy, all at once. But I think that's how I'd describe you."

I laugh lightly. "I turn you on and I make you happy?"

"Yes. You do. Now call me on video. I want to see your face as you walk home."

I give him what he wants. I want it too. I switch to a video call, and there Fitz is, looking so unbelievably handsome in—

"Are you wearing a fucking suit?"

Fitz wiggles his brows. "I am. Heading to a preseason game."

I shake my head in appreciation. "You look incredible," I say, drinking in how handsome he is in a tailored dark-blue suit, clearly custom-fitted, as well as a crisp shirt and light-green tie. "Mmm. That tie. If I were there, I would put it on you."

His lips curve up. "You would?"

"Drape it around your neck, line it up, loop the tail over . . ." I'm getting ridiculously aroused as I walk home, telling Fitz how I want to knot his tie. If I were to put on his tie, my hands would be on him. "Thread the fabric through, tighten the knot, and adjust it against your neck."

He breathes out hard, his chest rising and falling, his fingers tugging at his collar. "Look what you're doing to me. You're turning me on telling me how you're going to accessorize me."

"You're not the only one turned on." My whole body is buzzing. "I think all of South Bank must know I have a hard-on."

"Thanks for mentioning your dick. Now I'm rock hard too."

"You were pretty hard already, I bet."

"I was," Fitz says as he unknots the neckwear.

I blink, processing what he's doing. "Are you going to get undressed right now? While I'm on the street?"

"I am. I'm too worked up not to."

I glance around. "I'm almost home. Just wait. I can't have everyone seeing you."

"Better walk fast, babe."

"You dickhead," I say, but I'm smiling as I pick up the pace while he tosses the tie to the floor. Soon I'm at my building, up the stairs, in my flat, and slamming the door shut just as he parks himself on his couch, unzipping his trousers and taking out his cock.

I don't even make it to the couch. I'm standing against the door, one hand on the phone, the other unzipping my jeans. In seconds, I'm stroking my dick and watching Fitz take his length in his hand, and it all feels so damn right.

Like this is where I'm supposed to be.

Reconnecting with him.

"Look at you," he growls as he watches me jerking myself. "God, I missed that. I miss you. Want to have my hands on you right now, my mouth everywhere."

I'm already breathing hard, close to the edge, pleasure

blasting through my veins as I watch him shuttling his fist up and down his cock, sitting like a king on his couch in that suit, looking so powerful. "I want to get on my knees right now. Take you in my mouth," I tell him, my voice hoarse with desire.

"Yes, that. Fuck, I want that." His eyes squeeze shut, and he groans his release. The sight of him coming in his hand sends me over the edge as an orgasm rockets through my body.

I pant, groan, and slump against the door.

When I open my eyes, he's sitting there, smirking. "I'm going to call you right back. I need to put on a new shirt," he says.

"You do that."

I hang up, head to the bathroom in this hazy, heady state, wash my hands, clean up. I return to the living room, flop down on the couch, and grab the phone when he calls back.

On video again.

"Hi," I say.

He's in his bedroom, the phone balanced on the bureau, and he's sliding his strong arms into a crisp, starched shirt. "Do I look more civilized?"

"I don't know how I'd keep my hands off you if I saw you wearing a suit in person."

He finishes sliding the top shirt button into the hole. "Don't ever say such a horrible thing. Keep your hands off me? That's crazy talk."

"Utter insanity. My hands would be *all* over you," I say with a smile. I park a palm behind my head, and he knots his tie again.

His gaze snags on mine. "You like watching me get dressed, don't you?"

"I do," I say.

"If you were here, would you tie my tie for me?"

"I absolutely would. Though I make no promises about whether I would put it on or take it off."

"Babe, I would just love if you were here," he says, soft and tender.

"Me too. But you're playing great. I'm proud of you," I say.

"Thank you."

"How's your pact? Aren't you breaking it by talking to me?"

Fitz shrugs. "Maybe. Don't care anymore. Don't care at all."

"Thank you for the jukebox. That was incredible." He deserves a million thank-yous.

"Does she like it?"

"She loves it. You made a very happy Maeve," I say, as he finishes with the tie.

"I'm going to the arena now. Come with me?"

I laugh. "Sure, Fitz. Take me in the car."

"If you were here, would you come to my game?"

"I would."

Fitz leaves his place, locks the door, and heads down the hall to a mirrored brass elevator.

As he makes his way to the game, I talk to him the whole time—about New York and hockey and life and missing him and missing me. When he arrives at the arena, he asks, "Can I call you later?"

"You better."

He gets out of the car, thanks the driver, then says to me, "Dean . . ."

My name is full of heat and need and want. I say his back the same way. "Fitz."

He smiles at me. "I love you. That is all."

"I love you," I tell him, and when the call ends, I think I understand how it feels to be happy again.

The question is what to do about it.

* * *

We fall into a rhythm, just like we did when Fitz was here.

We talk at night—we FaceTime, we get off. We talk again in the morning. We text during the day.

He no longer cares about the pact.

He's playing great, and he says it's because I give him a good luck charm before every game. That's what he calls it now when I dirty talk him before he heads to the ice. It's our thing, and it works.

One night, after I tell him about a book I just finished, he says he has *special news* for me. He holds up a sheet of paper. "I asked the team doc to test for everything."

That gets my attention, and I sit up, peering more closely at the report. "That's excellent news."

"Clean bill of health, babe."

I stretch my arm to my bedside table, reach into a drawer, and show him mine, pressing it to the screen. "Same here."

His blue eyes darken, glimmering with desire and dirty deeds. "Can we go bare when I see you again?"

The prospect of doing that for the first time is insanely arousing. "Yes."

"I never have before. Not with anyone."

"Nor have I," I say.

The conversation quickly turns fantastically filthy as I tell him how good it's going to feel, and he shows me how much he likes it when I talk like that.

* * *

Soon, the season starts in earnest, and his team wins the first game. I call him briefly from the bar to congratulate him.

"Great game," I say when he answers.

"If you were here, you'd go out with us to celebrate, right?"

"Maybe," I say.

"You don't want to hang out with my teammates?"

I laugh. "No offense to your teammates, but it's you I want to see."

"That is the perfect answer," Fitz says, then he kisses the screen.

When he's home, he calls me again. The time difference works for us, since it's three in the morning for me and I'm getting into bed.

He asks about my night at the bar, and I tell him about all of the customers and how the jukebox has gone over. We do what we do—we talk.

"I have three days off," he says, so much hope in his voice. "Starting next Monday. Ten days from now."

I know what he's going to say next. I know he is forging full speed ahead. But I want to be the one to offer, rather than to be asked.

"I'll come see you," I say.

His grin is wider than it's ever been, his eyes brighter. "You will?"

"I will. I want to. More than anything."

"I'm getting you a ticket right now," Fitz says, walking through his apartment, presumably on the hunt for his laptop. "You cool with that? With me getting it? You better be, because I have a fuck-ton of miles, and I am spending them on you. Just say yes."

I remember that word. *Surrender.*

Is this what surrender is? Saying yes even when you worry you'll succumb to the mistakes of the past?

Maybe it is.

Maybe I don't know.

Maybe the past no longer matters.

All I know is it feels good to say yes to him. It always has. "I already said yes. It's kind of all I can say to you."

He punches the air. "I can't wait. I'm going to build a time machine so it can be next week."

"Don't be silly. All you need to do is learn how to apparate. That's a much more useful skill."

Fitz groans in happiness. "Do you know when I started to fall in love with you?"

I laugh. "No, I don't."

"When I learned you liked Harry Potter too. And now, do you know what that 'apparate' comment means?"

"What does it mean?"

"That I'm in love with you even more," he says.

When he says that, a warm, hazy feeling spreads over my body once again.

This is happiness, and I want it.

And I'm starting to see how it's possible to have it.

But I shouldn't make assumptions.

Pretty soon, though, I'm going to need to figure out how to take that step. I have a question to ask him, and I have to pose it carefully because any future happiness hangs on his answer.

THE NEXT DAY

Also known as the day I make my plans.

43

DEAN

The river is a comforting constant in London, and that's where I go with my dad on Saturday before I go into work.

We walk alongside the water, Dad reminiscing, me making plans.

"I used to bring you here when you were young," he says.

"So, like a few years ago," I tease.

"You're still mostly young."

"I'll be thirty-two soon. So old. Does that mean I should start doing that whole *it's my twenty-ninth birthday for the fourth year in a row* thing?"

He chuckles lightly, then sighs contentedly. "And you always loved it, coming to the river," he says, sliding back into nostalgia. "We were here every weekend when you were six, seven, eight."

"I did?" I ask, eager to hear more. I remember this, but not from his point of view.

"You just wanted to be near it. Of course, you had so much energy. You were always moving around. I had to run you like a dog along the water."

Rolling my eyes, I laugh. "Thanks, Dad."

"Your mum always came with us."

I nod. "I remember."

He stops as we near London Bridge, and he points to it. "The two of you would stand there on the bridge and make wishes over the water." There is no recrimination in his voice, only the warmth of memories.

"I remember that too," I say, a little softly, as the images of those moments play before my eyes. "I wonder what I wished for."

He sets his arm around my shoulders, his voice a little more serious. "I know what I wished for."

I look at him curiously, a strange lump forming in my throat. "What did you wish for?"

He squeezes my arm. "For you to be happy."

And that lump grows tighter, a knot now clogging my throat, and I don't know if I can speak. Or if I could, what I'd say. I bite the inside of my lip because I have a feeling about what's coming.

But he's undeterred, determined to keep on. "And I have a feeling that wish is coming true."

I furrow my brow, head pounding with the intense turn he's taken. I'm not sure I can handle it, so I try to sidestep. "I've been happy."

He shakes his head. "That's not what I'm talking about, and I think you know it."

I look at the water, thinking about certainty and uncertainty, things we know, things we don't know. The chances we take. This time, I face the reality of what I'm going to do head-on. "I know what you mean, Dad."

"Do you though?" he asks. This is a true father-son talk. No more cheek. No more sarcasm. It's all been washed away.

I exhale deeply. "I do know."

He doesn't let it stand at that—typical of him. He's fixed me with a stare that won't let go until he's sure I know my mind. "So, what are you going to do when you see him next week?"

"That's the question, isn't it?" I won't be able to dance around it either. I'll have to say more, say everything, when I see Fitz.

Determined, Dad waits for me, finally prompting, "Well? Are you going to go after your happiness?" His mouth relaxes into a tiny smile that grows when it spreads to his eyes, where it becomes a gleam of possibility. "Are you going to make those wishes come true?"

I draw a deep breath, then ask the hardest question of all, the one that weighs on me. "Will you be upset if I go?"

"No." He yanks me in for a huge hug. "And I'd be shocked if you didn't."

And then, a tear slides down his face, and somehow that makes the choice crystal clear.

A FEW DAYS LATER

Also known as the day I decide to speed up time.

44

FITZ

If I thought time passed slowly before, it's nothing compared to the snail's pace at which it moves now that I have a fixed date to anticipate.

Now that Dean has a ticket to New York.

I call him when I wake on Tuesday. "I'm going to see you in five days," I say when he answers. He's running in the park, looking sexy as hell in a T-shirt, the waistband of his running shorts visible at the edge of the screen.

"You are, and you better have your arse at the airport to pick me up, because I'll need my lips on you the second I'm on American soil."

I scoff. "Like I wouldn't pick you up. What do you take me for? Some guy who doesn't know how to romance his boyfriend?"

That's the first time I've called him that. *Boyfriend.* But it feels right.

Dean's quiet for a moment as he runs, staring at me on the phone instead of watching the trail. "I'm your boyfriend?"

"Yes," I say emphatically. "You are. Don't even try to get out of it."

"I wouldn't dare."

I stretch in bed, the sun beating through the window. "Do you want me to make plans to take you to . . . where was it you wanted to go? Empire State Building and Statue of Liberty?"

He laughs. "Do you think we're actually getting out of bed?"

Stroking my chin, I pretend to consider this, then answer truthfully. "No."

"You're very smart, Fitz." He peers a little more closely at me on the screen. "What are you up to today?"

"Early morning paintball. Feel free to shudder in horror."

Dean does.

"And then I'll work out with Ransom, grab some lunch. We don't have another game till—"

"Thursday."

I shake my head in appreciation as I swing my legs over the side of the bed. "You're going to need to wear my jersey next."

His eyes bug out, and the cackle that comes from his mouth is epic. Dean actually stops running, sets his hands on his thighs, and tries to stop laughing. When he looks at the phone again, he arches one brow. "In the span of two minutes, you've called me your boyfriend and said I need to wear your jersey?"

I shrug hopefully. "I'll take one out of two?"

"You can have the first. I'm not doing the second."

"Fine, be that way," I tease. "Are you working today?"

"Yes, I need to deal with the books this afternoon. Then I'll just be serving all night long."

"Call me later. I'm going to hit the shower."

"C'mon, take me into the shower," Dean says as he resumes his pace.

"You say that like I'd even consider anything else," I say, accepting his challenge as I angle the phone so he can see I sleep naked.

"Fitz," he says in a warning.

"What?" I play dumb as I stroll into the bathroom, giving him a full view of my morning semi.

Dean swivels the phone screen, showing me the scenery behind and beside him. "Do you not realize I'm in the park?"

I shrug as I reach the shower, stretch my free hand in, and turn it on. "Doesn't bother me."

He shakes his head. "Nope. You're mine. Just mine. No one else gets to see you naked. Boyfriend rules."

That word. I love it. It's a great word, but it doesn't fit entirely right, and I'm not sure why. "Fair enough. But I will be getting off to you in the shower."

He winks at me. "I know." Then he slows down, bringing the phone closer to his face, maybe so no one can see me. "See you soon. Also, I fucking love you."

I tell him the same, then I say goodbye, set the phone down, and step under the stream of water.

As I shower, I mull over the word *boyfriend* while my mind races back to that last evening in London at his flat, when we shared the shower and his things.

My brain rushes ahead to the next morning at his table, when he made me breakfast.

And how I felt something like déjà vu, but for the future. *Forward vu.*

Only then, the image was hazy, incomplete. Now, I can see that breakfast more clearly. I see it day after day after day.

And my heart goes wild, pounding madly against my chest.

The picture fills in, and I understand what I was already starting to want before I left London, before I even realized it.

I know now what I desperately want, and it's *not* to count the days till I see him. It's not for him to be my boyfriend. It's not for me to call him later.

I rinse the soap off, turn off the shower, and grab a towel.

It's not any of those things.

It's to do for Dean what I've done for my family. Because that's what you do when you love someone.

You don't do things halfway.

You're either all in, or you're not.

First, I go to the airline website. Then, I text my buddies and cancel paintball. Next, I call Ransom. "I can't work out today."

"Cool. Everything okay?"

"Yes," I say as I get dressed, pulling on clothes quickly. "I need to do something. I need to do it right now."

"What is it?" There's no teasing in his voice—I must sound as serious and determined as I feel.

I tell him my plan, and he lets loose another *whoa*. Then he says, "Clock's ticking. You better go. Do you need a ride to the airport?"

I laugh. "I can get a Lyft, but I appreciate the offer."

"Just sounded like fun. Are you sure?"

"You want to ride with me to the airport?"

"This is epic, so yes, I kind of do. I'm in Murray Hill, so I'm on the way. Also, there's a pizza place out by LaGuardia that was just reviewed on *Barstool Sports*, and I wanted to check it out."

"Of course you have an agenda."

"I do, but your agenda is awesome-r."

"Meet me in thirty minutes. I need to make a pit stop."

* * *

After my errand, I call a Lyft and we pick up Ransom. On the way, I give him the rest of the details.

"Not gonna lie, I had a feeling you'd do this," he says.

"You did?"

"You're not happy like you used to be." When we reach the airport, he says, "Go get your man."

"That's the goal."

When he hops back in the car, he gives the driver the address of the pizza place, and I go to get on a plane.

45

FITZ

I'm five time zones away from where I started. It's nearly midnight and I have to return to New York tomorrow, but tonight I'm standing in front of The Magpie.

The first time I walked into this bar more than one month ago, it changed my life. I hope walking in here tonight changes everything again.

I take a deep, fueling breath, like I'm prepping to go on the ice.

But this is nothing like going into a game. Nothing like the playoffs. I know how to prepare for a face-off. I've done it since I laced up my first pair of skates when I was four.

The mental preparation for a hockey game, where my job is to stop the opponent, is grueling in an entirely different way.

Nothing has prepared me for this.

Nothing except the last weeks of wanting, having, missing, loving, and needing.

Needing him more than anything else in my life.

I shove aside the nerves and push open the doors. I step

inside and look around. Jazzy, sexy music floats through the air, and women in dressy shirts and men in jeans are everywhere—the bar, the tables, the booths.

My eyes go to the bar, hunting for the most gorgeous man I've ever known. He's at the other end, mixing a drink. He's tall, sexy, and *mine*.

My heart slams against my rib cage like a dog scrabbling to be set free. It wants to bound across the floor and jump up on him and slather him in kisses.

Damn good thing that organ is in a cage where it belongs.

Dean slides a beer glass to the customer in front of him, then flashes a smile and says something. Maybe a thankyou, or giving him the total on the tab. Maybe a quip or a piece of advice.

I can't make it out from here, of course, and he hasn't noticed me.

Good.

That gives my jackhammering heart time to settle down.

Though slowing its wild pace seems impossible now that I've set eyes on him.

Seeing my man affirms that he's everything I need. Seeing him is exactly as I hoped, and somehow even better. Because I feel so certain about this. More than I've felt about anything else in my entire life.

I walk to the edge of the bar, and when he happens to glance my way and spots me, he does a double take, not even sure it's me. Then he does a triple take. He tries to school his expression but fails miserably, a wild grin spreading across his stunning face.

My Englishman heads down the length of the bar, his eyes on me the whole time as I walk to meet him at the end.

He stops. I stop.

A bar is between us.

His lips still curve in that grin, and he goes first. "So, this guy walks into my bar…"

"That's what I came here to tell you. I came here to tell you a story," I say, trying to calm my frenzied pulse.

He's quiet, taking in every word like he wants everything I have to say. "Tell me a story."

I draw a deep breath, so damn ready for this. "So, this guy walked into a bar one night. He went there to get a drink with his sister, but he was completely blown away by the hottest, sexiest man behind the counter."

Dean dips his head, smiling, and maybe trying to hide how big that smile is. He lifts his face and meets my eyes again, his hands gripping the edge of the bar. "Go on."

I tap my chest. "And this guy was completely determined to get the other guy's name, to get his number, to get him to go home with him. To get his man. Because he had to have him."

Dean can't stop smiling—his grin glimmers across his eyes. "He was very determined. That was one of the things the other guy found endearing about him," he says.

Hope wants to run away with me, but I continue the story at a steady pace, not wanting to rush it. The story of *us*. "And this guy kept finding ways to see the other guy. His sister even engineered one of those times, and it was worth it because it led to the best first kiss of his life."

His grin grows wider. "What do you know? I heard the same thing. Best first kiss of the other guy's life too."

His words embolden me. I would fly across the ocean again and again to hear them over and over. "And they spent a week together. They went to this cheesy bar where they were supposed to hit some softballs, but they got distracted. They had tea together, and they spent a lot of time in hotel rooms, and on Tower Bridge, and on a river-boat, and in the park, and in a club. And . . . they completely fell in love."

"They did," Dean says, and the laughter of people nearby barely registers. I only have eyes for him.

As I look at Dean Collins, it's not desire behind this glowing warmth inside me. It's love. It's hope. It is my absolute certainty in how I feel. I have never felt this way with anyone else. I don't think I *could* feel like this with anyone else. How could I, when everything belongs to the man in front of me? Every ounce of emotion, trust, love, and hope—they all reside with him.

"But then this guy . . . He couldn't stay. He had to go."

Dean's expression shifts, more serious now. "I think I know how this story ends. It ends with them being far apart. Is that the story you want to tell me?"

I shake my head, my eyes locked with his. "There's this other version of the story. It has a different ending."

In the softest voice I've ever heard, he whispers, sounding almost desperate, "Tell me that story, Fitz. Tell it to me now."

I nod to where I'm standing. "Come out from behind the bar, and I will."

Without breaking my gaze, he lifts the pass-through and steps forward, standing in front of me, a foot away. We don't touch, though, and I know why. Once we do, we will be putting on a show. I don't know that I could hold anything back unless I hold everything back, so my hands stay clenched in fists at my sides.

I have to say what I came to say before I can touch him.

I start over. I start a new story. The next chapter. "So, this guy walks into a bar tonight, and he has two days off before his Thursday night game, and the other guy is coming to see him next week, but this guy—he couldn't wait till then. He couldn't wait another minute." I step closer, needing to be near him, to be in his space as I take the narrative for myself. "All I could think about—literally the only thing in my head this morning after I called you my boyfriend—was that I had to get to England right away. Because the thing is, Dean . . ." I can't hold back now. I need to touch him. I reach for his face, to hold him. "I cannot stop thinking about you. I cannot stop thinking about us. I cannot stop thinking about how we can be together."

I take a beat to let my chest fill with air again. "That's why I got on a plane this morning—so I could come here tonight to ask you something."

46

DEAN

Mirage was my first thought when I saw Fitz at the end of my bar.

Then, *it's a trick of the mind.*

Seeing the face you most want to see. The one you dream of. The one you love madly.

I never expected him to show up like this. Not when I have a plane ticket for Sunday. Not when I'm supposed to be flying to see him in five nights. When I'd planned to tell him I'd move to New York for him.

That I'd be with him if he'd have me.

That I'd give up all this for him.

Because it's not giving up, it's getting him. And he's what I want most in the world.

Instead, he's here, and he has something to ask me. I'm not one to jump to conclusions, to make assumptions.

But even so, my heart is two steps ahead, hammering wildly, assuming desperately. I try to slow the stampede of emotions as I speak, but the words come out gravelly anyway. "What exactly are you proposing?"

His grin is wicked and satisfied as he says one word. *"That."*

I arch a brow, barely letting myself hope. I haven't let my mind go there. It would be too much. Too good. Too unreal. "That?"

His expression is fierce, and his eyes never stray from mine, and his gaze never breaks as he holds my face. "Marry me."

For a few seconds, I'm living in a dream, or maybe in a rom-com. The entire bar goes incredibly still, library-quiet, and I am aware out of the corner of my eye that everyone is now looking at us. That the noise and the bustle has died down as my customers figure out what's going on in this corner of the bar.

We are in the proverbial spotlight. And I should care. But I don't, because all I care about is him and the two words he just said. And the words he keeps saying, because he doesn't stop talking, because Fitz is a talker, and he can't ever stop running at the mouth, and I love it, I love everything he's saying, every single word.

"I don't know how any of this works, Dean," he says. "But I will do whatever it takes for you. I want you to come to New York with me and live with me and be with me. Now, tomorrow, always. And I will do whatever you need me to do to make that happen. Whatever I can do to make your life easier, to make our life together happen, I will do it. I will do whatever it takes to have you come to New York and be my husband."

The air rushes out of my lungs. I try to form words, but I can't think. I can only *feel* . . . feel this intensity, this passion, this wild, wonderful love.

And when I think I can't possibly feel anything more, he gets down on one knee, making it all so real.

Fitz reaches into his pocket, takes out a velvet box, and flips it open. A platinum band. It's simple, classy.

For me.

I am floored.

Utterly floored and still speechless.

I try to say something, to say yes, to say *God, I fucking love you so much*, but my throat is clogged with emotion—with happiness and so much love I don't know how to contain it, or if I even can.

He looks up at me, his blue eyes so vulnerable and so full of hope. "I have no idea if you'll even consider this, but I will regret it for the rest of my life if I don't ask you, because I want to spend the rest of my life with you. I love you so damn much. I love you more than anything. More than anyone. And I am heartsick without you."

My own heart is ten sizes too big. It beats outside my chest, and I can't contain it. Because my heart starts and ends with him.

There are a million questions, a thousand things I need to figure out, but there is only one answer in the entire world.

The one I've been saying to him all along. The place I knew I would go with him. "Yes."

But that isn't all I have to say. That word unlocks everything else inside me, all the things I feel every second. It frees the truest thing I've ever known. "You're the love of my life, James Fitzgerald. You are absolutely the love of my life."

His smile spreads slow and easy, like he's taking this in, like he's not sure I said that. Like he just discovered fire or magic, and this love is equally as wondrous.

It feels that way to me.

Fitz slides the ring on my finger, then threads his hand through mine. I yank him up, bring him to me, clasp his face, and kiss those lips I have missed every night and every morning.

I kiss the hell out of him.

I kiss him like it's the only thing I've wanted to do since he left.

Like he's the only one I ever want to kiss again.

Like he's the only man for me.

Because he is, and I love him so fucking much.

That is all.

When we break the kiss, we're eye to eye, face-to-face, and he looks drunk on happiness.

"Yes? You mean it? You will?" he asks again, maybe needing to make sure. "You'll marry me?"

"I mean it. Every word." I look around the bar, this little slice of my life here. The place that's been my home. Then I run my hand along Fitz's bearded jaw, and he moves with me, like he always has, leaning into my palm. "I've lived here my entire life," I say as I touch him. "And it's been an incredible life. One that was perfectly good until that day when *you* walked into it and upended everything. You changed everything. You took over my heart, mind, and body. So, the answer is yes. I'll go anywhere with you. You are my home."

The bar erupts into a wild cacophony of cheers and clapping and laughter. Now I know what it feels like to live in a rom-com, and it's so damn incredible.

I kiss him again.

I kiss the man I want to spend the rest of my life with.

And this kiss now? This is the greatest kiss of my life.

When we break apart, he's beaming like the sun. That's who he is. He curls his hands over my shoulders as he says, "I am so happy . . . you make me so happy. More than anything ever has. You. Just you."

I quirk up my lips. "The feeling is completely mutual."

And because we're us, we do it again. PDA is pretty much our MO. We kiss over and over, and we're most definitely putting on a show, and I don't care, because he is where I want to be.

Then Maeve calls out, "Get a room, get a room."

And we finally break the kiss.

Fitz wiggles his eyebrows at my friend, who's now a few feet away. "It's not a bad idea," he says.

I gesture to the bar. "I shouldn't leave. It's my shift."

Maeve laughs at me, puts her hands on my shoulders, and does her best to push me out the door.

"*Go.* Daisy's here to help me out," she says, gesturing to one of our bartenders. "Just go be with your man."

I turn to her. "I'll call you tomorrow. We'll sort it all out."

"We'll sort it *all* out," she repeats, then shoos me away.

I leave, take Fitz's hand, and say, "So, did you hear the one about a guy who walks out of a bar? Out of a bar and into the rest of his story with the love of his life."

"Sounds like a good story."

"It's a great one. It's ours."

47

DEAN

When we turn on my street, I tug his hand to make him stop.

"What is it, babe?"

"There's something I need to tell you," I say, and when his eyes flash with worry, I shake my head and smile to reassure him. "It's good. I promise."

Fitz threads both his hands through both of mine. "Tell me."

A flock of nerves takes flight inside me, but I find the guts to say what I need to say. "Next week, when I visit you —I'm still visiting you?"

"Damn straight."

I swallow, then finish my confession. "I was planning on asking if you wanted me to move there. To be with you."

He blinks. "Shut up," he says, jerking me closer.

"It's true. I was going to."

"You were?" His voice is stitched with wonder.

"I was."

"You were going to do that for me? For us?" Fitz asks, like I've told him he's won the lottery.

"I talked to my father yesterday, and it was clear—crystal clear. I knew I had to do it. To ask you if you'd want me to join you." I don't know why I'm still nervous telling him this. He just asked me to marry him, so I shouldn't be. But I am. Maybe because this is how I crack my heart open and let him see inside, like he did for me.

It's one thing to say yes.

It's another thing to ask.

And I want him to know what I'd do for him. That I'd have asked him to be with me too.

Fitz shakes his head in a kind of wild disbelief. He lets go of my hands and slides his palms up my chest, here on the street. "You keep doing this, Dean," he says, his voice going to that low and smoky zone that I love.

"Doing what?"

"You make me fall more in love with you every single day," he says, then he claims my lips in a kiss that leaves me woozy and lightheaded. "For the record, I love that you were going to ask to move to New York for us, and presumably move in with me, because I'm not letting you live anyplace else. But I need you to know that I want to be married to you *more* than I just want you in the same space as I am. I mean, I do want us to be in the same space. I want to wake up with you and go to bed with you and shower with you and shave with you. I want it all. But I don't *just* want that. I want to be with you for the rest of my life, and the fact that you were willing to move for me just makes me love you harder."

"I love you pretty hard too."

"Speaking of hard things," he says, arching an eyebrow as we resume our pace to my flat.

"Yes, let's. Let's speak of very hard things."

When we reach the door and I unlock it, Fitz runs a hand down my back and brings his lips to my ear. "*Trade-sies.* Tonight, I fuck you. Tomorrow morning, you fuck me."

I laugh. "I'm good with that. Very, very good with that."

So good with it that minutes later, we're naked in my bed, and he's on top of me, his hands wrapped around my wrists, his lips devouring mine, his cock rubbing against my shaft, driving me absolutely mad with lust.

When he breaks the kiss, I look up at his hands. "I see you still like to be in control," I tease.

"No. I just really want to fuck my man."

"The feeling is mutual."

Fitz reaches for the lube on the bedside table and works his magic in me with his fingers, making me moan and groan and practically beg.

"Ready?" he asks.

"You know I'm fucking ready. Just get inside me," I grit out, and he smiles at me, too sexy for words.

I'm so used to this part of sex—the prep, the condoms, the process—that it takes me a few seconds to register what he's doing.

And what he's *not* doing too.

He's pouring the lube in his hand, slicking up his cock.

And it's the sexiest thing I've ever seen because it's brand-new. Because of what it means.

Because it's part of this promise between us.

Only us.

Him and me.

There are no barriers—only trust.

And when he's ready, he moves that slick hand to my dick, strokes up, and notches the head of his cock against me. He gives my cock a tight squeeze as he pushes inside my body.

And it's like fireworks.

It's fucking extraordinary.

"Holy fuck," I groan.

Fitz grunts as he fills me, sliding deeper, bottoming out, then just going deliciously, torturously still inside me.

"That is . . ." He's just poised above me on his forearms, frozen for a few seconds. "Dean," he rasps.

"Yeah?"

"This feels *soooo* fucking good."

I rock my hips up against him and bend my knees, sliding them up my body, giving him more room to fuck hard. "Better than good."

He shudders as I move beneath him, just trembles all over, and then swears for days.

"Babe. You're killing me. I think I'm going to come in, like, two seconds."

I arch a brow. "I bet you can make it last. I bet you want to."

And that's all he needs. A little challenge. A little bossing around.

It does the trick. It stokes all the competitive fire in him, and he grits his teeth, fights off the prospect of a too-soon climax, then thrusts into me, his hand on my cock the whole time.

"Missed you, babe," he says as he strokes deep.

"Missed you so much," I murmur.

And then we're done talking. We're doing. We're fucking and sweating and groaning and grabbing.

And it's intense and powerful and electric.

It's everything it's ever been with us, and it's so much more.

Because now it's *this*—the start of a whole new life together.

48

FITZ

Turns out sex without condoms is pretty messy. Pretty sticky. But that's what showers are for.

I take a shower with my fiancé, and I go to bed with my fiancé, and I wake up with him too.

Well, I wake up with his hard dick pressed against one ass cheek, since Dean is wrapped around me, playing the big spoon.

But that's a damn good way to wake, in my book. "Mmm. How about a few inches lower?" I suggest, since I'm helpful like that.

"Good morning to me," he says in a husky voice that gets me even more turned on.

"Told you I could do it every night and every morning," I say, pushing my ass against his hard-on. He reaches for the lube.

"I never doubted you, Fitz. But it's always good for you to show me the evidence."

I grab his hand and jerk it around to my cock. "Here's your hard evidence."

Dean laughs loudly, and I do too, then my laughter ceases when his finger slides inside me.

I close my eyes and groan.

He groans too. The sounds he makes go straight to my dick, and I swear I'm steel right now, and he doesn't let go of me.

And soon, he has me ready, and with his hand on my favorite body part, he pushes inside.

He takes his time, letting me adjust, letting me take him. "You are so hot and tight," he murmurs, as he goes deeper in me.

I breathe out hard, getting used to the new sensations. The absolutely fucking amazing sensations. I honestly never thought I'd be into this back and forth of roles, into taking turns. But then, I never thought I'd be in bed with a man I was going to marry.

Dean adjusts my leg, giving himself all the access to where he wants to be, where I want him to be too.

Deep inside me.

His hand tightens on my cock, and wild lust rockets through my body.

"You are mine," he whispers hotly in my ear as I thrust into his fist, and he drives into my body, his other arm wrapping tight around my chest, pulling me against him.

I heat up like the sun, as he fucks me like this, our bodies tangled together. Doesn't take me long. I'm close, so damn close, and even closer when his lips roam across the back of my neck. My entire body, my mind, my fucking soul is bathed in bliss, in lust, in desire.

"Nothing is as good as this," Dean murmurs, biting my ear.

"Nothing," I repeat, and I sound just as lost as he is in the pleasure.

But I'm found too.

I'm where I want to be.

And after we come in another hot, sticky, perfectly sexy mess, we clean up and return to bed, where he takes my hand, threading his fingers through mine.

I look down at the ring on his finger, admiring it. "Looks hella hot, Dean."

"Yes, and I think you need one too." He holds up my hand, showing me our fingers twined together. "I can't have you walking around like this. All these bare fingers. I need everyone to know you're taken."

And I smile.

Yeah, I'm definitely taken.

"Feel free to put a ring on me, babe. Let the world know I'm going to marry the love of my life."

He squeezes my hand. "I fucking love you. That is all."

And *that* is everything.

THE NEXT FEW DAYS

Also known as the start of a new countdown.

49

DEAN

When I walk into The Magpie before we open the next night, a whoop and a holler greet me.

"Lover boy!" Maeve rushes out from behind the bar and over to me, jumping into my arms.

I grip her before we topple over. "Lovely to see you too."

"Tell me everything, you dog," she says when I set her down.

I arch a brow. "Everything?"

She rolls her eyes. "Great sex, blah, blah, perfect chemistry, blah, blah, happily ever after, blah, blah."

"Sounds about right," I say, laughing as I walk inside and grab stool at the bar.

She hops up next to me, rests her chin in her hand, and bats her eyes. "So, when is the wedding? Can I be your best woman? And how bloody fucking happy are you?"

"Next year. Obviously. And more than I ever thought possible."

She sets her hand on her heart and sighs. "I want to say I told you so, but I'm too excited for you to gloat."

"Gloat a little. You deserve to."

She squares her shoulders, preens, then pokes me in the chest. "Remember that night when I said I'd laugh so hard when love smacked you in the face and knocked you on the arse?"

I stare at the ceiling like I'm deep in thought. "What do you know? I recall it perfectly."

"I was right," she says, shimmying her shoulders.

"You were," I say, and once we've done the requisite recap, I take a breath and broach the subject we need to discuss. "So, I'm leaving soon."

"I know," she says, a little heavily.

"I'm going to miss you."

"I'm going to miss you too," she says, wiping her hand across her cheek as her eyes shine with tears. She purses her lips and looks away. "A lot," she adds, her voice breaking as tears slide down her cheeks.

I reach for her, drawing her into an embrace.

She cries quietly for a minute, then she pulls back, flaps her hand in front of her face, and composes her expression. "I'm all good. No more tears."

"We need to talk about this place and what this means. Especially since the loan is nearly paid off."

"Right. How do we work this out? I mean, I'll buy you out, of course."

I shake my head. "No."

"What?" Then she blinks, an alternative occurring to her. "Oh, you want to be a silent partner from the US? I'm sure we can sort that out."

I take her hand. "Listen, I talked to Fitz about this. And I hope this isn't presumptuous. But we really want to do this for you. Because here's the thing—everything is changing for me, and he wants to make it easy for both of us, for me and for you. So, think about it if you need to"—I take a beat—"but I want to give you my half."

Her jaw falls open. "What?" She looks like a cartoon character hit with a box of shock. "G-give it to me?" she asks, stumbling on the words.

"Yes."

"Ah, um, how?"

"Well, I can't run it anymore. And I bought my flat at a steal, and it's gone up in value, so when I sell it, I'll have enough for a lease on a new bar in New York. And I want you to have this place."

"But New York isn't cheap."

"Nor is London, as we both know." I scrub a hand across my jaw. Money matters can be touchy to discuss, but Maeve and I talk about everything, including finances. "Look, I'm going to be blunt here. My fiancé does well for himself. And I don't intend to dig my heels in and be pigheaded about things. That would be pointless. He takes care of the people he loves." It's such a privilege to be one of those people—to be *his* person. "When I'm in New York, the bar I open will be mine, and I'll be responsible for it. But I won't have to worry about rent or a mortgage, or things like that. So, yeah. I—" I stop, because I didn't make this decision alone. I made it with Fitz this morning before he returned to New York. "He and I—*we*—we want to do this for you."

Hearts seem to flutter above her head. "He wants you to have everything you want."

"He really does."

Maeve reaches for my arm and squeezes it. "Because you're what he wants most."

All I can do is smile, because that is the whole truth.

* * *

On Sunday evening, after six hours and fifty minutes in first class, I see Fitz waiting for me on the other side of security. The second I reach him, he wraps his arms around me, and we do that PDA thing we do.

We get in the town car he ordered, and as the driver whisks us into the city, Fitz peppers me with questions about the flight and The Magpie and my flat.

All stuff we talked about on the phone, but he likes to know where it stands and how the details are coming together. He wants to be a part of this change, to be with me as I unwind my life in England for a new one here.

Once we cross into Manhattan, he sweeps his arm out, indicating the city outside the windows. "So, this is the Big Apple, something New Yorkers never call it. What do you think?"

Laughing, I look around, soaking in the sights. "I'm taking it all in for the first time. I haven't formed an opinion yet."

He nudges me with his elbow. "C'mon. What are your pros and cons?"

I tap my chin. "I hear it doesn't rain as much."

"Definite pro."

"Also, rumor on the street is New York has great pizza."

"Yet another benefit."

"And my accent will stand out and make all my new customers swoon. So, big tips coming my way."

Fitz runs his hand over the back of my neck. "Told you you'd like it here."

"I guess the only thing left is to see how nice the view is from your place."

"The view is epic."

And he's not exaggerating. He lives on the twenty-fifth floor of a gorgeous building overlooking Gramercy Park. The city unfurls below us.

Later that night, after we reconnect in our favorite way, I stare out the floor-to-ceiling windows, drinking in the flickering lights, the skyscrapers, all the people walking on the streets below. "You have a great view."

Fitz moves behind me, shaking his head and circling his arms around my waist. "No. *We* do," he says, then he kisses my neck, brushing his beard against me in a distracting way.

I say nothing because it still feels so surreal, this mingling of everything. Also, because . . . that beard.

He cups my jaw and turns my face toward him, his eyes intense. "It's *ours*, Dean. You know that, right? Everything I have is yours."

I roll my eyes, not because I doubt him, but because I don't know what to say. His generosity is wonderful and staggering at times.

"I mean it," he says insistently. "And you better get used to it. Because I am going to shower my husband with everything."

He moves in for a kiss. I kiss him back, and when the kiss ends, I stare out the window again, savoring the view of my new city.

Soon, I'll sell my flat.

I'll pack up my things.

I'll say goodbye to my friends and my family.

I'll fly here for good.

I turn back to Fitz, feeling even more certainty about this choice. "I like it here."

He pumps a fist. "You'll love it soon enough."

"I have no doubt," I say, my lips curving up in a grin. "It's *our* home."

His eyes gleam. "It is. It's ours. Yours and mine."

The next morning, I get him a ring, and then I kiss him on Fifth Avenue with crowds of New Yorkers

rushing past us, the city around us, and our life ahead
of us.

NEXT YEAR

Also known as . . . and we live happily ever after.

50

FITZ

Best month of my life.

It's February, my team is kicking ass, I'm having a killer season, and my fiancé is about to open his new bar here in New York.

Of course, the month before was damn good too, because . . . Dean.

I could say the same for the one before that.

Hell, every day has been epic since he arrived in town.

Today is another epic day.

After an afternoon workout, I stop by the spot he leased ten blocks from where we live and survey the watering hole.

"It's so London," I say, taking in the dark wood, the pool tables, the trivia games, and the TV screens that will surely have his version of *football* playing.

"Not too shabby?" Dean asks as he pours me a stout, just like he did the night we met.

"It's awesome," I say, grabbing a stool at the bar and taking a drink.

Everything about the place feels so very Dean, from the

standards playing over the speakers to the name of the place—The Pub.

"It was my dad's idea," Dean had said when he decided on the name. "A few days after you left the first time, I was feeling particularly shitty, and he took me to a place just like this. Looked around, said it felt like home. I decided that was what I wanted here in New York."

And that's what he made happen.

This weekend, it opens, and I can't wait to be here with him when it does.

"Does it make you miss London?" I ask him, only the slightest bit nervous that he'll say yes. That he'll long for what he left behind.

Dean shakes his head. "No. I have everything I want here."

There he goes, making me fall harder for him every damn day. "Good. Let's keep it that way."

"Works for me."

I point at the TV screen hanging in the corner. "You're going to carry hockey, though, when I play, right?"

"Maybe," my guy says with an easy shrug, setting his elbows on the counter, giving me those *do bad things to me* eyes. "Depends on whether you make it worth my while."

"I always do," I say, then I tell him to come around to this side because I need a picture of us.

Dean joins me for a selfie and gives me a sexy grin as I snap a shot of us in his bar.

"And will you use that on your next road trip?" he asks when I show him the image.

My eyes travel up and down his body. "Not if you video chat with me like I want you to."

"Insatiable," he scoffs, then slides a hand along my thigh before he returns to the bar.

"Just like you," I toss out.

"Absolutely, Fitzgerald. Absolutely."

I shoot him a curious look. "You're calling me by my full last name now?"

Dean tilts his head as if he just realized what he said. "Huh. I guess I hear it all the time during your games. Maybe I'll call you Fitzgerald in front of everyone else and Fitz in the bedroom."

"You do that, babe. Want to know why?"

"Tell me why."

"Because Fitzgerald sounds hot AF in your accent, and Fitz sounds like *sex* on your lips."

Dean taps his chin. "So basically, I turn you on no matter which variation of your name I use?"

I laugh. "Sounds about right."

"Works for me, then . . . *Fitzgerald.*"

A little later, we leave together, headed to meet some of our friends in New York for a little get-together.

Our friends.

Because that's another thing I love about my man. He's so damn charming that he gets along with everyone.

We head to a restaurant on the Upper East Side.

Logan spots us first and calls us over to the bar, where he has his arm wrapped around his new woman, Bryn, a take-no-prisoners brunette who keeps my bud on his toes.

"Laser tag. What are your thoughts on that? I'm looking for a summer league," he says, then nods at Dean. "You want to play laser tag with us?"

Dean strokes his chin. "Let me think on that. Wait. I have an answer. Thanks, but no thanks."

I shrug. "He's a sports snob. What can I say?"

"You can say you'll play," Logan says, clapping my shoulder then chanting, "Do it. Do it. Do it."

"You know I'm always down for it."

Bryn squeezes Logan's arm. "But look, sweetie, if you

can't get it together for laser tag, you can just join the hula-hooping class that Amelia and I are taking."

Logan shakes his head, but he's smiling, and I'm sure he's thrilled that his new woman loves doing sports with his daughter.

Summer comes in next with her hubs, Oliver. Dean and Oliver catch up on all things British, sliding quickly into talk of London and what's going on there, while Summer and I chat about how her new fitness center is doing.

Soon, Leo joins the crew, and after quick hellos, he claps Dean on the back. "Check this out," Leo says, then grabs his phone and shows Dean a picture. "This table is from the dark ages of the fifties. I picked it up last weekend at a garage sale."

"That one needs a fuck-ton of work," Dean says, studying the shot.

"I know, right?" Leo says, sounding ridiculously excited. "I'm thinking power sanders, protective goggles, the whole nine yards. You down with that?"

"Power sanders get me very excited, so yeah. Count me in. Your warehouse space?" Dean asks, and I try to contain my grin as they chat, but it's hard as hell, since I love that these two bonded over the whole furniture restoration thing, and now they're good buds.

"This weekend. Saturday. Be there early," Leo says.

Dean shudders. "I can't wake early. It's against my nature. But noon sounds great."

Leo laughs. "I'll see you at noon."

When the hostess pops over to tell us the table is ready, the whole crew heads away from the bar.

I grab Dean's hand, holding him back for a second. "I told you that you and Leo would get along."

"You were right," he says.

"I'm glad," I tell him. "I'm glad you like it here."

Dean slides a hand along my back. "Ah, but that is where you're wrong. I don't like it here."

I freeze. "What?"

He leans closer and whispers in my ear, "I love it here."

That makes me hella happy.

He has his own friends, his own business, and his own life.

But my favorite part of his life is that he shares it with me.

51

DEAN

That suit.

My fiancé looks fantastic in his suit a few weeks later.

It is dark gray, hugs his muscular frame, and makes me want to strip him down to nothing.

But I behave. I already had him in nothing, giving him his good luck charm before the game, and getting my own too. Pregame rituals are so important to follow.

Now, I help Fitz button his shirt, then I grab a purple tie for him from the closet. I fasten it around his neck, adjusting the length then knotting it. "Later, if you're particularly good at that whole ice-defending thing you do, maybe you'll get another reward."

His blue eyes spark with dirty wishes. "Maybe? You'd never deny me, babe."

"True." I smack his ass. "Get to the arena. Playoffs start soon, and you need to continue hitting homers till then. I'll see you there tonight."

Fitz laughs as I walk him to the door. Before he leaves, though, he grabs the waistband of my jeans, bringing me against him. "You coming to my games never gets old."

"I know," I say with a smile. "But you need to go, or you'll be late for kickoff."

He rolls his eyes. "I fucking love you. That is all."

"The feeling is mutual."

* * *

A little later, I stop by The Pub, checking to make sure my employees have everything under control for tonight, then I meet up with Leo to head to the arena.

"I have a new book for you. It's all about a Ponzi scheme on Wall Street. Totally brilliant," I say, and as we walk across town, I give him my synopsis of the tale of greed and excess I just finished, since we have similar taste in books.

"I'll check it out," he says, but he sounds a little distracted.

He's that way at the game too.

Normally, he's all *rah-rah, go, team, go*, but when the good guys score, he doesn't even cheer.

I sit back down, take a drink of my beer, and arch a brow. "What's the story? You're a little out of sorts."

He drags a hand through his hair. "It's Lulu."

I blink, surprised to hear that name said that way. "Lulu? Your best friend's wife?"

"Yes." He says it heavily.

"Oh," I say it heavily too, since I have a feeling this conversation is about to become more intense than the game. "Is there something going on with you and her?"

Leo shakes his head adamantly, like he can't stop shaking it. "No, just no. No, no, no."

"So, what is it?"

He takes a drink of his beer, sets it down, and sighs. "Do you have any idea how lucky you are that you're not madly in love with your best friend's wife? That you haven't been for years?"

The logic there kind of falls apart for me, but now's not the time to break it down. "You've been in love with Lulu since she married Tripp several years ago?"

"Since *before* she married him," he admits. "And there is nothing I can do about it."

"Well, yeah. Since she's married and all."

"I know. I know," he says.

Then he keeps talking. He doesn't shut up. He tells me about the day he met Lulu. He tells me about how Tripp fell for her too. He tells me about Tripp's battles with alcohol, and how he and Lulu are trying to help him get to rehab, and it's all really fucking intense, since he's crazy for her too.

"But there's nothing I can do."

I nod, wishing I could dig into a secret box of bartender advice and give him the perfect solution for being in love with his best friend's wife.

"All you can do is be his friend. And be her friend. That's all you can do," I say.

"Yeah. It is," he echoes.

* * *

Later, after Fitz wins, notching an epic slap shot that I cheer the loudest for, my fiancé curls up with me in bed. "Did you have a good time at the game?"

"Always."

"And how's Leo?"

I shake my head. "You can't imagine the ass-kicking that love is serving him right now."

"Yeah?"

I don't go into the details. It's not my story to tell.

Instead, I give him a one-sentence summary. "It makes what we went through to get here seem easy."

Fitz arches a brow. "Was it hard though?"

"I dunno. Was it?"

"It's hard now." He nudges me with his pelvis.

I crack up, feeling the evidence. "You have such a one-track mind."

"I know, but some things are always hard, babe. I can't help it. I'm in bed with you. It's just always going to be hard."

"Get your lips on mine."

When he kisses me, all thoughts of other people's love lives fall out of my head, because mine is just too damn good.

And it's not because we're lucky.

It's because we made it happen.

And this summer, I'm marrying him.

THE FIRST EPILOGUE

Fitz

I was right.

My mom loves Dean.

All my sisters do too. Emma, Carrie, and Sarah. They're all here in New York for a June wedding.

We'll meet them in Central Park later.

For now, I'm getting ready at our home with my guy. My fiancé. The other groom.

We're not doing the whole *don't see each other before the ceremony* thing. That's not our style.

Our style is this—he wears a tailored dark-blue suit. Mine is lighter blue. I fasten his tie. He knots mine.

And then I step back and take a look at the man who's going to be my husband. "You clean up well, Dean Collins."

"Same to you, James Fitzgerald."

"Picture time," I say, holding up my phone in the living room as I snap a selfie on our wedding day. I show it to him.

"Keeping it. Definitely keeping it," he says.

And we head to the park in a limo together. We walk in together. And we meet our families together.

That's how we walk down the aisle, which is really the stone walkway at Bethesda Terrace. Hand in hand, my mom on one side, his dad on the other, then it's just us at the front with a justice of the peace.

Everyone I care about is here. Everyone he cares about is here too. All his friends from London, Naveen and Anya, Taron and his fiancé, Maeve and Sam, and Dean's father and his girlfriend, Penny.

My friends from New York, who are now our friends.

Most of my teammates too.

Everyone we love.

But I only have eyes for one person.

"Do you, James Fitzgerald, take this man to be your husband?" the justice of the peace asks on a warm summer day as the sun shines brightly above us.

I say the easiest words ever. "I do."

"And do you, Dean Collins, take this man to be *your* husband?"

The guy I love madly, beyond anything, more than anyone else in the whole universe, locks his eyes with mine and makes me the happiest man in the world when he says, "I do."

And then I kiss the groom.

Something I plan to do every day for the rest of my life.

MAEVE'S EPILOGUE

A few weeks ago

After I close one evening in May, I survey the pool table in a corner of The Magpie, the one I decided to get because it reminds me of Dean, as if a little piece of my friend is still here.

I can hear him in my head, assessing the guys, deciding which one'll tempt me tonight.

One of the benefits of the game Dean and I played was that it kept me from jumping into a bad choice. And I've made some. Plenty of guys seem good on paper and then turn out to be total wastes of time.

Take Jeremy, the best and worst of them. Went to Cambridge, nabbed a fancy law degree, dressed like James Bond. He wrote poetry on the side and would read it to me while we sat on the balcony.

It was perfect. Except, of course, for how he was doing private poetry readings for some other woman at the same time.

But that's all in the past, because I've found the perfect relationship. I pour my soul into this one, and in return, it just gets better and better. It's a lot of work, but The Magpie will never let me down.

I find the flyer for the tasting event on my desk. The Bars and Wineries of London tasting tomorrow. While there I'll have the chance to talk up what I love.

Makes missing my best friend a little bit easier.

* * *

The next morning, I'm one of the first to arrive at the event hotel, dressed in leggings and a casual top, with my dress and heels packed in a bag.

I start hanging up the faux flowers and lights I picked out for the booth, and then I grab the glassware and liquor bottles for our sample cocktail.

"Look who didn't tell me she'd be here." The deep baritone voice sends a spark along my skin. I turn to find Sam's dark eyes glinting at me, paired with his sexy, crooked grin, like gin and vermouth.

"Sam, you sneaky man. I could say the same—why didn't you tell me you were going to be here? I saw you a couple of weeks ago, and you never mentioned it."

"A man's got to have some mystery," he says.

"Well, your secret's out of the bag now. Good to see you."

That's the truth. It's no hardship to be looking at his fabulous face. With a strong jaw, smoldering eyes, and just the right amount of scruff, he's always been easy on the eyes. Plus, his sexy American accent just does it for me.

Not that I gave him a second thought until recently. When I first met him a few years ago, he was married, which established him firmly in the "just mates" column.

As a friend of Dean's, we always found ourselves at the same parties and events and I got to know him better after his split, and he became my friend too.

"And you. Looks like I lucked out with my booth neighbor," Sam says, drawing me into a hug. He feels so solid pressed against me, and he smells like clean sandalwood. I catch myself breathing him in and step back.

"How's Sticks and Stones doing?"

"No complaints. The bigger question is how are you doing without Dean?"

"I miss him terribly, especially when I need someone to lift heavy things or reach high shelves. Speaking of, I have to go find a ladder to get these tassels hung up."

I hold up the gold-and-silver tassels I brought to liven up the top of the booth.

"He's not the only tall guy around, you know. I can give you a hand."

"Oh, I'm fine," I say. I've gotten used to going it alone. "I'll just stretch high."

Sam laughs, low and hearty. "What kind of friend would I be if I didn't step in to help?"

I glance behind me at the booth.

But on the other hand, I could use the help. "I do need to get changed. Would you be willing to hang some stuff up while I run to the loo?"

Sam frowns. "Wait a minute. You're not going to wear those fine leggings?"

Oh, did he just compliment my legs? I think he did, and I liked it.

"Sadly, no. I need to look like a professional. Ergo, no yoga pants."

Sam sighs. "Such a shame. But I guess I'll help you out anyway."

I laugh and grab my bag of clothes. A rush of heat runs down the back of my neck at feeling Sam's eyes on me.

I tell myself not to read too much into Sam and his flirtations, and head for the restroom, where I swap gym clothes for the red dress I picked for the occasion.

I slip on my heels and head back to the booth. My mouth falls open when I see that Sam not only has finished hanging the tassels but also has set out my flyers for The Magpie.

"Booth decorator extraordinaire."

"Indeed I am," he says, and when he turns around, his eyes take an obvious detour up my body.

"And with that dress, I don't know that I'll be able to pay attention to my booth."

I roll my eyes, though I don't mind the compliment. "Please. It'll be easy. You'll have so many ladies flocking to you. Just like they do in life."

"Do they flock to me? I hadn't noticed."

I laugh. "Oh no, you're not trapping me into admitting that."

But it's hard to tear my gaze away from the handsome man as he walks to his booth beside mine.

Uh-oh.

I know this feeling.

This feeling can only lead to trouble.

It's the same one that led me to think that Jeremy was a good guy.

If anything, liking Sam would be even riskier. The inevitable crash and burn would hurt more because he wouldn't be some random guy. I would lose a friend.

So, I need to pull it together and ignore the remnant of heat skating along the back of my neck.

Even though it feels so good.

* * *

By the time the event's over, I've made more small talk than I ever thought possible—which, as an experienced bartender, is saying something—and have run out of ways to describe The Magpie's "modern, inventive energy." I've also served hundreds of old-fashioneds, and I'm sure I smell like orange and whiskey.

As I pack up the glassware and the decorations Sam stops by, smiles and starts taking down my higher decorations.

"You read my mind," I say, setting a hand briefly on his shoulder. His strong, firm shoulder. "Dean used to help me with stuff like that. Too bad the prat had to go and fall in love."

Sam laughs. "From what I hear, someone did push him along the way."

I shrug, grabbing some of the flyers and tucking them in a box. "Who am I to stand in the way of true love?"

"You really knew right away that they'd be good for each other?"

I grin, nodding. "With those two? Absolutely. Or at least I knew they had incredibly hot chemistry."

"And that translates to love?"

"I think you could argue that true love needs true chemistry."

"Now you're philosophizing, Maeve."

"It needs more than that, obviously," I say. "You need trust and commitment and honesty. But to get off the ground, maybe, love needs chemistry. You need to be with someone who gets you."

"Sounds like you're speaking from experience," Sam says thoughtfully.

The conversation is dancing too close to the topic of

romantic history, and I'm not inclined to dive into my past heartbreak. Not with Sam.

So I answer, "Only because it feels like everyone I know is falling in love these days."

"Tell me about it," Sam says in a beleaguered voice. "I have my friend Tom's engagement party to go to next weekend. I already know I'm going to have to field tons of 'Where's Emily?' questions from people who don't know about the divorce."

"That has to be rough."

Now we're not just dancing near the topic of broken hearts. We've landed on it.

"So . . . have you dated?" I ask. "Since . . ."

"I sort of took a break. I'm in no hurry to go through all that again."

My heart jumps a little at that.

"I know what you mean," I say. And because I do understand, and because he's a friend, it only seems right to offer to help.

"What about a friend? Would it help to go to the party with someone you're just mates with?"

"Are you offering your services?"

"That makes it sound so improper," I say.

"Sometimes improper is a very good thing."

"Indeed it is," I add.

"And proper or improper, it would be nice to go with a friend. I could return the favor at any time."

"I do have a charity event I have to go to in a few weeks," I say. "Dean always went with me, but since he's gone, it'd be great to have a friend there."

There's more to it, but I'm not quite ready to give him all the details. If he says yes, I can fill him in later.

"I'd be happy to volunteer my services."

"All the proper and improper ones?" I ask, a little flirty.

Fine, *a lot* flirty.

"All of the above."

I pretend with all my might that this is nothing. Just a flirty friend, just two events.

What could go wrong?

* * *

On the day of the engagement party, Sam texts that he'll pick me up at my flat. Since it's a daytime party, I choose a fit-and-flare dress, light pink with a simple tulip pattern on the skirt, and I fashion my hair into a French twist. My picture could go in a wiki entry for "daytime social occasion."

When I open the door, Sam's eyes slowly widen. He swallows a little roughly and clears his throat. "Wow. You look . . . stunning."

Stunning doesn't sound just-friendly, but I like it.

"I'm just trying to help you make a good impression."

"Oh, you're definitely going to make a good impression. On me," he says, and oh my, did he just go there?

I don't mind that he did.

But I'm also not entirely sure if we *should* be playing these flirty games, so once we're inside the Lyft, I ask about Tom, his engaged friend.

"We've become pretty good buds through our running group," he says as we swing past the park. "It's my relatively new hobby."

"New, as in post-divorce?"

"Yes. Try not to be blown away by the coolness of it. But yup. I needed to do something to get out of the house."

I pat his hand. "It sounds like you were trying to make the best of things."

I don't press the subject, but I'm learning that I like that

Sam can talk about it. He doesn't hide what he's gone through. He's spoken more openly than I have about my relationship ending.

Maybe it wouldn't be so bad to open up.

"This stuff's always hard, isn't it?" I ask, a little wistfully, as the car slows at a light. "Engagement parties and weddings. After you've . . . gone through a breakup. They were hard for me right after anyway. Are you okay? With going?"

For a moment, Sam stares out the window. I wonder if I've gone too far, but then he smiles. "Yeah, I'm okay. I'm better since you're here."

He reaches over to squeeze my hand. Just a friendly squeeze, but it sends shivers all up and down my body.

Alarm bells go off again, warning me to keep this chummy. But I'm not having the easiest time of that. And I don't entirely want to listen to the alarm.

Especially as I drink him in. His sharp jawline, freshly shaved. The way he runs his hands through his dark hair. The way his eyes light up when he talks.

The way he makes me feel safe.

Then, of course, there's the fact that his hand still lingers on mine.

He glances down at it and then at me. For a moment, all I can do is look into his eyes.

The eyes of a thoughtful, funny, *single* man.

The car pulls to a halt at Roehampton Club, jolting us out of the moment.

At the event, we say hello to the guests of honor then wander through the crowds, nibbling on the crab-stuffed mushrooms and spring rolls. Sam keeps me laughing with jokes and stories from his American childhood. We drink pinot grigio as he tells me about the major differences between Los Angeles and New York, saying that Los

Angeles has better views, but New York has more honest people, and then saying London's a perfect mix of the two.

Soon, the DJ starts up with toasts to the happy couple. Soon enough, he's calling everyone to the dance floor, and Sam stands and extends his hand to me.

"How about a dance?"

The prospect sends tingles down my spine, and it's the tingles that sound those warning bells again. Laughing is one thing. Shivers are another. Shivers lead to *more*, and *more* leads to heartbreak.

Correction: tingles and shivers can lead to more, but they don't have to. I'm only agreeing to a dance. Nothing wrong with that.

I think of Dean and Fitz, careening forward into the unknown together. That is frightening. This is just a dance.

Sam leads me to the floor by the hand, but there's a fast song playing, which is perfect. It's all fun and games and whirling and laughing. We get our groove on for two more songs before the DJ switches it up with a slower tune.

A couple's tune.

I sense more than see Sam's questioning look. No pressure, just wondering. I'm not sure I'm ready for his arms around me, even in public.

I adore flirting with him. So why balk at a slow dance? But the question isn't so much can I trust him, but can I trust myself? I'm not sure so I say I'm ready for a drink.

Later, he takes me home, and he's quite proper as he says goodbye.

A blip—more than a blip, if I'm honest—of disappointment surprises me. I wouldn't have minded an improper goodbye.

* * *

A few days after the engagement party, a bouquet of flowers arrives for me at The Magpie.

I eye them curiously, and the note too.

Maeve,

Thank you for suffering through that with me. It might be the most fun I've ever had at a required social gathering.

Yours, Sam

How did he know about the sunflowers? It's not as if I've broadcasted that they're my favorite. How could he know that they remind me of summer days and fresh starts?

I text Dean immediately. He's the only one I've told about my love of sunflowers—I gushed to him about getting them for the opening of The Magpie.

Maeve: Did you tell him?

Dean: Tell who what?

I bet I can imagine his face right now. Hell, I don't need to imagine it. I FaceTime him, and immediately a satisfied-looking Dean shows up on my screen. Looks like he's at his new bar—The Pub.

"You told him, didn't you? About these?"

I flip the screen so he can see the sunflowers, and then I flip back to me. Dean dares to look innocent. Not just pretending-to-look-innocent either. Actually innocent.

"I honestly have no idea what you're talking about. But are those from a guy? Are you dating?"

"Sam sent these. As a thank you for going to his friend's party."

Dean laughs. "So you *are* dating."

I roll my eyes. "Never mind. But you didn't tell him about the flowers?"

"I swear I didn't. I don't have that much of a cupid in me. Plus, some men, you know, remember things about the people they like."

I hum, kind of doubtful, then say goodbye.

I pace around The Magpie, then get out my phone, snap a picture, and send it to Sam.

Maeve: Thank you for these. How'd you know they're my favorite?

Sam: Good! I was hoping that hadn't changed. You mentioned it a while back. Something about the way they make everything seem just a little lighter, right?

The memory comes back to me all of a sudden. Sam, Naveen, Anya, Dean—all of us walking along the Thames last summer. We talked about our perfect Sunday, and I'd casually mentioned that every Sunday should start with fresh flowers.

Sunflowers, in particular.

For exactly the reason he'd said.

But that was almost a year ago. How in the world had he remembered?

Sam: It always stuck with me. Now, I can't see a sunflower without thinking about you.

Maeve: That's the sweetest thing anyone's ever said to me. Really, thank you. I don't know how I'll make it up to you after the charity event.

For a minute, the bouncing dots keep appearing and disappearing on my screen. Then, finally, a message pops up.

Sam: You could wear those yoga pants again.

Maeve: The yoga pants really do it for you, huh?

Sam: Or jeans. Or anything, actually. I'm not really particular. You look good in everything, Maeve.

Maeve: You do too.

I want to keep flirting. But I'm still so wary.

What if we don't like dating as much as we like being friends? There's no reset button. I dwell on it for a day, and then two.

But surely if I can be friends with a gorgeous, sweet,

kind man who somehow remembered my favorite flower, then being more than friends shouldn't intimidate me.

Finally, I decide it's time. If my best friend can move across an ocean, I can let go of my hurt.

And give a real date a real chance.

* * *

The Night of Lost Stars I twist my hair up into a chignon and choose some chandelier earrings that brush my neck. After some consideration, I pick out a violet dress with a slit up the side. I swipe on some lipstick, steeling myself for the emotions that inevitably come my way at this event each year.

I take in a breath just as my doorbell rings.

I pull on my heels and grab my clutch. On the way out, I glance at myself in the mirror. Tendrils of hair frame my face, and not even an eyelash is out of place.

I'm ready.

Sam meets me at the door looking insanely sexy in a fitted suit. He sees me and whistles.

"Damn," he says. "This is how you should dress all the time."

I laugh. "Likewise. I don't know if I've ever seen you in a suit."

"Get used to it," he says. "If I have to wear this to get you to wear that, then suits are my new wardrobe."

Sam's already called a Lyft for us, and it pulls up just as we reach the pavement. He opens the back door for me, and we slide in.

He clears his throat. "So, what's this event tonight about? What're we saving? Animals? Babies?"

I don't answer right away. I take a breath first, wishing there weren't another person here. Still, our driver hasn't so much as glanced back since we got in, so I shouldn't use him as an excuse.

Time for honesty. Full-on.

"It's to support ALS research, actually," I say, sounding just a little bit fragile. "Which . . . my dad died from."

"Oh," Sam says, his deep brown eyes going soft and sincere. "Maeve, I'm so sorry. I didn't know."

"It's okay," I say. "It was seven years ago. But my mum and I used to always go to this together. And then, Dean used to go with me, but now . . ."

"Now I'm here," he says. "And I've already made a joke of it."

"No," I say. "I'm glad you're here. Honestly, I don't know that I've ever told someone about my dad without crying. And now, look. Mascara still firmly in place."

I laugh, and Sam laughs with me.

I feel lighter about this than I ever expected.

"Well, then, let's go raise as much money as we can in your dad's honor," he says as we pull into the event. "Can I bid on a boat? I've always wanted to bid on a boat."

Tsking, I shake my head. "Boys and their toys." Soon, Sam's taking my hand and walking me into Novotel London West. We make our way to the event space, passing people who look like they're made of money.

We check out the auction items, browsing through signed movie posters and football jerseys and, finally, a signed Ed Sheeran guitar. It's white and glittery with a gold signature on the front.

"My mum says his songs remind her of my dad."

"Then let's bid on it."

Sam looks down at the bidding card. "One thousand pounds. I'll split it with you. We have to go in on this."

I shoot him a skeptical glance. "Sam, do you even like Ed Sheeran?"

"Doesn't matter," he says, dead certain. "We're doing this."

"How are we going to split a guitar in half?"

"We'll have joint custody. Half the time at my place, half the time at yours."

"Ridiculous," I say, but I'm laughing, and that feels good too.

"It'll give you a reason to visit," he says in a flirty tone.

While I reel a bit at the idea of going to Sam's home, he's putting down a bid for the guitar. We're outbid for it before we've gotten more than ten paces away, but that's okay because we're having fun.

As the night winds down, Sam and I call another car. We tumble in, laughing about everything and nothing at all. We pull up to my flat, and there's no question—I've never ended this evening feeling this light or this good.

Sam did that. Sam, who kept my spirits up during the event. Sam, who remembered the sunflowers. Sam, who's kind and funny and thoughtful.

He walks me up to my steps and takes my hand to kiss my knuckles.

"We'll have to do this again sometime," he says, his lips curving into a knowing grin. "You know, I've got this wedding to go to. Not sure if you'd be interested. It's transatlantic."

"You don't say?"

He laughs, and I decide it's time for fun. For chances. For choices.

I nibble on my lip, meet his gaze, and go for it. "Would you like to kiss me? Because I'd really like to kiss you."

"What do you know? I'd love to kiss you too."

He cups my cheek, brings his lips to mine, and dusts a soft, gentle kiss to my lips.

One that sends tingles down my spine.

And one that doesn't stay soft for long.

I kiss him back harder, and he tugs me closer, and soon we're kissing like we don't want to come up for air.

We make our way up to my flat, kicking off heels and shoes and losing ourselves in each other. I catch a glimpse of the table where the sunflowers have lasted remarkably well in their vase, and I smile, as sure as I ever have been about a decision in my life.

* * *

After a beautiful wedding ceremony, Sam holds my hand as we watch Dean and Fitz take their first dance in the middle of the Loeb Boathouse's dance floor. As they finish, Sam presses a kiss against my temple, and warmth thrills through me.

How could I have ever thought to say no to this?

I laugh and lean against him. He's running his hand along my knee when the DJ changes the song to "Thinking Out Loud."

"Oh my God," I say. "This is the guitar!"

"What?" Sam says, and then he listens. "Is this Ed . . . what's-his-name? The guy with the guitar that we bid on?"

I nod and laugh harder. "The guitar we were robbed of."

"It's a sign," Sam says. He stands up next to me and holds out his hand. "We didn't get a chance to slow dance before," he says with a smile. "How about we fix that?"

My hand slides into his, and we glide over to the dance floor. I catch sight of Dean and Fitz dancing too, and my heart gives a tiny flip.

Remember when we promised this wouldn't be us? I think. And as if he can hear me, Dean glances my way. He smiles and shakes his head before turning back to Fitz, looking like a guy who can't believe his luck.

I laugh as Sam twirls me, and when he catches me, we're closer than ever. I look up into his eyes and find his are gazing right into mine.

"So, what're we going to do now that we're out of parties and events to go to?" Sam asks.

I pretend to think about it. "Hmm, I guess we'll just have to keep having mind-blowing sex all the time."

"Oh man," he says. "Not sure I'll be able to make that work."

"No?"

"I'd have to make it official first. Officially date," he says. "And you'll have to meet my friends."

I laugh, and he catches my mouth in a kiss. It's a shiver that doesn't go away, spreading from where his lips touch mine.

This, I could do forever.

And maybe, just maybe, I will.

THAT NIGHT AND ON INTO THE NEXT FEW YEARS

Also Known As, what happens next after you change your life for love…

ONE LAST EPILOGUE

Dean

After I dance with my husband's mum and all his sisters, and after he dances with Maeve and Anya and Summer and Bryn, I toss my suit jacket on the back of a chair. Eager to steal a moment away from everyone else, I make my way toward the terrace overlooking the lake at Central Park, tossing a glance at the man I just married.

I tip my forehead in the direction I'm heading, my eyes saying *Join me*. Since I'd like a moment alone with him, and I've barely had that all night. With a knowing nod, he sheds his jacket on a chair too and follows me outside.

Resting my elbows on the railing, I gaze at the lights of New York as Fitz slides a hand up my back, draping his arm around my shoulder. "Hey you."

"Hi." It's so simple, those words from each of us. Nothing special. But it's how we greet each other when it's only us. It's our language, it's how we reconnect.

Glancing around the quiet terrace, he squeezes my shoulder. "You angling for a quickie out here?"

I roll my eyes. "No. Sorry to break your heart there."

He frowns, snapping his fingers. "Dammit."

I make a shooing gesture. "By all means, go back inside, then."

He laughs, squeezing me harder. "Fine, so you just needed a moment alone with me for a hot kiss. I'll settle for that, as long as you admit you can't resist me."

I loop an arm around his waist. "I think we already established that one a long, long time ago, Fitz."

"I'm happy to keep establishing that fact every damn day."

"Then where's the hot kiss?"

"Oh, now you want it?"

"Don't I always?"

He obliges, giving me a searing kiss here on the patio with all of our guests inside. "That's just a teaser for later."

I hold up a finger to make a point. "Which will *not* be a quickie."

"No fucking way, babe. We'll make it last on our wedding night."

"Like we always do," I say with a smile, then turn back to the skyline.

He stares out at the city too, then takes a deep breath, exhaling, sounding ridiculously content. "Mr. Collins."

He says my name like he's tasting it, like he's savoring it on his tongue.

"Mr. Fitzgerald," I say.

He returns his gaze to me, his tone less playful, more earnest. "You look good married."

A warm, buzzy sensation winds through my body, and I don't think it's from the champagne I've drunk tonight. "And why's that?"

He brushes his knuckles along my jaw. "Because you look happy."

"Of course I am."

"Yeah?" There's the slightest bit of nerves in his voice, like the night at the club in London when we danced and he asked if I minded dancing in public.

"Why do you ask? Do you really wonder if I am?"

Briefly, he nuzzles my neck, then pulls back. "I just like to make sure."

I loop a hand around his neck, threading my fingers through his hair. "I am very, very happy."

"It's a good look on you," Fitz says.

"Keep putting it there," I say, before I realize the double entendre. But I bet he'll pick up on it in three, two, one . . .

"I will. I promise. Always." Then he brings his mouth to my ear. "Also, I'll keep putting it everywhere." And he pushes his pelvis against me.

I crack up. "I knew it. I was counting down in my head. I fucking knew you'd be unable to resist that."

"How can I resist when you make it so easy?" He runs his hand around the back of my neck, an appreciative rumble in his throat as he hauls me close. The two of us, we've never been good at keeping our hands off each other. "Speaking of easy . . ."

"Are you trying to cop a feel *again?*"

Fitz shakes his head. "Just trying to kiss the groom one more time."

"Let me help you, then."

I grab his face and bring his lips to mine, kissing him for the hundredth time today.

I close my eyes and savor every second of my mouth on his. My tongue sliding between his lips, the hunger in our kiss, the way it makes my head hazy and my chest hot.

Mostly, how it never gets old.

Which is why I should stop.

I set my hand on his chest, gently breaking the contact.

He pouts. "I'm so sad. Why'd you stop a hot wedding kiss, babe?"

"Because I like it too much. Always have."

"You say that like it's a bad thing."

"It's a good thing. It's a great thing." I tip my forehead to the floor-to-ceiling windows that give a perfect view of all our guests inside the boathouse. "But it's also a dangerous thing, since I suspect we'll have to go back in there, and I don't want to be wildly aroused the rest of the night."

He glances downward toward his crotch. "That ship already sailed for me."

I give him a serious look. "I have faith in you. You can soften."

"You shouldn't have any faith in that. Ever. I'm pretty much a lost cause the rest of the night. We could just skip out early . . ."

"Patience, Fitz. Patience. Good things *come* to those who wait."

He growls. "Now I'm more turned on. Thanks. Thanks a lot." Then he shrugs his broad shoulders. "Whatever. I don't care. As if they can't all figure out I want to shag you," he says, dipping into his English accent tool kit.

"Classy."

"C'mon, Dean. It's obvious. Anyone who looks at us is jealous."

"Is that so?" I ask, loving his confidence, loving the way he talks about us, how he sees us, what we have. What we're so damn lucky to have.

"Of course. We have it all. Love and sex. Sex and love. And all that goes with it. Happiness." Fitz reaches for my hand, threading his fingers through mine. "Have I told you how glad I am you moved here?"

He tells me that every day. And every day I say the same thing in return. I tell him that now too. "Best decision I ever made."

He taps his chin. "Wait. Technically, wouldn't the best decision you ever made be agreeing to a fling with me?"

I stare at the inky sky, filled with stars. "Hmm. Fair point. That was a good one too. Since, without it, you'd never have known I'd rock your world."

"Exactly. So maybe *that* was your best decision. I think mine was walking into your bar."

"Obviously," I say, then my brow knits as my brain snags on a detail I've never asked him. Funny, that after nearly a year together, I never thought to ask him *why*. "By the way, why did you go to my bar that night? Was it just coincidence?"

Fitz grins. "You think it was fate, don't you?"

I laugh. "I don't believe in fate."

"Of course you don't."

"And why do you say that?"

"Because you believe in facts and logic and pros and cons."

"So, did you make a list of pros and cons that night of various bars to go to?" I ask.

"That's your style, babe. You want to know why I was there?"

"Yeah. I do. That's why I'm asking. I'm assuming it was just random. Was it? Random?"

He lifts a brow wolfishly. "Or are you thinking maybe I looked up the hottest bartenders in London? Found a website? Like a top ten list of sexy Brits. And I ran my finger over it, stopped, pointed at the one who looked like Michael B. Jordan, and said, 'Damn, I hope he likes dick'?"

I press my palm over his mouth. "Shut up. Just shut up. You're not allowed to speak anymore."

He bites my palm, and when I remove my hand, he's laughing.

"Oliver told me about The Magpie," he says, still chuckling.

"Oliver? Really?"

Fitz nods.

"But I'd never met him. He'd heard about the bar?"

Fitz strokes his beard. "If memory serves, last summer when I told him and Logan I was headed to England with Emma, he said, 'Don't forget to check out The Magpie. Some of my mates over there were raving about it. It's their favorite local bar.'"

I nod, understanding now. "And you thought, naturally, *I hope the hot bartender there likes dick?*"

"Fuck yeah."

I laugh. "Yet another reason I love you. So fucking relentless."

"I am absolutely relentless. And admit it," he says, poking me. "Admit you're glad I went there. Admit you're so fucking happy I went to The Magpie to check out the rumor about the hot bartender."

I lean in close, brushing my lips against his ear. "You know how much I like that you showed up. As in . . . *love.*" I pull away, taking a moment to savor the view—his blue eyes, his chiseled jaw, his trim beard, and most of all, his smile. It just does something to me every time he flashes it my way. "And I should thank Oliver for the tip."

"Wait. Want to know what else the guys said to me when they mentioned it?"

"I do."

Fitz's expression softens, sliding into that smile that's my undoing. "Logan said, 'Maybe you'll meet someone with an accent just like Oliver's who'll sweep you off your feet.'"

"So, really, both of your mates were right. I definitely owe them a thanks."

He nudges my side. "What will you say? Thanks for sending that irresistible sex god into my bar?"

"Yes. That. Precisely that," I deadpan. I stare off in the distance. "Funny. You went from sex god to besotted fool in love in, what was it, five days in London?"

"That's all it took?" Fitz asks dryly. "I thought it was less."

"If memory serves."

"Then I'm guilty as charged. I'm both." He taps his chest, owning it. "I'm *still* both. I can multitask."

"You are definitely both," I say. "Those are among your pros."

"You better not keep a list of my cons."

"Wouldn't you like to know?" I tease.

Fitz grabs my arm. His eyes plead with me. "Say it's all pros. Your list."

"Say it or mean it?" I toss back.

"Both."

I run my hand over his where he's gripping me, giving him the reassurance he sometimes seeks. And he always deserves. "Don't ever forget it only took me five days to fall in love with you too. So, yes, the list is all pros. You are all pros. Now, let's be good boys and go see our guests."

He grabs my ass, squeezing. "Good. And then a little later, I am going to strip you naked and have my way with you. Because I am seriously hot for my husband."

"Yet another pro. Also, *ditto*." I smooth a hand down my tie, then straighten his. "There. We look presentable now."

"We won't later," he adds.

"I know. Trust me, I know."

We head back inside, scanning the guests. Summer and Oliver are sharing a slice of cake. Logan and Bryn are dancing slowly. Ransom stands at the bar, his elbow resting on it. He tips his forehead at Fitz, who nods back at him. His teammate then returns his focus to a pretty redhead, who's laughing and, it seems, making him laugh.

"He does seem rather hooked on Teagan," I whisper.

Fitz peers at his friend. "Yeah? How can you tell?"

"He looks at her the way you and I looked at each other when we first met. Perhaps at the teahouse. Wait. That was a little risqué. Possibly how we looked at each other at Sticks and Stones."

Tilting his head, Fitz regards them like he's gathering data. "Or maybe how we were on the Harry Potter bridge. Or outside the Tube station?"

I toss him a wry grin. "Well, if he looks at her the way we did outside the Tube station, this whole boathouse will go up in flames. I know I did. That's when you told me how much you loved fucking me."

He laughs heartily, draping his arm around my shoulders. "Let's go with the riverboat cruise, then. That was moderately chaste for us. But I was also pretty damn hooked on you by then. And that means he's screwed if she doesn't feel the same."

"Do you think he's even aware he's got it bad for Bryn's best friend?"

Fitz shrugs, lowering his voice another notch. Not sure. But he had his heart broken a while ago, and at laser tag the other week, Bryn and I were saying she'd be good for him. Whether he figures that out is anyone's guess, but she did win him at the charity auction."

"The one you're never participating in again?"

Fitz holds up his hand, running his thumb over his platinum band. "Um, yeah. Taken. Hello? But that raises an interesting point. Would you have bid on me? Like, say you never met me, hypothetically. And you went to the auction and saw me onstage. In the Win a Date with a Player auction."

I laugh. "You're assuming I'd have been at the auction."

"Work with me. Pretend you were. Pretend I'm onstage all smoldering and sexy. You'd have bid on me, right?"

This man. He has always made me laugh. "No. Of course not."

"Why not? I'm irresistible. You said it yourself."

I set a hand on his back. "I've seen the way you stare at me. I'd never need to bid on you. You'd have jumped off the stage and into the audience just to ask me out on a date."

Fitz pretends to consider this. "You are so cocky, but also so right."

We swing past Teagan and Ransom, and Fitz mouths to him, *Go for it.*

Ransom points to his ear, mouthing back, *I can't hear you*, then smiles at Teagan once again, looking wrapped up in whatever they're saying.

"Some guys don't see what's in front of them," Fitz says.

That's definitely true, not just for guys, but for everyone. I look over at Maeve and Sam, holding tight to each other on the dance floor. I flash back on that moment at the sushi lunch last year, when something seemed to be brewing. That was months ago, but Maeve needed that time, needed those months. Seeing her now, she's ready for all that love has to offer her.

Perhaps that's the true key to happiness. *Seeing* it. Recognizing it. Having the guts to go for it. To know you deserve it. I reach for my husband's hand, thread my fingers through his, look at our joined hands, then meet his eyes.

"I am not one of those guys. I know exactly what I have in front of me."

His grin melts me. *"Everything."*

And I give him his favorite word from me. "Yes."

Soon enough, we say goodbye to all our friends and family, and we head to the hotel, making good on all our wedding night promises.

* * *

The next morning, we catch a flight to Europe, and we go to Copenhagen, like we talked about doing one morning when we were tangled up in the sheets of a hotel bed in London.

The capital of Denmark is both picturesque and cosmopolitan, with cobbled streets right alongside skyscrapers. We spend our days wandering around the city, taking boat rides and bike rides, and checking out the sights, doing what we've always done together.

Talking, laughing, having *the best time*.

One evening, we stop at a bar and grab beers to drink outside, when I spot a tall, strapping blond Dane walk by.

Fitz scoots closer to me, nodding to the guy. "Told you the men were hot."

I arch a brow. "Are you honestly going to perv on other men on our fucking honeymoon?"

Licking his lips, he gives me a salacious grin. He laughs, then shakes his head. "No. I can't even pretend. Not even in a fantasy. But you know what I want?"

"What do you want?"

"I want your fantasies, Dean. Tell me what you'd do to me right now. If we were in our room? Whisper it in my ear."

I run my hand over the ink on his muscular arm. "Ah,

that I can do. I can definitely tell you all the filthy things I want to do with this body. I like that a lot better." I move in closer, flicking my tongue over his earlobe. "Bite your neck."

"Do it now."

"With pleasure," I say, as I brush my lips downward then nip the flesh of his neck.

He shivers, then closes his eyes. "What you do to me . . ." His voice trails off.

"And what exactly do I do to you, Mr. Fitzgerald?"

He groans as I say his name, since he loves whenever I use it. Any and all variations of it. "You turn me on, Dean."

"Good answer."

"You're the only one I want."

I bend my face to him again, rubbing my day-old stubble against his neck. "Good. Because all my fantasies are about you too."

"Tell me another one," he says, adjusting himself in his chair, his eyes still closed, the expression on his face one of clear arousal.

"Some are pretty simple. Right now, I'd take you back to the room. Throw you on the bed. Tease your stomach with little kisses. Nibble on your thighs. Bite your arse. Lick you. Torment you. Not even touch your cock till you were begging."

He opens his eyes, narrowing them. "You're so cruel."

"That may be true, but you'd be rewarded for enduring my cruelty."

"How so?"

"I'd put you on your hands and knees, get inside you," I say, as his expression goes slack-jawed. "Cover your body with mine. *Take* you. *Please* you. *Fuck* you. And finish what I'm starting right here."

Fitz sits up straight, blinking, sex written in his eyes.

"Now. Do that to me now." He reaches into his wallet, fishes around for some kroner, and tosses them on the table. Then he grabs my hand, tugging at me.

I lift my beer. It's half full. "I'm not done. Don't you want to enjoy the scenery some more?"

"I want to enjoy *your* scenery."

I hold up a finger, making him wait as I take another swallow, even though I want that fantasy as badly as he does. Then I set the glass down, as his eyes sear me, like he's saying he's going to punish me for making him wait another damn second to deliver.

If hot, hard, hungry sex with my husband is a punishment, then I'll be bad every day.

And in our hotel room, we're so bad that it's damn good as we enjoy the scenery so very much, exactly as I told him we would.

* * *

Later that night, when we head out to dinner at a swank new eatery Naveen raved about, Fitz drapes an arm around me, as a couple of guys walk past us, looking our way. "They want what we have," he says, all confident, as he often is.

"Yeah? What's that? Reservations at a hard-to-get-into restaurant? It did take me some finagling to snag it."

He stops, cups my cheeks, and looks me in the eyes. He goes serious. Intensely so. "Do you have any idea how fucking amazing it is to know that one person can be everything to you?"

My heart thumps harder. I match his tone when I answer. "I do."

"It's incredible that one person can be it for you. Can be your great and fantastic love."

And the organ beats louder, only for him. My voice softens to a whisper as I look at the man I love. "I know what you mean. I have mine, and it is fucking amazing to be with you."

"Same, babe. It's the same for me."

We continue on, walking down the street, wrapped up in each other.

This is happiness, and I've got it.

We've got it in each other.

* * *

The next summer we go to Italy. We have more to celebrate. Not just a one-year anniversary.

But a Stanley Cup.

Fitz is still pretty over the moon about winning it. Understandable. Though he said his favorite part was when I wore his jersey to the winning game.

Not true.

I didn't. I just wore a team jersey.

But he has an active imagination, and he pretends I wore his number. I let him have this fantasy. I let him have all his fantasies.

Since most of his mirror mine.

The following summer, we go back to England for a few weeks, then to Prague and Amsterdam.

It's everything we once imagined it would be.

And when we return to New York, the next season starts. He's busy again, and so am I.

But we text and talk, and I video chat him the morning he turns thirty, since he's in Toronto for the last game in a long road trip.

He stretches in his hotel bed. "I'm so sad I can't have a birthday morning BJ."

"I'm devastated too. I can't think of a better present to give you." But, in fact, I have other gifts for him.

When he returns the next night, while I'm at The Pub, he'll find it on the kitchen counter.

A note that says: *Remember that time you walked into my bar? You said some things were hard to resist. You said, too, that you'd show me if I told you what time I got off. Tonight, I get off at one. I'll show you what's hard to resist, after I make you a martini that goes to your head. Pros of being married to a bar owner.*

But first, Leo arrives at The Pub in the early evening. We chat for a few minutes, as he tells me all about what went down when Lulu showed up at some sort of chocolate event, and then he helped her get a job at his company.

"Level with me. Are you prepared to work with her?" I ask my friend.

"She's a contractor. We're not going to be in the same offices."

"You completely dodged the question," I point out, since things are different now with her. Well, they *could* be different, since his friend Tripp died a few years ago, shortly after I became friends with Leo.

"It'll be fine. We're friends," Leo says of Lulu. "We've been through plenty, as you know. And plenty of people who have history work together."

Laughing, I slap my palm on the bar. "That is the best understatement among all the understatements in contention for Understatement of the Century."

Leo grins, shrugging. "Who doesn't have history?"

"You two have so much history you could write a new textbook." But then I stop the ribbing. "Listen, all I'm saying is, once upon a time, you were in love with her. Now all you have to do is keep it on the level as you work with her. It ought to be easy, right?"

"Piece of cake."

But when Lulu strolls in, and Leo gives her a look like she's the answer to all his prayers, I have a feeling he's going to be back here in a few days, needing a much stronger drink.

And I'll be here when he needs me.

* * *

Later, after I close the bar and clean up, there's a knock.

My reaction is Pavlovian. My skin heats up. My dick starts to harden as I walk to the door.

Blue eyes, hot as sin, greet me as I open it.

"I believe you said you'd make me a martini," Fitz says in a low rumble.

"You want the kind that goes to your head?"

"Yeah, I do," he says, and his gaze is hungry already, since he's been on the road for a week.

In an instant, the air between us is charged.

Flickering with arousal. With the promise of hot, dirty deeds.

Three years in, it's still there.

It's still pulsing.

It's still powerful.

This connection. This intimacy. This desire.

He grabs my face and devours my lips.

We kiss hungrily for a few minutes, then I break the kiss and pull him to the bar, away from the doorway and from the eyes of anyone on the street past midnight. "Sit. Have your drink."

"*Someday*," he says, echoing the words we both voiced at the club the night I said I'd make it for him. Our wish to have all our somedays together.

"You get all your somedays, Fitz." I hand him a martini.

Fitz knocks back a thirsty drink as Sam Smith plays on the sound system. "I want all my somedays," he says, desire in his voice as he hands the cocktail to me. I find the spot on the glass where his lips were and drink from there, meeting his gaze the whole time, as a pulse seems to beat between us.

He groans his appreciation. "It's already working."

"Is it now?" I put down the glass.

His eyes won't leave me. They stay on me, full of heat. "You go to my fucking head, Dean." My husband stands, walks behind the bar, and grabs the waistband of my jeans. He jerks me toward him, our bodies pressing together. "That drink makes me want you. Or maybe it was a week on the road. Seven lonely fucking nights."

"You missed my cock."

He runs a thumb along my jaw. "Missed your cock. Missed your face. Missed your sarcasm." He grips my chin harder. "Let me fuck you here."

I shake my head. "No. We're not fucking behind the bar. I can't in good conscience serve a customer knowing we screwed here."

"I want to, babe," he says, on a needy, hungry plea. "What if I do chores, like you and Maeve?"

I laugh. "Wait a second. Chores are in the running? That might change everything."

His eyes twinkle with mischief. "Let's start a new game. For every dirty deed you let me do to you here in your bar, I'll owe you a chore." He brings his lips to my ear, licking and biting, driving me wild. "And you know what'll get me to sanitize the ice bins for you."

A groan works its way up my chest as I picture our X-rated exchange rate. "I do enjoy when you work your magic in that department. You have a wicked tongue."

Fitz flicks the tip of it against my earlobe. "You love all the things I do to you with my tongue."

My temperature shoots up a hundred degrees. "I love all your secret, dirty tricks." For a few seconds, I linger on the images, on all the ways he drives me out of my mind with pleasure. But I also find so much pleasure in having fun with him, teasing him. I inch away so I can tip my forehead to the game room. "Only, I *really* need someone to paint the game room."

His hands grip my hips now, and he yanks me against him so I can feel the full length of his erection. "Let me fuck you here, and I'll paint it this weekend," he offers.

Even though I'm tempted, I laugh. "Hmm. You seem hard up, so this negotiation might be mine to win. How about a blow job for a paint job?"

"Tradesies. I'll do it."

"You must be really horny, Fitz."

"So fucking horny you can't believe it."

"Why don't you prove it to me? So I can be sure I believe it. Feel free to get on the floor and suck my cock." I point downward. Where I want him.

His brow furrows. "Wait. I thought I was getting blown?"

I adopt a surprised expression. "Oh, you don't like blowing me?"

"Fuck you. I love it. I'll show you how much. Happily."

And lucky me. On his birthday night—fine, it's a day later, but we're celebrating tonight—my husband gets down on his knees, unzips my jeans, and takes me in his hungry mouth.

My body burns the second he makes contact, and I grunt out a *yes*.

I run a hand over his beard, loving the feel of it on my

thighs as he draws me deep, his cheeks hollowing out like a hungry man as I fill his mouth.

Sparks race across my skin, making me hot, making me wild. His eyes glint, as he moans against my shaft. Taking me deeper, sucking me so damn ravenously that it's like electricity is flickering throughout my entire body.

"Yes, that. Fucking that," I say, groaning as his tongue spirals along my length. I curl my hands around his head, fingers roping through his hair, moans falling from my lips. I rock into his mouth as pleasure intensifies in my spine then breaks, detonating as I come down his throat.

He rises and clasps my cheeks, claiming my mouth. Our lips crash together, and we kiss, rough and consuming. When he breaks it, he breathes out hard, his eyes still glimmering with lust. "I fucking love doing that to you. Every single time."

"What do you know? The feeling is mutual." I slide a hand along his shirt, into the waistband of his jeans, over his hard-on. "And now I get to take my turn."

"Happy birthday to me," he murmurs as I reach inside his boxer briefs, lust sizzling over my skin as I run my palm over his length.

"Here's another gift, birthday boy," I say as I get on my knees, taking him in my mouth.

"This is my favorite present," he rasps out, staring at me as I draw him in deep, filthy words escaping his lips with every lick and suck.

Words that only stoke my desire, as I show him how very mutual all these feelings are.

And since it's his birthday, we don't stop there.

We've always excelled at making it last. An hour later at home, we're ready for another round.

"Birthday sex is the best," Fitz says as we tumble to the bed. "Let's have birthday sex every day."

As I slide my hands down his naked body, I say, "I'm pretty sure we do. But while we're keeping score for this new bar game, you do know that if you want to fuck me for another birthday present, you're also going to need to scrub all the floors this weekend too? In addition to the paint job?"

"Worth it. So worth it."

And yes, it is absolutely worth it.

* * *

A few days later, I give him another present when I fly his family in for the weekend, surprising him.

The look on Fitz's face when he sees all the people he loves is worth it too. Being able to do this for him is worth every decision I've ever made in the last few years.

He's worth everything to me.

Especially when he helps me paint the bar.

Not as a payment. Just because that's who he is.

Because he likes to help.

When we're done, he turns to me, giving me that smile that melts me. "Hey you."

"Hi." I gesture to the new colors on the wall. "I fucking love you. That is all."

"I fucking love you too. Always."

"Always," I repeat.

I'm so damn lucky to have this. Love and sex and happiness and support.

And family.

Most of all, *that*.

All in the same person.

This man. This life. This big and wonderful and passionate love. It's mine and it's his and it's ours.

The End

If you enjoy MM romance, I have another one coming soon! ONE TIME ONLY is a wildly sexy romance between a rock star and his bodyguard and it's available everywhere to order!

Want more Dean and Fitz? Sign up here to receive a bonus scene sent straight to your inbox!

(If you've already signed up for my newsletter, be sure to sign up again! It's the only way to receive the bonus scene, but rest assured you won't be double subscribed to the list!)

Ransom's story is next as these sexy, single men find their happily ever afters. Preorder THANKS FOR LAST NIGHT!

Curious about Leo? He has a story to tell in BIRTHDAY SUIT, available everywhere.

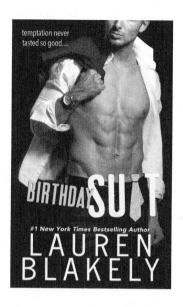

Sign up for my newsletter to make sure you don't miss a single sexy new book!

ALSO BY LAUREN BLAKELY

FULL PACKAGE, the #1 New York Times Bestselling romantic comedy!

BIG ROCK, the hit New York Times Bestselling standalone romantic comedy!

THE SEXY ONE, a New York Times Bestselling standalone romance!

THE KNOCKED UP PLAN, a multi-week USA Today and Amazon Charts Bestselling standalone romance!

MOST VALUABLE PLAYBOY, a sexy multi-week USA Today Bestselling sports romance! And its companion sports romance, MOST LIKELY TO SCORE!

WANDERLUST, a USA Today Bestselling contemporary romance!

COME AS YOU ARE, a Wall Street Journal and multi-week USA Today Bestselling contemporary romance!

PART-TIME LOVER, a multi-week USA Today Bestselling contemporary romance!

UNBREAK MY HEART, an emotional second chance USA Today Bestselling contemporary romance!

BEST LAID PLANS, a sexy friends-to-lovers USA Today Bestselling romance!

THE HEARTBREAKERS! The USA Today and WSJ Bestselling

rock star series of standalone!

P.S. IT'S ALWAYS BEEN YOU, a sweeping, second chance romance!

A GUY WALKS INTO MY BAR, a sexy, passionate, utterly addictive standalone MM romance!

CONTACT

I love hearing from readers! You can find me on Twitter at LaurenBlakely3, Instagram at LaurenBlakelyBooks, Facebook at LaurenBlakelyBooks, or online at LaurenBlakely.com. You can also email me at laurenblakelybooks@gmail.com

Printed in Great Britain
by Amazon